EXODUS

THE
DOLPH/IN SAGA

A NOVEL
BY
MARTIN.A.ENTICKNAP

First published printing, July 1999

cover wrap around image:
"The Last Day at Starnay"
created by Martin A. Enticknap

cover design, typography, and text production:
Parris Graphics & Printing
Murfreesboro, Tennessee, USA

Library of Congress Catalog Card Number: 99-95234

ISBN: 1-928798-35-7

type: Fiction?

The author: Martin A. Enticknap,
may be contacted by mail through the publisher.

Copies of **EXODUS: the Dolph/in Saga** are available through:
Amazon.com.
http://www.amazon.com

and also through the publisher:

Armstrong Valley Publishing Company
P.O. Box 1275
Murfreesboro, TN 37133-1275, USA
Phone: 1-615-895-5445
Fax: 1-615-893-2688

Dedicated to
My Daughter Cassie.
Who was born in the same year that this novel came to life...
And to all Cetaceans everywhere.......

And Finally.......
To Jen , for her editing of the
Original manuscript from 1990 to 1992,
For showing faith in this novel,
And for her love and patience over the years,
Thank you.....

Acknowledgement

Goes to Robert S. Sanders, Jr, who I had the good fortune to meet while I was resting in a remote mountain refuge hut in June 1994. A friendship which has successfully spanned more than just two continents, and proven to be a creative and thought provoking force in both our lives. His belief in this novel has brought this publication about. This novel, completed in 1992 and revised once in 1994, would have been lost had it not been the time and effort that Robert gave to scanning and editing the only one of two hard copies and spending hours converting to a PC readable file format, and that was at the beginning of our friendship! To you my friend a special Thank you indeed!!

The Last Day at Starnay

CHAPTERS OF EXODUS

yen = second, minute, moment
clar = hour
tay = day
veul = week
jeanth = month
season = year
dee(s) = foot, feet
klee = kilometer

Introduction to Exodus from the Author

In ancient times, when shaman gathered on the plains, huddled around the fire in caves, when they talked in temples of civilisations which have long been forgotten or become Myth, they shared a secret. A legacy shown to them by the elder race, who in turn were shown by the sea people. We know them as Cetaceans - Dolphins and Whales whom we barely understand. But once long ago they shared with us water-time and the power of the *song*.

The evidence exists in the remains of legends, folklore and tribal traditions of many of the races over the millennia. The last fragments were quickly lost as their people no longer sang because the "Civilised Ones" came and swallowed them up. But in spite of being eaten, some of their magic and wisdom survives. We see this change as a product of the last three hundred years as The *Europeans* expanded outwards to exploit new lands. In truth it's part of a cycle that goes back as far as humanity does.

To the Cetaceans what we may call the soul they would call the *song*. Now the nature of that *song* is what is important - it should be considered a Harmonic, a vibrational frequency which resonates in harmony. The nature of Water-time ranges from the simple mind to mind sharing to a complex pattern involving sight, sound, touch, and taste. A Watersinger is someone using the expression of his/her *song* or soul infused outwards to water-time and beyond. To change the very nature of reality - the combined Harmonic of life itself. As in all things some are good, bad or indifferent, and you will meet and share the water-time of several in this novel - an expression of that *song*.

Some of the words in this novel may not trip off the tongue lightly, *others hear the harmony and have no trouble*, but the Harmonic they represent is a glimmer of the whole. Names such as Mel-e-gar or Tan-e-lea for example are easy, representing three tones combined with a visual shell. Translating isn't easy but this way preserves the essence of the combined Harmonic. A word like Aiouqes for example will be pronounced differently by the reader and will blend with *their* harmony to create something new and I would not impugn that by fixing their pronunciation in stone. If you like, they become the representation of the Chaos element of the *song*. This is important in any Harmonic construction.

Returning to the Shaman and why I pulled something from us into an introduction about them and the Worlds of Dolph/in kind, contrary to popular belief you cannot teach enlightenment. *Something Mel-e-gar and Tan-e-lea learn.* It's a journey exploring the Harmonic. You either discover this for yourself or like the Watersingers in this book you may be born with a slightly greater instinctive understanding of the potential of it. When Humanity was far more open about what is now considered by many to be mystical nonsense, the truth was expressed in the *song*, and they discovered that the most enlightened of their number, (*not meaning superior intellect*) could be catalysts. These walking time bombs who without needing to even open their mouths had the effect of changing those around them thus creating the raw creative pulse which causes other *songs* to harmonise. Those affected would sometimes curse the ones responsible. Because if the responding *song (and they all respond one way or the other*) is out of tune, it's not nice to suddenly come face to face with your own discords. But a few would rise to the challenge - to begin their own unique journey, to really ***dare*** to explore strange new worlds in the comprehension of the divinity of reality, their part in it and the effect they have with the other *songs* around them. To care beyond their own frame of reference, to discard the straight jacket of dogma and to make the world a more colourful and exciting place to live, taking as much care as they could to help others do the same. They would show others by example rather than preach - If I'm not too careful this will sound as if I'm doing just that! However that cobbled road is a road best stepped upon *lightly*.

Returning to the shaman, they found new ways, and lost part of the plot. Ritual became more important, words turned to ashes and the paint on the pictures quickly went mouldy until somebody came along and redressed it - a touch up job. So it has continued century after century. The world is full to the brim of it! You see it.

There have been many individuals who expressed the power of the Harmonic and captivated generations. But the *songs* have lost much of their power, often through neglect or deliberately altered to tell a new story that in itself negates the random element which makes the harmony most powerful. That's why the story must keep a full range and the Harmonic should only be felt and not seen. *Then it's seen.* Millennia ago a man expressed, *in story form*, a universal Harmonic. Then they killed him and wrote down their version thus changing the Harmony. His *song* was only expressed once in its unadulterated form, before others came along and paraphrased him. It changed and ultimately has largely been lost. This shows how an individual, expressing a universal Harmonic cannot rely on it *not* being changed by others. The sound is fluid to the interaction of other *songs*. Therefore the dangers of becoming a follower are apparent, especially if you cannot be sure the source hasn't already been tampered with. Blindly obeying another *song* may leave you - *the follower* in danger of being served up as roast lamb! Tasty but not so lucky for you.

In truth the path to enlightenment doesn't exist. You create enlightenment for yourself. This endeavor can be risky and you may get burnt along the way. You even risk your life in the fulfilment of all those glorious colours and rich tones that make up your unique *song*. Because those that wrap themselves in fear, afraid of the unknown will always attack the unusual and unique. If we let them win we lose our *song*. So know this, singing that *song* is the most powerful expression of your life. Go for it, be not afraid, and if you are still reading this - enjoy the story, and enjoy the Harmonic - I hope it inspires you to go out there and explore for yourself. That's *your* truth, as individual as yourself and as you go - take care of each other, even if you *have* to say goodbye to allow them to say hello to their truths. Someday we may sing well enough to understand those that brought the legacy long ago, which we let slip into the crack in the dusty floorboards of history - So, when you pass a Dolphin or Whale or any of the Cetaceans look them in the eye and say *Thanks*. I can assure you they will understand. And if you can try and stop people from eating them or killing them for so called scientific research (***Norway and Japan I'm talking to you***. - *That should kill any sales in those countries.*) - then do so.

You wouldn't like it if your Mother was harpooned, dragged out of her front door and gutted on the street - Would You? So you can imagine how they might feel - and you never know the **consequences** of *that* Harmonic!

Martin A. Enticknap, Sanday, Orkney, 7:18 AM, 20th May 1999

We dreamt, We listened, We waited
For another voice in the darkness.
But they were already here.
We just could not conceive that
They would be as they have always been.

Through time and stars they came
For a home to find
And here they stayed
To make their race as *Dolphin kind.*

This is their beginning.....

PROLOGUE

Part One .

1629 S.T. [19055 S.C.]

Gei-e-gar stood at the edge of the forest, the giant Aiouqes standing tall and comforting at his back. Danetar was low in the sky behind the Duorsilear mountains. The final calls of the Leujan were sharp in the still air as the sky-flyers made their way to their roosts in the high canopy behind him. Like a signal being given he returned their call with a long weary sigh and began the climb to a cave in the highest mountain of the range, called Duors. As he climbed over the grey granite rocks tinged with the faint touch of twilight he remembered he was laying to rest not only the end of the present cycle but also those lives that had lived once so far in the midst of time and so near in their hopes for the future.

It had been the first time in dolph history that a guardian of the forest of Duorsilear had been chosen to head the main Council on Delikadove. Some thought it was a strange choice as Gei-e-gar spent a great deal of his time, as all guardians before him, in the forest. But he knew why and they gave him the understanding that his tenure of office would only be for a season and then he would be free to make his excuses and resign. That was acceptable to him because spending his time in the city of Colisee listening to the problems of his fellow dolphs for the rest of his tays was not his idea of fun! No, the only problem he had was the price he had to pay for such a short tenure.

He had been given two tasks, (that had been set out in secret at the highest level of the Council), and no one was to know, not now and not ever, for the sake of future generations and it was his responsibility to implement them.

The first task was to wipe the entire age of Tawnal from every reference in dolph culture. One thousand six hundred and twenty-nine seasons were to be absorbed in the cycle that preceded it. The age of Celsen, instead of ending in **17426**, would be brought forward to end as **19055 S.C**. It was a strange feeling to know that the season of his birth and the past sixty-three seasons of his life would no longer exist as a date in time. He had argued with them saying that changing the name of the cycle would not undo what had happened in the last decade of Celsen. After all it was on record that the Grand-elders of that time had unanimously agreed to begin the Cycle of Tawnal as a reminder of the Legacy that the Strangers had left.

The second task was the destruction of the Crystal that was the main cause for contention in the Council. There were in fact two, the other being the main library crystal which now resided in the chambers at Colisee while the preparations for the special network to alter all information crystals on the entire planet could be activated. There was a certain irony to the situation in knowing that the knowledge that the Strangers had brought with them was now going to be used to wipe out any reference that they ever existed at all!

Twilight was fast approaching, the first stars appearing as he paused to rest for a yen. A cool breath of wind made him shiver, making him raise his body temperature to compensate. Gei-e-gar looked back, the forest a rich green, darkening as he watched and he couldn't help the sigh which escaped as he turned to regard his continuing path. He wasn't used to the burdens that they had placed upon him. He moved closer to the rock wall on his left, away from the edge of the path, scattering bits of rock and stones. Some gleamed white catching the last rays of Danetar. With a clench of his teeth he resumed his climb, his mind going back to the meeting with the Head of the Council.

On the tenth tay of discussions Chy-e-lea had taken him to one side and allowed him full access to the truth behind the distorted Legend that had arisen after the Strangers had disappeared as mysteriously as they had arrived in **17416 S.C.** He had no choice but to admit that the impact of such information if on general release could potentially be disastrous for dolph society. But part of him also felt that the Crystal which was marked for destruction held ideas that could expand dolph culture in ways that would be positive, and for him the most attractive was the idea of going to other worlds even though the methods of implementation appalled him.

For an eternity dolphs had accepted and made use of and had been used by the Shakeilar knowing that they were another species from a different part of the galaxy and not once in all that time had the Shakeilar divulged any method that the dolphs could use. In the long relationship only a handful of dolphs had asked and each time were told that the techniques the Shakeilar used would not be of any use to the dolphs. Which was true as dolphs could not fly by kinetic energy and would die in the airless void of space. So it had been accepted that dolphs would forever remain in the cradle of Delikadove until they found their own way to travel among the stars.

The Crystal showed that dolphs would only develop the skills necessary if a fundamental change in dolph society occurred. The main change needed was to break the reliance on the Shakeilar and abandon the comfort of the cities and begin to create their own by using the resources available around them. Which in the long term could result in the devastation of large parts of Delikadove. That was seen as a high price for that kind of progression, if you could call it that. There was one other way, known as The Gateway and the price for that was a life and only one dolph could pass through. So you would have to persuade half the population that their life force combined with a Shakeilar crystal would enable the other half to pass through their own individual gateway to another planet if they were lucky! There were hints that another power source could be used but no details were given.

Those were the two main reasons which made it a dangerous knowledge indeed! In the time since the Strangers left there had only been six Watersingers and none were ever informed of the Crystal's existence, as it was decided that their power of watersong combined with the knowledge could be dangerous. It was deemed fortunate that the time of the Strangers had occurred in the two hundred and fifty season gap between Watersingers and the origin of the library crystal was easily dealt with as there had always been a central crystal for storing information and this was just the latest version.

In the end he had to agree. If it made him feel any better it was pointed out that it had taken generations of deliberation by the High Council to finally lay the matter to rest simply because the appeal of trying to discover an alternative power source had kept the select few captivated for nearly two millennia.

PROLOGUE

Gei-e-gar, his mind elsewhere, stumbled, almost missing the break in the path. He narrowed his eyes, peering into the gloom. A thin mist was rising, slowly creeping up the mountainside. He looked over the edge as it rose from below. He didn't have long to reach his destination. Taking more care he edged down to the narrow ledge which twisted back up leading in a zig zag to the cave. His feeling of melancholy deepened and the fading tay made him not only weary but also heart sick. He rubbed his chest feeling the pain, and remembered.

The season had passed without incident. The library crystal was declared harmless as it was nothing more than a very efficient storage crystal, capable so far of storing the entire dolph/inal and general history of Delikadove without ever being full. With an added bonus of having different levels of access so sensitive, information could be stored that was so secure that any dolph who did not have permission would find that the crystal would record the identity and inform the required sources. Not that it had ever been used by anyone not authorised by the High Council in the sixteen hundred and thirty-six seasons that it had been in operation.

It did its required task with ease and sent out the message to all the information crystals to change S.T. to S.C. by using cities like so many rivers to flow the information without every dolph on Delikadove converging on the city to have their crystals altered. There were a few murmurings among the general population but only because they had to remember to make the change when discussing some event. As there had always been adjustments made to the length of cycles it didn't make that much difference and Gei-e-gar knew that the coming celebration to mark the beginning of a new cycle in four tays time was taking much of the attention away from the reason behind it. Not that many knew, only the High Council, and those who had lived over sixteen hundred seasons ago were not in any position to complain about it!

That was sickening to Gei-e-gar. At least within the crystal it wouldn't be completely forgotten, as he had laid the substructure open to lay the imprint of those events. The sky, now a deep purple with streaks of orange, allowed more stars to shine and the clouds drifted open. He stopped, his climb complete, and paused taking deep breaths whilst watching the twin moons rise to their zenith point.

He couldn't procrastinate by standing there hoping to delay, so at the dark entrance he lifted the Crystal up. Blue, red, and white light shone out sweeping away the pale light of the moons giving him more than enough light to enter the cave. The crunch of his dees upon the grey sandy floor sounded loud in the hollowness of the cave, but as he carefully moved among the sharp points of crystalline rock that hung from the ceiling and rose from the floor the sound became familiar and he felt a little better. It was peaceful. He passed through seven caverns before stopping before something that was alien to dolphs.

They had been crafted by strange hands, two pillars of a soft white crystal rock, flaked with green and gold. The left pillar was decorated with what looked like a vine wrapped round it. The other was ridged in vertical lines. They seem to guard the entrance. His eyes were drawn to the top piece which had been smoothed flat. Indented were two symbols: a *J* on the left in green and an *M* on the right in gold. Gei-e-gar didn't know what they meant but they seemed important and somehow shouldn't be forgotten.

Feeling resolute he took a deep breath and entered into the cavern. There in front of him was why he had come to this forbidden place, a place he had visited with his sonling. Sharing this secret made him feel less alone. Bringing his light lower he saw the lip of a shaft that was only three dees wide in the cave floor. Kneeling, he looked down and remembered when as a youngling he had stumbled upon this place, which as an Elder he had learnt was forbidden for dolphs to enter. He had thrown pebbles down the shaft - counting how long it would take for the pebbles to reach the bottom to tell him how deep it was. But no matter how long he waited, (*invariably falling asleep*) he never heard if any of the pebbles ever reached the bottom. He often imagined that they were still falling, like tiny memories of his youngling tays falling for an eternity.

Putting aside such thoughts he held the shining colourful crystal over the hole, then opened his hand. As it fell a great beam of light shot upwards hitting the cave ceiling, splaying out a rainbow of colour as if grasping for something to hold onto. But there was nothing to stop its momentum, no suspension of gravity to halt its inextricable fall and still the light refused to fade. For what seemed a remarkable length of time a flicker of colour licked the lip of the shaft until the distance became too great and slowly the light faded. Finally there was only darkness to keep Gei-e-gar company.

Had he done right? Was this the right thing to do? The compromise that he had come to with Chy-e-lea in secret - Only those two knowing that the Crystal would not be taken to the volcano of Tethilay. *To be thrown into the fiery crater of molten rock, lost forever but instead taking a chance in Gei-e-gar's faith that if one tay it was ever needed the crystal might find its way into the right hands?*

He knew he would never know. He had done what he felt was the right thing to do. That was all the comfort he could take, but there were burdens upon his spirit that quickly stole that warmth from his fragile spirit. Shivering from an inner rather than an outer wave of cold he curled himself upon the cave floor to wait for the dawn - A new tay, a new Cycle of Gealasor when his sonling would come and fetch him with a crystal to light his way as they had done as a game countless times before. But this was no game and as sleep stole him away promising peaceful oblivion a barb pricked him and he bled a memory. *With an awful clarity the voice of the Crystal rang out making tears slowly roll down his cheeks as he sobbed his pain and guilt into the darkness.*

For one of two Strangers who hadn't disappeared at all.......

Part Two.

Over Three thousand seasons later......

1215 S.N.

It was always a surprise. Something unexpected each time he ventured forth to walk his thoughts away from the city of Santiier, to climb the tree covered hill which at a certain point seemed to lean slightly to his left, as if wanting him to find it. He followed the creature path that was scratched away from the yellow moss to reveal the rich earth loam of the woodland floor, that on this tay was damp from the recent rain and felt so cool under dee. It brought a wide smile that made the sharp grey lines of his face soften and for a yen he no longer looked as one with the Kerg. Not so hard and sharp indeed. His black oval eyes sparkled with inner fire as he called his laughter to his most secret place and ran, springing each step along the path which at the turn round the hill opened wide. He came to a breathless halt in open sight of Danetar's bright light. The purple blue of the sky with only a scattering of clouds stretched out over the vista of the valley before him, steep cliffs on either side, with a scattering of trees amongst the yellow grass. The white purple foam of the rushing stream snaked down from the Frelegar mountains in the south.

Now he felt safe away from the prying eyes of his own kind. He carried with him the woven basket of Oilan wood which contained his lunch of dried fish and the small orange and white fruits of the Oilan tree. Underneath the silver leaves which it all rested upon was the Crystal which had thwarted any attempt by him to access it. His secret, his passion had kept him occupied with its mystery for nearly two seasons. Changing the basket to his right hand, the urge building as he hefted it, he felt the pull of his desire to find the centre of this place. He followed the stream south letting the warmth of Danetar fill him as he scanned the horizon. He had only walked for a clar when the valley widened further. Alone and majestic there it stood. The stream seemed to give it a respectful distance as it curved away - into the side of the cliff, leaving the slightly raised grass platform alone. The golden yellow hue of the bark made the tree seem magical. To many it would seem to be just a tree. But to him it was something else, something that said to him to stay and be at peace. That whenever he desired a safe and a warm welcome this was the place. *To him sanctuary.*

He slowed his pace and came to a halt just underneath the upswept canopy high above his head. The tree's golden silver oval leaves seemed to shimmer with extra life. He had to crane his neck right back, looking up the hundred and fifty dees to see into the depth of the crown of the tree. He held his gaze and then allowed it to slowly drop, following a pathway down the golden bark to the base. So perfect, so very beautiful. Taking the final steps he reached out and touched the smooth bark. It was warm and he carefully placed his basket at the root of the tree. He then used both hands to bid his hello to his golden tree before turning and sitting down, allowing his back to rest in relief and finally really relaxing.

He closed his eyes and his mind wandered back to his home city of Gothina, to the mountains of Duorsilear and of the Aiouqes. Once a few seasons before he had heard their call. To be a forest guardian, to apprentice himself to those magnificent trees but his other desire would not allow him to think about a life in seclusion away from his first love. The desire for knowledge, to be a maker of things. To create new ways for his kind. *To change the dolphs' dependence upon the Shakeilar! Why not use the power which was held within them for more than comfort of shelter, for more than providing water and food?*

His teachers had told of the symbiotic relationship between them, the benefits that had allowed dolphs to pursue the creative arts. Of earth, air and water. Of space and time and a million other subjects which occupied the minds. *But what was the use of such knowledge if you didn't use it to change the dolph's place on this world or even to take them away to explore the twin moons or even further to the very reach of space where he, as everyone knew the Shakeilar themselves had come from. To go where they had been. What was so wrong with it?* That was the eternal question at which his teachers only smiled and said, "Strange ideas, young Pha-e-gar but interesting," *in a tone that to him was so patronizing it would make him scream in frustration!* They told him he was gifted, he was brilliant and yes, some of his ideas may be used one tay. *But what good was that?! Why not now?* It was a cycle which he had not yet broken. He did know he wasn't alone. There were some others who had questioned and there were increasing rumours and furtive talk among some Elders and even Grand-elders that changes were long overdue. A movement of sorts had begun and the leader Xrl-e-lea, an intense dolph who Pha-e-gar felt for the time being was too extreme with her talk of building a new society away from the mainstream. He wanted to work within and not outside. But then again maybe one tay he might have to.

As always the tree took his sense of frustration away and he felt better, enough to open his eyes and lift the basket which held his food on his lap. This was something physical, a sign of change. A simple thing a basket but so new for a dolph. He had found a way to weave small stripped branches together, it had been a start. He didn't carry the Shakeilar crystal shelter with him as those that ventured away from the cities would normally do. He had learnt to build a shelter from branches and leaves woven to make a canopy. Not as efficient as the Shakeilar shelter that would grow and open on command, making a portable home where ever one desired and as he had to admit was more comfortable. But like the basket his shelters were his creation and not the Shakeilar's. He didn't need them to live. He had learnt to hunt, had even tasted the forbidden fruit of Muala flesh, the red meat which if known by his peers would make them shudder in horror. He had made bone implements, used the thick hide which when stretched and bound to branches had improved his design of his own shelter. All small steps and when he was ready he would show the High Council that dolphs could venture forth no longer bound by the Shakeilar, a freedom which tasted so sweet to him.

But then again the Shakeilar did have one thing which held him in awe. It was the power which they generated to change their crystalline mass density which could divide to either provide a small home or an entire city! Now that was a power which if harnessed could take the dolphs anywhere. He had learnt as many before that the Shakeilar needed the creative mind of the dolphs to build the pattern which formed the cities. It took a great deal of effort and usually the Healers had to form into large groups to slowly pour their collective will, bound by the vision of the shape to be able to create something that large. Once the pattern had been fixed and the growth had finished then the occupancy of the city by the dolphs kept the city vibrant and alive. Could even expand further if the need arose, with very little effort. It seemed once the cycle of energy had begun it would continue indefinitely keeping it as new and as fresh as from the very first tay. It was very simple, a process of fissionable fusion of energy that made the Shakeilar what they were, but for a dolph to find a way to do the same was impossible unless they learn to challenge the physical laws to build by their will and Pha-e-gar as those before him knew this would need changes that would mean dolph culture, their very way of life would be totally swept away and that would of course not go unchallenged!

Pha-e-gar had long mused that if dolphs now this instant left the cities and began again it would take several thousand seasons for them to climb up that particular mountain. Which would take too long for him! He wanted to see it in his life time which always returned him to the paradox that the Shakeilar held the answer to jump them forward. If only there was a way to tap into the power within them to use it as a tool to create cities from the mountains, to build .... *well, baskets that could hold dolphs to fly!* That would be something to fly over their world. To see Delikadove from the air and then ultimately to fly further to the stars themselves. Just dreams he knew and as he stared at his rather simple basket the overwhelming enormity of it filled him to an almost crushing point.

He didn't allow the hot sting of tears that burned at his eyes to fall. Instead he stared at the basket, took off the covering leaves and took some dried fish and began to chew, grinding on the dry taste to take his mind away from such useless thoughts. Only as he lifted the fruit to quench his thirst did he remember the Crystal which had lain forgotten at the bottom. He reached under the bed of leaves and brought it forth. It was a rather dull looking blue green crystal which he had found at the bottom of a river bed by the dee of the Duorsilear mountains on his many excursions away from his home of Gothina. That was two seasons ago and now he was here, on a different continent and in a valley south of his new home of Santiier, the great learning city where he was to choose his life's work. As he turned the Crystal in his hands, allowing the cool smoothness of the surface to calm his spirit he thought on his latest assignment. As his teachers had decided to try him in all departments to somehow find a challenge that would excite his restless and inquisitive mind they had recently chosen him to be apprentice to the Healing centre. Now that did bring a smile when he thought of his teacher.

Her name was Eil-e-lea, tall, graceful and she moved with such fluid movement that she could pass as silently as a cloud. She had been so different; she would often listen when others would just walk away, the first real friend he had ever had. From her light blue eyes to the warmth of her touch she made Pha-e-gar forget how out of place he felt with his own kind. He supposed he was a little in love with her; he was certainly in awe of her. He had watched as she had healed the sick with an ease which left many floundering in her wake. He had even learnt something of the theory of the art which she called water-time, some ancient method left over from those far tays when the ocean was the home of dolphs. She told him how it helped her to see inside to feel the very pain of her patients and from the starting point she could feed the energy to heal them. A mixing and balancing of two fields was the best understanding which Pha-e-gar had. *It seemed more mystical nonsense to him at first and to anyone else he would still say so but somehow Eil-e-lea made it sound right, even dare he think it logical!*

Now what he had to admit made his stomach twist in knots for it was his cool analytical mind which enabled him to weld his own logic with a flair far above most of his teachers and that was the foundation which he lived by. So her water-time was in many ways the complete opposite and this he knew had been one of the main reasons the dolphs had stayed so bound to the Shakeilar. So he didn't try to make sense of it and when his thoughts might betray him into thinking there might be something to it he was quick to change the direction such as now by returning his attention to his crystal.

Now he held in his hands something which defied the rules, the very order of things, a Shakeilar crystal that wasn't of the Shakeilar. When he had found it he did at first believe he had found an ancient Shakeilar crystal lost since the tay of spawning when the Shakeilar first came to Delikadove those countless eons ago. There were times in the past that Shakeilar crystals had been found and they were always taken to be appraised to see if the life energy was strong enough to be brought back to join with the other Shakeilar. Often they had been too lost for too long and could only be used as a storage crystal. Occasionally some had been near enough to dolph habitation to have the internal energy field kept going. When Pha-e-gar had found this one it had flared into a momentary spasm of blue, white, and red light which had flared so brightly when he had first held it but then died away leaving the blue green dull opaque sheen empty of any life. So he had taken it home and for a time left it with his other crystals. Those he used to store information for later use. It was only his innate curiosity about the flare of light that had kept him going back and examining it closer until he found its unique nature.

He had tried the usual method of measuring the internal power sign by placing it within a power bowl. Every Shakeilar home had a place where acting like a junction a dolph could tap the main power source to revitalise old crystals, to allow them to be used for information storage, if the balance of energy taken would allow them to be used in that way. It was also the way a Shakeilar could call forth one of its own if the life force still resided in the crystal. The result was instantaneous and if it still lived a message would be sent to the main library and a high Grand-elder would come to take the Shakeilar crystal away to be added to those that would some tay be used for other cities.

It was by the sight of a cycle of internal light bursting forth and commencing a pattern that the dolph would know the Shakeilar lived. There was also the instinctive sense of the normal subtle communication between dolph and Shakeilar. His Crystal had failed this test and at first he had consigned it to be used as a storage medium. But it failed to take and he had then concluded that it must be a native form of crystal. But it was not rough. It had been shaped sometime in the past because natural rock crystal was not found in perfect polished spheres. Again the Shakeilar did that job. It used its power to compress and mould rock crystal into any shape a dolph could wish. It also allowed a certain artistic flair of the dolph to bring out the natural colours and bring the best shape forth. Those became decorations in dolph homes. *Quite rare as there were not many willing to go looking for pieces of rock!*

So for awhile he let it be a curiosity piece in his home but when he was sent to Santiier he had access to new crystals that had been designed to read the crystal structure of other Shakeilar. There had been experiments into how the power of the Shakeilar changed the internal structure that had led to an understanding that the dead crystals could be used as tools by forming a structured pattern of light inside that could be used to either store information directly from the dolph mind or to be used as a tool for performing a desired function. Most of these were kept for the use in the high learning centres and the Healers had access to quite a few. There had been more demand but as it was a finite resource they were seen as precious and their use restricted.

Pha-e-gar had often thought that it had shown a beginning in change of attitude towards the Shakeilar but it was only the dead ones that were used this way and of course they were totally dependant on the power of the very much alive Shakeilar. So the dead became just crystals sometimes prefixed as in Healing crystal, Magnifying crystal, Dream, Dolph/

inal, Shaper and many others. It had led him to wonder whether it would be possible to dominate the Shakeilar's mind and direct its power by virtue of his will. After all the Shakeilar would never willingly allow dolphs to put it in any kind of danger. He knew that many dolphs did not consider the Shakeilar to be very aware and had taken the relationship with a very complacent attitude. A mistake to ever underestimate the *power* of the Shakeilar, they may appear to be the dominated ones but the dolphs should remember that they are living in the comfort that the Shakeilar allowed them to and not the other way round.

So it was with a Magnifier crystal that he had used persuasion to obtain for his own private use that had revealed in the projection of light on his home wall the internal structure of his Crystal. He learnt that it had some similarities with the Shakeilar but it also had a dense structure at the centre which looked like nothing he had ever seen. A crystal inside another crystal was his conclusion but the tight structure at the centre had such a high mass ratio that defied the normal laws that would have formed a natural rock crystal. *So it was something new but what? This had been his question and of course what use was it?* There was something about it that drew him to it. He often carried it around and like this tay he would sit holding it hoping that his mind would give him some answers if he held and stared at it long enough. Not really logical but it was a puzzle and that was something that Pha-e-gar always found irresistible. He had considered going to his teachers and had even contemplated telling his friend Eil-e-lea but something kept him from doing so. He was not ready yet to share it. It was his after all.

He was so deep in his contemplation, the rest of his food forgotten that he did not notice the shadow that fell across him. It was only with the realisation of his sudden lack of light that he looked up to see why. He almost jumped out of his skin in fright. She as always moved in silence and gave a smile at his momentary fright.

"*Sorry*, I didn't mean to startle you Pha-e-gar."

"I....I.." he began but fell silent as a sense of panic overtook him and he tried to bury his Crystal back into the basket, *hoping she hadn't seen it*. A ridiculous thing to think but he really hoped she hadn't.

She in turn did nothing to betray that she had noticed his furtive movements as she sat crosslegged in front of him waiting with patience until he had settled down. She really had flustered him and she could feel that with any wrong move on her part he would bolt away and she didn't want that to happen.

His fear had turned to panic, then anger. Anger at her intrusion and *why was she always so calm? So peaceful to look at! So beautiful to look at he also meant!* Now he felt embarrassed to have such thoughts in her company. Pha-e-gar licked at his now very dry lips and tried to stop his heart from beating so loud. He was only just barely an Elder of fifteen seasons while she was at least twenty seasons or more than he and most important of all she was his teacher. He just had to get a grip on himself and *anyway what was she doing here? How did she find his most secret place?* His anger started to reassert itself and the heat he felt suddenly changed to a coldness which made him glare accusingly at her.

"What are *you* doing here?!" he fairly spat out the words at her. She just smiled and with a quick motion placed her fine tapered fingers onto his cold sweating brow. He felt an immediate flush of warmth at her touch then a calmness swept over him. His anger quickly dissipated.

"Pha-e-gar, you must not get so *excited* and to answer your question I followed you here. I have been concerned for you these past tays. You have seemed so preoccupied and distant from your studies. *I would like to help if I can.*"

Her words were softly spoken and the real concern that was so apparent in her blue eyes made him bow his head no longer able to hold her gaze. She only meant well and any more thoughts of her intrusion turned to a desire to share with her. But that thought for a yen brought back a flush of almost insane fear that no one should take his crystal from him.

"You can't have it......" cried Pha-e-gar, his black eyes now raised up to lock with hers, "You *can't......*" But he couldn't hold it and he let his gaze drop once more.

Her brow crinkled with concern and the momentary madness in his eyes made her wonder why the crystal which she had, of course seen him holding so tightly should have such a hold over him. Having made the decision she allowed her sense of water-time to flicker outwards. A soft probe of her most gentle stream reached to feel the contours of his troubled mind. Almost immediately she withdrew, the pain and confusion mixed with guilt at his feelings for her and the tight knot of blackness at the centre that spoke only of the Crystal and nothing else. An obsession, Eil-e-lea felt that truth and the edge into madness or as many called it Sky Happy. As a Healer she felt compelled to help him and as a friend she so wanted to. Maybe she should have probed him before but that would have crossed the boundary which she didn't cross unless the dolph in question was her patient. Now of course she must see him as such.

"*Pha-e-gar,*" she whispered, *"Let me help. You know you can trust me."* He didn't respond just stared at the basket and only the flicker of his eyes made apparent the war that was going on inside him. She had to allow him the first step, otherwise anything she tried to do would dry her streams to impotence. So she sat and waited.

He was so confused, he felt bad that he had shouted at her and maybe she could help. *Why not trust her?* She didn't have to hold it and he could just show her the Crystal. But inside he could hear another voice saying *"NO! No! She would take it from you and you would be lost without it!"* It made sense didn't it. *What if she only followed me to take it away?* Maybe they; the Grand-elders, the teachers had somehow found out about it and wanted it for themselves. Back and forth his mind went trying to find a path that would make some action possible. Maybe it was the way she sat so calm, not judging just so patient with him. So kind and with her he didn't feel so alone. *Yes, he would dare to trust her, if not her who could he ever?*

Eil-e-lea had slowed her breathing down and had made herself so still as if she was no longer there while she waited for him to decide. She had to catch herself though when his hand disappeared into the basket and the light of Danetar caught the blue green sheen of the Crystal making it look far less dull than it had before. She really had to hold her hands still because the compulsion to reach out for it almost became overwhelming and that in itself was highly curious to say the least. *What is going on here?* her waters flickered as he raised his hand to allow her to see the Crystal in all its glory. His smile was rather fixed but he had made the gesture.

So it was time to ask. "*Now* Pha-e-gar tell me about it; tell me in any way you like but *talk to me*."

And like a river undammed his words gushed forth, in such speed that she had to really concentrate to understand all he said. He talked with such animation that he placed the Crystal between them on the yellow grass to allow his hands free movement. The passion for his ideas and dreams he painted with such colour that she was held quite spellbound by him. He talked and talked and she listened. Danetar began to dip behind the Frelegar mountains and a cool breeze brushed against them as the shadows grew longer and the first star was born into the coming twilight. When his words became a trickle and the look of fatigue shadowed his eyes she dared to speak.

"Pha-e-gar, I believe I might be able to help you with your crystal."

"But *how...*" His voice held such despair that she reached out to him and held him close, allowing the fatigue to take him and when she felt him relax into her she used a little of her water-time to reach out and touch him to sleep. Then she whispered to him, *"Later, now rest Pha-e-gar. Let sleep hold you for awhile."*

She gently laid him back against the tree and from behind her where she had placed it unseen by him, reached for her Shakeilar crystal and bid it open to be their shelter for the night. With a shimmer of purple and silver the globe expanded quickly under her direction and grew over them sliding smoothly under Pha-e-gar and herself to enclose them in the dome of its welcome embrace. The purple light flickered to a soft hue and a slight red glow grew from the centre casting warmth and shadow to flicker against the smooth curved walls. His crystal that had lain for the yen forgotten on the grass was now like them inside the shelter, the Shakeilar not forgetting to include that as it brought them inside. It now rested against the centre core from which the fire warmth came.

With a flicker of her water she asked the Shakeilar to bring forth her Healing crystal. A blue and silver orb popped up through the smooth floor and hovered by its own power a dee in front of her. She made the command and it moved silently to lay gently into her waiting cupped hands. The solid weight and welcome glow of warmth filled her as the tingle of energy claimed her and with a slight flicker made a cast of blue light to reach out to Pha-e-gar's sleeping form, to cloak him into a healing slumber. With that done she stretched herself out relaxing each muscle, each bone to settle into proper rest and she then turned onto her side and stared at the red centre. Only occasionally did she allow her eyes to wander from the blue green Crystal, now sheened with reflective red to the steady, sleeping form of Pha-e-gar. She did not let sleep take her but resided in that twilight state, relaxed but alert for any change in her patient as she waited.

Three clars passed, and she was just counting to the fourth when Pha-e-gar began to stir. He yawned, it was such an expansive and relaxed yawn that it made Eil-e-lea smile and she sat up while bidding the light of the shelter to increase. As it was warm enough she allowed the Shakeilar to withdraw the fire warmth. It slowly disappeared into the floor. The Shakeilar made one last ripple and the floor was as smooth and untouched as if nothing had ever been there. The Crystal rolled forth and came to rest in the centre.

Pha-e-gar broke the silence, "It's still here then, I thought maybe I dreamt it all." He managed a quirky smile and Eil-e-lea felt hope for the first time. Maybe its hold over him had relaxed while he had slept. He looked calm and his eyes looked at her with a directness which further confirmed her feeling that he may be over the worst. She had healed many before just by listening and allowing dolphs to unburden their worries and fears to her. But she still knew that at this the most delicate stage she would do nothing to disturb that feeling. She gave him a reassuring smile and allowed him the next move.

Sensing this he added, "You can hold it if you like." Even though he was inside a Shakeilar shelter he did feel better. Some of his *fear* of the power, yes, he could admit that now, had left him. With Eil-e-lea everything seemed okay. He did not feel she would do anything to harm him or take anything that he would not give freely.

They sat in silence, facing each other, the Crystal in between them as lifeless as always and she felt the time was right to begin. Taking her healing crystal in her right hand she reached out with her left and picked the Crystal up. With palms open she balanced both and explained to Pha-e-gar what she intended. "After you had told me all you had tried and all you knew of the Crystal, I began to wonder whether there was duality inside. A crystal within a crystal-perhaps sometime in the past something has happened to cause an internal fracture, separating the inner life from the outer shell. Maybe over time that centre collapsed within itself, like a star that dies. All light falling to the centre, all energy absorbed into the higher density field that it creates."

"You mean like a black hole!" exclaimed Pha-e-gar, "Why, *yes* that would make sense. Funny I didn't think of that before."

"Maybe you were too close to the problem to be able to see clearly."

That made him laugh, "Very true," he paused for a beat, "You make such sense I don't know why I didn't listen to you better before!" She smiled in understanding and allowed it to pass without comment. She returned her attention to the crystals and even though he was unaware of it she could see the change in him, the open posture, the clear eyes and the way his smiles spoke of increasing adoration. It was not uncommon for a pupil to feel a bond with their teacher and with patient and healer that seems much like love and in Pha-e-gar's case she was in the position of both. That did trouble her water-time but there was nothing she could do. After all she was about to, if she was right, answer his most fervent wish and solve the mystery of the Crystal. *It was one river which she was bound to ride and she hoped that there wasn't a waterfall at the end of it!*

"Are you ready Pha-e-gar?"

"Now you sound like my *teacher*.." She couldn't help but notice the light in his eyes dim for a yen but he seemed to shake himself and the full open sparkle came back, maybe brighter than before as if her words had touched a raw nerve and he was beginning to over compensate for the fear he must feel. She just had to hope that Pha-e-gar would in time understand the boundaries that had to exist.

Opening her healing state she allowed her waters to reach out and fill her crystal, readying the time of fusion. Her senses shifted and her eyes saw blue light all round, a slight shimmer of silver energy that laced the light as it began to move towards Pha-e-gar's Crystal.

He watched as the shelter filled with the strange blue fire and as Eil-e-lea's eyes closed her face seemed to relax. He was so taken with watching her that he almost missed the transition. It was as if the light at the centre of her crystal flared then seemed to move sideways, reaching out for his Crystal. A yen of panic as space itself seemed to shift and then there was only one crystal where there had been two. The blue and silver light flared up and Pha-e-gar shrank back as the light seemed to spin wildly, the Crystal now spinning on Eil-e-lea's palm. The Crystal had expanded to twice its size as a pulse of red light suddenly broke forth shattering the blue, and sending shards of fractured light in all directions of the shelter. They impacted on his face and chest sending cold shivers through him. As his fear mounted he could do nothing but stare wide eyed as a white light joined the red, dissipating more of the blue and silver. It was raining light. A battle seemed to be going on and then another light broke through, this time a dark blue which totally wiped any vestige of Eil-e-lea's crystal's own light from existence. The three lights pulsated in an orderly rhythm, pounding a beat which struck within his mind like rock falls onto unprotected warm flesh of helpless bodies.

The pain was so great that he could no longer open his eyes but somehow he could still see. The shelter was a wild state of red, white and blue light which seemed to spin all around. Eil-e-lea looked like a wraith of insubstantial form, her hands now dropped to her sides. The Crystal with the power fully flowing was spinning in mid-air and he watched in silent horror as Eil-e-lea crumpled and fell in a heap upon the floor. It was then she suddenly shifted and before a spasm wreaked havoc through her body she managed to cry to him, "*Beware*!"

Her lips did not move and her eyes now empty of life, stared sightless up at him. His last sight of his friend and teacher was as her body under its own will curled up into the foetal position and was forever still. Then the world exploded.

Black, but not, empty but not. There was nothing, *he knew he was Pha-e-gar but he wasn't sure why. That didn't make any sense. Shelter? Shakeilar? Answers or questions? He had no body, where did that go? Strange and I feel empty, hollow, just nothing then. Was as they said Sky happy, the blackness of madness? Where was he? Must be somewhere? I am here am I not? Can anybody answer me? Was there anybody to listen?* That brought him a clear vision of a happy smiling vision of Eil-e-lea. *Yes, I know her, she was my friend wasn't she? Is this Chisharnlay? The place for all who sing the deathsong? Why won't anybody answer me?*

He didn't know how long he asked questions hoping that someone would answer. He did not know what had happened inside the shelter or what they had released from the rather dull looking crystal. But he wasn't sure he liked it at all. Which of course he didn't. It was only after he had begun another set of meaningless questions. *Well they are if you have no one to answer them but yourself. Because you always know the answer Don't you? No, not always.* When an equally disembodied voice decided to join him.

You don't know much do you? And before he could answer that the voice added, *No, don't answer. It was a silly question.*

Actually the shock of hearing again a voice other than his own made any comment impossible.

Typical, here I am, I come to join you and you are the one who has been trying to contact me and you now play dumb. Typical, typical!

The voice repeated the word, *Typical,* several hundred times before Pha-e-gar found the courage and the voice to finally speak back. It was only by listening to it rant on that he also realised that the voice was lea. *A very definite She!*

So he asked the obvious, *You are a lea aren't you?*

A what? came the indignant reply then a pause of silence before she muttered, *Oh yes Lea, yes I am a lea. Dear me it's been so long since I've talked with anyone I must I have gone a little funny in the head. Ha! Now that is funny, I haven't had one of those for a very long time. But I suppose that is what I get for being more inquisitive than I should. Left it well alone I can tell you.*

Left what alone? he could not help but enquire. He was feeling less disorientated now that he had someone to talk to.

The Crystal of course! Should have left it in that cavern with him. I really wish I had....

Her voice sounded so lost and forlorn that Pha-e-gar could feel her pain. He had so many questions but at that yen it didn't seem right to ask any.

All I want to do is go home! Is that so bad?

He wasn't sure she was speaking to him or just speaking out loud, that is, if what they were doing was really speaking in the literal sense. His mind felt as if thick mist had descended as he tried to make sense of things so he was left with only one course and that was to ask another question, *Where are we? And before you answer that who are you?*

No need to shout, I'm not deaf. Well with no ears I suppose I should be. Sorry, just playing with you there. First of all-You, well part of you is inside the Crystal, your mind that is. And secondly my name.. Well that is difficult..Now let me think... I'm sure I had one but it has been so long... Hang on just let me think for awhile.... No! It's all right I remember, they called me Tawny!! Tawny is my name!

Strange name ..... he answered, *Not a name I've heard of being used by a dolph.* He thought for a yen then added, *A Shakeilar name!*

A Shakeilar! Tawny shouted back at him, *I'm a Hu-* She cut herself short.

A Hu? asked Pha-e-gar, now more puzzled than ever ,*What's a Hu?*

I'm sorry, forget I said that, then added as an after thought, *and you will....*

What do you mean I will?

Look just forget it, you have lots of questions and I can't really answer them. Almost as if it had just occurred to her she then asked him, *By the way what is your name?*

Pha-e-gar.

Pha-e-gar...Tawny repeated the name as if it had meant something. Something she had long forgotten and to his amazement she shouted with barely controlled excitement, *Of Course! **Pha-e-gar!!** Why I had forgotten, It has been so long..* There were sounds of tears in her voice as she croaked out, *Oh yes, you poor thing I had so forgotten*, But then in the next breath the excitement returned to her voice and she cried out to him, ***You** can help me. You can begin the beginning and I can go home!*

For the first time in his state of bleak limbo the warning of Eil-e-lea whispered in the back of his mind, ***Beware!*** But he had to know, he had to get out of here so he thought to balance it so he could also be free of the crystal.

Ah Tawny.. he tentatively began, *If I help you will you help me to return to my world.*

What! Yes, of course, your world; Delikadove.. she sounded distracted as if she was trying to work something out, *My world; Earth.....*

Earth? Is that a place? He couldn't help but ask.

I wish you would be quiet but yes. Oh you know of it as Edenlea.

Now that left him further confused, because he like all dolphs had heard that name before as the old name for the sea of Delikadove in the far tays when they were only as dolphin and not dolph. *So was she then an ancient dolphin trapped in the crystal?* As always Pha-e-gar was left with more questions than answers and he felt by the irritated tone of her voice that this time he wouldn't ask even though it burned inside him to do so.

So Pha-e-gar, I will return you to your world but to help me you must first access the central core matrix. She could feel his question but she just shushed him and finished with, *It's the centre of the crystal, the high density part, what your friend was explaining to you and before you say anything I was aware of what was going on but it took the special mind or water-time of Eil-e-lea to allow me to finally have a voice. Now* ***go...***

Even though at her final word he could feel the sudden upsurge in power which was making a light begin to appear at the edge of his vision, the mention of his friend reminded him and he had to know, *Is she all right!* His final words were screamed into the sudden silence and he would never be sure if he heard Tawny say *Yes* or *No.*

Everything changed and one dream came true. For there were stars and he was among them. Going so fast they seemed to blur and he felt filled with delight as he sped through them towards a growing globe of white and blue. As he came nearer he saw the blue planet and as the wave of white cloud swept over him he saw the rich blue green sea of an alien world. His dream and he was being given a look at another world. He knew it was not Delikadove and any question of its name was for the first an unasked and unwanted to know question. Just the thrill flying high over and round seeing continents of various sizes go past. He smelt the rich salt in the air and cries of such different sky-flyers.

But all too soon he began to slow down and he began to fall, so fast he couldn't stop but he could make out an island in the middle of an ocean. Trees, mountains, and the sound of life reached him. When he thought he would be crushed against the ground he was placed upon a yellow sandy beach. The sky was clear with the light of a sun high in the sky, a light sea breeze and the taste of salt upon his tongue. He stood, his toes in the dry sand feeling pleasant and warm. There were the strange trees lining the upper shore line and among them a grey, red moss covered rock sat alone, as if guarding the beach. A strange thought but no stranger than the experience so far. So when the rock moved from its place to stand before him and a rich strong granite voice said, *Welcome. Access is granted.*

He did the only thing possible; he *fainted.*

Before he returned to Delikadove he dreamed a thousand dreams, learnt the unenviable truth of his future and if he was still capable he would wish he had listened to a friend. But then the name that would blind him and bind him to free the lost one would be a name of power.

That name is ....

From Twenty Nine Thousand and Fifty Eight Seasons ago to Present time*.

Recent Cycles of Seasons On Delikadove

Age of Celsen **17426** Seasons long [Later Extended to **19055**]
Age of Tawnal **1629** Seasons long [Absorbed into previous Cycle]
Age of Gealasor **2731** Seasons long
Age of Neimas **7268** Seasons long

Recent Cycles of Seasons On Edenlea

Age of Edenlea **4** Seasons long and *Continuing...*

Authors Note: * Over 35 Million Years Ago

EDENLEA

4 S.E. (Seasons of Edenlea)

Tan-e-lea, like most youngling dolphins, enjoyed asking questions and on this tay she chose to share sounds with her Grand-elder;

"Can I ask a question?"

"When did you ever have to *ask*?" laughed Mel-e-gar.

"You seemed deep in water-time...I wasn't sure if I should disturb you.." replied Tan-e-lea.

"I have many things to see in water-time, but I would not let that stop me from answering any question from you Tan-e-lea." He looked at her and motioned with his flipper for her to get closer and as she responded, he helped her keep pace as he dived deeper. "Go on, ask your question."

"What is the green that doesn't move and flow like water? I saw some earlier totay and it made me want to go there."

"Ahh! You must mean *un-water*. It is that which holds our world in place and once many seasons ago we came from there. But now we cannot return, for if we tried we would die."

"But Why! If we came from there why can't we return Grand-elder?"

He smiled and sounded, "You are of the water part of this world. *More so than the rest of us...*" He stopped and turned into a wave, flipping himself over in a somersault, splashing back into the sea.

Tan-e-lea was not put off and followed her Grand-elder's example; crying with joy as she imitated his manoeuvre to perfection. She came to his side once more and sounded, "Continue..*please*.."

Mel-e-gar knew he had sounded too much to his son's youngling. It was not her time to know such things, she would learn the truth soon enough. But not now and he gave her an honest reply, "I cannot tell you anymore at this time, but I will when you attain a few more seasons. Now go and play *Tan-e-lea!*" giving her a gentle push into an oncoming wave.

"*Yes, Grand-elder..*"

She wasn't happy with his reply but she could not refuse him. Tan-e-lea swam back to join her sisterling and brotherlings, her waters deep in water-time. So many things she wanted to know about her life and her world.

Their home at this time was a large expanse of Edenlea, far from the shores of un-water. Each school of dolphins had an area to themselves, not strict boundaries but by mutual consent they abided by an informal pact. Of course they visited each other often, especially the younglings who were forever playing together.

As dusk fell they arrived home. Solarn had melted the sky on the rim of the world to a red and orange splash which reflected back its image from the water. You could easily have imagined the water boiling as the sun sank beneath the waves.

It always fascinated Tan-e-lea to watch this spectacle each evening. On this particular eve she was with her brotherling. Her Elders had gone to meet with the Elders of the other schools and this time her sisterling and her oldest brotherling were included, leaving Zar-e-gar to keep an eye on Tan-e-lea. A task he didn't mind in the least as her continuous questioning invited his waters to work in creative water-time.

"Why does the light go and darkness come?" she asked.

"I'm surprised you haven't asked before," replied Zar-e-gar.

"I wanted to find my own answer through water-time...But I haven't found it..*So...*"

"You see the light, the round sphere in the sky during light time?"

"Yes!" she replied, the excitement rising in her sound, "It gives us life *and* without it we would not be."

He gazed at her with deep fondness as her innocent eyes took in all he sounded, "Well we call the light *Solarn* and we, that is *Edenlea* travels round it once every season -"

"But *why* light and dark?" interrupted Tan-e-lea.

"If you let me finish little one..*I shall*!" he sounded splashing water at her.

She responded by splashing back and they were soon diving and leaping, swimming this way and that. Laughing sounds filled the air as they exploded to the surface together and embraced, beak to beak. Still laughing they came to rest so that Zar-e-gar could continue.

After swallowing a fish he had found while they had played he sounded, "Mmm! good Tooka..Where was I? Yes...Well..As the world spins it gives a different face to the light causing parts to face away and that causes the darkness to come!"

"I think I understand," Tan-e-lea sounded, "*But why does it happen?!*"

"Well....." He looked at her and was taken by water-time, *Good point! Why indeed..* But instead sounded, "Enough questions! You'll learn soon enough. *Go on*! Go and find your friends."

Again she was not happy with this reply and knew her brotherling either didn't know or wasn't going to tell! So she went to find her friends from the other schools.

He watched his sisterling swim away and returned to finding fish, his favourite pastime. *He did indulge in water-time but not that deep!*

* * *

At the meeting of the Elders Kel-e-lea was bored with the continuous sounds of the others. She didn't see any reason to pay attention and instead swam through the others, weaving patterns through the water. Now and again she would give a friendly bump on the tail of her brotherling, causing him to give her an annoyed look.

Haw-e-gar now very irritated with her, sounded, "You should pay attention!"

"I don't want to!" Kel-e-lea replied as she circled him, "And I'm not going to!"

In reply he gave her a warning sound as their Grand-elder swam over. He was not best pleased by her antics. "You *must* pay attention Kel-e-lea!" rebuked Mel-e-gar, "We invited all the younglings from the age of ten seasons for a good reason."

Kel-e-lea stopped her playfulness, came up to her Grand-elder, looked him in the eye and sounded, "*But Why*!" and proceeded to weave a water pattern around him, her eyes twinkling with mischief. She feared no one but she loved her Grand-elder deeply and his sounds made her realise that there were things more important than her love of water weaving, so she listened.

Mel-e-gar knew Kel-e-lea was just being herself and he found it hard to suppress his laughter at her audacity. But she must learn the *Why's* of their new home so he proceeded to sing her a *watersong*.

Haw-e-gar was so surprised that he flipped beak over tail and dived below, his own annoyance forgotten as his waters delved into past water-time, back in his old home.

His Grand-elder was the only one who could sing watersongs, a talent rarely found among their kind and everyone was surprised that Tan-e-lea was born with the same gift. Especially in the same family, for the gift only appeared every ten generations in their old home. The Elders who studied the deeper water-time found it was not hereditary and no one could explain its origins. It was a great power and could be used in many different ways. But Haw-e-gar remembered his first experience of his Grand-elder's use of the watersong, when he was a youngling of two seasons.

He had managed to be left behind when his family had been caught in a storm; the purple sea was a violent place to be in such times. The rain and wind stirred the sea, creating waves many *dees* high. One moment he was by his motherling's side, the next he found himself alone. Haw-e-gar couldn't understand what had happened. Many times he looked above the waves searching with increased desperation and he cried his sounds. But no matter how he much he called there was no answer. He felt so lost and alone, soon becoming very tired and then his will began to fail him. After awhile all he could do was to float and let the waves take him. He began to turn inward to the deepest levels of water-time, the place to hide within himself.

For him it seemed as if many clars had passed, maybe even tays, when he heard a strange water sound. It sounded of warm comforts, a friendly and loving sound. It penetrated to his wanderings in water-time, making him slowly stir and reach out to this wonderful safe sound. He had not heard of the watersong, so his young mind did not realise that the sounds he listened to belonged to his Grand-elder.

He started to feel a strange tingling sensation which soon spread through his entire form.

What was happening? he sounded and it made him come out of water-time to open his eyes. Tentatively he raised his eye lids. Before him he saw the beak of his Grand-elder, who smiled and sounded, *You are safe now.*.

Haw-e-gar was amazed and he sounded a note of joy, but then the image began to shimmer and fade. His joy turned to alarm and he leapt towards the last whisper of the image. As he passed through it, he heard the song and knew he was safe.

He found himself in front of his Grand-elder, "Are you real?" he gently asked, touching Mel-e-gar's beak, expecting it to disappear at any moment.

"Yes, my *little* grandling...I am very real."

It made him jump. He hadn't been sure that he would get a reply. He then leapt forward and embraced his Grand-elder. "*Thank You! Thank You!*" his sound rang out in joy. "I was lost! I *couldn't* find you....and..I...went deep into my water-time!"

"I know Haw-e-gar! Here are your motherling and fatherling. Go to them," replied his Grand-elder.

He swam to them and his concerned Elderlings embraced and kissed him, laughing with joy, so glad to have their first born safe and sound.

Later as they played, Haw-e-gar asked his Grand-elder how they had found him and Mel-e-gar told him of the power of the watersong. When they realised he had disappeared in the storm and that in the bad conditions their sound would be lost, his Grand-elder had used his watersong to find him. The power of the watersong was in the nature of it. The song sounded in water-time and could travel to any water-time it was directed at. When his Grand-elder had made contact he used his creative abilities to turn the song into a gateway. When Haw-e-gar had leapt at the image, it had brought him back to the originator of the song.

"How wonderful Grand-elder," Haw-e-gar said. "Can you teach me! *Can you*?!" The prospect of such a thing excited him.

"No..my dear youngling...*It cannot be taught.* You have to be born with it," answered Mel-e-gar. He knew that his answer would disappoint his grandling but it couldn't be helped.

Haw-e-gar was disappointed but after a while he soon forgot about it and when in the future he heard his Grand-elder sing, his water-time went to the terror and then the joy when he felt the power of the watersong. These delvings into past water-time made Haw-e-gar look towards his sisterling with very mixed feelings.

The sound rose and all who could feel, felt the power grow stronger. Kel-e-lea didn't know what to do. She hadn't expected this. Her eyes grew bigger and she looked at her Grand-elder in amazement as the sound took hold and she slipped into deep water-time. She learnt about some of the past waters of their kind, revealing a few of the *Whys* that her Grand-elder knew she had to know.

The song caressed her and her water-time opened and flowered, making joy in her heart. She would always be mischievous but now she knew that playing with water weaving was one thing but sometimes there are times when even she must learn about other things.

Her Grand-elder started changing the song so his grandling could see something else, something very special. Kel-e-lea began to come out of her water-time and with her emergence the song faded away.

She looked at her Grand-elder and sounded, "I'm sorry...But thank you so much!" And with that she leapt towards the surface of the sea, breaking through into the night sky sounding her joy at what she had learnt and of course the vision of her talent that he had bestowed upon her. She dived back into the sea and swam quickly towards her friends, making a few water patterns as she went.

Mel-e-gar was satisfied with his work and proceeded back to the meeting to continue mixing his sound with the other Elders. But his water-time went out to Kel-e-lea, *So incorrigible!* Laughing all the while.

Haw-e-gar swam back to join the meeting, hoping that his sisterling would now stop her teasing, then again.. *No! I doubt it!* he sounded to himself. Even he had to laugh at her ways. But he did enjoy the look on her face when his Grand-elder had begun his song.

That shut her up! He chuckled to himself as he settled down to hear the sounds of the Elders.

* * *

Ser-e-gar swam away from the meeting with his mate Car-e-lea. They had decided to swim to the shore of an island twenty klees away from their home. They both indulged in water-time as they moved swiftly through the Edenlea, both occupied by past times, a different sea and different lives.

Car-e-lea swam closer to Ser-e-gar, diving below him and coming up to slide her warm form over his. He responded by nuzzling her neck, making warm loving sounds. They were soon entwining themselves around each other, all past water-times forgotten as they played like younglings, chasing this way and that, diving in and out of the water, joined together as one. Happy sounds filled the water and sky as they touched, caressed and joined their water-times to celebrate their long seasons together.

Ser-e-gar whispered sounds to her. *My Car-e-lea... We have seen many times but these new waters bring us different challenges...*

I know... she whispered and dived through a shoal of Tooka, snatching one as she passed through. She held it in her beak and came back to Ser-e-gar and passed it to him.

He gulped down the fish and sounded, *Why thank you...*and returned the gesture by snatching up a larger fish and presented it to her.

She laughed and sounded, *Too big!* but took it and swam to the surface and tossed the fish into the air. It flashed up high into the sky and fell back to her waiting beak, sliding neatly down her throat. She came back to him and sounded, *Beat that if you can!*

So as they journeyed towards the water surrounding their island they continued the game. By the time they had finished eating and laughing they were gorged but happy.

Ser-e-gar spied the island and turning to his mate sounded, *There it is!* He raced ahead, speeding through the water at a tremendous rate.

Car-e-lea caught up to him sounding, *You'd better slow down or you'll bump your beak on the shore!*

He changed direction and broke through the breaking waves as they pounded the beach. As he flew through the air his body shimmered and changed. Twisting his form around he approached the sea shore tail first. When his tail touched the land, it sparkled with light and split into two. Instead of a tail...Two silver-grey dees, attached to long silver-grey legs. He called out to Car-e-lea, "The un-water is quite fine!"

He watched as she repeated his manoeuvre, but far more graceful in its execution. He sounded his joy when she landed gracefully by his side.

"Now that is what I call an *exhilarating* experience!" She laughed and put a newly formed webbed hand on his shoulder.

"It's a pity that our younglings cannot be here with us.." remarked Ser-e-gar.

Car-e-lea nodded her high domed head and sadly agreed, "I know, it was one of the reasons we left our old home."

They turned and looked towards the sea. Solarn was rising above the horizon, bringing the dawn of a new tay. It was a beautiful morning. Solarn shone its warming light on the two dolphs, making their wet glistening forms sparkle and shimmer as they walked along the edge of the shore. They dug their five, webbed toed dees into the sand, leaving strange deeprints behind them.

Ser-e-gar stopped and sat down on the sand, beckoning Car-e-lea to do the same. They stretched out and basked in the sun. No danger for them but their water-times turned once again to their younglings, *At least they would be safe in Edenlea.*

* * *

Tan-e-lea watched, her grey beak bobbing up and down as the flow of Edenlea carried her nearer to the beach. She kept blinking her eyes, trying to change the image that she beheld. Her parentlings were oblivious to her as she carefully circled around the bay. Her waters delved deeper into water-time, trying to make sense of the vision she had witnessed.

Tan-e-lea had been playing with her friends in the early morning, before Solarn had risen. The wind was still and the stars shone in a clear dark sky. The sounds of the Elderlings finishing their meeting came through the water. She broke from a game with a youngling named Rea-e-gar; a friend who constantly made her laugh at his antics.

He was surprised as she turned and left without any warning sound. He called out goodbye but Tan-e-lea didn't make any sound in response. "Typical Lea!" he sounded and went to find another friend who would indulge him in his particular sense of humour.

What had made her break from her game had been her parentlings leaving the meeting. She had a question for her Fatherling, a question that had been making her water-time deeper than usual. As she swam closer to them her senses made her slow down. Normally she would have sounded to them but something made her stop and she was also curious about their destination. For they were swimming with strong strokes away from their home waters. Her curiosity grew as each klee took her parentlings further away, so she followed them at a discreet distance. *Where were they going?* her water-time sounded.

Tan-e-lea caught fish as she went. It was hard work following them and her young form needed much energy to keep pace. She watched as they played and made such happy sounds that Tan-e-lea felt great joy. It was something to see, their love for each other sweeping the water with such abandonment. She felt a little guilty, this spying on her parentlings but she so much wanted to know where they were going. But they swam faster than she and soon they were out of sight. Tan-e-lea felt too tired to continue. *Must rest* she sounded and swam to the surface and floated, letting her tired flippers go limp. Tan-e-lea was stubborn and was determined to carry on. She knew the general direction that they had gone but she knew that by the time she was rested they might be far out of her reach.

She relaxed and delved into water-time, seeking an answer. Then with a splash and a twist she leapt in joy as an idea came to her. The power of the revelation had caused her to leap high into the air and as she fell back towards the blue water, she hoped her parentlings had not seen her. After all that would spoil everything.

Her idea was simple for one who had the power of the watersong, even if she had never tried it before. *I can do it!* she sounded and proceeded to sing a *watersong*.

Now her Grand-elder had told her the principle of transition through space, that is from one point to another point. He would never, in his wildest water-time have considered that such a youngling as Tan-e-lea would ever be able to do it. After all it was one of the higher arts. It had taken him nearly two seasons to perfect, with many mishaps on the way. She giggled at the memory of her Grand-elder telling his wild stories and when she had asked him if she could learn *water-moving*, as he called it, he had gently laughed and said that she must wait until her fourteenth season. Having only just reached her second, it seemed such a long time away, totally *unreal* to Tan-e-lea.

But at this time her young waters, not being given to beliefs in unreal water-time, proceeded to sing her song. Her slim, silver-grey form began to glow and shimmer, the water around her taking on an eerie light. Small splashes of silver dyed the water and her waters heard the sound of the song. Of rain falling on leaves in a forest, of young sky-flyers crying to their motherlings when they have been brought food and of Edenlea breaking its waves on a far shore. Tan-e-lea felt soothed by it and her form filled with so much energy that she felt she would burst. Instead she felt a warm rush of air surround her, making her open her eyes for the first time since she had begun, not daring to before, in case her song hadn't worked.

That's funny! her water-time not yet realising the truth. Then she screeched in alarm as she made the connection, that she was about fifty dees above *Edenlea!* All this took only a yen and what she found funny, was the sight of an island from a vantage point in the sky. The next yen she was falling fast towards the water. Tan-e-lea was stunned as her form plunged from the sky at a colossal rate. Luckily she was heading for the safety of Edenlea, beak first! Otherwise the fall might have killed her.

The impact of the water discharged her fear and the release of so much tension made her laugh, her sounds crying out for all to hear. She didn't care. She was safe in the warm caress of Edenlea.

Soon her laughter died down and she swam back to the surface to see where she was. She realised as she took in her surroundings that she must have transported herself to the other side of the island, about ten klees away from her parentlings. The sounds she had heard when she had sung her song were the sounds of the island. Except for the rain, for Solarn was beginning to rise above the horizon and it wasn't raining here. Tan-e-lea swam through the water, keeping within sight of the island. *That must be part of un-water!* her waters sounded as the excitement grew inside her. She delved deep in water-time pondering the mistake she must have made but she did not have enough knowledge to know what had gone wrong. All she knew was that she had overshot her mark by about twelve klees as far as the dimension of water goes, but why she had ended up fifty dees up in the air was another matter entirely.

As Tan-e-lea came round the island she saw two forms swimming through the water. *She had caught up!* she sounded and watched as her fatherling leapt out of the water and she realised in alarm that he would hit the shore. She nearly cried out to warn him but the sound stuck in her throat as she witnessed the change. Her young waters couldn't believe it. It was impossible, then she saw her motherling do the same. ***No..no..*** her water-time sounded, ***It cannot be!***

From her safe distance she saw her parentlings walk across the sand, *Grand-elder said they couldn't live on un-water,* her waters sounded, *but they are alive!* and to her they looked very different.

She went deeper and deeper into water-time, her distress mounting as each ripple made little sense. *Why had her Grand-elder told an untruth? It didn't make sense to her.* Tan-e-lea tried to make herself calm down and to see things more clearly. After awhile she succeeded and she found what she had been looking for, the water-time of his words filling her:

...But now we cannot return, for if we tried we would die. And when she had questioned him further he had sounded, *...You are of the water part of this world. More so than the rest of us...* Then he wouldn't tell her any more. At least she knew why he had stopped, but he had told an untruth and that hurt Tan-e-lea. The second part puzzled her, *Was there something different about me!* She sounded to herself and it came to her, there was only one way to find out....

* * *

7255 S.N.

Car-e-lea felt safe with Ser-e-gar as they both wandered through each other's water-times, caressing each other with waters of their early tays together.

She had just reached her twelfth season when she had first met Ser-e-gar. It was while she wandered the streets of the old city, a derelict place full of strange sounds which to her always sounded so very sad. She was gazing up at a high domed building which had no sharp angles. They were rounded and once she could imagine flowed like the waves of Geailea. Even now the building still shone with a sparkling silver hue as the rays of Danetar shone its red light upon it.

"Incredible still isn't it?"

The sound made her jump back in alarm, her dees stumbling on the fallen debris making her fall neatly into a pair of waiting arms.

"You should be more *careful* Car-e-lea!" laughed Ser-e-gar as he helped her regain her balance.

"Who are you?" asked Car-e-lea feeling embarrassed that she had been caught unaware by this stranger. "And..how do you know my name?" She enquired further turning round in his arms but feeling unable to pull away from this strange dolph.

"My name is Ser-e-gar and I know who you are because I asked your friend; Bel-e-lea. And..I.." Now it was his turn to stumble, but on words not on stone. "..I wanted to meet with you..." He let go of her, his confidence floundering under her inquiring gaze. He met her eyes with his own and drank his fill of her green and grey eyes, the most beautiful that he had ever seen. Ser-e-gar for a moment was lost for words.

Car-e-lea decided to come to his rescue. "Yes it is *incredible*!" Returning him to his original question, and slipping her hand into his, she walked into the building.

He let her lead him in, feeling grateful to her for changing the subject. They both looked around the circular room they had entered, gazing in awe at the way the walls seemed to flow and weave around them, still shimmering with a blue radiance. It made them both feel as if they had stepped into the sea of Geailea. In the middle of the room was an altar made from green and blue crystals that refracted the light that shone from the walls. To them both it seemed as if the crystals gave the walls an illusion of movement.

"Amazing!" exclaimed Ser-e-gar. "I have heard of the ancients building such places, but I didn't realise that any still existed!" He reluctantly let go of Car-e-lea's hand and walked further into the chamber. He came to the crystal altar and moved his hands over it. The light changed as he did so, casting his own silver grey skin with a hue of green and blue.

"Look!" cried Car-e-lea. Ser-e-gar looked up and what he saw was strange indeed! His hands were still on the crystals as he watched his own colour added to the spectrum of light, making the walls bleed with his silver grey. The colours seemed to dance and slip into each other, joining and separating the flow over the walls and ceiling.

Then a voice boomed out to pierce their awe:

"You Must Leave This Place - Younglings of *Edenlea*!"

The name struck a familiar tone in Ser-e-gar, something his fatherling had spoken on in past tays. His waters were caught between the past and future as he tried to pull his hands away from the crystals, but they seemed to be immobilized. A strange force was holding him in place. He looked pleadingly at Car-e-lea. She could still hear the echo of the voice in her waters and for a yen she too felt unable to move. But she struggled away her confusion and rushed to Ser-e-gar's side, feeling a great deal more than she believed she should for this strangely compelling dolph.

As she placed her own hands on his the light changed once more. Now the light that radiated from the crystals began to pulsate in an eerie rhythm. They both felt as if the very sea of Geailea was about to gush forth. Then it changed again and as the weight they had felt lifted, it made them feel warm and safe in a way strangely unlike anything they had ever felt before.

For the last time the strange voice spoke:

"YOU ARE NOW JOINED! NOW *LEAVE-EEE*!"

It echoed round and round the chamber then the light flashed into such a blinding bright intensity that it made them both hold their hands over their eyes. They did not at first realise that they were both free of the force that had held them. As their eyes adjusted they found themselves on a high, red grassy plain. The city had completely disappeared.

They were both bewildered. *Where had the city gone?!* Ser-e-gar turned and faced Car-e-lea. "Has anybody ever told you that you are very beautiful?"

She laughed and said, "Now that is what I call *changing* the subject!" and flung her arms around him, holding tightly as if he too might vanish into thin air. She whispered into his ear, "*I love you too..*" Car-e-lea felt the truth of her words tug at her heart and she ached for him as they stood on the high plain, where only yens before there had stood an old city of the ancients.

For them both it was a beginning that had changed their lives. If a yen can be a life time, then their lives had always been entwined. They left the hilltop, making their way to one of the last cities to be inhabited by their race. Plesilea lay by the shore of Geailea, at the mouth of the river Jeralea. As they ran down the hill they were met by a crowd of dolphs that came rushing up to them-so many voices with so many questions which exploded in upon them. The sound was deafening. Ser-e-gar held his hands up for silence as he and Car-e-lea came to an abrupt halt half way down the hill. Soon they were both encircled by the mass of curious dolphs, all seeking answers from them. In response to Ser-e-gar's signal they soon quietened down. He turned to Car-e-lea and said, "You tell them, after all it was your find."

She smiled at him and turned to the crowd and told them what had happened-how she had gone exploring the old city looking for answers to questions about her race. (The ancient times of their world had fascinated Car-e-lea ever since she was a small youngling.) Her meeting with Ser-e-gar and what the voice had told them - on reflection this was a great deal. *That is, as far as Ser-e-gar and herself were concerned!* When she told them of the flash of light followed by finding themselves on a red hillside, where a city had once stood, the crowd went into an uproar, crying out even more questions.

Neither of them knew how to answer them for that was all they knew and as they waited for the crowd to quieten down they were aware of it parting in two. A dolph came striding up through the passage that had been made.

As he came nearer Car-e-lea cried out, "*Mel-e-gar!*" You could hear the awe in her voice.

Then Ser-e-gar surprised her by crying out, "Fatherling!"

That made Car-e-lea stare in wonder at Ser-e-gar. "You mean he's *your* Fatherling!"

"Yes..Didn't you know!" laughed Ser-e-gar.

"*No...*" she whispered.

Mel-e-gar was an imposing figure of a dolph if you didn't know him and his presence certainly overwhelmed Car-e-lea. She stood there silent under his probing gaze. He was tall for a dolph. Most only reach the height of twelve dees but he was nearly seventeen dees high which made everyone crane their silver grey necks up to look him in the face. Well worth the look, for he had a high domed head that came down in a gentle slope to form a pear shaped face. The most compelling feature being the grey blue eyes that seemed to read your waters as easily as the flow of Geailea.

He reached out and pulled his youngling to him. "I see you have found yourself a friend to play with.." joked Mel-e-gar.

Ser-e-gar grinned broadly showing the rows of tightly packed teeth that gleamed brightly in the afternoon light of Danetar. "Yes I have!" grinning even more.

Mel-e-gar turned to Car-e-lea and said, "I knew your Fatherling very well." As if reading her waters he continued, "*I miss him too...*"

Car-e-lea read the kindness in his eyes, grateful for the recognition of her loss.

He had died in the summer, killed whilst exploring the remains of Zylasayer, a city near the Bylinkan mountains, not that far away from where they were all gathered. An old building had collapsed killing not only him but several of his party also.

This came as a surprise to Ser-e-gar. He had not realised that he had been chasing the daughterling of Jan-e-gar, a renowned explorer of the old ways. His heart went out to Car-e-lea and grabbing her hand he pulled her to him, including her in his family. After all he had lost his Motherling during the return of the Great Deathsong two seasons before and knew the pain of her loss.

They stood holding each other within Mel-e-gar's strong embrace for a few yens and then Mel-e-gar told them it was time to go. He called out to the crowd to join him in the Council chambers within the clar. For only he knew the truth behind the events that had befallen his youngling and his new friend or should he say *mate*!

Car-e-lea and Ser-e-gar were abruptly brought back from the wanderings in past water-time by a loud wet slap on the sand. They both sat up and stared in disbelief at the sight before them. For there on the shore was a dolphin and as it turned its eyes towards them, they realised with an awful sinking feeling that the dolphin was their daughterling *Tan-e-lea...*

* * *

Mel-e-gar felt a shock of pain course through his form. The vision that shattered his wanderings in water-time was the first stage of the deathsong. It made him cry out in alarm! *No...It cannot be! Not Tan-e-lea!!* He tried to shake the vision from his water-time, trying hard to pull his sounds together. As Mel-e-gar brought some measure of control over his water-time he managed to ease the pain that the shock of the song had brought him.

As all dolphins are linked through the deepest part of their water-time, it was possible for any of them to call in times of trouble. Or if that link was as interwoven as it was for Mel-e-gar and Tan-e-lea it made it an empathic sound, so he would feel what she felt in times of great danger.

Mel-e-gar had not long finished teaching the younglings in the ways of their home and had then gone off to find Tan-e-lea because somewhere deep within his water-time he knew that his youngest grandling was not happy with their earlier discussion in sound. It had made a ripple that would grow into something that would have to be dealt with soon. *But even the **Great Mel-e-gar** can miss the obvious,* he ruefully sounded.

The pain subsided as he put into place well practised blocks to protect himself, for he knew that a powerful link can bring an empath the same death as the one who is going through the deathsong. Mel-e-gar began to reach out and soon he sensed the combined sounds of Ser-e-gar and Car-e-lea. Their shock came to him in waves and he had to renew his blocks so that their pain did not overwhelm him. As a clear picture began to form he saw the beach and the still form of Tan-e-lea.

Mel-e-gar knew that they could not help their daughterling while they were on un-water. She was too far up the beach for them to pull her to safety, and Tan-e-lea could not help herself as her watersong did not work out of Edenlea.

Mel-e-gar began to sing. It made his body gradually glow with brighter and more luminous shades of silver and grey, radiating into Edenlea, making the life forms that were living in the vicinity dance through the water in raptures of great pleasure as the watersong drew on their energy, building into a crescendo that blasted the water away from Mel-e-gar in great waves. With a flash of dazzling silver he was gone.

Now Kel-e-lea was playing happily with the other dolphins as she too vanished from Edenlea bringing a rush of water to fill the void left behind her. Her water-time felt the reassurance of the presence of her Grand-elder. *What is happening?* she sounded to herself. Being so young she was surprised when an answer came to her from Mel-e-gar.

I need your help, he sounded gently, not wishing to cause Kel-e-lea too much alarm and went on to explain to her what had happened to her sisterling.

You need my help! she sounded as the shock of the vision washed over her.

Yes.. he laughed, *I do indeed..I need the help of your special talent. Now you will understand what I sounded to you earlier on. But even I did not see in the water-time that it would be this soon that we would have need of the Waterweaver.*

The Waterweaver, sounded Kel-e-lea. It felt good that at last she could use what she had believed to be nothing more than a toy in her play time.

This exchange between the two only lasted for a brief yen in time as Kel-e-lea materialised beside her Grand-elder. She felt herself supported by the gentle touch of Mel-e-gar's flipper, helping her keep up as he sped through Edenlea at a tremendous rate. So fast that to Kel-e-lea it seemed that the world of Edenlea was but a blur of blue and green as the warm waters passed over their sleek forms.

Mel-e-gar used the passing of water-time to explain his plan to help her sisterling. He had to omit that her parentlings were with Tan-e-lea, for it would have to wait until a meeting of the Council before he could divulge that knowledge to the rest of the younglings. It was the first time in his wanderings in water-time that Mel-e-gar questioned the wisdom of keeping back so much of their past times. But he told himself they couldn't start to break the rules that had been made with the best of intentions if they were to survive in this their New Edenlea.

About two klees from un-water Mel-e-gar stopped and reached for the water-times of Ser-e-gar and Car-e-lea. *Leave this place. I will bring Tan-e-lea to you when she is safe! Now go!*

He felt the relief as they understood his message for with those brief sounds came the full picture of the reasons they must leave the youngest of their younglings.

* * *

Solarn was still shining brightly on the two dolphs as they sat cradling Tan-e-lea on the shore of the island. They were still recovering from the shock of seeing their daughterling stranded on un-water. Many questions passed through both Ser-e-gar and Car-e-lea's water-time. *What had made Tan-e-lea follow them?*

There seemed no answer except for their daughterling's insatiable thirst for knowledge.

Ser-e-gar looked at the glistening form of Tan-e-lea and his love for her passed through him into her still form. "*Please* save my daughterling!" he cried. It had turned a beautiful tay into a nightmare when they had been awakened from their water-time to find Tan-e-lea on the beach. He felt helpless because he knew that she was too far up the beach for them to drag her to the water.

Car-e-lea took hold of his hand and said, "I will go and bring some of Edenlea to her."

"You must find something to carry it in *and*," He turned to her and gazed into her eyes and sounded, "Be careful not to let too much water touch you!"

Car-e-lea was far more practical than Ser-e-gar and she responded by giving him an *I know* look. She laid Tan-e-lea's beak gently onto the sandy beach and walked to the tree line searching for something which would hold water. For if enough of Edenlea touched her skin she would be transformed back into a dolphin and then have to change back again, wasting water-time. Soon after searching the line of trees she found a broken shell. It had once been the home of one of Edenlea's many creatures - *a Galdane,* she recalled as she carried the dry black shell to the water's edge. Carefully she dipped it into the water and so the shell became a cup of life giving water.

Car-e-lea walked slowly over to Tan-e-lea and holding the shell over her daughterling poured some of Edenlea over her dry beak, massaging the water into Tan-e-lea so her skin didn't dry and crack under the rays of Solarn. After Car-e-lea had finished she kissed Tan-e-lea and hugged her beak in her arms.

Tan-e-lea remained oblivious to her motherling for she was swimming deep in a realm of water-time. She kept seeing different forms flash past her and every now and then she could discern a face, that kept appearing then disappearing from her water-time. Gradually the face began to hold more meaning to her. It was her Grand-elder. He seemed to be trying to tell her something but as the deathsong took hold she slipped further away from him. A feeling of peace transported her down to the depths of a new kind of water-time. Then there was light. So much light that she had to blink to regain her sight. As her eyes became accustomed to the light she saw a strange vision.

Tan-e-lea found herself in a place that she had never been, a place that her water-time was incapable of translating into terms that she could understand. Tan-e-lea was in a large building. The ceiling stretched far above her head and the colours of blue-green and silver-grey danced over the walls like the passing of many waves of Edenlea.

Her young water-time gazed in wonder at the sights that came to her. She wondered where she could be and what sort of place could have the feelings of the very depths of her home-Edenlea but still not be Edenlea? She walked across the room and came to an altar that held a collection of crystals that reflected the light from the walls. *How beautiful!* she sounded and she reached for them. As her hands touched them she changed as waves of light flowed through her, causing her to feel great pleasure then great sadness as if something wonderful had been and then had passed from life leaving a tear to fall and splash onto the crystals. When the tear touched they seemed to grow larger and the vision that Tan-e-lea saw changed again.

This time she found herself standing on a hilltop of red grass, something she had never seen before. Then she stopped, *her water-time realising that she was standing on un-water using five toed dees! But where was her tail?* The realisation that she had somehow, in this place, become what she had seen but had found hard to believe, when she had witnessed her parentlings standing on the island. The concept had blown her water-time apart then. But now she was thrown into an even greater confusion. *For how had she become like them and where was this place?*

Before she could formulate any answer to the many questions that had come upon her the scene changed once again and with it a feeling of despair because her water-time had let her see wonders but had left her more confused than ever. Then as her feelings of despair started to grow she felt the warm embrace of Edenlea.

Car-e-lea felt Tan-e-lea grow even more still and the warmth of her daughterling's form seeped into the sand. She looked to Ser-e-gar and saw tears running down his face. "*She is leaving us..*" he quietly sounded. As they both reached out to each other in their despair they felt a glowing presence fill their water-time and their feelings changed to happiness as they felt the contact of Mel-e-gar and hope grew in their hearts.

As Mel-e-gar told them what was needed from them they both looked at their daughterling and sounded, "Wait little one, *please* wait a little longer. Your Grand-elder is coming to help you!" They then reluctantly laid Tan-e-lea's beak gently down and Car-e-lea kissed her goodbye and took hold of Ser-e-gar's hand and sounded, "It's time to go. She will be *fine*.."

Ser-e-gar found it hard to respond to his mate's sound but he slowly acknowledged her and sounded, "Yes..I will come."

They left Tan-e-lea on the beach and walked to the line of trees and stopped and turned to face Edenlea. They silently gathered themselves and ran towards the waves. As they approached the first line of waves, they launched themselves into the air. Their silver-grey forms flashed through the air and as they reached the pinnacle of height they straightened their forms in perfect union falling towards Edenlea. Reaching it, their bodies seem to explode into a cascade of light as the power of transformation brought them back to the womb of Edenlea.

Ser-e-gar and Car-e-lea were not long in reaching Haw-e-gar and Zar-e-gar. It felt good to them to be back, where they were beginning to realise was the best place for them.

Mel-e-gar was glad to see his youngling and mate back where they belonged and watched within his water-time as they swam back to their other younglings.

He turned in the water and faced Kel-e-lea, "You can now begin." He sounded and she responded by singing her song, the Song of a Waterweaver.

Mel-e-gar helped guide Kel-e-lea as she began her song and he knew now that despite his earlier reservation, the secrets of the old time would have to be brought out into the open, so nothing like this could ever happen again.

As Kel-e-lea's song grew in power a new kind of light filled the depth of Edenlea. A few dees in front of them a swirl of water began to spin around a central axis, spewing off shards of green, yellow and blue light in all directions. At its centre a white light began to form and within its centre a purple light grew out to touch the waters with greedy tentacles. It pulled water in on itself and began to mix a powerful potion that slowly shifted and changed, creating a bubble many dees in diameter. Kel-e-lea concentrated even more as the power she welded began to grow, making her form glow a bright beautiful shade of purple, a strange sight not witnessed since ages past.

Mel-e-gar helped her as she sang her song, giving advice as the pull of the song made her cry out with joy. He found that he didn't have to do much for she showed herself to be a master of her craft. Before them the bubble or maybe it should be called an orb grew larger as each moment of water-time passed, its purple sheen lighting their beaks with its eerie glow. Then Kel-e-lea let out a last cry of her song and the light started to fade from her form, which now began to heave in the water as the pressure released itself. She did a backward flip through the water of Edenlea, surprising Mel-e-gar as waves of warm water washed over him.

"I did It! I did It!" she sounded with delight. A few dees away a purple orb speckled with pear shaped drops of blue hung motionless in the water.

"Yes you have certainly done it," he agreed laughing at the joy that was spread all over her cute dolphin face. “Now I must do my part..You may *leave* if you like,” he jokingly sounded.

“Leave!” Kel-e-lea cried, “You must be joking!”

His form shook with laughter at the indignant look in her eyes, “Well settle down and I’ll begin.”

Kel-e-lea looked fondly on her Grand-elder as he began his song. And it was her turn to look on with amazement as the power of his watersong took hold of the orb and as it seemed to glow with his light of silver and grey, it flashed a brilliant white then vanished.

Now Mel-e-gar turned his water-time to sending the orb to Tan-e-lea. He saw her lying motionless on the shore and as he sang a new tune to his watersong the purple orb hovered above Tan-e-lea and began to descend towards her. He adjusted his song once more and the orb slowly began to envelop Tan-e-lea. Soon she was obscured within the orb. Only a shadow of herself could be seen. Mel-e-gar brought his song to a new depth and the purple orb flashed twice then vanished from un-water and so with it did Tan-e-lea, bringing her home.

Kel-e-lea sounded with amazement as the orb reappeared and then vanished leaving an even more startled Tan-e-lea in its place.

“Grand-elder!” she sounded with surprise, “Oh Grand-elder I know! Why did-”

He interrupted her and sounded, “Quiet now young one..We have much to sound on. But let’s travel in water-time later, we must get you back to your parentlings.” And he gave her a look which silenced her sounds.

Kel-e-lea witnessed this exchange and questions began to form within her water-time that she would like answers to but before she could begin Mel-e-gar gathered them both to him and with a sound of delight which made their questions fall to the depth of Edenlea, he took them home by the power of his watersong.

THE COUNCIL

Early, the following tay Mel-e-gar left the school and followed the current south, his waters reviewing the events of the previous tay. He gave only a cursory glance as he passed the island, breathing the salty air before diving back beneath the waves as he altered his course slightly east, taking him away from the main flow as he weaved his way through several smaller islands until he was sure of his position. Then with a cry of his song his body shimmered with silver light and he transported himself seventy klees further east. His reappearance caused a shoal of Tooka to scatter in all directions as he headed for the surface to check that he had not gone too far. As his beak broke through he saw that his song had been true and he had found what he had been searching for. It was not often that he used his song randomly in travelling through Edenlea but as he needed to traverse a greater distance in the shortest time he had taken the chance. In the distance a large island dominated the horizon. With a flick of his tail he descended, his sounds soon picking up the shadowy outline of the reef which he had been hoping for. The perfect place for the younglings to explore while the Grand-elders and Elders, including several Younglings who had passed their twelfth- the age of maturity, had the Council meeting to honour the new season.

Apart from the convoluted reef which ran like many streams over the ocean floor it was the island itself which Mel-e-gar found himself drawn to. It was dominated by a large volcano that made his waters twinge with a flicker of pain bringing a clear picture of another place only a few short seasons ago. Only Que-e-lea-the Nursery Motherling and Jer-e-lea would know the significance even though most of the younglings had seen that other island's bleak, barren south shore, without ever realising what lay hidden on the north side.

Giving himself a yen to let his waters settle he rested upon the surface watching Solarn's light sparkle on the yellow beach, while making the foliage of the forest that seemed to have swept up the sides of the volcano appear like a great dark green wave, broken only by thin streams of molten lava that ran along ancient beds among the trees.

Deciding he had seen enough he slipped below the surface and began to swim back to the nine families that comprised the school, who would be waiting for his return.

The nursery motherling had been busy among the families, bringing all the younglings together and choosing Jer-e-lea, a youngling of ten seasons to act as the head of those younglings between three and eleven seasons in the absence of their respective parentlings. It was her task to make sure that they did not stray too far from the school. To assist her with this she had three helpers, one of which was Kel-e-lea who was the same age as herself and who had helped to share a sometimes troublesome water-time before. The other two were Fer-e-gar, a gar of nine seasons and then there was Tey-e-lea, the youngest of the trio at six seasons young. This helped in looking after the wide age group of young dolphins as it meant they could communicate to all of the younglings at their different levels of development, leaving Que-e-lea with her main task of looking after the remaining eight younglings from the age of two seasons and younger, which included Tan-e-lea.

The preparations were in full swing when Jer-e-lea and Que-e-lea heard the sound of Mel-e-gar in their water-time. They were both busy organising the younglings to move to an area of Edenlea which they had agreed was safe for their charges to play in undisturbed. So they broke from their tasks and sounded to their deputies to take over. Que-e-lea had chosen Tan-e-lea as hers on this tay.

They both swam through Edenlea sharing water-time as they went to meet Mel-e-gar. They saw him playing with Zar-e-gar and as they approached Zar-e-gar gave Mel-e-gar a playful slap with his tail, then swung round and planted a kiss on his beak. He then sped off through the blue-green water chasing a particularly large fish. They both laughed as Zar-e-gar dived underneath the fish, giving it a thwack with his tail, flinging the fish upwards, breaking the surface of Edenlea, to continue its untimely flight through the early morning sky, and as it came spinning back down Zar-e-gar leapt through the surface and neatly caught the fish in his beak. He then twisted himself in mid-air and plunged through the waves to finally stop in front of Mel-e-gar.

“Breakfast!” laughed Zar-e-gar and passed the fish to Mel-e-gar who grinned at him while accepting the fish, which quickly slid down Mel-e-gar’s throat.

“Ah! The best way of having breakfast! Letting one of the younglings do the fishing for a change!” laughed Mel-e-gar. He then motioned to Zar-e-gar to come closer, who immediately complied and Mel-e-gar whispered something to Zar-e-gar. Whatever it was, it made Zar-e-gar burst into a roaring sound of almost cackling laughter. He then turned from them and quickly swam through the rich waters of Edenlea laughing as he went.

“Now there goes a dolphin who is in love with finding fish, the bigger and tastier the better it seems,” chuckled Mel-e-gar.

Still chuckling he turned his attention to Que-e-lea and Jer-e-lea. As they came closer his water-time remarked on how similar they looked. Now Que-e-lea being of sixty seasons was the larger of the two but with her grey blue eyes which twinkled great amusement, they were almost identical. Her sleek lines over a form of twelve dees long had silver streaks that flowed over her like a phosphorus wave. Jer-e-lea seemed to have the same grace and markings on her smaller form of six dees. But she did have one difference. Her eyes had a green-blue hue to them which made them almost glow as the light of Solarn filtered through Edenlea. Then Mel-e-gar’s water-time quivered, *Why of course!* he sounded to himself, *Que-e-lea was Jer-e-lea’s Great Aunt-ling. My waters must be evaporating..!* and laughed as water-time told him that with sixty three dolphins to guide it wasn’t surprising that his water-time paused for a moment.

“Welcome Que-e-lea and Jer-e-lea!” he sounded. “We have much to discuss on this tay. Come and we will swim through water-time together.”

His much larger form swam between them and beckoned them with his flippers to come close to him.

Que-e-lea gave Jer-e-lea an, *I know what that means*, look and swam after Mel-e-gar. Soon they were swimming through Edenlea, diving and playing as they explored each other’s water-time.

Que-e-lea was the first to make a contribution to their combined water-time. *I have chosen the place for totay’s nursery.*

Good, responded Mel-e-gar, *but I have somewhere else, a very special place to take the younglings this time. There is a coral reef about a klee from an island of un-water, which makes it a journey of two tays from here.*

Now that threw them both into confusion and it was Jer-e-lea who responded to Mel-e-gar. *Why so far?*

And before he could reply Que-e-lea sounded, *Yes, the younglings would find such a journey very tiring and we do not know those waters of which you sound.*

I know but I have my reasons for such a journey. He turned and patted Que-e-lea's under belly which quite shocked her.

She replied, *Now you must have taken leave of your senses!*

Your water-time has been growing in straight lines my dear youngling! To take such offence! he laughed.

Jer-e-lea was shocked by this exchange between two Elders. But then she had not seen these two play their particular game before. She decided the best course was to be quiet for a yen.

Que-e-lea now getting into the swing of their game responded. *And your water-time is growing dry in your old age!*

Mel-e-gar *roared* and dived over Jer-e-lea quite startling her and then came underneath to give Que-e-lea a tremendous blow to her under side, which knocked her beak over tail, slicing through the water causing her to spin seemingly out of control.

It was so funny to see that Jer-e-lea burst out *laughing*, her sound carrying through the water to Que-e-lea.

As their water-time was still linked Que-e-lea responded, *You're a great help*! But she soon joined the laughter that Jer-e-lea seemed unable to control.

After awhile they came together again and continued their swim.

Mel-e-gar and Que-e-lea shared their water-time with Jer-e-lea and their sounds told her of the seasons before when Mel-e-gar and Que-e-lea first became friends in their old home. Which soon explained why they mixed their water-time in this way.

7225 S.N.

They told her of a night when their old world was in the throes of change and they had met in the coastal city of Yengile on the northern continent. Que-e-lea had just begun her training as a nursery motherling to a group in that city and it was Mel-e-gar's task to check her progress. As she was only thirteen seasons young when she started, some made it clear that her water-time was a bit immature for such a responsible job. The water-time of many younglings was very precious and great care was taken on their first education. So they chose carefully who they appointed. Mel-e-gar was one of those who questioned the wisdom of appointing one so young.

Mel-e-gar had begun experimenting on different ways of using his power of the watersong and this night he did not expect to be called away from his studying in water-time to oversee a young apprentice nursery motherling. Considering he had objected to her position he was surprised that the Council had insisted that he, as Head of the Council should pay her a visit. But never one to turn down a task, he went along to the purple beach of Yengile City.

His home was in a semi-underwater city which he had helped to design eight seasons before which in return they had named it the City of Melegarn in honour of him. It was about thirty klees away from Yengile and he decided to surprise his charge by swimming to her location.

A beautiful night.. his waters rippled as the two moons, Jedikar and Leatar, rose high in the night sky as he made his way through the streets of his city. The streets wound their way round buildings that all shimmered by the light of their moons. Beautiful greens, blues, reds, yellows and some with a silver sheen that sparkled and flowed across the wavy edges of the buildings. They were created to be smooth to the touch and they all felt alive.

Mel-e-gar had not met Que-e-lea before. He had only been told about her by the Council meeting that evening. So he wondered what she was like. "Well I'll soon find out," he sounded out loud as he passed a group of dolphs walking to the submerged part of the city. They looked at him as he overtook them and as they started to respond to his remark, so he returned their gaze, smiled and waved them on. *I must stop sounding to myself! Otherwise I'll keep getting in water-time with too many dolphs!*

He had noticed that as his work progressed, the way dolphs communicated was rapidly changing. Instead of "Thoughts" or "Mind", in was coming more the way of Edenlea, *The Way of the Water-time.*

He came to what he called the launch platform, where those who wished to transform in a more dramatic way could if they so wished. He had made sure that any dolphs that took the gentler way could slip into the ocean of Geailea by way of the swimming tube, where you could slide gently into the sea- not that the change was any less spectacular but the dramatic appeal of the launch pad appealed to Mel-e-gar's sense of humour and adventure. Many of his fellow dolphs agreed with him.

On this eve there were many preparing to go to the submerged part of the city. He waited his turn like everyone else and soon he was ready to go home, as he saw it. Mel-e-gar ran along the long piece of Shakeilar. When he reached the end he launched himself into the air, going up into the sky maybe as much as fifty dees. He could hear the *gasps* from the crowd below as they watched him do a triple somersault in the air. After all it was not every tay that they witnessed the architect of their city display his talent so openly. For Mel-e-gar was different in that he changed shape in mid air and not on contact with Geailea. He used his power to bring a cloud of water vapour to descend from the sky and wrap itself around him like a cloak. As it touched, his body shimmered and changed. His form of seventeen dees long grew by five and he made a spectacular *splash* as he smoothly dived beak first into the embrace of Geailea.

Mel-e-gar dived deep then began his swim to Yengile City. It wasn't long before he came within two klees of the beach. His speed changed and then he launched from the water, spinning in mid air, his form changing once again. As he changed he could hear squeals of alarm. *A bit too close!* his water-time told him as he landed on the soft sand. But it was so exhilarating. He laughed out loud much to the displeasure of an angry looking dolph who marched up to him. Now this dolph was only six dees high, so Mel-e-gar had to kneel down to get closer. His silver grey hand stopped her oncoming charge.

"Whoa!" he said.

"Whoa! *Yourself*. Who the..? What the..? *Are You*?!" shouted back the angry dolph.

He calmly appraised the dolph before him, "Well I could ask the same, but I don't think I have to. For you *must be* Que-e-lea.."

This stopped another torrent of abuse and she pulled herself up and replied. "Well at least you've got that right. Now would you mind telling me who the..*You are*?!"

"My you are a rude youngling!" he said and walked over to the other younglings on the beach. They all looked up at him, their silver grey mouths hanging open. There were ten in all and they looked up in wonder at this large dolph before them.

A young dolph blinked twice and screwed up her courage and blurted out, "It's *Mel-e-gar*!"

Mel-e-gar turned and sat by this young dolph, still choosing to ignore Que-e-lea, who by now was standing by her dolphs, putting out protective hands around two of them. She was still fuming at the interruption but she realised that she had just insulted a Grand-elder and not just any Elder, but Mel-e-gar himself, the champion of Edenlea.

Well I'll be..How should I know? She thought rather shame faced. Taking the hand of each of the young dolphs by her side she walked over to Mel-e-gar and said, "Next time please let me know you are coming so you don't startle my charges like that!"

She has spirit, I give that much to her, his waters observed as he looked down at Que-e-lea. Even sitting he was several dees taller than she. "Yes, you are right I should have warned you but then again, what better way of testing out my new pupil!" he replied grinning at her, his eyes smiling warmly, making his face light up. It made the younglings come scurrying over to meet this large imposing but friendly dolph.

"I apologise for my outburst Mel-e-gar." But her young face still had a defiant look about it.

"Come and sit Que-e-lea," and he motioned with his hand for her to join him on the beach.

The night wore on and the two dolphs, one large and one small but large in spirit, began to talk and soon they became good friends. Mel-e-gar's opposition to her appointment disappeared at that first meeting and he learnt that the number of seasons that a dolph had passed had no bearing on their ability to do their task.

"Now I understand," sounded Jer-e-lea as they finished their story and she looked at them in a new light.

Mel-e-gar turned to Que-e-lea and smiled. "When are you going to ask if Jer-e-lea wants to be your pupil?"

"Why not now?" she replied and turned her attention to Jer-e-lea and asked, "So after hearing about the trials of one Nursery motherling, do you think you could handle such a job?" as she tapped her flipper on Jer-e-lea's beak.

Now Jer-e-lea had not been expecting that and she found that no sound would come from her beak. So she answered in water-time, *Yes! Yes! I would love to!* They all laughed and played as they began to head back towards the school of dolphins.

* * *

Tan-e-lea was teaching the younglings in her charge how to catch fish. They were all making great laughing sounds as Tan-e-lea dashed this way and that through the early morning water. She was having great fun getting the others to swim through a passing shoal to try and snatch their breakfast. Now the fish were not co-operating at all, and the youngest of the dolphins found it a great deal of effort to catch a fish in their beaks. What made it harder for them was Tan-e-lea being dragged through the water by a fish that wasn't a fish but a Reakea that had wandered past, oblivious to the antics of the dolphins. It was not pleased when one grabbed its short stubby tail and seemed determined to hang on. Tan-e-lea enjoyed the ride as the creature struggled to break free from this annoyance, even though every so often her beak would bump into the hard shell that covered most of the Reakea's body, as it twisted through the water, causing her beak to grow increasingly sore.

It wasn't long before her antics brought the attention of the elder younglings and soon the water was filled with the roar of cheering dolphins. "Hang on!" they sounded. "Don't let the *Reakea* go!"

The Reakea decided to end the game by twisting its body, making Tan-e-lea lose her now tenuous grip. She flipped backwards through the water and was about to swim away when the Reakea swung round and snapped at her tail. It just missed as Tan-e-lea flipped her tail out of the way.

"That will teach you!" sounded Zar-e-gar as he joined the school.

Tan-e-lea was relieved that it hadn't made contact, but she was surprised that the Reakea had responded that way. *I was only playing,* sounded Tan-e-lea to herself.

Yes, you may well have been, intruded Zar-e-gar on her water-time, *but the Reakea doesn't know that. Hasn't anyone told you that you do not interfere with those creatures in that way. They are not known as Snapping Reakea for nothing. Those jaws could have torn into your tail making a real mess of it. You were very lucky. I believe you were supposed to be keeping an eye on these younglings! And not teaching them silly tricks.*

Tan-e-lea had not expected such an outburst from her brotherling but she realised that she had not been very responsible with her charges. *I am sorry Zar-e-gar!*

Okay, Tan-e-lea but remember to show a little respect to the other creatures that also inhabit our home. With that he left her to delve into her water-time and hopefully she would remember this particular lesson. Now Zar-e-gar was not known as a great delver into water-time but he knew a great deal about their home in Edenlea, the dangers and the pleasures that were to be found. But even he could see the funny side to her display. He *laughed* at the image it brought forth.

His water-time transferred him to the joke that his Grand-elder had whispered to him early that morning. It made him laugh even more as the image of himself being born with a fish in his beak formed in his water-time. That brought other images of their old home, of purple seas and an array of fish in so many forms, more diverse than those he had so far encountered here. With it brought a special water-time spilling forth and ripples of great pleasure flooded his being. *Arh! Vue-e-lea...*

Now that was a dolphin that brought pleasure as well as some tears to Zar-e-gar. She taught him a great deal about fish and all the creatures that inhabited his old home, of the Kerg that lived in the orange sky as well as the great seas. Vue-e-lea considered it to be the greatest finder of fish that their old world knew and all Zar-e-gar's lessons revolved around it. "*To be a Kerg*.." she would sound, always with a tinge of sadness as that was her dream.

Zar-e-gar hoped that one tay she would come to his new home as he missed her so much. The Elders had told him that like so many others she had to stay behind. There had been no contact with their old home for more than two seasons and he continued to wonder why. That time played for him as he swam to join Fer-e-gar and Tey-e-lea in their task of taking all the younglings to the reef that Mel-e-gar had shown him in his water-time.

Tan-e-lea had just finished sharing water-time with the seven younglings her age and younger, passing on the lesson that Zar-e-gar had shown her when she received the call from Que-e-lea to join her and the other younglings. "Come on!" she sounded and led them away through the sparkling water. Solarn was rising higher into the clear blue sky, telling her that much of the morning had passed. They swam together, playing as they went, in the things that pleased their young water-time.

* * *

Que-e-lea had enjoyed sharing water-time with Mel-e-gar; it always gave her a tingle of delight just to be with him. She had hoped that he would share more than water-time with her but she knew that his time was running short, but then she laughed to herself that is what many had sounded on before. A hundred and ten seasons he had seen so far and she hoped many more to come. Some of the Elders speculated on what kept him going. For on average they passed into that other sphere, known as the deathsong at around eighty seasons. Whereas his longevity had become legendary, which made him something of an enigma to the rest of the dolphins.

He shared water-time like everyone else and she knew him better than most but still there seemed to be an air of mystery about him. One part she had found most invigorating was his water-time. It was so much Edenlea, *as if he was Edenlea....* She had searched her water-time before trying to see the truth behind that idea, a part which she never dared share with any other. After all a hundred seasons had passed since he started to share his water-time, his dream and prophecy of a new future for all of the dolphs and dolphins. While six generations had been born in that time and then a few short seasons ago they had come to their new Edenlea. *That was what made him such a legend after all.*

She looked to her side and watched the young form of her apprentice Jer-e-lea and saw a better future for them all.

Que-e-lea stopped her delving into water-time and sounded to Jer-e-lea, "You have made the choice, young one to try and show the younglings what it is to be a *dolphin* and you cried with joy when we asked you, 'Why?'"

Jer-e-lea looked at her and smiled, "I like to share *water-time* with them and it tells me that my way is also with them."

Her answer made Que-e-lea swim faster and her water-time was pleased with the response. Her companion swam faster to keep up and then Que-e-lea swam a little faster which made a game for them both. They chased each other back to the nursery of dolphins, sharing in a way that Que-e-lea had not enjoyed since the old times and for the first time she realised that now she felt at home.

As they arrived back at the nursery they saw that things were well in place for them to start the journey to the Reef, a place they had both had no idea how to get to. "Mel-e-gar told us we would have a guide, Jer-e-lea. Who do you feel will be his candidate for the job?" giving Jer-e-lea a wink as a certain dolphin went swimming past, chasing a particularly fat fish.

"My water-time tells me *nothing*!" laughed Jer-e-lea which made them both shake with laughter as they turned and gave chase to that certain fish chasing dolphin.

It wasn't long before they had all re-grouped and Zar-e-gar had shared with Que-e-lea and Jer-e-lea his vision in water-time of the place he himself had been shown. So with twenty younglings gathered about them they swam through the warm embrace of Edenlea to the Coral Reef. None of the younglings had experienced a journey of such length without the help and guidance of their parentlings, so it was a real adventure for them all. The excitement flowed through them as their young water-time revelled in the new sights and sounds of uncharted waters.

* * *

Mel-e-gar had serious water-time to dive into which made his form become very still in the water. *How much should be shown to them and how will they understand?* These kinds of water-time had been before for him and it was never an easy task to undertake. He was about a thousand klees away from the School of dolphins, a place he had transported himself to using the watersong. It was further away than was normal for the Council meeting but then this was no ordinary meeting he reminded himself. He continued to wander the waterways of his water-time going through all that had led up to their move to Edenlea. Streams led him to see again the paths of others and soon he dove down to investigate the one he held closest to his heart; Tan-e-lea.

Even at two seasons young she had been able to use the transporting effect of the watersong, something he hadn't expected. *A vast and powerful talent she possessed and where will that lead her?* rippled his water. All these water-times challenged him and he decided to use another aspect of his watersong; the ability to suspend time, something he had only discovered in the last season and would only last for a clar before the effort caused the song to dissipate, leaving him drained. So he was always careful to keep an eye on his sense of dolph/inal time and to halt it long before it would do so naturally.

The song sounded like the call of a Kerg, a high pitched tone that made the water around dance in agitation. His watersong twisted and the sound changed to the patter of rain on the surface of the seas. Then silence.

Nothing seemed to move and Mel-e-gar opened his eyes and swam through the still water. Everything he touched twitched once then was still, as time continued for him but for nothing else. He swam and explored waters that he hadn't visited for many seasons, in a past time when he first explored this strange but familiar place. He leapt from the seas onto many parts of un water, where life forms lived and breathed without ever knowing the delight of Edenlea. But it reminded him of his other home and that was enough for him. This place was untouched by any sentient life, unchanged and virgin. But one tay he knew that would change. Maybe his kind would do so. There have been sounds in the Council of Grand-elders of moving and building on un-water and maybe they will but only for a short time. It's the other that worried him- that small furry creature that had once sat on his hand which had made him see a different destiny. But that was far into a future that he and the Elders didn't belong to and where the younglings were only the beginning.

Enough! his water-time cried and he moved back into the stream of time. But one last tantalising ripple made itself felt. *If I can suspend time can I pass further into it?* He smiled at his audacity for letting such ripples tease him so.

Right, he sounded, *it's time to call the meeting*. Now Mel-e-gar used his transportation song to its fullest effect. It always pleased him when it worked well. Summoning up the song, his beak broke the surface of Edenlea and his song burst forth. Light seemed to streak from the sky. The clouds raced across, heavy and black then they burst. It rained down so hard that it made Mel-e-gar gasp. He shook with delight as the rain sparkled with shimmering colours that made dancing rainbows over the surface of the sea. Solarn broke through the clouds and shone its warmth on Mel-e-gar's beak. His song rose another pitch and the water exploded in gushes, forty dees into the air. As each plume fell a dolphin crying with joy was left in its place. Soon the sea around him was full of dolphins, and soon their forms were diving into the light of Solarn and back to feel the warmth of the sea.

As the last of the dolphins appeared the rain stopped and the water became calm. All forty three dolphins that made up the Council came together. Car-e-lea and Ser-e-gar with Haw-e-gar swam up and made sounds of joy with Mel-e-gar as their water-time remembered the last time such an event took place, when he had first brought them to their new home.

It wasn't long before they were gathered together in three circles: the inner circle of the twelve youngling Council, then around them swam the eighteen members of the Elder Council, last of all the nine members of the Grand-elder Council. They were only a few klees away from a small continent which lay in between the two great land masses of un-water. They swam in a circular spiral around the southern tip, feeding as they gave birth to their sounds of change.

Mel-e-gar soon made his sound heard above the others and called the meeting to start. "This is no ordinary meeting as many of you know and all have made their sounds clear to me, that they feel it is time to tell all the truth of why we have come here."

There were sounds of agreement from the inner Council who felt that if they had been included in seasons past some things may never have happened.

"I have been chosen by the Grand-elders to tell the whole story to you all." He stopped and looked closely at the rest of them. "But first I want Haw-e-gar as the representative of the younglings to make his sounds clear." He motioned for Haw-e-gar to begin.

Now Haw-e-gar had spent a great deal of water-time on what he was going to sound on and not without a feeling of nervousness he began.

"I.. on.. *behalf-*" He stopped and made his sound clearer, "Of the younglings here and those that are with the Nursery say that no knowledge that affects us all..." He paused again and the rest of his sound was shouted, "Should be held from us!"

Mel-e-gar smiled to himself, not a bad opening question, something that he had already decided upon and which the rest of the Grand-elders and Elders had agreed to. So his reply was simply:

"We agree to your *demand*!" he sounded with a stern look at Haw-e-gar.

Haw-e-gar had expected some argument over this and his beak was a picture to behold which made Mel-e-gar and the rest laugh out loud. The tension eased and Haw-e-gar realised that whatever reason the Elders and Grand-elders had for keeping back information it was done for the best of intentions.

Mel-e-gar heard his sound and warmth flowed to Haw-e-gar, but his sound grew heavy as he knew that it was time to show the Younglings the truth. "Before I begin I want to change the way this Council is held. Will all of you get into your family groups and come and swim nearer to the un-water." The circles split up and soon nine family groups swam with Mel-e-gar within a klee of the shore. He stopped and turned in the water and swam to the surface. As each beak bobbed to join him he began.

"Three seasons ago, we came from a place much like this, the only differences are the colours of sea, sky and un-water..!"

All eyes surveyed the scene of the blue sky and blue-green water which lapped gently around them. To the north un-water could be seen, with its sandy shore and trees that stretched as far as the eye could see.

Mel-e-gar motioned with his flipper at the Sun called Solarn. "He asked the younglings" What is different about the *Solarn* from our old home?"

A youngling called Yen-e-lea answered, "Ours was called *Danetar* and it shone a pinkish red."

"Good," Mel-e-gar sounded, "And do you know why they are different?"

This made her feel somewhat foolish for Yen-e-lea had never dived that deep into water-time. Well it never really interested her enough to enquire. All she knew was the light here was stronger than their old home. Her response was a tentative, "*No...*"

Mel-e-gar was not that surprised for Yen-e-lea had her water-time on other things. "Anybody know?"

"Yes. *I do*," said a quiet sound.

Mel-e-gar reached out with his water-time and encouraged the sound of the youngling to continue.

"Well, our Danetar is more than twice the age of Solarn. It being much older means its light isn't as strong as this one," the sound replied.

Mel-e-gar couldn't see the speaker as she was hiding behind her Parentling. "A strong clear sound for such a shy creature," he replied. "Please come over here youngling so we can all share your wisdom." Mel-e-gar was impressed as there had not been much sign of the deeper water-time as far as the sounds of the sky were concerned among the younglings.

The Youngling came forward and she was a beautiful slim silver back dolphin with an unusual stream of black wavy lines running down both sides. Mel-e-gar saw that it was the daughter of Arl-e-gar and Gis-e-lea, her name being Jux-e-lea. His water-time told him it was an appropriate name for she was named after the southern star of their old home called *Juxelayer*. When she had come right up to Mel-e-gar he saw that her eyes were a green speckled with silver and black. Now Mel-e-gar was moved by this beautiful dolphin and he felt something stir that hadn't stirred in a long while. He called out jokingly, "Is she *mated* yet?!"

There was a roar of laughter and calls of, "Are you *asking*?"

Jux-e-lea was quite taken by the idea as she had felt deep feelings in her water-time for Mel-e-gar for quite some time, and her water-time nearly flipped at his response.

Mel-e-gar realising the response he was getting from her gently coaxed her waters to calmness and bade her to continue with her sounds.

Jux-e-lea being of fourteen seasons was a mature youngling of vision and she knew that it was impossible for her and Mel-e-gar. But somewhere deep within her water-time a hope remained and so she continued, "We also had two moons while this place has only one which makes the seas of our Edenlea far calmer than those of Delikadove. Also the difference in light and atmosphere content, being slightly richer in oxygen, makes the sky blue and the sea blue/green while our old home had purple seas." She stopped and looked at Mel-e-gar awaiting his sound.

Again Mel-e-gar was impressed with her sound and replied, "I am pleased to have such a knowledgeable response. Thank you Jux-e-lea." He motioned for her to join her family. They stopped for a small while to gather their water-time around them as they all sensed the beginnings of his oratory.

Mel-e-gar had decided to share his water-time by getting all the dolphins to interlink with him. This type of water-time was a very personal joining. Many of them had not experienced such an emotional bonding before and it took some gentle guidance to coax them into mixing their water-time together. The best way of describing it was like so many streams leading into- rather than out of- a strong flowing river.

The process took some time but soon all were joined, sharing the same sphere of water-time. Mel-e-gar could feel and see many different colours to the streams and for him a great sense of their harmony came upon him. He decided to weave the water-time together, further mixing to reveal to them the events that had led to them leaving Delikadove.

For them all it was like passing back in time and they experienced what it was like in the beginning;

On a hillside of red grass a group of dolphins materialised. At the head was a large dolphin that was standing on two silver grey legs. They were now dolphs. The younglings had never before experienced the sensation and to them it was something they could never have dreamed possible. But instead of standing on un-water they were standing on a land mass that dominated a very different world. The perspective for them was to say the very least unusual, because they had only seen the shoreline of a distant rocky island in the purple sea of Hederlike.

"You.." He gathered the younglings around him, "Were born different and only this way can you understand our past. The great events of water-time that for you can never be the same again."

Questions started to form in their water-time but Mel-e-gar told them to wait, for all their questions would be answered. He started to walk down the hillside, the orange sky was filled with the sounds of the Kerg. It made Mel-e-gar think of Zar-e-gar and he laughed. *Born with a fish in his mouth...* he chuckled to himself. The rest of the dolphs shared the story and a light breeze of laughter made itself heard.

They walked for some time sharing the sights, sounds and smells of Delikadove. Soon they had to climb a bigger hill that was dominated by plants that seemed to whisper their names in the wind. For the Younglings who were now quite taken up in their new sensations this phenomenon was very intriguing and Mel-e-gar's grandling, Haw-e-gar turned to his Grand-elder and asked, "What are *they*..?"

"They are called *Leiner*, and they have the capacity to mirror your sound."

"You mean they share our *water-time*!" exclaimed Haw-e-gar.

Mel-e-gar laughed and replied, "Yes. In a way they do but they seem to only call out your name." He gazed at Haw-e-gar and realised with some regret, what a handsome dolph he would have made. But the illusion he had woven for all the younglings was impressive. Maybe they wouldn't have been quite the same if they had been born as those before but still they looked convincing.

For awhile Mel-e-gar and the younglings walked over the hills, leaving all the other Elders behind and none of the younglings seemed to notice as each new discovery they made took all their attention. As they wandered around talking amongst themselves Mel-e-gar dropped back and sat down. He enjoyed watching them discover creatures that for them had no name.

He watched as Danetar slowly moved towards the horizon and he realised that dusk was about to fall. He had just made up his mind that it was time to move on when he felt a small hand intertwine with his and the touch brought a smile to his silvery lips.

"Hello *Jux-e-lea*.." and he turned his head to look at a dolph that could never have existed in real time. Her colouring would have made her unique. Black streaks flowed from her head down to the base of her spine, where they forked to travel down her slim legs. She didn't speak but just sat next to him, her hand entwined with his. So Mel-e-gar spoke to her. "Your water wonders at what this all means..." She didn't reply so he continued, "When I swam in my water-time I saw that you all had to know what it felt like to be a dolph. So I wove this for you all.." He paused and then said, "How do you feel now that you know how different we once were?"

Jux-e-lea was confused, her water-time seeming to be a stormy place with high peaked waves that made her feel excited, yet afraid of what Mel-e-gar would reveal. Part of her wanted to know but another shied away from the knowledge he would bring. She wasn't sure that she could trust herself to speak in sound that was not the same as the water sounds of Edenlea. But she tried, "It doesn't *feel* like *me*.." and looked up at Mel-e-gar.

"I'm glad that you feel that way for there were risks in doing this to you all." He gently squeezed her hand, then stood up, pulling Jux-e-lea to her dees. "We must do one more thing before we go.." Mel-e-gar called the younglings together and they climbed what was the final hill.

They reached the summit just as Danetar disappeared behind the Bylinkan mountains. Down below at the base of the hill sprawled a city that none of the younglings had ever seen. It stretched for thirty klees around the hills they had climbed. It seemed to pulsate with life, as the lights of the city came on. Shining domes of the city's main buildings dominated the scene. Orange, green, and silvery blue lights flowed over the domes, from one to another, a pulsation of rhythm that left the Younglings rooted to the spot in awe. Even Mel-e-gar felt the life that flowed through the city and he filled his water-time with the sight of his first home. A slight breeze blew from the south bringing with it the sounds of the city. A cacophony of different tunes played on many diverse instruments that were the dolphs that lived there.

Mel-e-gar broke the spell by saying, "That my dear young dolphins is where our story begins; the city we called *Plesilea...*"

As he spoke the name the city seemed to shimmer and fade from their sight and they soon realised that Mel-e-gar had brought them back home. All the younglings were filled with what they had seen and soon questions poured forth, but with it Mel-e-gar also could feel within the water-time a sense of relief. The sense of being in an alien land permutated the younglings' water-time and part of Mel-e-gar felt sad for them but also he was pleased that they did indeed feel that the waters of Edenlea was home.

The Grand-elders and Elders took their younglings away in their family groups to play, letting all their water-times settle back down and to prepare themselves for what was to come.

Mel-e-gar and his family swam south into deeper waters and searched for fish to eat.

Car-e-lea and Ser-e-gar shared their water-time making ripples of past tays in their old home. They too had watched as Mel-e-gar had shown the younglings the city and their past had come flooding back.

Do you miss the old times Ser-e-gar? sounded Car-e-lea.

Yes sometimes... He trailed off as another water ripple of time took him back to Delikadove. *Do you?* he enquired.

Car-e-lea swam through her water-time and felt again her young tays as a dolph when she went with her fatherling exploring some old forgotten place. His delight at each new find, confirmed his theories about their long past. Yes she did miss it but like her fatherling before, her sense of adventure had brought her here and her sense of *survival*!

She dived deeper making sounds to Ser-e-gar to follow and they danced through the waving fronds of the seaweed and chased the many creatures that lived there. As she caught a grey fish in her beak she gave her answer, *Yes I do, but I feel my fatherling would sound his delight that I share his wonder at all the new water-times we will share.* She then turned and sliced through the water to gently join with Ser-e-gar. They played for some time in the shallow waters and after they had both had their fill of fish they swam back to join with the rest of the dolphins to share with them all in discovering their own story.

SANCTUARY

It was **7162 S.N.**

The number of seasons that had passed in the cycle of the Neimas, a life form that had lived on Delikadove but had perished in the great fire when a meteorite had fallen on their home. It was a solitary creature that was known for its ability to turn rock into food. It was considered an honour to partake of a feast once every ninth tay with a Neimas. A custom which all the dolphs valued for it also shared with you its sense of peace and tranquillity. They would invite a dolph to lie next to its long furry body and tell it stories and in return it would give you a piece of its food. The food was called Teaka. It tasted very sweet but very light at the same time, a yellow and red food that looked like it had been taken from a cloud. Its fluffy consistency made it feel insubstantial, but one mouthful is all you could eat and no hunger came to you for two tays. The dolphs practised in the material arts have tried for many seasons to copy this but they have never managed to do so. Their loss was greatly felt. So as a mark of respect for the kindness that they always showed, they began the cycle of the Neimas.

It was the evening of the twenty-ninth tay of the eighth jeanth of this season that Mel-e-gar was born, out in a sheltered bay about twelve klees from the city of Plesilea. His motherling and fatherling were very happy that their first born had made it safely into the world. All leas of the city gave birth out in the safe waters in the ocean of Geailea.

As was the custom they threw him onto the red beach to see if he would transform into a dolph. Mel-e-gar's first experience was the warm waters and it was a shock to his water-time to be treated this way, something that all dolphs never forget. He spun through the air and landed dees first, which surprised his parentlings, for normally they would land in a huddle unable to stand for at least two tays. His parentlings were so amazed that they floated in the cove staring in disbelief as the young Mel-e-gar walked quite easily over the sandy shore. His first sound was a yell for them to come and get him. They both dove out of the water and he watched as their bodies sparkled a fierce blue, laced with the green glow of the two moons as they changed into dolphs. They landed with a wet *thunk*! on the sand and he ran to them and cried to be held.

Mel-e-gar was the first to display that kind of agility at birth but he wasn't the last, for the following season every dolph that was born did the same. It wasn't long before their race realized that they were changing.

His early seasons were very happy but uneventful. He grew up like the rest until he reached his seventh season; that was when he first sang a watersong. Stranger still for the last record of a Watersinger, about two hundred and fifty seasons before, showed that they could begin at birth. They used to call it the birthing song. So everyone was surprised that he had the talent. Mel-e-gar's parentlings were guiding him into the material sciences as they were once called, so they were not prepared for having a Watersinger in their home. There were no records of how to sing the watersong as it was crafted by the singer and only the singer created the rules. It was an exciting time for him as he swam in the waters of his home, trying out his watersong.

7171 S.N.

On his ninth season Mel-e-gar was going to be taken to see the Sanctuary of past Watersingers. The season of growth and renewal was upon the land of Delikadove and he awoke from his sleep excited at the prospect of seeing where past Watersingers had worked. He climbed from his sleeping place which was oval in shape and was designed to let dolphs get the maximum rest. It recreated if you wished the depth and feeling of the womb or could be as light and as airy as sleeping on the highest mountain top. So it satisfied the twin aspect of the dolphs. He ran though his home calling for his parentlings to awaken.

They lived in a building that could also change its shape. For the substance of Shakeilar could be as hard as stone or as soft and as warm as the down on a young Kerg's back. There were seven rooms on this tay. Normally there would only be four, but the extras were being used by his parentlings' guests. They were looking after three young dolphs whose parentlings were away from Plesilea on a field trip to investigate why the Muala were on the move in the western continent, leaving their normal habitat.

Zes-e-gar and Tor-e-lea heard the sounds of their youngling and awoke from their sleep to get their first meal of the tay ready, calling out to him to get the others from their slumber. Mel-e-gar did as he was told and roused the others. As they sat round the centre pool of his home he talked with the other younglings: Wel-e-lea at five seasons with her sisterling Ler-e-lea at three and her brotherling Jey-e-gar at two. They all loved to come and stay with Mel-e-gar for he told them the most fantastic stories of a place he called Edenlea and a family of dolphs who lived there as dolphins who never left their home waters to go onto the land. The very idea was alien to them and they laughed at Mel-e-gar's imagination.

"You mean they don't venture onto *dry land*!" cried Ler-e-lea, "That just isn't *possible..!*" She put a hand on Mel-e-gar's shoulder and patted it gently and said, "I like your stories Mel-e-gar but sometimes you defy description!" She laughed and jumped into the pool dragging Mel-e-gar with her.

They played like this and Mel-e-gar teased her by saying, "Maybe it *isn't* just a story!"

"Don't take any notice of him. He is just teasing you!" said Wel-e-lea as she looked on in indignation at their playfulness. She didn't think they should be playing like that at breakfast. Her manner was that of a motherling looking in disapproval at her youngling's behaviour. "Come on out of there!" she cried as Mel-e-gar's parentlings walked into the room. She turned to them and said, "I've told *them*!"

Zes-e-gar turned to Tor-e-lea and said, "I think our youngling has been stirring things again." They both laughed and told the younglings to get ready to go. For they had decided that Mel-e-gar's first trip to the Sanctuary would be best in the company of his friends. It was midtay before they left their abode and with Mel-e-gar striding ahead they walked through the city streets. He knew where it was and he was impatient now to get there.

The Sanctuary was in the middle of the city, surrounded by the twelve domed Council chambers. The only way to enter was by a high arched walk way that ran in a sinuous path through the centre of the building. Mel-e-gar found the high walls and rippled archways breathtaking and he felt his blood run faster as they slowly moved along the curving path.

"It's beautiful isn't it?" he remarked to his fatherling as they came to the entrance that would lead into the area where the Sanctuary stood.

"Yes Mel-e-gar it certainly is and this Council chamber like many of the others in our cities took many seasons to complete. But it is the only one that was designed around a Watersinger's Sanctuary." He then took hold of Mel-e-gar's shoulders and turned him to face the entrance. "Now we must leave you for only you can pass through."

Mel-e-gar looked up at his fatherling in confusion and said, "But I thought all of you would be coming."

"You didn't do your homework," remarked his Motherling. "You may have known where it was but you have not thought on what it is! That place is reserved for the next *Watersinger*. Only your song can get you through." She lowered herself down so her head was equal with his and kissed Mel-e-gar and as a single tear dropped gently onto the silvery floor, took him in her arms and whispered, "Be *careful...*"

Her remark hung in the air and it slowly dawned on Mel-e-gar that he was risking more than he had realised. Before, it was more of a game and he hadn't considered the seriousness of what he was about to do. He stilled his trembling feelings and drew his parentlings to him and hugged them both. His small frame clung to them for a few yens. Then he let go and turned to his friends to say goodbye.

Wel-e-lea the oldest of the trio went up to him and took his hand in hers and said, "You are still *short* for a dolph."

He laughed and said "Well you are too *tall*!" He hugged her and turned to Ler-e-lea, "You take care of your brotherling and don't let your sisterling *boss* you too much."

Tears started to fall down her face and she looked at Mel-e-gar and through the tears cried, "Don't forget to come back.." And she ran from him back the way they had come.

"She'll be fine," assured his Motherling as Mel-e-gar watched Ler-e-lea disappear round the corner of the path.

Jey-e-gar stood firm, his young mind not quite understanding where his friend was going but knew that it was Elder business and that was good enough for him. He just hoped that he would see Mel-e-gar again. Mel-e-gar knelt down and whispered into Jey-e-gar's ear. It left Jey-e-gar looking wide eyed but with a broad smile that lit up his face. Mel-e-gar turned away from them and walked up to the blue oval door and sang one note. He saw the door shiver then it sparkled with a thousand small fire lights. He turned once more and looked at his parentlings and friends then stepped through and was gone from their sight.

"Do you think he'll be all right?" asked Zes-e-gar looking at the door with a frown upon his broad face.

Tor-e-lea a dee taller than her mate, replied, "Yes..I think he will." She reached out and took hold of Jey-e-gar's and Wel-e-lea's hands and walked back leaving Zes-e-gar with his thoughts as he considered his sonling's future.

Walking back through the city streets Tor-e-lea suddenly stopped and bent down and asked Jey-e-gar, "What did my sonling say to you?"

Jey-e-gar smiled and replied, "You will see me in your *water-time*!"

For a brief yen Tor-e-lea was puzzled then she burst out laughing, and she carried on laughing as they walked home, her mind remembering her sonling's stories of Edenlea.

They found Ler-e-lea huddled in her bed chamber fast asleep. Her face was stained by the tears she must have wept. Tor-e-lea watched her for awhile then left to get the evening meal prepared.

She didn't see a smile slowly spread across Ler-e-lea's face or hear the contented sigh as she slept dreaming of Mel-e-gar.

* * *

Mel-e-gar stood rooted to the spot as he gazed at the building before him. His first thought was that it reminded him of a rain drop hanging from a leaf of a Redisea tree. But this rain drop was suspended in mid air. There was a path that circled the Sanctuary and he had expected to be able to see the walls of the Chamber surrounding it. Instead there was a shimmering wall of blue and silver that looked like a frozen wave of immense proportions. He slowly walked round trying to see if there was an entrance to pass through. But he couldn't find it and carried on walking trying to figure out what to do next. He had no idea how long he had walked when he decided to stop pacing round as it didn't seem to be getting him any closer to a solution.

He sat down on the path and just stared at the rain drop. *Well where is the door?* he asked himself in desperation. *Maybe if I touched it..* He let the thought hover in his mind, reluctant to touch such a beautiful thing.

"Well, do something you fool!"

Mel-e-gar shot up and looked wildly around him trying to find the speaker.

"Don't just stand there! Do something about it!! You are *supposed* to be a *Watersinger* after all!" exclaimed the voice.

Mel-e-gar started to walk around the rain drop trying to find the owner of the voice. *What is going on?!* he muttered to himself.

"Look! You are doing it again. Stop that at once you *stupid* dolph!" shouted the voice.

Mel-e-gar was more annoyed than afraid of the disembodied voice. He decided to talk to it instead. "Well, maybe you wouldn't mind telling me who you are!" he shouted back at the voice as he continued to try and find the owner.

"At least that's a start! And stop moving around. You are making me feel quite *ill,* all that pacing!" The voice continued to make tutting noises as Mel-e-gar ignored the bit about pacing and tried to figure out what was going on. He hadn't expected this. Which made him *chuckle* because come to think of it he hadn't any idea what he would find in this place.

"Well...!" And there were sounds of somebody tapping his dee on a floor.

Mel-e-gar laughed out loud as the image of an old dolph came into his head, sitting on a rock in the middle of an ocean. He chuckled as he said. "Well if what I just saw is correct then it's a neat trick that *tapping*!" He stopped his pacing and walked over to the rain drop and touched it.

"That's *better*!" said the voice, "Now what else are you going to do?"

Mel-e-gar felt the rain drop pulsate under his hand and the colours shifted to orange and yellow. He ignored the voice and set his mind to sing a watersong of opening.

"Very good!" continued the voice as the song changed form and the notes seemed to hang in the air like stars in the sky. "I like that," the voice said. "*Getting better!*"

Mel-e-gar moved up a scale and he felt himself tingle with emotion as he passed through. It was certainly worth the effort as he found himself standing in a large room that had thousands of colours shimmering and moving like waves all round him. "Beautiful.." he murmured as he took in his surroundings. In the middle of the room that must have been a hundred dees in width, was an array of crystals and sitting on a rock by it was a dolph. "A very old dolph by the look of him!" he found himself saying out loud.

The dolph grinned at him and said. "Well that may be the case young dolph but don't judge too quickly."

He grinned back not in the least fazed as he was beginning to like what was happening to him. He walked over to the old dolph and said, "My name is Mel-e-gar. Perhaps you wouldn't mind telling me who you are?"

"Good.." replied the dolph liking what he saw. "My name is *Pel-e-gar*, the last Watersinger at your service."

Now Mel-e-gar, realising that he was talking to somebody who had entered the deathsong over two hundred and fifty seasons before, felt his mouth grow dry and he responded by stammering, "But.. How.. can.. That.. *Be*?!"

"Told you not to judge too quickly!" laughed Pel-e-gar as he stood up and walked up to Mel-e-gar and took hold of his hand and led him to the crystal array. "Now my young dolph feel the *heart* of a Watersinger," and he placed Mel-e-gar's hand onto the crystals.

A flame thirty dees high leapt up into the air as the crystals responded to his touch. Mel-e-gar nearly pulled back but the flame did not harm him and it felt like the crystals were absorbing his very identity. A serenity took hold of him as he moved further into the crystals. It is so peaceful here he thought as the lights in his mind started to flow gently over his thoughts making them more *fluid* and changing them.

He had no conception of time in the place. His mind seemed to wander and he felt like he was flying over mountains and oceans of his world. He saw the changes that were coming and some of them made him shudder, but the lights soothed him and spoke to him of the true meaning of the water-time which was something Mel-e-gar had known as an idea and not as a way of being. The old seeing crystals in the library of the city had told him of the legends that surrounded Edenlea and the time when the water-time held sway over Delikadove. The concepts were still used but the feeling of them had been lost for generation upon countless generation. That in part he had come to understand better than any dolph before, except that is for the Watersingers and maybe the Healers who had some measure of water-time. For they knew and they alone kept the dream alive, because some tay they knew it would be needed again.

Mel-e-gar blinked twice and the images faded. He looked at the crystals and watched as the flame died down to nestle within the confines of the crystal array. Then everything went dark. Pel-e-gar caught him as he slumped to the floor and carried him to his stone and sang a song. The rock cracked open and spread itself like a blanket on the floor. He laid Mel-e-gar upon it and stepped back and sang once more. The rock wrapped itself around Mel-e-gar and twinkled with a mischievous fire and vanished, taking its passenger to another part of the Sanctuary.

Pel-e-gar smiled as he said out loud, "I like to keep a tidy *home*!" Still laughing he walked to the crystals and spoke to them. "Do you believe he will?"

A loud voice boomed back:

"Yes indeed he is the one we have waited these past seasons for."

"Good. Now can I get some rest?" his tone tired. "It's time I left this place. My job is now done." He was weary, for he longed to be able to enter the deathsong in peace.

"Yes you are *free....*" The voice of the crystals died away and Pel-e-gar found himself fade with it, "Peace in your water-time Mel-e-gar. I don't envy you your task...task.. task..."

His last word echoed around the room before the lights themselves faded from the walls and all grew still.

Waiting......

Mel-e-gar woke from his sleep feeling refreshed. He at first didn't know where he was but he guessed that Pel-e-gar had laid him here to sleep. *I wonder where he is?* he thought as he sat up and took in his surroundings. It was circular like before and there were pictures on the walls. Now there were not many artists on Delikadove so the fact that there seemed to be thousands of pictures, hung on every spare place intrigued him. He walked over and examined them. A sound made him turn round. "That's *curious..*"

In the place where he had slept there now stood the rock that Pel-e-gar had sat on. His mind taken from the paintings he jokingly said, "Do you know where *Pel-e-gar's* gone?" He didn't expect a reply but that is what he received.

"He is now at peace, gone to swim in the sea of the deathsong," replied *the* Rock rather wistfully.

Mel-e-gar stepped back a pace and shook himself. *I must be dreaming*, he thought, *because I've never heard of rocks that can talk.*

You are wrong on the first part but not on the second, spoke *the* Rock in Mel-e-gar's mind.

You are right there for sure, retorted Mel-e-gar, *But I am new at this.*

True...Very true..But I bet I can teach you a thing or two.

Mel-e-gar realised that *the* Rock was speaking within his mind, in fact in his *water-time*, a truly different sensation for not only did he hear the words he felt them as well. The most curious aspect was that the words were in true tones. Some sounded like rain falling gently on a rock, while others sounded like the waves beating on a distant shore, yet like the sound the Kerg makes when it calls for a mate. Then it changed again; each time Mel-e-gar felt, heard and saw the meaning of *the* Rock. He already used the ability to see by sound when he swam in the oceans as all dolphs could but this was much more than that. It made his watersong seem clumsy in comparison.

Do you have a name? he enquired of *the* Rock, liking the depth with which he could express himself.

No.. the reply came, *I'm just known as the* ***Rock***, putting the emphasis on the last word.

Mel-e-gar found this quite funny and it made him giggle like a new born dolph. Soon he was roaring with laughter. It seemed so funny.. The ***Rock***.. he repeated to himself.

The Rock joined in saying, *It is..* They both laughed, and both kept repeating the words over and over again, each time finding it funnier and funnier.

After they had calmed down, *the* Rock slid over to Mel-e-gar and said in a voice that would seem to need lips to speak. "Let's talk like this for awhile as you must not forget that is the way your kind still communicates the most."

Mel-e-gar found this quite reasonable and he returned his attention back to the pictures, "I've never seen *so many*.." he said in awe. "Who are they?"

"They are all past Watersingers who have passed this way in the water-times of Delikadove and beyond." *The* Rock slid along showing him the pictures and the names of them all.

Mel-e-gar returned to a blank space he had noticed earlier and asked, "Who is that reserved for?" As he finished speaking the words the place on the wall seemed to blink and there now filling the space was a portrait of Pel-e-gar, sitting on a rock in the middle of a purple sea.

"Now you *see*.." replied *the* Rock.

A ripple went through Mel-e-gar as he realized there were no more spaces on the wall. It stayed with him as he looked around again at all the different faces of ancient Watersingers and he gave in to the ripple and asked, "Is there no space for me?"

Now *the* Rock stopped and it seemed to be delving very deep before it answered. But instead of answering it asked Mel-e-gar how young was he?

"I was nine seasons young six jeanths ago."

"Arh..Young, very young but it's better that you are, replied *the* Rock.

"Why?" enquired Mel-e-gar.

"Normally of past tays they sent a new Watersinger when she or he had passed their twelfth season. It is unusual for one as young as you."

This puzzled Mel-e-gar for he was told that he was a late developer as far as a Watersinger was concerned and *the* Rock's reply didn't make much sense. He instead dove into his water-time and tried to work it out. *The* Rock seeing this joined Mel-e-gar, *Come with me and I'll show you.*

He welcomed *the* Rock's company and they both joined in water-time and they swam together through a purple ocean, becoming more entwined as they went.

For awhile Pel-e-gar had grown weary with the waiting and had begun to believe that there would be no more and like you he saw no extra space in the hall of the Watersingers and nearly came to the same conclusion. But his water-time told him to be patient and he was. He nearly missed you altogether because you showed no sign, but when you reached your seventh season and sang your first note he became excited. He searched the crystal records for a precedent and came up with nothing.

He said over and over again that you couldn't be. But as I pointed out, you were and it couldn't be denied. Over the jeanth he became more agitated and tired with the waiting. He saw fit to change the rules. Well he was right, some things stay the same because of tradition and laziness. He sent a dream to your Motherling and told her to send you to us when she felt you were ready. When the tay came Pel-e-gar was overjoyed and he laughed and danced for ages in his water-time.

So you must not let his initial manner bother you. As you can now understand he has waited for two hundred and fifty seasons for your coming and all he ever wanted was to continue with his journey and enter the deathsong.

Mel-e-gar *sighed* within his water-time and a bubble came to the surface and joined the air above, taking with it any confusion or ignorance about the *why's* he had felt earlier. But he still wanted to know if he would have to endure that kind of waiting and if so why no space. *Would his wait be forever?* That ripple he didn't like and *the* Rock showed him more.

"You *my* dear dolph are the *last* Watersinger of *Delikadove* and I am not allowed to tell you any more than *that*. So be pleased that you have no wait *here....*" the last being said rather than by water sounds.

It gave more ripples to Mel-e-gar's waters but he left it and joined *the* Rock. He looked around the room and said, "Is there any more to the Sanctuary and where do I go from here?"

"This is all and now you must leave for my work is also done." *The* Rock slid across the floor and touched the wall that Mel-e-gar had slept by and *it* motioned in water-time for Mel-e-gar to follow. The wall shimmered and disappeared. They both entered the crystal room together.

"Your last task you will find when you touch the crystals." *The* Rock seemed to glow for an instant and before Mel-e-gar could ask *the* Rock where *it* was going, *it* disappeared and Mel-e-gar was left alone.

He had grown fond of *the* Rock and was saddened that *it* had gone. But as that rippled through his water-time he heard a faint chuckling whisper say, "*See you around...Little dolph..*"

Mel-e-gar called out, "Now that is all I wanted to know. It made him feel warm inside and he laughed once more with *the* Rock.

He stepped over to the crystals and slowly he laid his hands upon them. The flame returned and he saw that his colour was added to the flame; his water-time balanced out and a harmony of song poured forth. It echoed around his water-time and filled the room with its beauty and Mel-e-gar did what he was asked.

On a hillside where one of the older cities stood, a small place near its centre began to glow and for a yen that was as brief as a sigh, the city looked new and life poured forth. For a sweet yen the city of Beslika looked newly born, but the light faded and the city returned to its decaying condition. A new building appeared that almost teased the city with promise but its fresh arches that seemed to reach for the sky came tumbling down to join with the rest and silence fell once more on a dead City.

Mel-e-gar opened his eyes and looked around and saw that the crystal room had changed. It looked as if it had aged a thousand seasons in a blink of an eye. The crystal array still shone but that too soon died. Mel-e-gar did the unexpected and laughed and he was still laughing at the joke as he left the building and passed into a dusty street. He stopped outside and looked up at the building and all was like most places that had been left for life to take back. It had to appear to the uneducated eye a ruin and just a ruin. The two moons shone their light upon a more confident dolph and he with new hope and vision in his water-time ran down the hill to Plesilea.

He felt that he had grown with the knowledge that Pel-e-gar had shown him, as if he had aged a number of seasons. The confidence grew as he walked through the city's streets.

He looked around at the dancing lights of the buildings and he watched as one of them flexed itself and grew a few dees wider on each side. *Must have company,* he sounded to himself. That brought him back to reality, for his water-time produced images of the friends he had left the tay before. He smiled at the images and his feelings went out to them.

He followed the winding streets playing with his new waters and he hoped that Ler-e-lea would forgive him for upsetting her. The feeling he received was that she already had. The streets were deserted at this time of night so Mel-e-gar had the city to himself. He wandered around for awhile toying with the idea of visiting the library to check on some of the images he had seen concerning Edenlea and he also wanted to know if there was any information on *the* Rock. "Now that would be interesting wouldn't it?" he asked the wall he was passing. The wall gave a ripple in response and Mel-e-gar laughed.

After several clars of wandering the streets he decided it would be best to go home. With that decision made he ran down the street he recognised, almost bursting with joy as he saw his home at the end. He slowed down and walked up to the blue shimmering marker of his home and touched it. But nothing happened. Puzzled but not unduly concerned he tried again. This time a tune played back. *That's new*, he sounded and waited for a response. He was puzzled because normally all he would have to do would be to touch the marker and part of the wall would disappear allowing him entry. The musical tone continued to play as Mel-e-gar stood in front of his home thoroughly puzzled.

"What is going on?" he called out, desperation creeping into his voice. By now his water-time was convulsing and it made him feel quite ill.

"*Will nobody answer...*" he whispered. The despair was growing for he knew something was very wrong. For a yen he even entertained the idea that he had come to the wrong house, but his water-time dismissed that as quite ridiculous. He was about to reach up to the marker to try again when an opening appeared.

He breathed a sigh of relief. "Where have-" He stopped, open mouthed as he looked at the dolph that was standing in the opening. "It *can't be*.." he cried.

"Hello, can I help you?" asked the dolph looking at Mel-e-gar, wondering why the dolph looked so upset.

"No!" Mel-e-gar cried, "I mean Yes! How is it that *you've* changed?!"

The dolph looked more puzzled. "Look maybe you should come in. My parentlings are out at the yen but my sisterling and brotherling are here." She motioned for Mel-e-gar to enter.

He almost stumbled into the house. He looked around at his home, or what used to be his home. He couldn't believe it. His parentlings must have moved. But his water-time insisted that only two tays had passed. So what it showed him couldn't be and the dolph who stood before him couldn't be who he believed it was.

The dolph was getting more concerned as she looked up at the strange but familiar dolph, who looked as if he was about to collapse. He was covered in dust and looked very tired. She motioned with her hand and the floor bulged up. "Come and sit down and we will talk."

Mel-e-gar automatically sat down on the now soft mound that the floor had grown to accommodate him. He sank into it and sighed, "How is it that you have changed so much..?"

The dolph sat on her cushioned floor and shook her head and replied, "I don't know what you mean?" She reached out and grasped one of his hands. The touch brought her more than she could have dreamed. She almost screamed in shock. Tears started to run down her face and an old memory of a friend she had said goodbye to many seasons before came to her.

The revelation made her cry uncontrollably and she sobbed, "I thought you were gone *forever*! I thought you had passed into the deathsong."

Her whole body shook with the emotional out pouring and Mel-e-gar reached over and took her in his arms. "It's all right, *Ler-e-lea*. I'm back."

They hugged each other for a long while and then she cried out again, "That means you don't know!" She drew herself away from him and clasped his face in her hands and said, "Mel-e-gar your parentlings are gone!"

He pulled himself away from her and stood up, his whole body starting to shake as he realized the meaning of her words. He fell to his knees and he lifted his head back and screamed, "NOOoooo!" The tears poured forth as the truth struck him, that his parentlings had passed into the deathsong. Gone to *Chisharnlay*.

He cried and his water-time opened up. He saw the opening and dived in. Then a blackness took him on an enormous wave of grief.

Ler-e-lea called out for her family to help, but they were already rushing to her side. "Help *him*!" pointing at the crumpled heap on the floor.

Wel-e-lea and Jey-e-gar went over and turned Mel-e-gar over. His face looked white and drawn and they looked at him, not quite believing it. The Mel-e-gar they had known had only been nine seasons old and at best he wasn't more than five dees in height. The Mel-e-gar they now both looked at was now of thirteen seasons and at least nine dees.

"It is *him*, isn't it?" asked Jey-e-gar of Wel-e-lea.

"Yes brotherling, our friend is back with us." She motioned with her hand and the floor grew up around his still form and took him to a Sleeping-chamber.

Later that evening the three sat around the centre pool and remembered the last time they had done so. They shared the grief they had felt when after a jeanth had passed he hadn't returned. Now four seasons later he finally turns up expecting to see things as they had been.

"He had no idea that so much time had passed, had he Ler-e-lea?" asked Wel-e-lea.

She sat huddled between her sisterling and brotherling. Wiping the tears away she said, "No, he looked at me and recognised me almost immediately, while I didn't him. But the shock on his face tells me that before coming here tonight he had no idea at all."

"*Poor Mel-e-gar*!" added Jey-e-gar his feelings scattered inside him as his young mind tried to make sense of it all. But he couldn't, nor could the others. They went to their Sleeping-chambers and hoped the next tay would bring answers to their questions.

Mel-e-gar searched his water-time for his parentlings. The depth he swam while he slept took him to places where he had never been before. At first the waters were murky and filled with strange images that he couldn't identify, but which made him shiver with fear. He was still crying in his water-time and the tears mingled with the depths and soon they changed to spheres of light. They flowed away from him and he felt their pull taking him deeper. He expected to find the waters darker but instead he was surprised that his tears had led him to a spark of light. He began to feel light and free as he sped up his swimming to get to the light as fast as possible. The black water changed and slivers of light pierced the gloom. He started to feel excitement which was at odds with his grief but Mel-e-gar only wanted to know what had happened while he had been in the Sanctuary. The light bled the darkness away making it easier for him to see.

He nearly stopped in astonishment as in the distance he saw his world, spinning in a black velvet sky that was cluttered with the expressions of a million stars. But he couldn't stop and he found himself falling towards the planet. He closed his eyes as he fell through the atmosphere expecting to be burnt to a cinder, quite forgetting that he was sound asleep at home. Then a light burst through him and the embrace of the sea engulfed his form as it slid him gently into the depth below.

Mel-e-gar didn't know how long he swam but it seemed an age as he searched the waters. The feelings that his water-time showed him brought a smile to his lips as he danced through shoals of fish and the creatures that lived in peace within a sea of Delikadove. A peace descended upon him and he felt as warm and as safe as if he were being held by his parentlings.

He realised that he still had his eyes shut and when he opened them he looked into the gaze of his motherling. He shouted with joy and the tears started to fall again as he gazed into her warm, laughing eyes.

"It's all right my sweet sonling; lie still and be at *peace*. Nothing will harm you here." She bent over and kissed him and his heart soared.

"It was just a *dream*!" he cried and snuggled up to her chest and lost himself in the sensation of being held in her arms as a new born dolph.

His water-time seemed to encourage this state of peacefulness but then he remembered his fatherling. His body tensed and he started to shake with the feeling of despair that he had felt when Ler-e-lea had told him that they had passed into the deathsong.

His motherling, feeling him going tense said, "Everything is fine. Your *fatherling* is here."

Mel-e-gar looked around him and the scene shifted.

He was standing by one of the decaying buildings of the old city of Beslika holding his fatherling's hand. He looked up at him and smiled. His fatherling was telling him about the city which had ceased to be a home for the dolphs for more than nine thousand seasons.

"The reason why the city has become a ruin is that the Shakeilar, which is the same substance that all our cities are made up of caught a disease which led to them entering the *deathsong...*" His fatherling paused and reached down and lifted Mel-e-gar up so he could show him a building in the distance. "Look!" he pointed and Mel-e-gar watched as a building with three domes collapsed into dust. "Now that was a great place," his fatherling said, a touch of sadness tingeing his words.

The young Mel-e-gar not yet knowing much of his world asked, "Why?"

His fatherling looked deep within Mel-e-gar's eyes and instead of answering his question said, "Remember that everything has a time of passing, when life is returned to the deathsong to bring forth new life."

That wasn't the answer Mel-e-gar had expected and he looked at his fatherling in surprise. He was about to ask again when the image shimmered and he felt himself return to his Motherling's arms.

His water-time now told him that this was a dream and they were both gone from his life. It was hard for Mel-e-gar but part of him accepted the truth and he looked up at her and asked the question that he knew would shatter the illusion. "Have *you* really gone to the deathsong...?"

She looked sad yet happy and spoke to him in such of a gentle tone that Mel-e-gar would remember it the rest of his tays. "When you left us we returned home and decided to take your friends away on a trip. I knew that you would be gone for awhile and I felt that it would be better for the younglings if they had other things to occupy their minds. So we took them to a place that you liked to play."

She stopped and laughed at the memory and continued with her answer, "It was a great time. We stayed for seven tays on the beach and your fatherling surprised us by telling us he had asked the Council to accept his proposal for naming the cove after you and they readily agreed. The younglings thought it a great idea and I have been looking forward to telling you that on your return. So *my dear* youngling you have a place that bears your name."

Mel-e-gar was soothed by her words and he relaxed completely in her arms and remembered that the place she spoke of was about thirty klees away from Yengile City, with its purple beaches. His water-time returned his attention back to his motherling.

"We played and told each other stories and the younglings told us more about *Edenlea* and even Wel-e-lea joined in the fun." His motherling stroked his head and in a whisper filled with emotion said, "*We had no idea the tay would end in the way it did.*"

Mel-e-gar felt the ripples of sadness that flowed through her form as she told him of their fate, "The younglings were lucky that they didn't join us and if it hadn't been for Wel-e-lea's quick reactions I think they would now be with us instead of with you.

"We were swimming about ten klees from the beach, enjoying the warm waters as evening fell on our last tay. Your fatherling was exploring ahead when he turned suddenly in the water and made sounds of alarm. I didn't know what could have disturbed him so much that he was making such sounds. I swam to him and had to dive deeper to catch him as he seemed to be following something. Now being that deep in the water it was very dark and I used my sounds to find him. It wasn't long before I knew what was disturbing our peace. There in the water ahead of me, with your fatherling's tail in its jaws was a *Keaverkack*, over forty dees in length, its purple body glowing in the dark. They are not normally found so close to the shores of our lands. They normally live in the depths of the seas about four thousand klees away and I wondered what it was doing here.

"Your fatherling told me to warn the others but as I turned to call them, another Keaverkack caught me in the side, its powerful jaws tearing into me. I cried out as loud as I could and my sounds could just make out Wel-e-lea coming closer. I made sounds to her to leave and she seemed to spin in the water in alarm and suddenly she changed course and dived below me. I felt her beak ram into the creature, causing it to lose its grip upon me. I thanked her for her bravery and telling her I would be fine I told her to take the younglings away. She made sounds of distress and swam from me. I know now she was successful in getting the younglings to safety.

"I was bleeding badly from the tear in my side and I tried to free your fatherling but he told me to leave and get help. I decided to try myself knowing that if I left him he would die. I copied Wel-e-leas example and butted the Keaverkack in the side. But no matter how many times I tried it wouldn't let go and then I saw the other come for me again. I was too far away from the shore to try and escape so I fought. But soon there were more of them with us and they tore into us both. I knew we had no hope so I swam to your fatherling and using my flippers, held onto him as they attacked for the last time..."

Mel-e-gar was horrified and he twisted in his motherling's arms to reach up and hold her face with his hands. His touch caused the scene to change and he found himself facing her and his fatherling in his old bed chamber. His height was equal now to his motherling's and it was strange for him to be looking down at his fatherling. They smiled as he kissed them. Mel-e-gar could still feel what they had felt and he cried with them as they re-lived their last times.

He saw them enter the deathsong together, while the Keaverkack tore them apart. Their last sound was a cry that caused the water to boil, making the Keaverkack writhe in agony, trying to rid their bodies of their now poisonous dinner.

"*Hopefully* they will not attack our kind again," said his fatherling as the image of their deathsong left Mel-e-gar's water-time, "and I am glad that we distracted the Keaverkack long enough for the younglings to get to safety." He looked intently at Mel-e-gar and said, "And you can find out why they came so close to shore in the first place."

"I *will...*" Mel-e-gar's voice trailed off as the image of his parentlings started to shimmer and fade. He knew it was time to leave them and continue with his life. He hugged them both for the last time and they left him by saying, "You have hard times as well as beautiful tays ahead of you but remember this; Chisharnlay is only the beginning for us. Be happy and look to the future, for your time is coming Mel-e-gar and this is but a small ripple in *your water-time*."

With that said they faded from view and Mel-e-gar found himself lying under a star filled sky on a mountain top. He lifted his hand and the image vanished to leave the ceiling of his home in its place. He now knew within his water-time that his parentlings were happy and he smiled, remembering them as they were.

Wel-e-lea, Ler-e-lea and Jey-e-gar were sitting round the pool eating their morning meal when Mel-e-gar walked in. He strode over and sat by them, none seemingly daring to speak. They all looked at him and each saw a very different dolph from the night before. He looked refreshed and very peaceful as he helped himself to the cooked fish which lay steaming on a platter that hovered a few dees above the floor. The silence continued as he took a bite from the fish, grinding it down using his many teeth. Everything, bones included slid down his eager throat.

It was Jey-e-gar who broke the silence, "It's good to have you back Mel-e-gar!" It was enough to break the spell and they all crowded round him, taking turns hugging and kissing him.

He laughed and said, "That is much better; it's good to hear laughter again." He leaned over and rinsed his hands in the pool and sat back on a mound that grew from the floor and waited for his friends to begin asking their many questions. It didn't take them long to do so and Mel-e-gar told them all he had witnessed in the Sanctuary.

They found it fascinating when he told them of *The* Rock, and Ler-e-lea asked him if he thought that *it* was made of Shakeilar. He told them that he didn't know if *the* Rock was a rock at all. Maybe *it* was something to do with Pel-e-gar but he didn't think so. Wel-e-lea told him what she had seen and he told them that he had dreamt of his parentlings. She confirmed what they had told him. Mel-e-gar had known that he had seen the truth and it had made it easier for his friends that he accepted what had happened. After all it had been four seasons ago for them. This brought Mel-e-gar to the questions which he couldn't answer; *Why had he no idea that so much time had passed and why had he aged in the time if his water-time told him that two tays were all that had passed?*

They told Mel-e-gar that a message had been sent to tell the Council that he was alive and they in return sent a message that they would send a representative round to ask him what had happened. He knew that in the next few tays he would be repeating the story many times over. His water-time returned him to his parentlings and his friends withdrew to let him remember in peace.

Later that tay his friends' parentlings returned and it was an emotional meeting for them all. They had heard the news as they had walked through the city as everyone was most eager to talk about it. There had been a crowd of dolphs eagerly awaiting for more news outside their home and Cla-e-lea, the motherling had told them to leave them alone. The dolphs respecting their privacy, a little embarrassed that they had stepped over the boundaries of polite behaviour, withdrew and went home to wait for more. The Council let it be known that a special session would be convened as soon as they had Mel-e-gar's permission. For now that he was past his twelfth season he was eligible to take his place on the Council.

In the evening the whole family and Mel-e-gar swapped news and he listened with interest as Cla-e-lea and Kin-e-gar told him that they had been investigating many cases of creatures leaving their own habitats and venturing into areas that were unsuitable for them. The problems of whole species starving to death or becoming victim to predators that would not normally prey on them. There had been a series of incidents over the whole world of Delikadove. The dolphs, such as themselves who studied the sciences had no explanation for the strange behaviour which included the Keaverkacks killing Mel-e-gar's parentlings. He asked them if the weather patterns had changed in ways whilst he had been gone that would explain the changes that were happening. But no, everything had been thoroughly investigated and still they had no answers.

Then Mel-e-gar felt a ripple in his water-time and he returned to the vision of his fatherling telling him about the disease which had wiped out the city of Beslika. He played with the ripple for awhile then he asked, "When was the last change in solar activity of Danetar?"

It was Cla-e-lea who answered, "About ten thousand seasons ago in the age of Gealasor." She saw what he was getting at and left her seat to return with a seeing crystal. "Now let me check in here." They watched as she held the crystal with both hands and closed her eyes. "Yes...You *could* be right Mel-e-gar.." muttered Cla-e-lea and opened her eyes.

Mel-e-gar waited as did the rest for her to put the crystal away and when she returned she told them what she had seen.

"The age of Gealasor began ten thousands seasons ago and it was named after a massive solar storm which in time affected our world. Many dolphs predicted that we would go through a series of calamities which indeed we did. One was the destruction of Beslika a thousand seasons later. It ended with the destruction of the *Neimas* which brought to a close the age of the Gealasor."

Jey-e-gar listened attentively to his Motherling and he was puzzled by the last part of her answer, "Didn't the Neimas die when a meteorite hit their home?" he enquired not understanding the connection.

"Yes indeed Jey-e-gar but that was caused by a change in the gravity of Danetar which pulled a chunk from the meteor belt which circles the outer planet of Punagor."

He still wasn't satisfied and asked, "But that was *long* after the solar storm."

"Yes, but it was one of the effects of the solar storm which didn't have any impact on our solar system until much later."

Jey-e-gar was amazed that something could last that long and being of only six seasons his mind had trouble with the concept of something that could last for nearly four thousand seasons.

She sympathised with her sonling because even she found the scope of time that the solar storm had precedence over, hard to imagine. She returned her attention back to Mel-e-gar and said, "So you could be right. For we noticed a small solar storm about six seasons ago but it wasn't out of the ordinary, just a normal storm." She paused and shook her head and then said, "It's not that strange that nobody made the connection, but maybe we should have."

At this point Kin-e-gar spoke up, "You have just made the point, that the storm was quite normal at this stage in Danetar's cycle so I don't see that it could have the effect of driving the many species that we have both observed away from their habitats."

Cla-e-lea replied, "Yes, I know but couldn't there be a connection somewhere?" She was convinced that Mel-e-gar might have the answer and she was reluctant to let the idea go. She threw it back to Mel-e-gar, "Well, what do you say?"

He had listened to them both and his water-time sifted the idea and he saw the connection, "I believe that you are both right." He looked at them both and grinned as they returned his gaze amazed at his reply. Together they said, "How do you come to that conclusion?"

Instead of replying straight away he summoned his watersong and made use of the pool. They looked on, open mouthed as Mel-e-gar's song scooped some of the water from the pool and shaped it into a representation of their solar system. It wasn't long before a mini version of Danetar and the five planets that circled it hung in the air above them. He showed them through a normal cycle and then froze the image and changed the light spectrum. "There is your answer," he answered, pointing at the violet light that seemed to wash over the planets from Danetar as he made them move one orbit around it.

"The light you see is the radiation that is flooding our world and that is what is changing us all. The point is that the solar storm in itself was harmless but it triggered an invisible flood of radiation across the spectrum which has been impacting on Delikadove for *six seasons*!"

The parentlings knew about radiation but they had not expected that it would be the answer to the mystery. Mel-e-gar sang a note and the image vanished, leaving a heavy silence behind. He saw that they were having trouble with the concept and asked, "Has anyone tested for an increase in the ultra violet emissions from Danetar?"

Cla-e-lea was stunned and for a yen couldn't answer, not only because Mel-e-gar had so easily shown them an error in their thinking but also for his demonstration of the power of the watersong. She gathered her wits and replied, "Mel-e-gar, that was amazing! And to answer your question, no they haven't!"

"I didn't think they *had* but you will find that the increase may also be affecting the magnetic field of Delikadove which in turn could be affecting the internal sound of the many creatures who make use of it."

Mel-e-gar felt it strange that he knew so much and he realized that although it may have seemed like only a yen of time in the Sanctuary it had nevertheless imparted in him knowledge that would normally have taken him seasons to learn. Which explained why he had aged and not known it. Perhaps Pel-e-gar had exchanged his seasons for that knowledge.

They all had more questions for him as the night wore on and he answered them as best as he could. The watersong fascinated them all and his knowledge of their world was even more amazing. Cla-e-lea and Kin-e-gar made it clear that they hoped he would stay, after all it was his home.

Ler-e-lea on hearing this flung herself upon him and hugged him so tight that Mel-e-gar thought he would burst. "You will *won't you*?" she shouted and they laughed as Mel-e-gar agreed that he would be glad to join their family. As they talked into the night Mel-e-gar felt at home once more.

* * *

UN-WATER

The voices faded into the background and the image seemed to blink once, then disappear from the dolphins' collective water-time. They all felt drained from watching the events of their past and Mel-e-gar made it clear that they would continue to see more later. But he wanted them all, even the Elders to look within their water-time and to let the past sink within themselves and remember how far they had come. The dolphins scattered in the water and some chose to swim away and be alone with their feelings. Others decided to stay in groups and play. Many went further away from the shore, out to the richer fishing grounds of Edenlea.

Mel-e-gar's family didn't venture far from him and he watched as Haw-e-gar chased Ser-e-gar through the water. His own water-time was still very deep but part of him watched them and he was glad that Edenlea was a safer place for them than their old world. The only danger that they had come across were the Keaka, similar to the Keaverkack but easier to deal with. His water-time told him that they had changed so much, that defence against potential predators was well developed through the use of the water sounds. They knew how to collectively fight the Keaka, using the lessons of the many battles on their old world, a concept which was new to them, to have to sometimes kill another creature in self defence. His water-time rippled with sadness that they had to learn such a lesson but he knew it was necessary that they should be able to do so.

He spent the rest of the tay swimming among the dolphins, exchanging a sound here and there. He felt the disturbances in the water-time of the younglings as they came to terms with what they had seen. Many of them were also eager to see more and Mel-e-gar told them that he would begin again in a tay or two.

* * *

Que-e-lea swam at the head of the younglings as they followed Zar-e-gar through the warm sunny waters in the afternoon of the second tay of their journey. She saw Zar-e-gar turn in the water and shout, "There *it is!*" The excitement flowed through the younglings as they all realized that they were nearly there. She called back to Jer-e-lea to make sure all of them were together and to take charge while she went ahead with Zar-e-gar to make sure that it was a good place for them to stay. It wasn't that she didn't trust Mel-e-gar but she always made sure herself. *After all being a Nursery motherling was a serious business.*

She broke away from the school and caught up with Zar-e-gar. Side by side they dived out of the water and broke through the waves and checked out the island ahead. In the distance she could make out a large mountain that dominated the island and only after she had swum a few more klees did she realise that it was an active volcano. There were trails of lava flowing down the sides into the vast vegetation which seemed to cover the island.

Que-e-lea merged her water-time with Zar-e-gar and sounded, *How active is it?* pointing with her beak at the volcano as they broke through the water for the umpteenth time.

Not very! sounded Zar-e-gar. *Mel-e-gar told me that it would be quite safe for us to explore the shallow waters around the island, as he has used his watersong to check on the volcano's condition*! Zar-e-gar found the idea very funny, for his water-time found a lot of things that Mel-e-gar did were beyond his understanding.

Que-e-lea agreed with that and responded, *I bet you haven't even heard the name before! Or even know what it is!*

Zar-e-gar laughed and sounded, *Yes, before Mel-e-gar showed me this place I had no idea such things existed on un-water! So I've learnt something new...*

Que-e-lea realized that Zar-e-gar had no more interest in what happened on un-water than the rest of the younglings, which she knew was the way things were to be. But she found it fascinating, as she had explored a volcano on Delikadove many seasons before with Mel-e-gar and found the experience exhilarating. Her water-time was sure that she would find time to explore the island when the younglings were busy sleeping and feeding later that evening.

Together they dived down through the clear water and skimmed the sea bed watching the many creatures scurry past. Zar-e-gar twisted away from Que-e-lea and chased a fish that he hadn't seen before. *Don't go far!* sounded Que-e-lea as he disappeared behind a rocky shelf. She smiled and turned back to meet the rest of the dolphins. She was laughing to herself as she sighted them in the water.

Jer-e-lea swam up to her and kept pace at her side. *What's so funny?* she sounded.

Oh it's just Zar-e-gar chasing a new fish. I believe he's quite obsessed by them!

They both laughed and Que-e-lea told her that the waters were quite safe. They guided the eleven younglings to the waters around the island and soon they were all playing happily and Que-e-lea made sure that they all had a good feed before they split up into groups to explore. It wasn't a hard job as she had four good deputies to help her. Tey-e-lea and Fer-e-gar took four while Jer-e-lea and Kel-e-lea took charge of the rest. Solarn slowly disappeared behind the island and dusk fell bringing a cool wind that stirred the waters above but which didn't disturb the scenes of joy down in the depths below.

Que-e-lea watched as Kel-e-lea and her sisterling Tan-e-lea explored the coral reef that seemed to snake around the island about fours klees from the shore. As the light was almost gone they used their sounds to see. She swam over and joined with their water-time as Tan-e-lea asked her sisterling, *What is it?* as she poked her beak at the maze of growth, where a teeming mass of creatures that existed in and around the reef went about their business. She found it fascinating as her sounds revealed more to her water-time.

Kel-e-lea paused in her water-time and looked at her sisterling and sounded, *Beats me!* They giggled and Que-e-lea joined in and sounded, *Well Mel-e-gar calls it coral and he says that many places have it living around the waters of un-water.*

She told them to follow her and they explored the reef together, sharing the many sights of their water-time. Que-e-lea had not seen anything like it before in Edenlea but it reminded her of Shakeilar. An idea formed within her water-time and she withdrew from the younglings, telling them she wouldn't be long.

Que-e-lea swam away and used her sounds to explore the reef even further, *Amazing*! she sounded as she realised that the coral was indeed a form of Shakeilar. *Now let's see if this has any effect.* Using her water-time to talk to the reef, *Hello, can you hear me?*

Part of her felt foolish as the coral seemed to decline in giving a reply. But not put off she carried on weaving in and out the reef, trying different places as she went. After several clars had passed she realized that the coral may indeed be like Shakeilar but a more primitive form, unfortunately a non sentient life form. *A pity..* she sounded. Her water-time was intrigued that this world should have the beginnings of Shakeilar. *I wonder if it will manage to evolve like ours did?* The question brought memories of Delikadove and she realised that it didn't really matter if it didn't because at least she had a lovely reminder of her old home. With that last ripple in her water-time she left the reef and went round to check on the youngling dolphins.

* * *

Tan-e-lea and Kel-e-lea left the coral reef and swam within two klees of the island. They poked their beaks above the waves and watched as a few wispy clouds scurried past in the star filled sky. Now Tan-e-lea's water-time was playing with an idea as she turned her beak and gazed at the island, feeling the familiar pull. It reminded her of her parentlings and the scenes she had witnessed. Her water-time began to bring the many emotions of confusion and fear to the surface. But she was more fascinated by the concept of walking on un-water like her parentlings. Soon her water-time brought waves of daring and her excitement steadily built up inside her.

Kel-e-lea was enjoying watching the silvery moon as it played hide and seek in the sky and so was at first oblivious to the change in her sisterling. However as the light shone down and cast shadows on the water she turned her beak and looked at her sisterling just as a moonbeam lit up her young form. The excitement that Tan-e-lea felt began to broadcast itself to Kel-e-lea and the water seemed to carry the energy to her. "What *in all* Edenlea has made you dance so?" she enquired of her sisterling, her water-time intrigued by the spectacle of her sisterling dancing in the water.

Tan-e-lea's sparkling eyes turned to Kel-e-lea and she gave a squeak in response then dived through the water, heading for the island.

Now where is she going?! sounded Kel-e-lea and gave chase. She didn't know what had taken her sisterling's water-time by storm but she was determined to find out. Being a lot bigger she soon caught up with Tan-e-lea and they dived in and out of the waves as they ploughed on towards the island.

"What is the matter with you?!!" she shouted at Tan-e-lea, "*What is wrong?*" She kept asking questions and Tan-e-lea who was by now quite oblivious to the sounds of her sisterling kept on ignoring her. Kel-e-lea was getting worried and a little irritated with her sisterling but she decided that it would be best to just follow and make sure that no harm came to her.

Tan-e-lea slowed as they came within a klee of the island and Kel-e-lea who overshot by several dees, flipped back and came alongside of her sisterling.

The water time of Tan-e-lea swirled around inside her, making her feel more determined to find a way to walk on un-water. *But how?* That was the problem. She sifted through the images of herself landing on un-water then suddenly being pulled back to the safety of Edenlea. The vision that haunted her the most was of herself standing in a strange place, with a large crystal and then the red hill. She was convinced that she had been there. It was too real not to have been. Her water-time seemed almost to boil inside her as she realised that if Kel-e-lea had helped to rescue her, perhaps her Water-weaving could help her to go back? A plan formed in her water-time, bringing a calm and an abiding sense of joy. *I can do it! I can!!* she sounded.

Can do what? sounded Kel-e-lea quite bemused at her antics. *What are we doing here*?

Tan-e-lea turned her excited beak towards her sisterling and sounded, *You know when you helped our Grand-elder save me from un-water, will you help me again?*

Kel-e-lea was horrified with the idea of Tan-e-lea being stranded again and retorted, *What in all the world is making your water-time so crazy*! But then her tone shifted as the questions she wondered at formed within her. *Why did you leap onto the shore in the first place?!*

Tan-e-lea laughed and sounded, *I was following our parentlings' example!* She was now so taken with the idea that she completely forgot Mel-e-gar's warning, not to reveal what had happened to her. Her rebellion was complete as she told Kel-e-lea the full story.

Now Kel-e-lea listened and as she absorbed the images that Tan-elea fed her she became intrigued and frightened all at the same time. There was so much she didn't know and Tan-e-lea told her that Mel-e-gar was at this yen revealing all to the Council.

When were we going to be told?! sounded Kel-e-lea in frustration at being a youngling.

Tan-e-lea suddenly realising what she had done began to shake and tears started to fall in her water-time. *I don't know!* she cried. The feeling that she had betrayed her Grand-elder ran wild within her.

Kel-e-lea seeing her distress calmed her sisterling down by saying, *Maybe he wants it to be this way*. A light of understanding filled her form as the realisation that Mel-e-gar did nothing without good reason and it was strange that he would leave their water-time in such confusion.

It didn't occur to them that Mel-e-gar may have failed to realise that by not fully explaining his warning it would leave Tan-e-lea's curiosity unsatisfied and combined with Kel-e-lea's own sense of adventure would create a storm waiting to break.

So with the assumption made that they understood his reasoning Tan-e-lea began to feel less guilty and so she asked the question again, *Will you help me Kel-e-lea?*

Yes! If you know how, sounded Kel-e-lea. The idea of going to the un-water filled her with excitement. She made sure that their water-times were properly joined and told Tan-e-lea to share her idea.

The moon seemed to be watching them as they shared their water-time, going over the plan several times. Kel-e-lea was disappointed that only her sisterling would be able to go as Tan-e-lea had no way of transforming her as well. But it would give her an opportunity to use her water-weaving once more and that in itself was gratifying to Kel-e-lea. They swam a little further out and dived to the bottom of Edenlea where they were to begin their experiment.

Tan-e-lea searched her water-time for the image of herself standing on what she believed to be a hill on un-water and then began her watersong. The use of the watersong to transmute a physical form was an old art that hadn't been used by dolphins for many millions of seasons. In fact it was the early Watersingers who had used the song when dolphins made their first attempts to colonise the land masses of Delikadove. This was unknown to Tan-e-lea but she seemed to tap that fruit of forgotten knowledge purely by accident. She had no idea what the result would be.

Her song flowed through her body, making her vibrate in the water and Kel-e-lea watched as Tan-e-lea's form started to change. Her body began to shrink as the watersong took a greater hold of her. Soon her tail split in two, forming two silver grey legs. Her torso bulged outwards, changing her lung capacity. The effect spread until arms and hands lengthened, breaking away from her flippers. A strange red and blue light made her body sparkle and it seemed to shimmer and swirl around her. Tan-e-lea changed the tempo of her song and before her head changed she began to sing a long note, that seemed to pause the effect, giving Kel-e-lea time to begin her water-weaving.

Kel-e-lea sent her power of sound and began to weave the water around her sisterling. Soon a purple light joined the dancing red and blue light. The water began to spin, weaving itself into a fine sheen, that cloaked Tan-e-lea completely. Her form was left suspended in the water as the cloak of water moulded itself around every part of her now transformed body. Kel-e-lea satisfied with the result, gave a twist to her water-weaving, causing Tan-e-lea to finish her note. The note faded away and Tan-e-lea's beak withdrew into her head making her face look flattened. Her jaw line became rounded and her eyes settled now into a forward position.

The disorientation was considerable for Tan-e-lea but she recalled from her water-time the way she had been in the dream and then the image of the dark sea came into focus. Kel-e-lea was just a blur of shadow a few dees to one side. Tan-e-lea tried to use her water-time to communicate with her sisterling. At first she didn't get any response, then it came.

Are you all right in there? called Kel-e-lea, her concern apparent as she looked on with wonder at her sisterling who lay in the water suspended from it, but still part of it. She nearly panicked as Tan-e-lea's water-time didn't at first respond.

I feel strange but I am all right. Our water-time is separated by the barrier of your water-weaving.

So it works! exclaimed Kel-e-lea. The hardest part for her had been to make a barrier of water, that would protect and enable her sisterling to retain the integrity of her new form on un-water. Allowing her to move easily when out of Edenlea had been tricky, but Kel-e-lea solved this by using the same method as before but in reverse. The other change was to make the bubble cling to the new contours of Tan-e-lea.

Yes, you have really done it, responded Tan-e-lea. The pause was pronounced as her water sound had to make the jump though the unusual nature of the water-weaving.

You'd better try the next part! sounded Kel-e-lea and she flipped backwards a few dees, settling down to watch as the strangest creature to ever come before her eyes began the song that would hopefully transport Tan-e-lea to the beach on an island of un-water.

Tan-e-lea gathered her watersong and in her water-time she visualised the beach. An explosion of energy lanced out in all directions. Millions of lights danced and exploded, causing different notes to be heard and felt by Kel-e-lea. Soon the water was filled with a tune that pulled on her water-time, causing a rush of emotion that leapt inside her and she somersaulted through the water in ecstasy. Great joy filled her body as the lights of many hues exploded for the last time. A rush of water filled the space as Tan-e-lea vanished from Edenlea.

Kel-e-lea quickly recovered from the shock wave and swam to the surface. She orientated on the island and then swam as fast as she could to see if her sisterling had made it. It didn't take her long and there standing on the beach was Tan-e-lea.

She really has gone and done it! her water-time sounded as she leapt through the breaking waves and signalled to her sisterling that she had seen her and swam back to wait for Tan-e-lea to return. They had several clars before Que-e-lea would begin to wonder where they had disappeared to and Kel-e-lea hoped that it would not be too soon.

* * *

Tan-e-lea's form sparkled with energy as she landed on the beach. Her water-time almost couldn't believe that it had worked so well but she knew the importance of maintaining the stability of her new body. She stood in the moonlight, and wiggled her toes in the sand, glad that there was no loss of sensation through her water barrier. Her form continued to glisten and sparkle with fire lights as she slowly walked along the beach, breathing the air slowly through her reshaped mouth and lungs. She felt so happy that she had broken through the barrier to the un-water, if only for a short while. Tan-e-lea knew that she could only stay for a few clars before the effort of maintaining her new form would exhaust her. She walked to the water's edge and looked out across Edenlea and by the light of the moon saw Kel-e-lea do her leap into the sky. She waved in response and turned and walked up to the line of trees.

The whole perspective was so strange to her that she almost believed that she was dreaming again. But no, the sounds of creatures that had no name could be heard in the wind, telling her that this was very real indeed. She slowly walked through the forest, using her hands to pull branches out of the way. The light was very dim and Tan-e-lea found that because she was still linked to the water she could use her sounds to pierce the darkness. That also revealed to her the many different creatures that were very active, scurrying up trees and running along the leaf strewn un-water. Now Tan-e-lea didn't have a lot of caution in her, as there were no real threats in Edenlea and as she explored the area there was no fear in her heart.

Her water-time was very calm and peaceful and she delighted herself by making sounds, rather deeper than her normal high tones she usually used while in Edenlea. It gave her a strange sensation to hear her sounds disappear almost instantly rather than the smooth echo that she was used to. It became a game to see how long she could make her sounds last as she become oblivious to her surroundings;

"Hello! *HELLO*!!" She called and giggled as her water-time wondered what Mel-e-gar would make of this. She talked to herself for quite some time, not realising that she was getting further away from the shore. Deeper she travelled, following a track here and there, then veering off through the trees, lost with the incredible sensations of touching, smelling, seeing, and hearing so many different things.

Several clars passed and Tan-e-lea came to the edge of the forest. At first she thought that somehow she had made her way back to the shore line of Edenlea. But she soon realised that she had come to a large expanse of grass covered un-water, with a large pool. The moon was lower in the sky, hiding behind the trees. She walked across the grassland and her sounds made out a circle of rocks that surrounded the pool. The beauty of the scene made her sigh as she walked over and jumped up to sit on the nearest rock. A fine growth of moss clung to it making a comfortable seat. She sat and swinging her short legs backwards and forwards, her dees cleared the ground with ease. The water of the pool seemed to be very active to Tan-e-lea's sound. Strange creatures seemed to croak, then jump a few dees onto the plants that spread themselves over the surface. Many small flying insects buzzed around and Tan-e-lea said hello to each one that buzzed past. She knew they were not sentient and couldn't reply but she remembered Zar-e-gar's sounds to give respect to other creatures. As he usually maintained, a dolphin's duty was always to say thank you to the fish before swallowing it.

A dim light started to spread on the horizon, picking out the odd tree here and there. Then the light shone on the pool, making it sparkle. Tan-e-lea was still sitting on the rock engrossed in watching a furry creature wash its paws with its tongue, then chatter away to her, making her laugh. She didn't realise at first that a new tay was starting. But as the light grew stronger it made the colours of the forest spring out at her and she jumped down in alarm, realising she was late. Tan-e-lea was about to run into the forest when she realized something odd. The skin on her arm was a dry silvery grey, without the sheen of the water-weave.

"No!" she cried, searching her water-time for the song of change. Her distress mounted as she realised that the song was no longer there. At first she nearly screamed in horror, believing the integrity of her form was about to collapse, leaving her to die as a stranded dolphin. But as her water-time started to fall apart, she stopped her panicking and saw that somehow the impossible had happened. She had managed to change herself so much that it had stayed, no longer needing the protection of the water-weave.

She walked around the pool, trying to figure it out. "How can this be?" she asked the furry creature, who was still cleaning its paws. It chattered back, as if to say, "*Who knows!*"

Tan-e-lea laughed and hunched down by the creature and said, "Well I know I don't." The creature hopped onto her knee and then scrambled up to sit on her shoulder. This made Tan-e-lea squeal with delight.

"Come on, we'd better get going." She turned and walked into the forest. Solarn was rising fast, lighting her way. She walked with her new friend, following the way that her water-time told her would be the quickest to the beach. Her joy was complete as the full ramifications of what she had managed to achieve filled her water-time. She stroked the creature as it balanced on her shoulder and said, "I can't wait to tell Kel-e-lea!"

Through the trees she soon saw the beach and she sighed with relief at getting back so easily. She lifted the creature from her shoulder and gently put it on the sand. The creature scurried off into the trees, where it paused and turned making its curious chattering noise before it disappeared amidst the green foliage. Tan-e-lea walked along the beach and soon came to the spot where she had materialised the previous evening. Remembering how her parentlings had left the water she knew that she would have to run and then jump into the air, hoping that she would change back to a dolphin when she slid back into Edenlea.

Tan-e-lea had hoped that she would see Kel-e-lea, but there was no sign of her sisterling.

"I'd better get on with it," she muttered and ran down the beach. When she reached the waterline she launched herself into the air. With a graceful dive she slid beneath the waves, but as she descended her body reacted with shock. She realised that no change had happened. Tan-e-lea had to fight to get back to the surface, as she had no idea how to swim using this form.

Her water-time was shattered. The idea that she could be stranded on un-water forever nearly crushed her. She struggled harder to get to the surface. When her head broke through, she pulled in hurried gulps of air.

It couldn't be..! her water-time sounded, *No! No! Don't let it be so!* She remembered Mel-e-gar and her family and the idea of being apart from them made her cry into the early morning wind. "AHH! Help me!!" Her young water-time was now truly falling apart and she blindly thrashed her way back to the shore. It was so terrible for her, trying to swim using an inadequate form, when only a few clars before she had been a young graceful dolphin. Now as she pulled herself up onto the beach she was a useless...*What*! She didn't know what dolphins were called when out of the water. Tan-e-lea lay in despair on the beach and the rays of Solarn shone on her miserable body on the sand.

"So you think yourself so clever! Silly *dolphin*!"

Tan-e-lea nearly had a fit as she believed that the voice was Mel-e-gar's. She lifted her head from the sand and looked up, shielding her eyes with a hand, as the light of Solarn shone in her face. She could just make out a bulky form standing over her.

She sat up to see properly and stared in disbelief as the voice said, "Never seen a *talking rock* before!"

It was too much for Tan-e-lea. Her water-time fell in, taking her down to the darkest depth of her being and oblivion.

"Where have I seen that sort of response before!" laughed *the* Rock and slowly spread itself over the unconscious form. "Here we go again. These *dolphs* can't keep out of trouble!"

The Rock paused as it finished storing Tan-e-lea inside *its* bulk and corrected itself, "Sorry, *dolphins*!" *It* then vanished from the beach. The waves soon filled in the indentation left behind by Tan-e-lea and Solarn held itself in the midtay sky oblivious to the dramas below.

* * *

Kel-e-lea swam in circles, waiting for Tan-e-lea to return. The wind picked up and the waves grew stronger as she repeatedly scanned the beach. Her water-time became deeper as the clars passed. It wasn't long before Solarn broke above the horizon, bringing a new tay. She could hear the early morning sky-flyers singing on the island and she knew that she couldn't wait any longer. The wind blew stronger, whipping up the waves as she turned from her vigil and dived to the calmer depths below. Her water-time went over and over the same problem. How was she going to tell Que-e-lea what had happened. With Tan-e-lea not returning from un-water she knew that something very wrong had happened to her sisterling. Her water-time mirrored the increasingly turbulent sea above and she did the only thing she could, that was to call Que-e-lea.

Her water-time became a river and it flowed through Edenlea, searching for Que-e-lea. Within yens it broke through and poured itself into Que-e-lea's water-time. It was quite a shock for the nursery motherling as the troubled waters mixed, revealing all. Que-e-lea had only just finished sharing her deeper water-time with Mel-e-gar when she received Kel-e-lea's worried flow. At first it seemed unreal as the images of Tan-e-lea transforming herself unfolded. Fortunately Mel-e-gar had just finished telling her what had happened to Tan-e-lea when she tried to follow her parentlings, so the inquisitive nature of the youngling was easier to understand. The fact that she had successfully used her watersong to such an extent was breathtaking. But it was also very flawed. Que-e-lea passed the images to Mel-e-gar and awaited his response. This was unknown territory for her and she wasn't sure which way she should respond. His reply came back that she should go and search the island. She also felt how deeply coloured his waters were by the sadness of his own misjudgement but for that yen he had to tell Ser-e-gar and Car-e-lea what had happened to their youngest.

The link broke and Que-e-lea quickly called out to Jer-e-lea to take charge of the Nursery while she was gone. Her apprentice accepted without question, which Que-e-lea was thankful for, as she didn't have time to explain the situation. Que-e-lea sped through the sea, bow breaking through the waves until she was in sight of Kel-e-lea. The youngling was struggling hard with her water-time and she didn't respond to Que-e-lea's presence.

It's all right, I'm here, sounded Que-e-lea, sliding her body next to Kel-e-lea. They circled together as Que-e-lea calmed the youngling down. It wasn't long before Kel-e-lea responded to the warmth that seemed to hold her and she broke from her water-time and swam for the surface. Her beak broke through and she rode the now heavy waves, peering in desperation at the beach.

Que-e-lea had kept pace and Kel-e-lea looked at her and asked, "Will she be all right?" Her whole form shook as she now realised what the consequence would be if Tan-e-lea's transformation had broken while she was still on un-water. Her sad pleading eyes turned to Que-e-lea as she repeated her sorrow, "Let her be safe!"

"Leave here and go back to the Nursery to help Jer-e-lea," replied Que-e-lea. "There is nothing more you can do. I must go and find her." She couldn't give false hope to Kel-e-lea and she knew that the best thing for her was to go and join the others. Before she turned from Kel-e-lea she sounded, "There is one thing you should know. Mel-e-gar knew that Tan-e-lea would try and get back to the un-water."

Kel-e-lea brightened a little as she replied, "Then I was right. I felt that he would not let Tan-e-lea have unresolved water-time unless he had a good reason to."

"Yes, But..." She hesitated. "But he had not seen that she would try in this way and most important of all, not so soon."

Somehow knowing her Grand-elder was not always completely right made Kel-e-lea shudder a little. Somehow her waters would never be the same again. Maybe it was harder being an Elder than she first had imagined.

For a few yens they both stayed close, comfort flowing from one to the other and Que-e-lea's water-time recalled the many occasions that Mel-e-gar had been so right and maybe part of her always expected him to be so. It wasn't fair and somehow it seemed important to remember that he was when all sounded just as fallible as the rest of them. *Well maybe not as often!* she ruefully sounded to herself.

Que-e-lea watched Kel-e-lea disappear beneath the surface before starting her approach. She dived through the waves and headed for un-water. Her speed increased as she checked the depth with her sound. Soon the sea bed rose to meet her and she knew it was time to ascend. Her form twisted away at the last yen, causing her to break through the waves. A shimmering light enveloped her as she arched through the early morning sky. Descending tail first, she felt the power of the transformation take hold. Her water-time expanded with pleasure, when her newly formed dees smacked into the sand, sending a shower of yellow particles into the sky. Que-e-lea stood for a yen to let the energy dissipate. She took a deep breath of the salt air, savouring the taste. She slowly walked across the sand, following the waterline and began to look for any sign of Tan-e-lea.

A multitude of heavy, grey clouds soon overshadowed Solarn and Que-e-lea felt the wind blow stronger as a storm started to brew. The temperature dropped as she scanned the beach, causing her water-time to respond by increasing her body temperature. There seemed to be no evidence to indicate that Tan-e-lea had ever been on un-water and Que-e-lea decided that her only course of action was to search the forest.

The sky seemed to get darker as she proceeded further into the trees. The broad leaves slapped her as she used her hands to make pathways among them. A flock of roosting sky-flyers, startled by the noise below, screeched loudly and flew into the air, making Que-e-lea jump back in surprise. She stumbled over a fallen branch and landed heavily into the undergrowth as a loud peal of thunder broke overhead. The heavens opened and a torrent of rain fell from the heavily laden clouds. The broad leaves of the forest gave her some protection but soon rivulets of water ran over her form. “A good job I’m a Grand-elder, otherwise I would be in trouble,” she remarked out loud.

She was grateful that she had been born twenty years before the time of the first major change in dolph physiology, unlike Ser-e-gar or the other Elders who would have had to have been inside the protective cover of Shakeilar if it ever rained. Because they were born without the conscious control over the power to transform into a dolphin. But they had retained the trigger the other way round. That was the other reason that Mel-e-gar had championed the cause for the return to the time of Edenlea. Nature itself seemed to demand it.

It wasn’t long before the rain drenched Que-e-lea found an opening in the trees to the grasslands beyond. She still hadn’t found any clue as to where Tan-e-lea could have gone but her water-time was determined to continue. The rain started to recede and the heavy clouds reluctantly gave back dominion over the sky to Solarn. Que-e-lea came across a pool with a circle of stones and rested for a yen. The creatures who had sheltered from the storm reappeared and she watched as a prickly beast waddled over to the pool and drank its fill. It was soon joined by several golden brown coated creatures only a couple of dees high. They trotted over on their three toes and snickered at Que-e-lea, quite unconcerned at her presence. Que-e-lea watched entranced as more life descended.

The strangest sight was a tall sky-flyer, that must have stood eight dees tall, with such small wings that Que-e-lea realized that it couldn’t fly. *How strange!* her water-time rippled, as she had never before seen such a thing. On Delikadove all the sky-flyers could fly and it didn’t seem sensible to her that they would ever choose not to use their wings. Then to evolve so that they became useless didn’t make much sense. Her curiosity piqued as she walked over to examine the creature, or un-flyer as she chose to call it. Being a couple of dees higher she reached down and stroked its head. Quite unperturbed the creature let Que-e-lea stroke down to its black and grey feathered back. It responded by rubbing its large curved beak against her arm.

"You really are amazing!" she remarked as her fingers descended to feel its small wings. "Do you know you have grown far too big to fly?!" She laughed and the un-flyer blinked its coal black eyes and bent down and scooped some water from the pool. It then held its head up, with its beak pointing at the sky to let the water slide down its throat.

Que-e-lea walked round the pool, leaving the many creatures to drink and walked across the grassy plains. She saw more of the small three toed creatures running across the plain. Everything was a marvel and she soaked up the sights, recording it all so she could pass it onto the others. In the distance the volcano she had seen only from the water loomed ahead. Another forest circled round and here and there small streams of lava flowed down its steep sides. The orange and red glow at the top told of more activity. Que-e-lea still saw no sign of Tan-e-lea and despite the wonders to be seen her water-time grew more restless as the tay marched on. *Where could she have gone?* Her sounds asked, but no answer was forthcoming.

The walk across the plains was uneventful and she was soon at the edge of the other forest. Taking her water-time in hand she steeled herself for the arduous climb, as the trees ascended up the rocky slopes of the volcano. Her legs grew tired and her body was whiplashed by the leaves, making progress painfully slow. The heat of the volcano made her reduce her body temperature to cope with it. Feeling more comfortable she climbed higher into the dense growth. She started to call out, "*Tan-e-lea!*" over and over again but still no response came. Her water-time began to get more desperate the higher she climbed. Then suddenly the trees were left behind and she was back in the open air. She had to scramble up a rocky overhang to get any further. She paused at the top and looked back. The view allowed her to just see the white foam of the distant shore, which made her water-time long to be back in the cool embrace of her home.

Que-e-lea realised that she would have to try and circle the volcano to find out what was on the other side. The rocky overhang gave her a broad platform for part of the way but then she came to a deep crevice. It was only about eighteen dees wide but at the bottom she could see the red glow of a lava stream. She backed off and readied herself to jump across. Her water-time eased the muscles in her legs, allowing her to take the run. With several great strides she leapt, her left dee landing just on the edge of the precipice, causing her to shift her weight forward. The extra momentum brought her safely to the other side. There she stood on trembling legs, for what seemed an age as she made her water-time calm down. Looking back she saw how close it had been, the rock had crumbled where her dee had landed and if she hadn't been quick, she would have fallen into the hot lava below. Not a nice picture in any one's water-time.

The rocky ledge she was on sloped back down to the forest. Que-e-lea breathed a sigh of relief and proceeded to carefully edge herself down. The rock was slippery from the rain and a couple of times she slid rather than walked down. As she came to the trees she saw that another precipice barred her way. It was a relatively fresh fracture as there were several trees with their roots sticking up in the lava stream below and this one was about twenty nine dees in width. She knew that it was going to get worse before it got any better.

The only thing to do was to estimate the gap and jump. On the other side there were breaks between the trees where Que-e-lea knew she had to land evenly or she was going to sing the deathsong a lot earlier than she had bargained for. The only way to do it was to scramble back up the slope and run down and launch herself off; the trouble was that the overhanging branches made it a perilous undertaking.

Que-e-lea scrambled up the slope and ran down. Her dees felt the edge and she launched herself into the air. She decided to treat it like a dive out of the sea by turning in mid air but as she descended she saw she had missed. Her fingers reached out and just managed to grab an overhanging branch of a fallen tree. She had missed only by a fraction and as she was now only a dee or two below the edge she used her other hand to reach up and by curving her fingers she plunged them into the soil creating an anchor. It gave her enough leverage to let go of the branch, then with a heave she pulled her torso up and over, swinging her legs up as she did so. She lay on her front length ways along the precipice and started to breathe again, her water-time hoping that all her effort would be worth it.

She scrambled to her dees and proceeded down the slope through the trees. The ground was a lot easier and Que-e-lea almost ran, feeling that the more distance she put between herself and the precipice the better she would feel. So it was with much surprise that the soft, leaf strewn ground gave way under her and she found herself falling through the darkest space imaginable. Her water-time froze as she fell and her last image was that of Tan-e-lea. *I'm sorry*.. was all she could manage, then nothing.

A million stars danced in the air and each colour of light painted itself onto the next, a continuous pulsating stream that went on forever. The whole whirling Kaleidoscope touched one part, then moved onto the next. The motionless body had no awareness, its life stilled by the movement of the stars. This process continued until a red glow permutated the skin. Then a healthy silver, grey sheen took over from the red and the chest moved, showing a normal breathing rhythm.

Que-e-lea opened her eyes and believing she had entered the deathsong, smiled and said, "It's nice to know there is Shakeilar here in Chisharnlay as well..." A feeling of peace flowed through her water-time as she continued to stare at the ceiling. Part of her wondered what was going to happen next.

"Get up! Get up! Can't have you lying about the place!!!" A voice exclaimed.

All Que-e-lea did was to smile serenely, not really hearing the voice. Nothing would disturb her from her peace. Well, that was the idea and she had a rude awakening as a force seemed to jerk her up onto her dees. One yen she was lying down, the next she was standing on very wobbly legs, as her body tried to regain its balance.

"After all I've done, you lie there with that stupid grin on your face. No thanks *whatsoever*!..." The voice continued to mutter and moan at *its* lot.

It took her a yen to realise that she was far from the deathsong. Her surroundings seemed to jump at her in stark relief. She was in a large room, made of three circles joined together. She was at one end and in the centre was a flame that danced in a cradle of crystals. It reminded her so much of Delikadove that her water-time began again to believe she had indeed entered the deathsong, as she knew that no building of Shakeilar existed on this world's un-water. The walls and ceiling had the familiar flow of colour that was so typical of her race's dwelling places. The confusion struggled inside her as she tried to figure out where she was.

The voice interceded, “Look, what is the matter with you? *Come on*, snap out of it!”

This time the voice did register on Que-e-lea and as she didn’t see anything else in the room except for the flame in the crystals, she walked over to it and said, “I’m sorry, but I don’t know where I am.”

“What are you talking to that for?!” the voice roared. “*And* move away. You might disturb it!”

Que-e-lea, her water-time becoming more even as each yen passed, had decided enough was enough. “Look stop being so rude and come out from where you are hiding!” She strode around the room as if she was talking to a youngling who had misbehaved. Her body stretched to its full stature as she glared around the room.

“You can start by looking behind you!” The voice retorted back.

She swung on her heels and there in front of her was a rock, about three dees in height. It had blue and red moss growing over the rippled surface. She knew that it hadn’t been there a few yens ago and she stared in disbelief. She was about to say, “I’ve never seen a-”

When *it* interjected, “No. Don’t say it! I have heard it a thousand times before!”

She stood there, opened mouthed for a few yens, then closed her mouth as her water-time told her she just looked silly. Que-e-lea crouched down and looked carefully at *the* Rock; she couldn’t see any form of appendage or a mouth to speak from and she wondered how *it* could move so quickly. Then a long forgotten water-time came to her of a story that she had heard Mel-e-gar tell a group of her younglings many seasons ago. “You!” she exclaimed. “I know of you!”

“At last, she’s *finally* figured it out!” *the* Rock replied.

Que-e-lea ignored the implied sarcasm by laughing instead and replying, “I’ve always wanted to meet *The Famous Rock*!”

The Rock murmured something in reply, which Que-e-lea failed to pick up and she watched as *it* slid over to a wall. There was a crackle of fire and the wall started to grow an appendage that flattened, then hollowed and filled with fish. The smell of roasted fish drifted over and Que-e-lea’s stomach began to howl with hunger.

“Come,” said *the* Rock. “Time to eat; then I will tell you what you want to know.”

Its tone was more reasonable and Que-e-lea noticed that *it* had a sound of sadness to *it*. Her water-time made her see Tan-e-lea and she nearly asked but something about the Rock made her stop. Instead she went over and began to eat. The floor bulged up and it gave her a soft place to sit upon. She went deep within her water-time as she looked around and a feeling of dread came over her. The image of Tan-e-lea kept flashing inside and she knew that something was very wrong. She finished eating and in response the wall produced a hollow, filled with water so she could wash the grease from her hands.

“How do you feel Que-e-lea?” *the* Rock asked, using a much softer tone. *It* slid along the floor and something took hold of her hand and pulled her from her seat. To Que-e-lea it almost felt like a hand, but then that would change to a feeling of a-, she couldn’t explain it. She instead accepted the touch and together they moved across the room.

“I feel fine, in fact I feel new..” Her voice trailed off as the feeling took hold. Inside something had changed; she didn't know what but it held her firm.

"Good, I'm glad that you do but I know you worry for Tan-e-lea." *The* Rock paused as Que-e-lea stumbled, all feeling leaving her legs.

"Come, you'd better lie down. The healing process is complete but you will need to rest after any exertion."

The Rock led her back to the place where she first awoke and she felt herself lying down on a soft bedding that the floor provided in an instant. Again the feeling of a hand that wasn't a hand stroked her head and after awhile she responded to the touch and relaxed. Tears came easily and she let the pent up feeling go. She cried steadily as *the* Rock told her what had happened.

"I found Tan-e-lea lying on the beach in a sorry state. She passed deep into her water-time and I brought her here. I tried the healing which worked so well for you, but with no response. She laid for several clars without ever giving sign that life still beat within her. I tried so many things. I searched her water-time and I never found her. It was as if she had gone into the deathsong leaving a breathing body behind. With you my job was easy. The injuries you sustained falling down the precipice were major and the burns that covered your body would seem to you terrible. But your life was strong and your water-time was eager to return. That was the difference."

The Rock paused in response to Que-e-lea as she moaned and cried for her loss and the family's loss. For a clar Que-e-lea's water-time came to terms with the fact that Tan-e-lea had indeed sung her last watersong. When she came to, she told *the* Rock to continue with the rest.

"I watched as her body, still retaining her dolph form, began to glow a strange green and it changed once to dolphin form then back to dolph. This went on for some time. It became a blur and I thought she might be trying to get back so I transported us to a distant part of Edenlea. The water seemed to flow into her, building the energy up. I tapped once more into her waters and for a yen I felt her presence but then it died. At that instant her body stabilised as that of a dolphin. But the energy continued to build." *The* Rock sounded heavy with emotion and Que-e-lea felt his pain as he continued. "Then...She exploded...a massive wave of energy hit me and I saw her, what was left..A shadow or a faint imprint in the water, then that too faded."

Que-e-lea seeing the events in her water-time tried to understand what had gone wrong, but she didn't have the knowledge that could help her. She sat up and reached out to *the* Rock and clung to *its* craggy surface, sharing the pain. Slowly for both, the pain ebbed away and she asked *the* Rock, "What did go wrong...?"

"Tan-e-lea used her watersong to transmute herself into a dolph. She had the power to do so and it worked for awhile. But when she tried to go back to Edenlea she didn't know how to switch it off. In fact she had managed to go beyond Kel-e-lea's water-weave and her body discarded it without her realising it. She was so happy with her achievement that she totally missed the point. Maybe if she had returned before her body had discarded the water-weave she might have been able to change back. But I don't believe so. There was one other thing that even Mel-e-gar couldn't have foreseen. The waters of Edenlea produced a very different Watersinger. Her power if it had stabilised would have far surpassed any gone before. It would have made Mel-e-gar look like a first born youngling, bare of knowledge in comparison."

Que-e-lea gasped at the idea. Her water-time found it hard to conceive of a power greater than Mel-e-gar. But then she was slightly biased. Her voice shaking with shock asked, "What about future Watersingers?" The image of the danger that might happen to some future dolphin appalled her.

"There will be no others..." replied *the* Rock.

"No *others*!?" Her water-time sighed in relief but then the image of Edenlea without a Watersinger brought her up short. "But don't we need them?"

"No, before on Delikadove the dolphs managed without a Watersinger for hundreds of seasons at a time. They were useful but Mel-e-gar was the last of those times. On this world, present and future dolphs will only be known as dolphins and here you have no need of the Watersingers. Once Mel-e-gar asked me if he was the last one, and for Delikadove he was. We had not expected the dolphins born on this world would ever produce the like again. The water here has the element of *Sealeta* missing. That was the cornerstone that the watersong works on and-,"

But how can Mel-e-gar's watersong work here?" she interrupted.

"Mel-e-gar has a gland that stores Sealeta and he found a way of secreting it when he sings; therefore it is added to the sea of Edenlea each time he sings. It will carry on producing until he too enters the deathsong. Now that I have answered your question I will continue. Tan-e-lea's song seemed to have a mixture of the inherited Sealeta and an element found on this world called; *Iridium*. It is normally rare here but a large quantity was deposited by a meteorite that struck about thirty million seasons ago. It killed three quarters of all life and made it possible for Mel-e-gar to safely bring you here. It also killed the predators that would have made life impossible. The other benefit was a shift in the orbit, to such an extent that ice caps started to form, which bring sporadic ice ages. That has produced a far better weather pattern and will continue to do so. That is why you see such variety of life on un-water and in Edenlea." *The* Rock stopped to let the mine of information sink in.

Que-e-lea's waters absorbed this new information and sifted it through. She came back to the Iridium and another question formed, "If the Iridium is still here and is mixed with future generations of Mel-e-gar's, won't that produce more Watersingers?"

"Maybe normally but I have checked the make up of the un-born dolphin that resides inside Car-e-lea-,"

"I didn't know she was *pregnant*!" exclaimed Que-e-lea, her water-time pleased that new life was on the way.

"Stop interrupting!" said *the* Rock, giving a strong message of annoyance. "Right, the reason is that she does not have Sealeta in her life blood. Furthermore no other dolphin has the gland to produce it or has the residue, like Tan-e-lea."

"So Tan-e-lea was the *last*......." replied Que-e-lea. A profound sadness held her as she organised the pictures in her water-time. A realisation that time had marched on filled her and she almost shouted at *The* Rock, "How do I get out of here?! I must get back to tell the others!"

The Rock tutted at her outburst, "I will send you back now if you wish!" and *it* muttered, "Is that all the thanks I get....?"

Que-e-lea laughed and replied, "Thank you Rock for all you have done." In a softer voice she added, "Especially for *Tan-e-lea...*"

One yen she was with *the* Rock, the next she was swimming in Edenlea, carrying a heavy burden for the family and the whole school. Que-e-lea had other questions she would have liked replies to. One was, What was the Rock doing on un-water in the first place? But that quickly sank to the bottom of her water-time as she spied Mel-e-gar and his family coming towards her. It didn't take long for her to tell them and they each reacted differently. Mel-e-gar stayed silent and Que-e-lea was aware that somehow he already knew. Car-e-lea and Ser-e-gar cried heavily into their water-time. Haw-e-gar reacted with total shock and he withdrew to the depths. Kel-e-lea felt it the hardest as she had been part of what had happened to Tan-e-lea. Zar-e-gar cried and went to search for another fish.

Later that tay, the whole school regrouped and they swam to the surface of Edenlea. With Mel-e-gar and his family in the middle, they watched the stars. The full moon shone its light down on the school of dolphins as Mel-e-gar led them in sharing the deathsong. A ritual to mark the passing of a dolphin. Their song shattered the quiet night and for many klees in all directions the sound of the song could be heard. Sky-flyers that had been roosting awoke and joined the cry, every creature feeling the sadness and then the joy as the dolphins wished Tan-e-lea a safe voyage.

The Rock also heard the song and *it* added *its* voice. After awhile the sound faded and *the* Rock slid over to the crystal array. *Its* rocky form began to change and soon two hands clasped the crystal, making the flame rise even higher. Its light expanded, shining onto the craggy features of *the* Rock. "It is done..."

A voice that sounded like a mountain roar replied, "GOOD....IS SHE READY?"

The Rock replied, "Yes." *It* made one stroke down with *its* hand and the far wall opened up. A shimmering curtain of blue fire danced across and with a further motion of *its* hand, the curtain vanished, revealing a vast cavern and at the bottom was a huge lake. *The* Rock entered and the curtain sprang back into place. *It* could feel the blue flames tickle *its* back. *It* bent down by the pool and cut the water with *its* hand. The water became crystal clear and *it* looked at the form that resided there.

A beautiful silver grey dolphin swam happily in the water. She saw *the* Rock and she dived clear of the lake, her body sparkling with a green fire as she landed softly on the cavern floor. "Hello Rock!" Her voice rang clear and it moved *the* Rock to tears. As *it* couldn't really cry tears, *it* cried inside. The large female dolph walked over and cradled *its* head in her arms. Her soft voice comforted *it*, "*It's all right...*They will be fine."

Her warmth filled *it* and *it* gently eased away and held her at arms length. *It* stared in wonder at the changes that transformed a once young and foolish dolphin. She was over eighteen dees in height now and her face appeared both young and old. The change *it* found most awe inspiring was her eyes. For now they shone green with a red fire that danced around her pure silver pupils. She grasped *its* hand and they walked out of the cavern. *It* didn't have to open the curtain. She sang a high sweet note and they passed through without hindrance, as smooth as a fast flowing river.

The crystal array began to vibrate as they entered the room and the fire exploded and was renewed. *Its* now deeper light shone brightly and *The* Rock gave thanks that at last the flame could now be truly eternal.

She stepped away from *the* Rock and sang her song. A song that told of time and worlds beyond worlds. The past, the present, and the future seemed to flow into her and her eyes bled. It ran down her face and spread outwards. Soon she was shrouded in silver. She just managed to say, "Goodbye Rock!" before winking out of existence.

The Rock said to the empty air, "*Goodbye Tan-e-lea....*"

* * *

SHAKEILAR

It was a very different meeting when they came together a jeanth later. The early death of Tan-e-lea had shaken the entire colony of dolphins. Mel-e-gar's family had urged him to continue with the telling of the story of why and how they had come to Edenlea. This time every dolphin was included and Mel-e-gar's original idea that the younglings under twelve seasons should be told later by their parentlings was now no longer relevant in the new circumstances. When Que-e-lea had told them that Tan-e-lea had entered the deathsong it raised questions in their waters that had to be answered. Mel-e-gar knew that this was finally the end of the old ways. Even he had been apt to hang on to the old procedures and it had taken the wise sounds of his own grandling; Haw-e-gar to finally change his water-time.

Mel-e-gar knew that his time was coming to an end and that in many ways the short seasons that had passed in Edenlea had made him more aware of that simple fact. So with that utmost in his water-time he transported the combined schools to the cooler waters of the northern hemisphere. The dolphins could see in the far distance the virgin white cliffs of the relatively new glaciers but it was a youngling who named them the waves of still water.

* * *

7182 S.N.

The deathsong of his parentlings was now a distant water-time and Mel-e-gar had spent a great deal of the intervening seasons in finding out why his world was changing. The three major seas of; Geailea, Hederlike, and Roulisad had become more treacherous for the dolphs and many had been killed by the Keaverkack who now infested most of the coastal waters. The dramatic reduction in the stocks of fish had meant that for the first time starvation was becoming a serious threat. His own plans for recreating Edenlea on Delikadove were in serious doubt if they couldn't solve the problem.

It was at the start of the hottest part of the season that Mel-e-gar travelled to the city of Desilata on the southern continent. The journey was made easy by having the use of the watersong, which made it possible for him to avoid the Keaverkack infested sea of Roulisad. His glowing form materialised just outside the city, where he was met by his old friend and playmate Ler-e-lea.

"Welcome Mel-e-gar, it's good to see you again," she said and stared up at him. "We have missed you.."

They warmly embraced and Mel-e-gar held her close and replied, "Yes, I've missed you too.." They shared a yen of silence, contemplating past waters before Mel-e-gar tentatively, almost guiltily asked, "It must be three seasons since you and your family left Plesilea. How are they?"

She heard the guilt in his voice and deciding to gently rebuke him replied, "They *are fine..*" She let go of him and turned towards the city adding, "But they have missed your company these past seasons. What have you been doing?!"

Mel-e-gar shook his head sadly and stated, "Still trying to find ways of solving the *Keaverkack* situation. It's been a hard problem to solve." He reached down and held her hand tightly hoping for forgiveness at his neglect and he was rewarded when she squeezed his hand in return. Her warmth of understanding flowed into him. Mel-e-gar sighed with quiet relief as Ler-e-lea made it clear that his answer was enough.

While they walked across the open grassland to the city she spoke of the rumour that had for many veuls passed among the inhabitants of Desilata; that there had been talk in the Council that he should be called upon to use the power of the watersong to move the Keaverkack to another part of Delikadove. He spent the time it took for them to reach the outskirts of the city to explain that until they found the reason why the Keaverkack had left their home waters he could not return them or place them in any other sea because he knew that until they had that answer they would only return.

Soon they were walking among the blue shimmering buildings of the city and he admired the very different formations of the Shakeilar. Desilata was laid out as a spiral and they had entered on the outer arm which meant there was only one continuous street that ultimately led to a centre spot. His waters became lighter as he allowed himself to be led to her home which was on the innermost ring. It was his first visit to the city and he liked what he saw. It wasn't long before they arrived and Ler-e-lea touched a blue and silver marker. An opening appeared and they walked through. His first sight was an immense pool that dominated the room. The outer rim was dotted with hollows. In each there was a different coloured crystal whose light refracted off the surface of the pool causing the colours to bleed into the water. It was a marvellous sight to behold. Mel-e-gar slowly walked round the pool, taking in the detail. He hadn't seen anything like it.

Ler-e-lea smiled, pleased with his reaction to her home. "Do you approve Mel-e-gar?"

She laughed when he turned and said, "*Not bad!*" She walked round the outer rim and gave a slight motion with her hand. The wall behind Mel-e-gar opened and she told him to follow. The next room was far smaller and the only thing in it was a single crystal that sat on a raised platform in the centre. Ler-e-lea tilted her hand slightly and two mounds grew from the floor.

"Come and rest yourself," indicating the opposite mound as she settled herself down on hers. He did as he was told and sank gratefully onto his. The mound grew around him, allowing his tired body to relax.

For a third time Ler-e-lea motioned with her hand and the floor obliged by opening and sending a platter of fish to hover gently four dees from the floor. She leaned over, picked a fish up and proceeded to eat it and between mouthfuls she said, "I heard that you were coming for the emergency meeting tonight. They say that Alk-e-lea has a proposal to put forth to you."

Mel-e-gar, now fully relaxed replied almost lazily, "Yes. They say she may have found a solution to the Keaverkack and for some reason she will not reveal all unless *I'm there*." He chuckled to himself as the image in his water-time amused him. "Well, I hope I may be of some help but if her solution does include moving the Keaverkack then they'd better forget it."

Ler-e-lea studied him carefully as he gave this reply and she could feel the depth of his feeling and she wasn't fooled by his almost nonchalant attitude. She decided to change the subject and said with a mischievous smile, "You will meet *Hil-e-gar* later."

For a yen Mel-e-gar didn't reply. Then as the name didn't register in his water-time his interest was aroused. He sat bolt upright as it hit him, "Your *mate*?!"

She laughed at the surprised expression on his face and teased him by saying. "I did leave a message for you to attend the *joining*! But as always your head has been absorbing too many crystals while Delikadove moves on."

Mel-e-gar apologised and then made matters worse by saying, "How long?"

This made Ler-e-lea roar with laughter and she had to put the fish she was holding back onto the platter before she dropped it on the floor. Her sides ached as she laughed even louder at the perplexed expression on Mel-e-gar's face. She sighed and said, "Mel-e-gar you really are something. I bet you don't even know where Wel-e-lea and Jey-e-gar are?" wagging her finger at him in admonishment.

"Are.. Well.. *aren't* they with you?" replied an even more confused Mel-e-gar as his water-time told him how out of touch he had become.

"No, you daft thing. Wel-e-lea mated a season ago and Jey-e-gar has only just passed his thirteenth season and has gone to join Nue-e-lea to study the science of the Puga."

That made his shame complete and he slumped back shaking his head over so much having happened with his friends. His water-time went back to the tay, three seasons before when the family left Plesilea to go to Colisee, a coastal city on the western continent and he had chosen to stay on at his old home, so he could continue with his work, whilst being close to the main library of Delikadove. He had known Ler-e-lea was living at Desilata when he received the message telling him that he would be met by her and so he had assumed that the rest of the family was with her. He apologised again but Ler-e-lea waved it aside still chuckling at her friend's perplexed expression.

"It's all right, Mel-e-gar," letting him off the hook. "I don't blame you!" She turned the conversation back to the matter in hand. "I'd better fill you in with some details. First of all I'm part of the meeting because of the knowledge I have gained, with the help of Hil-e-gar, on the Keaverkack."

Now this was something that Mel-e-gar had known about and he had heard of the stories of her bravery in studying the creatures at close quarters. But he hadn't heard Hil-e-gar's name mentioned at all. Feeling hungry he helped himself to the fish and while he ate, his water-time turned the information over. Between mouthfuls he asked, "So why haven't I heard of Hil-e-gar in all this?"

Ler-e-lea smiled as she thought on her mate's fine form and replied, "That is the way he likes to work. He says that he can do much more that way."

Choosing to leave it at that she was about to tell Mel-e-gar to finish the fish when at that yen Hil-e-gar entered the room. He nodded at Mel-e-gar and walked over to his mate to lift her from her seat for a warm embrace before she could say another word.

They stayed wrapped in each others arms while Mel-e-gar left his seat and walked back into the room with the pool giving his friend some privacy. His water-time was pleased that Ler-e-lea had found such happiness. Choosing not to change his form he dived into the pool and floated on his back, staring at the fluid motion of the ceiling. It mirrored the pool's movement and he felt it gently rock him to sleep.

Later that evening he walked with Ler-e-lea and Hil-e-gar to the meeting. It wasn't far and he found that it was the building at the centre of the spiral. He stopped outside and looked up at the impressive building. Two round spheres seemed to hover at the top and each gave off a different shade of blue, flowing down onto the main building, which was topped by nine curved arches. A hint of silver seemed to glow behind the different shades of blue giving a mesmerising quality which certainly had Mel-e-gar enthralled.

"*Come on*, we don't want to be late!" said Ler-e-lea pulling Mel-e-gar into the building. They entered a large chamber that was filled with dolphs. All were sitting around a central dais with three mounds. Mel-e-gar was about to follow Ler-e-lea and Hil-e-gar who were moving onto the back row when two dolphs came running up to him.

"Where do you think you are going?" called the tallest of the two, an imposing lea who seemed impatient for an answer. The other was a gar who grinned with mischievous delight at the confusion on Mel-e-gar's face.

He was about to answer when the lea grabbed his arm and pulled him away from Ler-e-lea while saying, "They've been *waiting* for you. Follow us." Mel-e-gar opened his mouth to reply, but then closed it again and did as he was told. They walked to the centre of the room where the lea bid him to sit on one of the mounds, while they settled down on the other two.

The chamber echoed with the sound of the many dolphs talking in low voices. He could feel an electricity of sound throb round the chamber as the dolphs, seeing the dais was now filled, turned their expectant eyes towards them. Mel-e-gar found the scrutiny of so many dolphs slightly unnerving and to settle his water-time he turned his attention towards the dolphs who sat with him. The lea, who was about twelve dees in height was whispering to her companion. His water-time inspected her. She had bright blue-grey eyes that shone with a commanding presence. Her fine chiselled features told him that she was an experienced dolph of about thirty three seasons. Her aura spoke of confidence and maybe a touch of an obsessive dolph/inality. She didn't seem to take any notice of Mel-e-gar as he continued to scrutinize her. He found her very attractive and he was growing more curious at every yen that passed. In the end he tore his gaze away from her and looked at her companion

To Mel-e-gar he had an air of easy grace and humour about him but Mel-e-gar couldn't place his age. The dolph caught Mel-e-gar's eye and winked. Mel-e-gar almost laughed out loud but the silence that abruptly descended on the chamber made him quickly swallow his laughter as the lea stood up and rested her hands on the crystal.

"Welcome my friends, we are here on this tay to discuss the situation of the Keaverkack." Her voice rang around the chamber, her bearing drawing their attention and as she spoke the crystal under her hands began to pulsate, its blue light bathing her form. "Some of you know me. Others are strangers but all of you are one family-" She paused then said, "We are here to end the Keaverkack infestation of our waters. For that reason I have invited-" She turned and indicated Mel-e-gar. "this dolph to attend the meeting." The crowd began to whisper and murmur, all eyes now on him.

He nodded his head in response and stood up. She whispered for him to join her and put his hands on the crystal. His touch invoked the crystal and a red and silver light now joined the blue light, joining them together. The other dolph who had been silent joined them and this time a yellow and silver light flowed from the crystal to join with the rest. To Mel-e-gar the whole process was fascinating but he was startled when the crystal began to speak.

"**Access is granted**," the voice intoned. "**Name; Alk-e-lea, student of Ancient Legends. Seasons young; thirty five...Name; Bue-e-gar, student of stars and constellations. Seasons young; seventy two...Name; Mel-e-gar, student of Edenlea. Seasons young; twenty**..." There were some gasps from the audience at the last part. For Mel-e-gar's height belied his age at being more than fourteen dees and the largest dolph so far recorded on Delikadove.

The slight echo of the crystal voice rang round the chamber, then silence fell once more. Mel-e-gar had many times come across stories that there had once existed crystals that could talk, but he hadn't expected to find one still in existence. He wondered what, ***Access is granted*** *meant and why such a formal introduction*? His face must have shown his curiosity, for Alk-e-lea whispered, "*It's registering our presence to see if we are fit to make use of its knowledge*."

This was an even greater revelation and he wasn't too sure if he liked the implication that knowledge would only be given to those that were fit to have it and by whose decree was such a decision made? Such ripples went through his water-time as Alk-e-lea began to speak again.

"Now that all of you are aware of who we are, we may now begin." The lights faded from their forms, sinking back into the crystal. It now only gave a dull glow as they went back to their seats. She indicated for Mel-e-gar and Bue-e-gar to sit while she continued to stand. The dolphs in the chamber found themselves under the scrutiny of her gaze and she shocked them all by saying, "We as a race are facing our *extinction*!!"

There was a roar of disagreement from the crowd and one voice could be heard above the rest. "It's not that bad. We have managed in hard times before and we will survive this!"

She held up her hands for silence and the voices, some still muttering, died down. "Yes-," pointing at the dolphs, "we may survive this but it is only the beginning of the troubles to come!" Before the dolphs could start again she raised her voice higher and with her eyes blazing said, "Now let me tell you what I have in mind to solve the problem of the Keaverkack! Without any more outbursts from the floor!!"

That was enough to silence the crowd and Mel-e-gar who was impressed by her performance found Bue-e-gar tugging at his arm. He turned from watching her and looked at Bue-e-gar whose grey, green eyes sparkled in the low blue light of the chamber. As a childlike grin spread across his face, he whispered, "She's *amazing*.. isn't she?"

Mel-e-gar nodded his head and his waters told him that Bue-e-gar was very much in love with her. He wondered if they were mated and he responded, "*Are you One?*" indicating with his eyes at Alk-e-lea. The broad grin and sly wink told him that they were. He became aware that Alk-e-lea had begun again.

"-are changing, there are signs that we are moving back to the seas and Mel-e-gar has a dream that we will recreate the idea and life of Edenlea.." That brought more murmurings from the dolphs and before any could raise the issue of the Keaverkack she said, "But that will not happen while the Keaverkack stay in our waters." She paused before she told them her solution. "I believe that the answer lies in the desert of *Arkelclared* on the eastern continent!"

That was enough to cause an uproar. Many dolphs stood up and shouted, "What use is that! No dolph has ever survived the *Arkelclared*!!"

"Please let me finish!" she commanded, her voice shaking with emotion as her eyes bore into the crowd, causing many to fall back into their seats dumbfounded.

Mel-e-gar's water-time was shocked by the response of the dolphs and he began to stand up when Bue-e-gar stopped him with a firm hand. "Don't, she can handle them. You must be new to this sort of thing. It's quite normal at these meetings."

Mel-e-gar relented and while Alk-e-lea talked of famine and disease, telling them that there was no choice, his water-time recalled what he knew of the desert that dominated the only continent on Delikadove which, as far as the library crystals told, no dolphs had ever inhabited. He was brought back from his water-time when he heard his name called. Almost automatically he stood up and he said, "*Yes?*"

Alk-e-lea turned to him and the crowd and said, "There is an ancient legend that tells of a group of dolphs that explored the desert many seasons ago. Only one returned and she brought with her a tale about a giant chamber and contact with a form of Shakeilar with immense powers. Unfortunately she passed into the deathsong before she could reveal much more. Her last words were that no dolph should ever enter the desert again, for no creature could withstand a power great enough to create worlds!"

She spoke with such passion that no dolph could speak against her and Mel-e-gar knew that somehow she was linked to the dolph in the legend. He now also knew what she wanted from him. It was no wonder that she had not spoken about it before.

He listened as Bue-e-gar told the assembly the changes in the condition of Danetar and that if it deteriorated any more then the problems they faced now would seem trivial by comparison. Mel-e-gar almost smiled to himself that Bue-e-gar was only there to reinforce the magnitude of disasters to come by making the case for Edenlea, by saying that dolphs may not be able to survive on the land for much longer. This made the Keaverkack their first priority. Mel-e-gar felt slightly redundant as he had not yet spoken and his water-time was troubled that the two dolphs were building him up into a saviour of Delikadove.

He decided to speak out. "That's *enough*!" Alk-e-lea and Bue-e-gar both stopped and stared in amazement at his outburst. He didn't give them a chance to interrupt and said, "That's a lot better. Now I know why I am here. You want me to go and contact this power you have spoken of but what makes you think that I can survive any better than the last poor dolph who ventured there?"

It was Alk-e-lea's turn to be impressed at the way Mel-e-gar had even managed to silence her. She smiled at him and said, "You have the power of the watersong and as a Watersinger you are the only one who stands any chance of coming back." Her words were softly spoken but loud enough for the crowds to hear and it made them stand and roar their approval. The sound was quite deafening and among the calls of agreement he was sure he could hear Ler-e-lea shouting the loudest.

"All right, I will only go if you have managed to figure out what has caused the

Keaverkack to leave their home waters and if you cannot then find some other dolph!" Mel-e-gar challenged and it was Bue-e-gar who answered.

"Myself and Ler-e-lea, with whom you are well acquainted and many others have discovered a massive new range of underwater fissures that are spewing hot lava into the sea. This effect has raised the temperature so much that the Keaverkack have no choice but to leave their home waters. If we wait a few seasons most of the Keaverkack will die from the change in depth and type of food they are now feeding on. A slow process but their bodies would pollute the inland waters for season upon season making it uninhabitable by us. So you see we do not have much choice but to ask you to go and see if you can find this Shakeilar and hope that its power may close the fissures. That is our hope, *will you...?*" His eyes now showed the full effect of his great age and Mel-e-gar responded by nodding his head in agreement.

That was enough. The chamber exploded with cheering dolphs rushing onto the dais to congratulate and thank them for what they had done and what he: Mel-e-gar was about to do. Many of the dolphs came from cities all over Delikadove and this only became apparent as Mel-e-gar walked among them and talked about the kind of future the dolphs wanted. Ler-e-lea joined him on the dais and with her mate they talked for many clars into the night.

The meeting ended far more informally than it had begun and Mel-e-gar was glad to finally leave. Alk-e-lea and Bue-e-gar joined them as they stepped into the warm night air. The five dolphs walked back to Ler-e-lea's home where she invited them all to stay. They agreed and the Shakeilar grew some more rooms. They left the discussion of the details until the next tay which Mel-e-gar's water-time knew would be for the best so he could get used to the idea of venturing into an area of Delikadove that still inspired fear in his race.

The following evening Mel-e-gar was ready to leave. "*So it's goodbye again Ler-e-lea,*" his voice full of emotion. "I hope I find the *answer...*" Mel-e-gar's waters were heavy and he let her wipe a tear from his eye.

She smiled up at him and said, "Just return safely." She could feel tears starting to form and breaking from the hug stood by the side of Hil-e-gar, who responded by putting a comforting arm around her waist. Alk-e-lea and Bue-e-gar said their goodbyes and the four dolphs stood back from Mel-e-gar as he prepared himself to invoke his watersong. They were all standing among a field of red and blue plants about two klees from Desilata. The two moons shone their welcoming light on the party below and watched as Mel-e-gar began to sing.

His song evoked different feelings among the four dolphs and all were held in awe of the raw power that made Mel-e-gar's body glow and shine with sparkling lights. His voice reached a high pitch and he lifted his hand, palm out and vanished. A roll of thunder broke the silence below and Ler-e-lea, her mind thinking of Mel-e-gar, walked back to the city with her friends. Not a word was spoken among them. All they could do now was to wait for him to return.

* * *

Mel-e-gar materialised by the only oasis to exist in the harsh desert of Arkelclared. He stood under the shade of a Calader tree, its broad green leaves protecting him from the rays of Danetar. A pool of water ten dees in width lay before him. This was surrounded by more of the seventy dee high trees. Beyond the trees he could see the orange desert stretch almost infinitely on all sides. Alk-e-lea had told him that the only reference point was the Oasis and he would have to search the desert on dee. He had to hope that he would stumble upon the great cavern. The only thing he carried was a small piece of Shakeilar. Its blue surface shone under the light as he placed it under the tree and sat down to wait for dusk.

They had talked about the time difference that would make it midtay at the Oasis whilst the city of Desilata, his leaving point would be under darkness. He had agreed that it would be best if he left while most of the dolphs of the city slept, to make sure that his leaving wouldn't become a spectacle. That meant he would have to wait for dusk when he arrived, but that couldn't be helped. Anyway it would give him time to review all he had been told the previous tay.

Mel-e-gar leant back and closed his eyes. His water-time rippled. *He now knew why it had thrown up the conclusion that Alk-e-lea was connected to the dolph who had survived the ill fated mission all those seasons ago. Her name had been Ual-e-lea and she was the direct ancestor of Alk-e-lea, a Great Grand-elder who had lived in the cycle of Kalan about seventy thousand seasons before. She had been a Watersinger and to Mel-e-gar that explained why she had managed to lead a group of ten dolphs into the desert. The reason had been purely for the quest of greater Knowledge. Even in their time the desert and the continent had never been explored. Why that was so had never been fully explained. Any reference to the reason that might have existed had been lost long before.*

In different periods of dolph history there had been times when crystals holding stored information had been destroyed by some disaster or other and never recovered, which left gaps in the hundred million season history of the dolph occupation on the land. The time before that was just called the cycle of Edenlea which as far as the dolphs had discovered went back a further two hundred million seasons. The great time scales involved had left their race sometimes slow to change but their ability to overcome any obstacle had seen them through some difficult times.

His water-time returned him from dwelling on the past and he opened his eyes to see that dusk was falling. He didn't relish the idea of walking through the desert but at least the wind which blew from the south would keep him cool. Bue-e-gar had told him that at first it would still be quite warm but when the twin moons reached their highest point it would drop drastically. If it became too cold he was to make use of the Shakeilar, which he would have to use during the tay. His body could cope with a slight deviation of temperature but the extremes that he would find here would test that to its limits. Mel-e-gar walked round the pool and picked a star in the sky to follow. After making his choice of a northern star he began his trek into the desert. Fortunately the moons gave plenty of light and he didn't have to call on the Shakeilar to light his way

After walking thirty klees Mel-e-gar retreated to his water-time and put his body on automatic. The dunes sometimes grew to great mounds that forced him to clamber up using hands and dees. How he was to find the cavern he didn't know and all Alk-e-lea had said was to use his instinct. He walked night after night. During the tays he sheltered inside the Shakeilar which could expand in size to form a curved shelter that mimicked the style of the orange sand dunes. He was impressed as he had never had any reason to make use of a *Travelling-shelter* before. There seemed to be no other life forms and after awhile he gave up looking. All he concentrated on was putting one dee forward at a time. The Shakeilar also provided a supply of fish and water. How that was done he didn't know. He just accepted it.

About twenty tays later, (Mel-e-gar couldn't be sure), he came to another Oasis, which surprised him as there was only supposed to be one. But pushing that from his water-time he thankfully collapsed under a tree and dozed off. His body was extremely tired from the effort of walking across sand that had a tendency to sink several dees under him. His sleep was full of sand and sand that never ended. His water-time mirrored the dryness, making him consider transporting back to the city of Desilata. But as the image of the blue city swam before his eyes he awoke and stared up into the tree.

No, he couldn't go back yet. He would try a different direction the next tay and walk some more. Mel-e-gar had forgotten how much hard work it was walking a distance more than several klees. Normally he used his watersong to transport himself to any place he wanted to go. He wished he could use it here but as there were no land marks except for sand he couldn't picture a destination, which was needed if he wanted to travel to it. (He had yet to perfect the ability to 'Far-see' with his water-time.) Ler-e-lea had provided the picture of the Oasis and the message he had received to go to her city had a picture of that destination. His water-time went over and over the simple fact that he would have to search on dee but firmly determined that one tay he would find a way round the need to know the precise point he was travelling to!

He brushed the sand from his body and walked over to the pool. His water-time registered the familiarity with his starting point and Mel-e-gar's heart froze as a dreadful idea poisoned his waters. *It couldn't be...* he whispered, but as he looked around him in the early morning light he couldn't deny it any longer, that he had somehow come full circle. The despair he felt was immeasurable and as he fell to his knees and cried, the hand holding the Shakeilar relaxed letting it roll across the sand and disappear beneath the surface of the pool. He dimly heard the *splash* and lunged forward. His head rested on the edge as he looked into the depth trying to see it. He was surprised how deep the pool looked and if he was to continue he would have to retrieve the Shakeilar. That was enough to stir him into scrambling to his dees and diving into the pool. As his form disappeared beneath the surface he transformed himself. Soon he was swimming down to the bottom of the pool as a dolphin and his water-time expanded washing away the feelings of despair.

Mel-e-gar felt free as he explored the depths. His whole body felt invigorated as his long, smooth form glided through the water. After awhile the water became darker as he descended further, leaving the light behind. He used his sound to pierce the depths but he still couldn't find the bottom of the pool. It was incredible that the pool could go down so far. After fifty dees he was still no nearer. There seemed to be no life of any sort in the pool and this made Mel-e-gar picture a nice fat fish which made him suddenly feel very hungry. It gave him an extra burst of speed and determination to find the Shakeilar as quickly as possible. Deeper he went, a hundred dees, three hundred, and on he swam. He stopped and rested for a few yens every now and then but he knew he would have to find the Shakeilar soon before he had to return to the surface to breathe.

At two thousand dees he at last came to the bottom. His sounds could make out a rocky formation. He swam towards it hoping that the Shakeilar would be nearby. This time he was rewarded; there nestled in a hollow of the rock lay the Shakeilar. Mel-e-gar grabbed it with his beak and turned to swim towards the surface. As his tail brushed the rocky formation he heard a sound like a heavy groan. He nearly dropped it again as he instinctively turned towards the sound. Thousands of giant bubbles burst from the floor of the pool and smashed into Mel-e-gar. It sent him spinning through the water, still trying to hold onto the Shakeilar.

Then a strong current pulled him further away from the surface. Mel-e-gar frantically tried to escape its grip as his lungs began to ache for the lack of oxygen. Almost bursting with the pressure he knew that he would never make it to the surface. As if that wasn't enough a burst of raw sound exploded inside his head. His water-time began to break up under the pressure making it hard for him to concentrate on trying to get away. It was almost like something was trying to break his will as well as drowning him. For Mel-e-gar there seemed no escape and he was close to giving up the struggle. He felt so tired and that made his will falter. In his water-time he could see a black wave bearing down on him and as it came closer he could make out another sound. Soon it became clearer and he heard a voice say:

Leave the Shakeilar here! Or Perish! The voice boomed inside Mel-e-gar's head, dulling his senses.

He couldn't let go even if he wanted to, as his beak was locked around the small piece of Shakeilar.

The voice suddenly changed pitch, maybe sensing his distress and then softly said, *You must....I do not wish to harm you...*

To Mel-e-gar that was a contradiction in terms as he felt his life slip away. But then it came to him that it was not yet his time and he refused to give up so easily. He gathered what strength was left and began to sing. Normally he would not use the watersong against any creature but this time he made an exception. The power grew and his body twisted this way and that in the water. The voice groaned in response and began to let go. More strength returned to Mel-e-gar as his song reached new heights of expression and power. The water began to boil and heave, multi-coloured lights exploding through the water in all directions. For a yen the current which had dragged Mel-e-gar through the water disappeared and with a powerful thrust of his tail Mel-e-gar broke free. He had to act quickly before his lungs collapsed. He changed the tune of the song causing a white light to wash through the water. When the light faded Mel-e-gar was gone.

His body sparkled into existence by the side of the pool and Mel-e-gar now in dolph form collapsed into the sand, taking as much air in as he could. He didn't know how long he lay there but it was dark again before he stirred. Mel-e-gar's water-time tried to understand what had happened and what he had encountered in the pool. At first he didn't make the connection but when he did, part of the story seemed to slot into place. The oasis wasn't just a starting point. It was also the destination! Ual-e-lea and her party of dolphs must have dived into the pool after they had wandered in the desert. But what they found eventually destroyed them. Even Ual-e-lea who had escaped was so weakened by the encounter that she passed into the deathsong a few tays after arriving back home! But his conclusions felt shapeless, his waters not really sure that his logical processes were correct. His feelings in sound and colour told him not to be so quick to conclude when he had only stirred a small ripple in a very large lake and even if he was correct it still left a big, Why? to be answered.

He picked up the Shakeilar off the sand and used the hand signal to open it. At first it flattened into a circle and then it started to expand. Mel-e-gar carefully placed it on the ground and stepped back to give it enough space to form. It grew larger until it covered an area of twenty three dees. Then it stretched itself upwards, curving over to make a roof. The colour pulsated once and settled down to an orange glow. When the shelter stood twenty four dees high in the sand, Mel-e-gar moved up to it and touched the side facing him. An opening appeared and he entered. In the middle, a mound grew up and opened, giving enough space for him to lie down in comfort. When he was settled in its warm soft folds he relaxed his water-time and tried something that had not been done for eons. He spoke to the Shakeilar.

The images that came were of colour and feelings of curiosity as the Shakeilar responded to his inquiring water-time. Slowly sounds began to form and it began to communicate back. Mel-e-gar found that his waters could translate the strange collection of feelings and colour into understandable sound,

A long-time...Why...So.. Long...?

Mel-e-gar felt the sadness seep into him and he knew his race had become so used to living with the Shakeilar that the communication had evolved into direct expression through a feeling or a motion of the hand. He hadn't realised that maybe they had lost something in the process and if it hadn't been for his experience in the pool his water-time would not have ventured down this particular stream. All this was passed straight to the Shakeilar.

We...Are...The...Same... Time...Is...Long...For...Us...

Was its response and Mel-e-gar understood that the Shakeilar was accepting its share of the blame for the lack of communication over the seasons that had passed since the two races first met.

We...Must...Change...Have.. To.. Be...Greater...To...Move...On...

This translated straight to Mel-e-gar's heart and he felt a great movement in his water-time. It added to his dream of the transition to Edenlea.

We...Are...Joined... To...Be... Of...Part... In...Edenlea...

Yes, that he had once visualised when he was a youngling swimming with his parentlings all those seasons ago and where he wanted the Shakeilar to share in the changes to come. Mel-e-gar changed his water-time and moved it to show the Shakeilar what had happened in the pool and why he was looking for the great chamber.

We...Have...Known... But...You...Go...back...

Somehow Mel-e-gar knew that was going to be the answer. He would have to try and communicate with the presence at the bottom of the pool. But there must be a better way of getting there. His water-time toyed with the idea of using the watersong to transport himself back down but as this formed in his waters the Shakeilar sent a shiver of pain.

No... Must...Not... Is...Same... You...Would...Be...Gone... I...Show...You...How..

Of course, that was the answer. The presence in the pool is a form of Shakeilar! That explained why the other dolphs were destroyed. Ual-e-lea must have used the watersong, as he had done, to save herself as well as the other dolphs. But it had resulted in their deaths. She must have had enough to transport herself back but the shock was still enough to have killed her. That was why she gave the warning, because she must have realised that any future exploration of the pool would have to be done by a Watersinger and that would spell his or her doom. But this Shakeilar he was in knew a way around it.

Yes... Now...

His water-time received the image and Mel-e-gar prepared himself for his next task. *Now that he knew what had to be done, it was ironic that it was a principle that a Watersinger learnt never to forget; That they must always use the watersong away from the buildings of Shakeilar as it had been handed down that otherwise the use could hurt them. Mel-e-gar had been lucky to escape the rebound effect of his own watersong.*

You...Leave...Me...here... Go... Alone... I...Wait...

Mel-e-gar knew that when he held the compact form of the Shakeilar, it was inside the protective aura of the watersong as the power always flowed away from a Watersinger. If it was turned inwards it would not only destroy the Shakeilar but himself. He wondered how it would protect itself if he left it behind by the pool.

I....Be...Safe... First...Eat.... Then...Go...!

The answer satisfied his water-time and after he had eaten his fill of fish that the shelter provided he left and walked to the edge of the pool. Danetar was high in the sky and another tay had passed. Mel-e-gar turned to watch the Shakeilar shrink in size to a small round chunk. Then it began to spin, sending a small shower of orange sand into the air. Within yens it had buried itself in the sand. Mel-e-gar smiled and began once more to sing his song. He felt the power pull him to a new destination.

He found himself in a cavern that was so big, he couldn't see the ceiling. It must have stretched for hundreds of klees, maybe even thousands in all directions. A lake flowed down the middle and as he walked to the edge, fascinated by the different colours that shone from the walls and the water, a giant white and grey tail fluke broke the surface and smashed down, sending a spray of water in all directions. Mel-e-gar was rooted to the spot as he watched the tail rise several times out of the water and slap the surface. For a yen it disappeared. Then the massive frame of the creature rose head first, sending a fountain of water from a large blow hole. Then another of the giant creatures appeared. It wasn't long before seven of the creatures were swimming together blowing their giant plumes of water into the air.

It was an incredible sight and Mel-e-gar calculated that the creatures must have been at least sixty dees in length. They had a look of a dolphin in a strange sort of way but the size was breathtaking. Their backs had ridges and their beaks were no longer really beaks. The bottom jaw looked like an upright bowl of Shakeilar that had also been stretched length ways, with a lid fastened on top. His water-time wondered how they ever came to be in a cavern below the surface of a desolate desert. He watched them play and they used their flippers to wave to him. It made him wish he could join them but he had to find the presence he had encountered before and hopefully finish his mission.

The sounds of the creatures echoed around the chamber as he followed the edge of the lake. The cavern floor was littered with crystals of many shapes and sizes. Each had its own unique colour that pulsated like a heartbeat. Mel-e-gar stopped every few dees and picked one of them up. They felt warm and cold all at the same time. Turning a beautiful pink crystal in his hands he noticed that the rhythm changed. It seemed to quicken then slow down as he turned it over. The surface was craggy and jagged but its semi clear surface was smooth and his water-time responded and sent him feelings that made him want to laugh, then cry. A strange mix of conflicting emotions stirred his heart. He carefully laid it down where he found it and each new crystal he encountered had a different effect. Some were very mellow. Others were frantic and crazy. This went on for some time as he went further along the length of the cavern.

Mel-e-gar noticed a left hand turn from the cavern. A wide tunnel stretched into the distance like an overgrown arm. Following his instincts he decided to explore. The surface was smooth and every few dees a crystal was embedded in the sides. The tunnel was about ten dees in width and forty high, giving him plenty of room. It began to slope down and Mel-e-gar paused and looked back. He couldn't see the entrance and wondered if he should go any further. But his curiosity took charge and he investigated further down the tunnel.

It twisted in all directions as he descended and soon he came to the end. It emptied him into a small dimly lit chamber full of shadows. The only colour amidst the shades of black and grey was the fluorescent light from red and blue moss growing on the sides, smothering the natural light that came from the walls. This made it impossible to see very clearly. Deciding to use his water sound Mel-e-gar found only confusion as something about the chamber caused it to echo erratically back at him. Being almost blind was not something he felt comfortable with but determined to continue he edged his way further into the chamber. He had walked only a few dees when he felt something hard underdee. He stooped down and looked closer at the object he had trodden on. For a yen a glimmer of pure white flickered but died as the chamber grew dimmer as the dark shadows consumed the remainder of the light. Now only having his sense of touch he picked up the object and hefted its long curved shape in his hands. As he tried to figure out what he was holding he followed the curve and its cold surface sent chills through his water-time.

Soon he was peering at the floor trying to see if any more were about. He carefully walked around and every now and then his dees would feel the cold touch of another. Only when he held them in a certain way to catch a little of the light that occasionally flicked did he see that they were all white in colour. Some were long and curved, and others were small and felt like broken twigs. He collected them together and making use of the odd flicker of light he judged the centre of the chamber and piled his strange collection of twigs there. His last finds were stacked in a corner, one on top of the other. To Mel-e-gar they felt like rounded shells and they weighed quite a bit. One by one he moved them over to the other things he found. He counted ten of the strange objects. Now all he needed was a bit more light and he would be able to see properly what he had found.

Almost as soon as the idea entered his water-time, the small cavern was suddenly flooded with a harsh white light. He blinked several times trying to adjust his eyes. When they cleared he looked around the chamber. Now he could see that the moss covered a great deal of the surface of the walls. Remembering his strange finds he looked down. His heart jumped up to his throat and the coldness he had earlier felt froze him to the spot. The objects he had found were bones and not just any old bones. They were all what was left of several dolphs. The round shell-like things were ten clean skulls and their empty eye sockets stared blindly up at him.

As the shock wore off Mel-e-gar hefted one of the skulls in his hands and said, "*Is this all that is left of ten dolphs that came here all those seasons ago?*" His voice echoed around the small chamber and Mel-e-gar knew that it was so. Now that he could look at them closely he saw that the skulls and bones were of dolph physique and not dolphin which meant they had come a great deal further than he had at first concluded. *If they made it this far what did kill them?* Many questions flowed through his water-time as he tried to evaluate what had really happened to Ual-e-lea's party.

He sat among the bones and carefully scrutinised them for any marks that might reveal what had happened, but they all seemed to be unmarked. *It was remarkable that they had not disintegrated long ago and it could only be the fact that they had lain undisturbed in the underground chamber away from any deteriorating factors*. When Mel-e-gar had finished his examination he walked over to the walls trying to discern why the chamber was now so brightly lit. He completed one circuit when the presence he had battled with earlier found him.

Welcome Dolph... the voice said, filling his waters with *its* presence, *Why have you entered my domain?*

Mel-e-gar at first didn't know if he could respond as he found it difficult to concentrate. But he struggled to the surface of his water-time and replied, *I have come for your help. I mean you no harm.*

The presence seemed to find this funny and *it* roared with laughter inside his head. *It* nearly blew him away and Mel-e-gar cringed under the impact as it seemed to go on for ages.

When the laughter cleared the presence spoke again, *You, little dolph..Mean me no harm!*

Its tone seemed to taunt him but Mel-e-gar didn't give way. *Well I didn't do so badly the last time we met!*

True..Little dolph. But I let you go.

Mel-e-gar realised that in part that may have been true but he did know that his watersong had hurt the presence. This didn't give him any satisfaction and he hoped that he wouldn't have to use it again. He decided to try and change the subject by saying, *I only came here for help but if you do not wish me to be here I will go.*

The voice chuckled in reply, *You have great strength little dolph and as you have done no harm in this place you may leave unhindered.*

One yen his waters felt as if it would burst its banks and then the next it would be nothing except the calm surface of a normal water-time. Mel-e-gar was so surprised that all his waters could say was, *Is that it?* Frustration rose inside him as the presence didn't seem to want to acknowledge his predicament. *But then why should it? It wasn't a dolph, who would help when asked. It wasn't like the Shakeilar he had known all his life who gave its service without question.* The feeling Mel-e-gar had was that the presence had only communicated because he had intruded into *its* domain.

Mel-e-gar decided to leave the small cavern and he re-entered the tunnel. *He wasn't sure if the presence was the one that Ual-e-lea had spoken of. It didn't have the feel of Shakeilar about it. The whole place may have been made of it but even that seemed wrong. The walls were too rigid and the feeling didn't have the same warmth as the Shakeilar his race had lived with for so long*. All these things went through his water-time as he stepped out of the tunnel back into the main cavern.

The water of the lake gave off a pale blue light and Mel-e-gar walked over to it hoping to see the strange creatures again. But the surface was calm and flat. No ripple or flukes disturbed it. He was disappointed and he walked along the edge scanning the water for any sign. His water-time grew more tired as klee after klee there was no movement in the lake. He wasn't sure what he could do next apart from leave.

No, he wasn't ready just yet to give up, and he searched his water-time for some way of attracting the presence's attention. *Yes! Maybe that would be enough!* he sounded as he looked at the inviting waters of the lake. Almost laughing with the simplicity of it he dived in. His body rippled and grew as he once more became a dolphin. His silver grey form glided down into the depth where Mel-e-gar saw a profusion of life. There were so many kinds of fish and creatures that swam all around him- he couldn't have begun to name them. The cool water caressed him as he played among the shoals of fish. He scooped a few small red and yellow fish up with his beak and let them slide down his throat. They tasted good and Mel-e-gar kept a look out for the creatures he had seen earlier. The lake was very deep and Mel-e-gar used his sounds to discern what moved in the darker waters.

It wasn't long before he found the dolphin like creatures. At a depth of a thousand dees the giant creatures slowly moved through the water. Mel-e-gar gave a good thrust with his tail and caught up to them. The closer he came the more detail he could make out. Their bodies had countless lines that rippled horizontally down their sides. The flippers were knobbly and strange growths seemed to cover their bulk. They didn't seem to mind as he swam around them. Mel-e-gar could make out four of the creatures and a couple of times he had to dodge their great tail flukes, which looked like a small creature had come along and taken thousands of tiny bites along the front edge. He wondered if it was so or if it was just the way they had grown. He swam to the head of one and saw the great mouth open. Mel-e-gar was amazed to find that the creatures had teeth that seemed to go on forever. It seemed to use the tightly packed teeth to strain the water, for what reason he couldn't be sure. The only thing that suggested itself was the creature was feeding.

Mel-e-gar's water-time was totally taken by the grace of the creatures and he could just discern on the outer reaches a sense of sound. His excitement grew as the sounds became clearer and his water-time flowed into theirs.

I bid you welcome to our waters young elder.

The sound was smooth and silky, with a feeling of immense age which carried itself to Mel-e-gar.

I thank you for allowing me to join in your water-time.

The creature slowly chuckled at this and with one of its flippers it guided Mel-e-gar to its side. With a flick of its flukes it pulled away from the others and headed for the surface.

What do they name you, youngling?

My name is Mel-e-gar. What do they call you? he replied.

The creature rolled its bulk and sounded, *Cual-e-lay*.

The name rolled through Mel-e-gar's water-time and he liked the feeling it gave him. He suddenly realised that the sounds were female and it was a she.

Cual-e-lay, you use lay instead of lea. Why is that? he asked, his water-time realising that she and the others were indeed like the dolph/ins.

She giggled at his question and pulled him even closer, letting her warmth fill him. *Many seasons ago we were once like you but as the seasons passed we changed in these waters. The change brought new ways and so did our sounds. For females it became Lay and for males it became Gla.*

How did you come to be down here? sounded Mel-e-gar and he cried for joy when she answered.

The bones you found in the small cavern were our ancestors and yes your water-time was close to that answer.

Not for the first time Mel-e-gar was glad that he had been wrong when he had believed the act of Ual-e-lea against the presence had killed her companions.

Cual-e-lay shared this sound and she told him about the beginning. *The one you call Ual-e-lea made contact with Serliker and it brought us here to this cavern-,* She paused and laughed, *I believe you have met!*

At least he now had a name for the presence and it invoked a question in his water-time, *Is it a form of Shakeilar?*

Of course, my dear youngling! But it is more than just a form of Shakeilar. It's the original! She let that sink into his water-time, enjoying the impact of her revelation on his young form.

The Original?! he mimicked not quite believing the sounds.

She patted his side with her flipper and her sounds divulged more as they continued to swim a few dees below the surface of the lake.

You have so much to learn and I can see that a great deal of past times has been lost. You only have a small part of the legend, so small as to make it meaningless.

It was in the cycle of Vewala, that a young dolph found a small round ball of rock that gave off bright colours. He took it to his parentlings who then shared it with the rest of the dolphs. In that era we had only just begun to colonize the land. It was made difficult by the fact that we had few means to make shelters and we still spent most of our times as dolphins, especially during the night.

The discovery of this seemly insignificant find changed the course of our times forever. At first no one could figure out what it was and the parentlings gave it back to their sonling. He played with it and purely by accident he discovered that he could talk to it. For several seasons he kept this quiet until one early tay he went to the place where he had hidden it- to find the ground littered with thousands upon thousands of them! More than enough to go round.

The seasons passed and the dolphs learnt that the Shakeilar were a life form and they began to help each other. The dolphs needed shelters and the Shakeilar wanted company. Beautiful in its simplicity. For the Shakeilar to grow it needed the creative force of the dolphs' minds and over the seasons that followed, both excelled themselves in the designs of the cities that grew on every continent, including this one... Cual-e-lay stopped her narrative and pushed Mel-e-gar forward with her flipper. She broke through the surface and joined Mel-e-gar as he looked around the cavern.

Mel-e-gar, her soft voice sang to him. *This place is the result of an act of blind jealousy.*

He wondered what she meant but still he didn't understand and he waited for her to continue. Cual-e-lay slapped her flukes on the water and he watched as the other creatures came from the depth and joined them. Soon twenty of the creatures surrounded Mel-e-gar and he watched as each slapped its flukes, sending great sprays of water into the air, many of which washed over him. The pace speeded up and as it became faster he wondered what they were doing. The answer came not from without but within his water-time as he felt their waters pass on section after section of past times. They were giving Cual-e-lay the rest of the story.

He found out later that the *Selahw*, that was the name of the new species that sprang from the dolph/ins, could hold thousands of detailed accounts of past times. When they wanted to share information among them they had a ritual of slapping their flukes to announce the intention. The Selahw didn't have to physically come together as they could pass what was needed over great distances. But if they were nearby they were happy to do so.

It wasn't long before they finished and they broke away and disappeared back beneath the surface. Cual-e-lay turned to Mel-e-gar and continued as if there had been no interruption of her sounds.

The young dolph lived for sixty seasons which was very old in those tays and he had kept the original piece of Shakeilar which had grown him a beautiful dwelling place. They shared happily many stories of their combined times. But what frustrated the dolph was that "Serliker" would not tell him where it came from and when the dolph knew the deathsong was near he persuaded Serliker to let him carry it for one last time.

He swam to this continent, which in those tays was covered with lush forests and it swarmed with different kinds of life. The dolphs had begun to colonize but the dolph knew a place in the heart of the forest, away from the new cities, a beautiful lake that he had spent many tays beside. The old dolph was near his deathsong and vowing that no other would share its time again, he threw the compact Serliker into the lake. As it disappeared into the lake he toppled in. The deathsong had begun. Because they were still linked the song was empowered with great energy and that combined with the anger and betrayal felt by Serliker exploded into a devastating energy wave which burned the face of the continent clean. In an instant whole species were wiped from Delikadove and thousands of dolphs in the few Shakeilar cities were destroyed...

The sadness and horror at what had happened all those seasons ago tore into Mel-e-gar and he felt Cual-e-lay bring a wave of soft comfort to his water-times. At least now he knew why the dolphs who came after buried this part of Delikadove's time. The dolph was never named by Cual-e-lay and when she told him that Serliker had fallen into a fissure that had opened beneath the lake, he knew why.

What it had fallen into was a small underground cavern and there it lay for an eternity, its power changed but it was useless without another life form to help it make use of it. Serliker knew that it would have to wait until someone, somehow found it. We cannot imagine what that must have felt like. The loneliness must have been incredible but it endured as their kind had done before...

When Ual-e-lea and her party of dolphs swam in the pool, Serliker couldn't believe its good fortune. It used its power to reach up and tap into their water-time, but found that they were more dolph than dolphin. This it understood so it pulled the now startled dolphs to the bottom of the pool. Ual-e-lea fought as you did, but her watersong wasn't powerful enough to free them. They were pulled into the fissure and now that it had access to their minds it used its great raw power to change the very nature of the small cavern. It grew from three dees to a thousand in yens. It placed the now unconscious dolphs on the ground and set to making this lake....

Cual-e-lay smiled at Mel-e-gar as his water-time saw that Ual-e-lea had made it down with the others but it made him wonder, *why she had returned in such poor shape that she had entered the deathsong?*

Wait, youngling and I will tell you the saddest part of our story. You must understand that Serliker was overjoyed, its past bitterness washed away by having company at last. But it didn't seem to consider the possibility that they wouldn't want to stay in the home it created. A blindness that has continued for these many seasons.

After Ual-e-lea awoke she stirred the rest of the dolphs and they began to explore the cavern. It was much smaller in comparison to now but still it covered a wide area. They spent the first few tays quite happy to swim and feed on the profusion of fish that Serliker had somehow stocked in the lake. When they found little to interest them Ual-e-lea told them it was time to leave. One of the dolphs spied the entrance of the tunnel and persuaded Ual-e-lea to let them stay a little longer.

He led them into the small cavern, the walls of which were encrusted with crystals of many colours and there on a pedestal lay Serliker. It introduced itself to them and welcomed them to their new home. When they protested it just laughed and said for them to enjoy themselves. Ual-e-lea went to grab it but Serliker finding her action threatening sent a pulsation of energy into her, badly burning her body. She was flung across the room and for a few yens she lay stunned on the floor. The other dolphs crowded round and used what water-time they had to ease her pain. Ual-e-lea didn't understand why it had attacked her so violently and when she had gathered her strength she went back over and told Serliker she and the others were leaving.

Again all it did was laugh and this made Ual-e-lea angry and she began to sing a watersong to transport them away. At first the energy was strong and it surrounded them all. They began to feel the familiar pull when something yanked them back. Ual-e-lea felt Serliker invade her water-time and it tried to take control. They battled and soon the chamber was filled with an energy that caused the walls to crumble, and the other dolphs began to burn. The shrieks of pain filled Ual-e-lea and she decided to have one last attempt to break free. Serliker was only amused at first but even it realised that if it held on any longer it would end up pushing them into the deathsong.

When it let go, the force of so much released energy completed her transportation and she disappeared from the cavern. The other dolphs fell to the ground still screaming in pain as the residue of the energy ate away at their forms. Somehow Serliker had separated them from the song. Maybe the rebound effect was responsible for them staying behind. Serliker seeing the appalling result joined with the dolphs and used its power to try and heal them. But they lay huddled on the floor without moving, their blackened bodies beyond repair. At first it believed that they would all die and it tried to find another way of healing them. Because there was still movement in their fragmented water-time it used it to transport them to the lake, utilising the trigger that would change them to dolphins. When the change came their forms began to heal and Serliker made a decision to remove their ability to change back to dolphs as it believed they would be useless in that form.

For many jeanths it looked after them, totally absorbed in the task and eventually they all recovered. Their water-time had expanded in ways that changed them forever. The shock eased and they soon adapted to living totally in the water. Over the thousands of seasons that passed they multiplied and each new generation changed a little more until we became what we are now. She ended her story by saying, *and here we will stay...*

Mel-e-gar was amazed that they had managed to keep a level water-time as what Serliker had done was very wrong. This went through his waters and he found it hard to come to terms with.

But Cual-e-lay helped him and sounded, *Serliker wasn't really to blame; it acted out of loneliness and a craving for company. In the time we have lived down here it has shared knowledge that spans many different worlds and times. Their race has shared with many different life forms and we, the Selahw, have a great deal to thank it for. This lake now covers an area that is equal to the continent above and is filled with places that fill our water-time with awe.*

Finally Mel-e-gar accepted her sounds and the feelings he felt against Serliker left his water-times. He slid from her side and swam towards the shore. When he was near the edge he let himself go and floated on the surface. He relaxed his water-time and turned the waves towards solving the problem of the Keaverkack, not yet seeing if Serliker would help him. Cual-e-lay joined him by the side of the lake. As the depth was fairly equal in every part she had no problem swimming by his side. Her water-time slipped easily back into his but she stayed silent as if allowing him to work through the problem without any comment from her. *Maybe she was waiting to see where his waters would go?* So he tried to see if there was a way to persuade Serliker to leave *its* cavern but that also left the problem of whether the Selahw could remain without Serliker. *How stable was their home?* There seemed no easy answers to the problems he faced.

The irony and saddest part of her story was that if Serliker had stopped and considered the arrival of Ual-e-lea and the others *it* would have seen that she as a Watersinger could have released *it* back to the world of the dolphs. But *its* own desire had blinded *itself* and committed *it* to a further seventy thousand seasons of exile.

As he went over this, taking Serliker's apparent short sightedness into consideration, *he wondered even if he did manage to get through to it whether its power could be harnessed to close the fissures in the ocean in any case?*

Cual-e-lay decided it was time to stop his waters because he had failed to consider one possibility, *Ah! My poor youngling if only that was so!* she sighed.

But if I could carry it with me when I leave here it might have the power to do so, answered Mel-e-gar, puzzled that Cual-e-lay was apparently now not considering it.

She stroked his water-time and with sounds of sadness she told him why. *You have taken it for granted that Serliker can leave by your carrying it out of here but unfortunately the power that was released when Serliker and Ual-e-lea battled it out had a rebound effect. It fused it to the pedestal in the cavern. It cannot be moved..*

Now that confused him even more because when she had told her story he just assumed Serliker had moved *itself* when *it* transported the injured dolphs to the lake, which to him seemed a reasonable assumption. As he may have heard and felt Serliker he certainly didn't see *it. So why didn't he see it?*

Instead of answering, Cual-e-lay just sounded, *It is there, go and look!*

This made his water-time more curious than ever. He bade farewell for the yen and swam away from her. He dived down and turned and swam as fast as he could for the surface. She watched as he launched himself from the water, somersaulting in the air, his dolphin form sparkling and changing. He landed neatly by the lake and looked back at Cual-e-lay who blew a great plume of water into the air, signalling him to go on.

* * *

KEAVERKACK

Several tays after Mel-e-gar's departure. Ler-e-lea and her mate Hil-e-gar were out in the deep waters of Roulisad, keeping a discreet distance away from the Keaverkack. The weather had changed from the normal fair conditions to a storm that was whipping up a wind which was tearing through the city of Desilata making it inadvisable for anyone to venture out in. However, it was ideal for their purpose of moving stealthily through the choppy waters, which at a thousand klees away from the shore were causing high frothy waves to churn the sea into a maelstrom. Every time they ascended for air they had to battle with the waves which tossed them about like so much scattered flotsam.

Hil-e-gar in particular was glad when they could descend to the calmer depths. For him the Keaverkack were positively welcoming in comparison to the storm. He followed Ler-e-lea's silver grey form as she returned to the place where they had both been watching the movements of the creatures as a shoal of fish swam among them giving themselves up as food. They were about three klees away from the Keaverkack and at a depth of five hundred dees which was enough distance for them to use their sounds to penetrate the gloomy waters and safe enough for a quick retreat if the Keaverkack should decide to dine on dolphin flesh.

Ler-e-lea had learned a great deal about the use of the water-time from her early seasons with Mel-e-gar and she had in turn passed her knowledge on to Hil-e-gar, who showed promise in using that fluid form of communication. All dolphs as dolphins had a measure of water-time but the passing seasons had made the use rare and for some it fell out of their lives altogether. But with Mel-e-gar's encouragement she had a greater command than she would have believed possible only a short time ago. So it was with ease that she passed into Hil-e-gar's water-time.

There are more of them than ever! she sounded.

I know, and from the recent attacks they are becoming bolder, responded Hil-e-gar and moved closer to her side, their slim forms almost touching as their sounds picked up the arrival of more of the beasts.

To believe that the few who attacked Mel-e-gar's parentlings were found dead as a result and we had made the assumption that they wouldn't do it again because of the poisonous effect we had on them. It didn't take long for them to overcome that problem.

Her sounds were mournful to his water-time and he stayed silent letting the feeling wash through him. He felt her release more of the grief she still felt about the incident. His left flipper stroked her side, encouraging her to press her body against him.

Her love for Hil-e-gar was a great sphere of light which lived in her heart and his reassurance and depth of life made things complete. She liked sharing her water-time and as they spied on the Keaverkack their bond grew stronger. She shifted her water-time and it flowed into his as the tay passed. By the evening a hundred of the Keaverkack had assembled, with the sounds of their great forms thrashing in the water as they filled themselves with fish.

It was ironic that it had taken a conflict over the seas for the Keaverkack to be properly studied. There had been no record in the library crystals other than the name and that they were creatures that lived in the depths of the oceans, never venturing closeer than four thousand klees off any land mass of Delikadove. For some reason they had been left alone, a reason that now was maybe clear as contact had proved to be dangerous and even fatal for the dolph/ins. But what puzzled Ler-e-lea the most was why that information had never been stored. Her friends at the meeting were unable to explain why except that maybe because the Keaverkack lived so far out and at such depths that no dolph had warranted them of interest for further study, which in itself was unusual as a major characteristic of their race was their insatiable appetite for exploration. For her it didn't make sense and Hil-e-gar and the others had expressed the same puzzlement.

Ler-e-lea's water-time swam about the anomaly as she and Hil-e-gar moved away from the Keaverkack and began the five tay journey home. Danetar had set and the last light faded from the sea as they broke through the waves and set course for the shore. They held their water-time together in mutual reassurance and with the peaceful silence embracing them they went home.

Over the next five tays they returned to observe the group of Keaverkack and witnessed the group grow larger. By the sixth tay there were more than a thousand swimming as one. Ler-e-lea tried to communicate with them but her water-time only received primitive but strong emotions that spoke of territory and food. There was no indication that they had other awareness. Their concerns were simple but necessary only for survival. In all her encounters with other creatures she had never come across such raw minds. Even the young that swam among them had no sense of anything but to quench their hunger. If they had spied herself and Hil-e-gar their minds were empty of it. All they seemed to do was eat. And by the quantity which they consumed she had real fears that the fish stocks of their oceans would be seriously damaged. Again this brought up a question that she couldn't answer; *What did they eat when they were in their home waters? For surely it must be more substantial than what they were now feeding on. The large teeth packed tightly together and powerful jaws spoke of much larger prey.*

Hil-e-gar broke into her water-time and sounded, *They sometimes seem agitated at what they consume as if it is too insubstantial for their hunger.*

Yes, I have felt that too and it worries me that as they grow more frustrated they might turn their attention towards us, she replied.

As the group had grown larger she and Hil-e-gar had moved further away relying on their sounds as they were swimming around the Keaverkack about four klees away. So far it had proved adequate as a safe guard from any surprise moves. But because they averaged on thirty to forty dees in length and had been shown to be powerful swimmers she had to hope that if trouble came she and Hil-e-gar would be able to get away.

The relative silence of their observation was broken by a high piercing whistle. It grew steadily higher, a pure note that cut through the water so sharply that Ler-e-lea expected the water to be parted into two. At first they couldn't fathom where it had come from as it seemed to strike from all sides cutting swathes through the water. Using their sounds they combined their water-time and tried to trace the source. But as they seemed to get closer it changed and threw their water-time into confusion.

In all tales of the Keaverkack and in all their own observation there had never been any trace of sound from the creatures. But Ler-e-lea knew that it was the only possible source. She had to struggle with her water-time as the sound continued to rise in pitch, cutting through her and making it difficult to concentrate her own sounds so she could see what was happening. All she could feel was the warmth of Hil-e-gar at her side and his rising panic as the sound stripped away his water-time. Thankful of Mel-e-gar's tuition she bridged the gap and managed to make her water-time flow into Hil-e-gar, filling the areas that were being stripped away. He was slipping from her as he retreated to the safety of the darker water of his mind. She called out for him to hold on but with the onslaught of the whistle he broke and she felt his form go limp. *NO*! she cried as the bond between them began to part. The cutting edge of the whistle was severing his link with her and the despair of the loss filled her.

Then silence, the sound didn't fade away. It just stopped, so abruptly that for a few yens it didn't register in Ler-e-lea's water-time. But as the realisation flowed through she found her sounds were intact and she quickly swept the area, one flipper holding Hil-e-gar up in the water. For a yen nothing registered but as the shock of the sound finally cleared she recoiled in alarm. From all sides came the Keaverkack, they were now close enough for their purple forms to be seen clearly and their open mouths spoke only of tearing flesh.

She tried her best to keep Hil-e-gar's limp form from descending to the ocean floor but his almost dead weight cried against her left flipper. But as she looked down she saw that they not only came from all sides but also from below. Their raw emotions flowed into her and she saw herself being torn to pieces by the blind hunger of the Keaverkack. Her only choice was to try and ascend to the surface and hope that she would be able to outswim them. But that fell from her waters as she knew she couldn't leave her mate. She knew he had not passed into the deathsong but if she didn't return him to the surface he would surely do so. Maybe it would be better this way for even she knew had he survived the sound intact he would be facing a far harsher death.

They were only yens from attacking and she faced them and waited for them to take her. Part of her wanted to try and break through but her sounds told her that with a thousand Keaverkack arrayed against her there would be no contest and she had no desire to hurry to her death. It was strange how the few yens that passed seemed eternal and her water-time mused on the fact that the Keaverkack could use sound to tear the mind away from its moorings. Why it wasn't used on earlier attacks she didn't know and now she had no one to ask. Strangely at the yen the Keaverkack fell upon her and as she felt Hil-e-gar torn from her side and as the water began to turn red she saw a different picture. For a brief yen she could have sworn that a strange red, brown furry creature chattered to her that she would be fine. Then her water-time retracted and she too went to the depth to escape the pain as razor sharp teeth began to tear her apart.

A flash of green, silvery light flashed into existence and a small part of its immensity penetrated her water-time and she embraced the call of the deathsong.

*   *   *

Mel-e-gar returned to the chamber and looked again to see if he could see the pedestal that Cual-e-lay had spoken off, but there was nothing except for the bones of the dolph explorers.

He felt waves of disappointment wash through his water-time as he realised that if he couldn't find Serliker then his mission couldn't succeed. He aimlessly walked around the cavern and his attention was drawn back to the bones. Something bothered him about the bones. When he found them he had noticed that they were of dolph physique and not dolphin. But if the information that Cual-e-lay gave was correct and he had no reason to doubt her water-time; *then how was it that they were of dolph, if when they had died they were the changed dolphin form? It didn't make any sense.*

He sat among the bones and examined them again. With his water-time held by the mystery of the bones he did not at first notice that the bones began to reflect a blue light and his back felt warm as if he was sitting too close to a fire crystal. That was enough to bring him back from his wanderings and now startled by the blue glow he dropped the skull he was holding. It made a clattering noise as it rolled away from him, disturbing the fine dust on the floor. The dust glowed briefly under the blue light and Mel-e-gar turned his head and gasped in surprise and relief. He came to his dees and turned round fully to look at the giver of the blue light.

Reaching five dees from the floor was a twisted column of white and silver rock. Upon the flat surface at the top rested a blue crystal that contained red sparks of light in it that seemed to shift position as Mel-e-gar's gaze washed over it. The blue light began to pulse and once more he felt the powerful waters that was Serliker enter his water-time.

Surprised small one! teased Serliker. *You do not look hard enough! Its* tone mocked Mel-e-gar and with his water-time now gripped tightly by Serliker he found he could not respond. But part of him found the situation familiar and an image of *the* Rock entered on a wave that made Serliker pull back in alarm.

You Know of...! screamed Serliker in panic as *it* fled from Mel-e-gar's waters. His head ached from the release of so much pressure and for a few yens he found it hard to put his water-time in order. He clasped his head in his hands and shook the feeling away. When he felt sure of himself he returned his gaze to Serliker and now the blue light was dull and a grey sheen seemed to flow through it. *What was going on?* For some reason *it* had reacted badly to the image of *the* Rock that had involuntarily entered his water-time. His frustration rose as he let his sense flow over Serliker. Now a wall of grey energy blocked any entry.

Talk about withdrawing into a shell. Now that made him laugh as an image of a Haldom came to him. The whole situation was ridiculous and with his water-time made up he started to leave the cavern. He had decided that it was time to look elsewhere for his answers. But something made him stop at the entrance and look back.

Deciding that maybe he should say something before he left, he said, "Goodbye *Serliker*!" A sudden wave of sadness fell upon him as he looked at the now very lonely looking Serliker and he raised a hand in farewell. He then finished with, "I'm sorry we couldn't have helped each other.."

Mel-e-gar walked back through the tunnel and his water-time went over the events. Something did strike him about Serliker. It reminded him not only of *the* Rock but also a very young dolph. A youngling that had misbehaved and had panicked at the knowledge that their Elder was going to reprimand them. That made him feel even more sorry for Serliker. To have endured such loneliness apart from *its* own kind. It was enough to make him turn around and head back. Maybe there was something he could do for *it* after all.

He ran back to the cavern and now no light glowed from Serliker and that made Mel-e-gar rush over and lay his hands upon *its* surface. His water-time found the presence muted and heavily shrouded. There seemed to be no indication of awareness on *its* part. His heart felt heavy as the misery of *its* plight entered his waters. Tears fell from Mel-e-gar's eyes and he clasped the crystal tightly. Then he raised his head and closed his eyes. The image of the fusion entered him and the power of his watersong came and like a bursting plume of water from a Selahw's breathing hole the energy impacted the cavern. Lights of many colours cloaked themselves around Mel-e-gar and Serliker. The tempo increased and the song of freedom and life cried their message and for a yen he felt as one with Serliker and with a final cry the energy tore the crystal from *its* exile upon the pedestal.

The cavern shook as the energy of the song impacted the cavern and as the ground grumbled and groaned beneath his dees he felt the awareness of Serliker burst forth and the joy and exaltation of *its* waters nearly caused him to drop the crystal. But now it was Serliker's turn to help Mel-e-gar. *It* sent energy flowing into *its* rescuer and as the exhaustion of his song fell upon him he felt a soft and warm embrace that lifted him from the floor. He was held suspended in the air as blue and red light wrapped him in a cocoon that eased his water-time to a gentle but deep sleep.

It was two tays later that Serliker released Mel-e-gar from his sleep and for the first time in the thousands of seasons that had passed Serliker (*In solid form*) was re-introduced to the Selahw. They in turn honoured *it* by saluting with a chorus of plumes of water that burst into the air and showered them both. Mel-e-gar laughed at the drenching he received and saw the delight of the Selahw who were obviously very fond of their once capturer but which they now saw as more of an Elder of their race. Serliker shone with renewed vigour and Mel-e-gar could feel that the bitterness of *its* exile was being speedily dispelled by *its* new joy.

The time was coming for answers to be given and while Mel-e-gar swam again with the Selahw, in particular Cual-e-lay, *it* showed that *it* could forgive by changing *its* shape to create a proper resting place for Mel-e-gar. *It* was small by the normal standards of Shakeilar dwelling places but *it* had a flare of originality by having a complicated spiral that twisted from the sides to loop back at the top then spread like a pool of water rippled by a stone, that poured in all directions till it solidified to create a resemblance of Mel-e-gar's face. The structure only stood six dees by twenty five but the colours of blue and red, tinged with silver swirled and danced over the surface making an illusion that the structure could on a whim change shape at any yen.

When Mel-e-gar had returned from his feeding he was in time to witness the final touch to his new but temporary home. Below the face Serliker had created his hands and there, dancing in a spin that caused red sparks to flare in all directions, spun the smaller form that he had first seen of Serliker. His water-time was awe struck and he was humbled by the honour that Serliker bestowed upon him and *it* showed a further measure that the blindness and anger that *it* had rightly felt because of the betrayal of the dolph with no name, had been put in its rightful place- in the past. Mel-e-gar dived from the lake and landed by Serliker and as the residue of energy from his change to dolph form dissipated his eyes shone with delight at the spectacle before him. His heart felt like it would burst with happiness and he knew that there was hope to be found in this place.

He walked to the entrance and crouched so he could pass through. Inside the floor was cushioned with soft blue mounds that rippled and beckoned enticingly. There was enough room for him to lie down and his eyes turned towards the ceiling. Now that was the biggest surprise and his voice caught in his throat. For it seemed that a universe slowly turned above his head. Countless millions of stars twinkled their lights and as he watched, the scene changed to give him the illusion of flight. He passed stars that were giving birth to planets and stars that grew to welcome them back to their fiery embrace. A profusion of time passed before his eyes. The birth and death of galaxies played out before him.

For the first time in a long time Mel-e-gar felt the simple joy of a youngling and a wide smile spread upon his face as he relaxed his water-time and allowed himself to be swept along by the vision of the journey that Serliker had taken countless eons ago to come to Delikadove. His water-time achieved perfect communion with the waters of Serliker and *it* told him the story of *its* beginning.

Out of countless billions of Galaxies that were home to billions more stars and planets there were many that held life upon them. At many stages of development and on one such planet there lived a race that had evolved to combine its life force with the very rock of its planet. That was who we were. We then found we could harness the raw power that all life forms gave off as thoughts and feelings. Each race of creature has a sharing of existence. This happens without the conscious knowledge of each race but it's a pool of knowledge and creativeness that can be tapped. For many it is never used to its full potential, even when the race has achieved sentience.

Which is ironic because part of that process is achieved when the combined creative will of a species reaches such diversity it spills back into each individual and that normally raises the awareness to a sentient level. Some like the dolphs attempted the next stage which is a closer awareness of the whole, like the water-time which shares mind to mind all that can be. This can create new abilities, such as the Watersinger.

Your race has gone through many changes. You achieved a communion of mind while still water bound and you used the power at its height to venture onto the land but as you became more earth bound you began to let go of that ability. But your race still produces a pure telepath in the form of a Watersinger every tenth generation. A quirk of your species perhaps. Your dream Mel-e-gar, is to recreate the legend of Edenlea, the Golden Age and you have been right that with the changes to come on this world it may be that your destiny must be that you return to the oceans. We shall see.

But to return to the Shakeilar. We shared and harnessed the energy of the other life forms and helped many on our own world to achieve sentience. This continued until our sun went Nova and the star took back its seed. We had already begun to search out new life forms among the nearby solar systems. The deathsong of our planet made us make a vow; to continue exploring and for ever more to seed ourselves as far as possible, so our unique race would continue to survive. Because we only travelled singly we as a race began to know the supreme extremes of loneliness. You can appreciate that contact was imperative. If each Shakeilar made successful contact then it would be able to trigger the process to spawn. Thus each could give birth to several thousand or even millions if the contact race had need for us.

This way we became dependant upon other life forms for survival. We took from the hosts the inspiration of creation to combine the energies so it could then share the art of the story with them. With some races like the dolphs they found that they were needed for dwelling places and others became oracles of Knowledge. On some worlds the interaction was limited to a solitary marker. Sometimes we consisted of a small group of large standing rocks/stones that the life forms would use to visit so they could dance and talk. Meeting places that would continue for centuries but as the race grew some forgot what the stones were and so they grew dormant with some dying of loneliness. Thus the bond of life and matter separated and silence fell.

But if there was no interaction then the individual Shakeilar would be helpless where it fell when it entered the planet's atmosphere, destined to die after enduring an eternity of loneliness. But if it was successful and the spawning had taken place then a Shakeilar was picked to be the new seed for the next planet in the vicinity. I was like many before and was picked to come to your world, a journey that took eons to complete.

In the beginning the power of movement was created by the harnessing of energy from each life form that interacted with it. So at first it was blind chance. In the beginning this did not matter to the whole but as the distances grew so did the loneliness for we found that we still desired to be in fairly close proximity to each other and when the distances became too great we began to suffer in ways we hadn't imagined. It was believed that each colony would be better if it did not retain contact and became more independent but it made matters worse. Then a disease appeared among us and many Shakeilar died. You see we were a race that shared everything and believed we knew better and we held that communion cheap.

Soon our minds could no longer conceive of any close mind contact over such great distances. So to cope with this we developed a communication system to span the galaxies and there we created a network of Sentinels to watch over each one. They have become the only contact that the Shakeilar race has with each of its parts. But they also have other tasks to perform. One is to make sure that we seed throughout this universe and ultimately beyond even that. Two is to make sure none of us overstep the boundary...

At this point Serliker ended *its* narrative and the images Mel-e-gar was receiving abruptly ended. The ceiling was now empty of stars and was replaced by fine laced blue light flowing above his head. His water-time felt swollen and it again reminded him of the time he had shared with *the* Rock. In response the lights flickered and briefly a grey sheen again appeared but it wasn't sustained and Serliker controlled *its* urge to withdraw.

Now it was time for Mel-e-gar to ask, *Why are you afraid of the Rock?* Part of Mel-e-gar knew the answer but he wanted the reason explained to him.

Its tone was filled with anguish when *it* answered. *The Rock is a Sentinel!* and with the sorrowful sigh of a youngling *it* cried, *And I have crossed the boundary which none should cross...*

There was a pause as Mel-e-gar had his suspicions confirmed.

But there is more to it than that? he gently enquired.

Why do you have to push?! Serliker cried. *The Rock is what you would call my Parentling. It is a terrible wrong that I have done..* The waves of sorrow flowed through their shared water-time and Mel-e-gar felt that he had to press on for he could not fathom the rule that Serliker had broken.

Share with me, tell me! He sent waves of comfort to *it* and said, *Maybe something could be done*. That was enough to send Serliker into convulsions of hysterical laughter and Mel-e-gar almost wished he hadn't voiced his feelings and he worried that Serliker's grip on *its* regained sanity would slip. But the water tears gushed forth and the pain that *it* had held inside was finally let go and when the weeping finished Mel-e-gar knew that the crisis had passed. It wasn't only the loneliness of *its* exile but the major part of *its* loss of sanity had been the overwhelming burden of guilt.

Serliker was still afraid to voice *its* perceived crime but finally after more coaxing *it* told Mel-e-gar. *I changed them.. I had no right..We are told that to change any sentient race is wrong and punishable by permanent exile on a dead moon or equivalent dead planet.*

Mel-e-gar almost laughed at the habit of Serliker to be so precise with *its* sounds. But he stopped himself and asked, *I take it you mean the Selahw!*

Yes! Yes! Of course! Serliker cried back.

But you saved them! replied Mel-e-gar.

But it was my fault. In my madness I exiled them here.

Mel-e-gar knew that it wasn't entirely Serliker's fault so he said, *Ual-e-lea was also responsible for what happened. She acted too impulsively and you were only defending yourself. She had her own share of guilt to carry as she did leave her companions behind to an unknown fate. Even though she presumed that they were dead she couldn't know for sure.*

There was no right or wrong in a situation that for the dolphs had been long since dead for the past seventy thousand seasons. But that was all Mel-e-gar could come up with. In truth Serliker was scared that *the* Rock would come for *it* when *it* escaped the confines of the cavern. But Mel-e-gar didn't believe *the* Rock would be harsh on *its* youngling as *it* had helped create a new offshoot of the dolphin race, maybe even speeding the natural evolution of the dolphin aspect. He used this reasoning on Serliker and eventually *it* settled back down to a more normal sense of water-time.

I have more questions Serliker, and I am sorry to have distressed you but I had no knowledge of your connection to the Rock.

Serliker's colour rippled and glowed, and *its* water-time sent warm waters to Mel-e-gar, *You are a fine dolph. I ask your forgiveness for the way I treated you when we first met. It* stopped, chuckled and continued, *You have shown more wisdom than I in this situation so I will comply and I will answer your questions.*

Mel-e-gar felt the sincerity in the colour of the sounds and replied, *There is nothing to forgive. I would find it hard to conceive of any way to survive such an exile and you have shown that in spite of all you have suffered you have tried your best to make amends for your actions. The Selahw are a marvellous addition to our kind. They will bring much needed wisdom to our race.*

I thank you for your kind sounds but we have another problem to solve...The Selahw's home will cease to continue if I leave.

Now that was something Mel-e-gar had considered. He had the feeling that Serliker and the Selahw were bound inextricably together. He had no answer to such a dilemma.

His waters considered for a time before replying, *Well, leave that for a yen and if we pull our water-time to another direction maybe inspiration will come to solve that problem.*

Serliker mumbled to *itself* then sounded, *What do you have in mind, young dolph?*

Mel-e-gar laughed and sounded, *Tell me about the bones. Tell me why they are in dolph form.*

It admired Mel-e-gar's persistence and *it* chuckled and replied, *Ah! Yes, I will tell you why. Then I will ask you a question.*

Their shared water-time sang with their combined laughter and Mel-e-gar sounded, *Okay, so tell me.*

After Ual-e-lea's party had been changed and they had successfully bred in their new home they in time grew old and they each had a wish. That wish was to become dolphs again at the time of their deathsong. Now I wasn't sure that was going to be possible because when I turned them into an energy form to heal their wounds I took away their ability to change back to dolph. My reason being that there was not enough genetic material to complete the sequence. If they had tried in their new form they would have triggered a genetic breakdown. For if the sequence could not be completed it would have caused the disintegration of their bodies. The end result would not have been pleasant, just a thick soup of blood and tissue. My task was difficult but there was one way. That was to combine them by using an energy weave to intermix them to produce a sharing of forms...

It paused when *it* felt Mel-e-gar's urgent enquiry.

That would mean they would have to enter the deathsong at the same time! The rest would have to choose to follow the one who was nearing the end!! Now Mel-e-gar was shocked that the nine other dolphs or Selahw would choose such a course. He knew it wasn't completely unknown for a dolph to enter the deathsong at its own behest if it felt that there was no more to accomplish, normally through extreme age or an illness that couldn't be helped by the healers. But this was completely different. He turned his waters back to Serliker and simply sounded, *Why?*

Now, even I was amazed that they would accept the concept, but when I saw their passionate desire within my water-time I understood. You see, Mel-e-gar they had come here together and they had no desire to slowly die one by one. They wanted to enter the deathsong together. When the seasons have advanced for you, you may yet see that their reasoning was true. For their love for each other bound them as one.

Mel-e-gar still found it hard to accept and then it occurred to him, *What about their younglings? How did they survive if all their parentlings went at once?*

Serliker laughed at Mel-e-gar's shocked sounds and replied, *Mel-e-gar! They had lived for two hundred seasons and more. There were sixteen generations born by then.*

Two hundred seasons! he exclaimed. *The normal life span of a dolph is only eighty at the most..* His sounds trailed off as the concept of such a long life span took hold.

Serliker waited for Mel-e-gar's water-time to absorb the information, then *it* sounded. *You have much to learn..*

The Rock once said something like that!

Hmmm... was Serliker's only response.

It made Mel-e-gar realise how much *it* was like *it's* parentling. But there was much truth in those sounds. There was so much to learn and understand. He let his water-time mull over that pertinacious feeling as he waited for Serliker to continue.

Mel-e-gar's sound had awakened Serliker's longing for the company of *its* own kind and now that the fear of *The* Rock was more shadow than substance *it* wanted very much to know *Its* parentling again. But for now *it* would complete *its* answer about the dolphs and return to those other matters later.

When I told them they bade me to fulfil their wish. I wrapped the ten Selahw in energy and while still retaining the integrity of their water-times I used the burst of energy of the Selahw who were entering the deathsong to combine them as one fluid soup of matter. Then I took them from the water and laid the pulsating mass on the shore. I used the memory that I held within my water-time to trigger the change to dolph form. The mass split into five forms which could hold the stability of the dolph shape. Two shared each body and their happiness was complete.

The energy sparked and flashed several times making five dolphs appear on the shore. The feelings which rushed into me made me ecstatic. The love and warmth as they examined themselves, using hands for the first time in two hundred seasons filled them with glee. I could only maintain the forms for a short while but they did not seem to feel any pain or sorrow. When after they had run and played like younglings I told them it was time to let go.

They regrouped and with their eyes closed each essence thanked me and bade me farewell. The energy began to rise as the last said goodbye. It took hold and then with a flash of brilliant silver and gold they flew out of their physical mass and rode the wave which sent them to the place of the deathsong; Chisharnlay.

Silence came and visited them both as they shared the images of that time long ago. Mel-e-gar broke the spell and sounded, *So that was how there were bones in the cavern..*

Well almost, replied Serliker, *But there is more.. When the deathsong had become a whisper I was left with a mass of protoplasm. I used the remains to fashion ten sets of bones to join me within my cavern. I felt it was one way of honouring them for their greatness of spirit.* Serliker finished with a sigh that spoke of that loss.

Mel-e-gar was satisfied that those ancient ancestors had lived a far better life than he had first perceived when he had stumbled upon them in the dark cavern. He was glad and those feelings made Serliker feel at peace for the first time.

Again, you have done me service by allowing this sharing to take place. But I must now ask you to show me your contact with the Rock! Serliker requested.

Mel-e-gar wasn't that surprised by the request and he happily allowed Serliker to see *its* parentling in action. That made Serliker laugh and for some time Mel-e-gar re-lived that first and only meeting with *the* Rock.

The water-time also showed Mel-e-gar's return home, the discovery that he had lost his parentlings and of the missing seasons. This made Serliker feel much pity for the price that *the* Rock had taken for *its* knowledge and there was a strange blank area within Mel-e-gar's water-time which *it* couldn't penetrate. *It* asked Mel-e-gar whether he realised this but all Mel-e-gar could sound was that he had been puzzled but had come to accept it as part of the *Mystery of the Rock*. All he could add was that he felt that in time he would know what lay in that strange emptiness.

Yet again you surprise me young one.

Mel-e-gar laughed and replied, *Much surprises me too!*

They shared much laughter at that. Then Serliker suddenly went serious and partly to itself *it* murmured, *My parentling has changed greatly since we were last together...*

This intrigued Mel-e-gar, so he sounded, *Well it has been a long time but how do you mean?*

A long time.. Hmmm...It certainly is, Well Mel-e-gar when I last saw the Rock it was much like myself. After all I was born from its mass. But now it has become more than the Shakeilar. It has changed in size and shape to a new stable form. I wouldn't have believed it possible. One thing about The Sentinels is that they have far greater control over their kinetic energy. In other words they can move where they will without the close contact of other life forms. But this is something more.. To think I was worried about its reaction!

Mel-e-gar's curiosity had grown each time Serliker added to his knowledge of the Shakeilar and this was no different. *What do you mean? Is there something wrong?* He was now worried as Serliker silently contemplated whatever held *its* attention.

Serliker expanded *its* water-time and *it* seemed to smooth the ripples from *its* surface and then finally replied, *It's nothing. I have been away so long that I forget that all things must change, even the Shakeilar.*

Mel-e-gar felt the answer was evasive and he nearly pressed but a ripple that turned into a wave in his water-time told him to let it go. There would be other times to find out what was really going on. For the more he ventured into *its* world and the Shakeilar's the more he felt that a larger picture was being created. *He wasn't sure he liked it but there didn't seem to be anything he could do about it.. Well not yet...*

It was time for him to change the subject, *Okay! Let's discuss the Selahw and the Keaverkack!! Then maybe we both can go home.*

Hmmm....

*   *   *

She was sitting in her room of study, going through all the information she could find in the crystals of the Library. A collection of fifteen were scattered on a white and yellow speckled ledge which grew from the walls to completely surround her. An uneducated eye would wonder how she had come to be in a room that showed no sign of an opening or how she could be sitting on a high backed mound that seemed to cradle her lithe form so comfortably in its centre. For she had only to enter her room and the ledge that crossed the entrance would part and then like liquid flow back to rejoin. Thus she could sit and turn any way and put a crystal on any part of the complete circle.

The ledge from the walls was about three dees wide which made it a comfortable position when any crystal rolled to the back, for nothing was out of reach. Sometimes if she was working late she would sleep snuggled in her mound. She liked the feel of the crystals tickling her mind as she slept. Not that she had much chance of that these tays for her new mate would demand her presence in their sleeping-chamber. A smile tugged at her mouth at the thought of her mate and she laughed out loud as the image completed. *They wouldn't believe it*, she thought, *that any dolph could melt her into submission!* But he had only to wear his most mischievous smile and her heart would melt and run along the floor to form a puddle of devotion at his dees. *More like a lake but that was real indulgence.* The blue and grey of her eyes were reflected in the smooth surface of the crystal she was holding and they sparkled with delight as her thoughts followed the line that they had taken.

Her pleasant thoughts were scattered to the four winds by a cry which tore into her mind, making her blood run cold. The cry was of hunger and the anticipation of its lust to be filled. The horror plunged her down to meet a savage spectre. The sound rose in pitch and a heart rendering scream became the chorus. The pain was intolerable but her body would not respond and she sat frozen to her seat. The cry was so piercing it cut into her and she could only feel that death would be welcome. It was the screaming which spoke of such intense pain that it was crushing her and she was helpless as it grew and grew. She felt herself being torn apart as the pitch reached its peak. The screaming continued and as the cry abruptly ended she realised that it was herself that had been screaming but it only made her screams that much more wretched as she lost control.

It took all his strength to restrain Alk-e-lea from tearing the flesh from her face. He pulled her hands down and the muscles in his arms rippled as tremors of strain began to run through him. But his determination to stop his love from hurting herself gave him enough to finally hold her down. The walls had withdrawn the ledge and now the room seemed bare except for a few scattered crystals, some of which were blackened and crushed by whatever had visited his mate. Slowly her body let go of the convulsions and the scream died from her. The look of horror that she had worn had nearly broken his heart when he had burst into her chamber. He had only just returned from visiting friends when the scream of terror had broken the tranquil silence of their home. Even the Shakeilar seemed to react to the sound and Bue-e-gar felt his seventy odd seasons for the first time as he sat cradling Alk-e-lea in his arms.

As she became aware of Bue-e-gar holding her she felt a wave of green light wash through, taking the pain and horror away. The empty calmness which came upon her suddenly filled as the light danced through her mind and a soft voice spoke to her.

You are needed...Go.... Go and help her....! Then it faded and Alk-e-lea sprang to her dees knocking Bue-e-gar to one side.

"*It's Ler-e-lea!* She is in *trouble*!"

She raced from the room before Bue-e-gar could draw breath. He did his best to leap to his dees but age made his leap far more gentle. He did his best to follow Alk-e-lea but by the time he reached the entrance of their home and stepped over the threshold, there was no sign of her in the early morning light. Only the call of the Kerg greeted him. He absently noticed the ground was wet and the small pools that had formed along the path to the main street of Desilata. He knew where she had gone and with a light breeze blowing in his face he began to follow its winding way. It wasn't long before he had reached a point where he could veer off to go over the open land that sprawled between the city and the sea. He knew that his mate would be several clars ahead of him by now so with slow but steady steps he began to walk across the expanse. *At least the weather was pleasant for it.*

Alk-e-lea ran like the wind and soon she came to the edge of the scrub land where the ground veered sharply down to the orange sands. At first she didn't see anything but as she raced down the beach she saw a grey mound huddled in the sand. Her pace quickened and she threw herself down beside it. By now Danetar had risen above the horizon. Its warm rays slowly crept up the beach to meet them. Slowly she turned the body over and the features of Ler-e-lea in dolph form could be seen clearly. The face was an expression of calmness and as Alk-e-lea's heart slowed down she quickly examined her for injuries. There wasn't even a scratch. Only a light dusting of orange sand interrupted the lines of her body. Ler-e-lea's breathing was steady and a great sigh of relief burst from Alk-e-lea as she realised that her friend seemed unharmed. But it was only as Ler-e-lea's eyelids fluttered that she remembered Hil-e-gar. From her crouched position she looked up and down the beach but there was no sign of Ler-e-lea's mate. All Alk-e-lea could think of was that he must have come ashore somewhere else.

Her attention was brought back to Ler-e-lea when she felt the eyes of her friend watching her. "Stay still. You are safe now." Ler-e-lea didn't immediately respond. She just continued to stare at Alk-e-lea but when she did open her mouth to speak there came only screams. It lasted only for a few yens, and Alk-e-lea watched helpless as the eyes of Ler-e-lea emptied of expression. Her composed face grew slack and she lay as if the morning of a new tay was too much and she had fled to escape its promises.

All Alk-e-lea could do was to pick up the limp form of her friend and carry her back home. Bue-e-gar met her as she climbed the incline to the scrub land. Their eyes met and he nodded in sympathy. Silently he did his own examination of Ler-e-lea. He used his water-time which was well developed to explore the frozen state of her mind and found a barrier of green light that would not let him pass. The more he pressed the firmer it became. In the end he had to give up and withdraw. Never in all his seasons as a healer and a student of the stars had he been defeated by a mind that appeared unwilling to be healed.

"It's beyond my skill..." was all he could say to Alk-e-lea's searching gaze. He turned towards the sea and watched as a flock of Kerg dived into the sea. Disappearing then reappearing with a fish that struggled to escape the confine of the beak. "At least they *struggle* for life.."

Now sure that the barrier wasn't preventing Ler-e-lea's recovery, more a manifestation of her desire not to, he consoled Alk-e-lea and they continued towards the city.

Alk-e-lea knew the longer her friend's mind stayed withdrawn her body while unharmed would eventually give up and die. It was past midtay when they returned home and with a heavy heart she laid Ler-e-lea in the newly formed sleep chamber. For the rest of the tay she stayed by her side and watched over her while Bue-e-gar arranged a search party for Hil-e-gar. On the following tay he and the others returned. There was no sign, not that Bue-e-gar had any hope of finding him as he felt part of the reason Ler-e-lea had withdrawn so far into a catatonic sleep was that Hil-e-gar had entered the deathsong. The only reason he had organised the search party was at Alk-e-lea's persistence.

Two tays later he managed to persuade her to allow Ler-e-lea to be moved so the Healers could take care of her. The city was alive with the talk of Ler-e-lea and Hil-e-gar. Many speculated on what had happened to them. Most believed that Hil-e-gar had been killed by the Keaverkack. But the biggest mystery of all was what had alerted Alk-e-lea in the first place. Such long distance communication was only possible when they were as dolphins. But even then that was limited. The only one who could have achieved it was a Watersinger which would mean that Mel-e-gar had alerted Alk-e-lea. That was dismissed when she let it be known with Bue-e-gar's help that it wasn't Mel-e-gar.

Ler-e-lea was still asleep a jeanth later when Alk-e-lea and Bue-e-gar were called to the main Council. She was surprised when they elected her to be leader. It became her task to organise the survival measures needed to help them combat the Keaverkack. But she still managed to visit Ler-e-lea every tay. She and Bue-e-gar had dolphs search all the knowledge of Delikadove for any way to break through the self imposed barrier. Time went swiftly but with no result for Ler-e-lea and on the second jeanth of Alk-e-lea's leadership rationing was introduced on Delikadove.

There was no part of the seas that were not infested with Keaverkack and the death toll grew. The call of these voracious beasts became known as the Siren of the Keaverkack. When the cries of the dying filled all the healing centres Alk-e-lea was called on to explain Mel-e-gar's absence. It had been more than three jeanths since he had left and many began to believe he had been destroyed by the power that was said to reside in the Arkelclared Desert. But she kept their hope alive by calling for dolphs to be posted as lookouts around all the inhabited continents. Within two tays of this being set up it produced an unexpected reward. For dolphs began to report that the Keaverkack who could now be seen thrashing around the shallow waters of the coasts had begun to withdraw. But still no word came of Mel-e-gar and when Alk-e-lea had discussed this with Bue-e-gar one late evening, he smiled his mischievous smile and said:

"He is out there! Why do you think the *Keaverkack* are withdrawing. *It's him*....He is doing it. *Somehow.....*"

* * *

Serliker was sitting happily on a new pedestal by the side of the lake, a better position to have direct contact with the Selahw. Five of which were giving a display of synchronised fluke slapping and combined with their marvellous breaching, which involved launching themselves out of the water and twisting in mid-air as they came crashing down, causing the water to explode into the air. The roar of their impact bellowed around the cavern. For Mel-e-gar who was joining in, it was the most joyful occasion in his life. To be dancing with such great creatures was a great honour and Cual-e-lay used her great beak to launch Mel-e-gar out of the water and they gently tossed him from one set of flukes to another. This went on for some time until Mel-e-gar grew tired and he and Cual-e-lay broke away from the rest and headed for the shore.

She stopped just short and he turned and dived beneath her and with his form touching her, he slid from her head to her tail and back again to her head. He repeated this and they shared great warmth as they revelled in the sensation of each other's touch. Mel-e-gar's water-time was filled with many feelings as he and Cual-e-lay shared themselves, a bonding that would hold true for as long as they wished it.

I will come back for you, he softly sounded and she blinked one great eye and whispered back, *Yes, you will.*. The water churned into froth as she playfully spun herself, holding

Mel-e-gar close to her warm side. They were lost to any curious eyes by a wall of white water and Mel-e-gar felt himself truly fuse with another's water-time.

His waters went over the three jeanths that had passed since the beginning of his mission. He had discovered many different things since then, but what had surprised him the most was his relationship with Cual-e-lay. Each spare yen that had not been used in discussing with Serliker the problems that had to be solved, he had spent with her and each yen brought a greater flow of feelings. It grew with such strength and passion that sometimes he imagined that he was a Selahw. She equalled this desire, and it made her sound her concern; the impossibility of a joining taking place. He knew that if he was a more equal mass of Cual-e-lay then it was possible but not while she was more than five times his size.

This problem he discussed with Serliker in yens when they rested from searching out other answers. When *it* felt that Mel-e-gar's desire was true *it* suddenly laughed and said, *My young lovesick dolphin, use your watersong and become a Selahw!*

With those sounds spoken Mel-e-gar received the picture of knowledge to accomplish the temporary transformation. But the question was whether their joining would be able to produce young. There was only one way to find out and when he had shared this with Cual-e-lay, the water was too small to hold her delight and she went to every Selahw and fish and told them.

So two tays before he was due to leave and with every Selahw watching he bade for Cual-e-lay to hold him to her side. When they were comfortable he began to sing. A song was born that changed the water to jewels of delight and every Selahw felt their laughter weave a blanket of joy around them. The energy made her body glow and shimmer and she felt him grow and expand. The displacement of water as a new Selahw came into being threw the other Selahw away and they laughed, but took it as their cue to leave. As the spectacular energy faded from the waters, two Selahw were seen beginning the dance of joining and they tumbled down to the depth, twisting and spiralling as they went, their water-times as closely melding together as their bodies were enjoying and Mel-e-gar and Cual-e-lay felt the completeness of their love.

Mel-e-gar had found his mate and Cual-e-lay had found hers. Neither could have foreseen such a unique joining taking place and on her part she was twice blessed, for this meant new blood would be added to their kind, making their race stronger in the future. They reached the depth required then returned to the surface and joined from head to tail they breached together. As they came down Mel-e-gar felt the energy take hold and he returned to his normal self. Now much smaller he slid from her grasp and together they swam through the cavern, exploring the depths and for two tays they made the best of times...

Mel-e-gar returned from his wanderings in water-time and he flowed his waters with Cual-e-lay and sounded, *It's time.. Keep safe my love...* He dived from the water and as he spun in the air, his form sparkling with energy he heard her say, *Be true...and remember your song can save you.*

His form changed as he landed beside Serliker and her sounds were now whispers that slowly faded but left a great warmth within him. He felt more able to complete the plan that he and Serliker with the help of the Selahw had formulated.

"Goodbye young dolph. *Don't forget to come back!*" were *its* parting words.

Mel-e-gar sounded in return, "I have *plenty* to come back *for*!" The sound of Serliker's laughter followed him as he began his walk down the beach. He had to get as far away as possible from Serliker, and when he judged about right he looked back and he could just see a faint blue glimmer that was Serliker. He then began his song, a song to transport not only himself but a new companion, Nual-e-gla. A plume of water spouted into the air as a Selahw signalled its readiness to go. A rise in tempo and the sweet sound of song reverberated around the cavern. The energy grew and then a thunderclap boomed around as Mel-e-gar and the Selahw were taken from the cavern.

* * *

They reappeared thirty dees above a stormy ocean in the dark! Mel-e-gar had to change his form as he fell towards the water and he slid beneath the choppy waves a few yens behind the Selahw. If the calculations that Serliker had made were correct then they were now swimming in the northern sea of Eaarklisade, the proper home of the Keaverkack. He used his sounds to penetrate the dark waters and he soon found a large group swimming southwards away from their position. Well that would have to change. Have to turn those beasts this way. But first thing's first. He swam to the Selahw and sounded within his water-time, *Are you ready Nual-e-gla?*

The massive bulk of the Selahw turned in the water and he rolled his large black eye and sounded, *I have been ready for longer than you have seen seasons.*

That made Mel-e-gar laugh and he watched Nual-e-gla slowly tilt in the water until his flukes just broke the surface of the sea and his head was pointing straight down. Then he sang the unique song of a Selahw, a song that told part of a story that spanned eons of time and told of the adventures of his kind as they had dominated their underground world. Mel-e-gar listened as the haunting sound flowed through the water and he knew it would soon be drawing the attention of the Keaverkack from all corners of Delikadove. The sound moved his soul and he waited for the savagery to commence.

Mel-e-gar began to swim around Nual-e-gla, singing a song of protection. He used the technique that Serliker had shown him. The energy began to grow around them, a wall of white energy that began to fuse the water together. It stretched for twenty dees in all directions. Soon the sphere of light was complete and Mel-e-gar came to rest by Nual-e-gla's side. *That should keep them busy!* he sounded and anchored the song within the Selahw's water-time, leaving him free to begin a new song.

In yens he vanished from the sea to reappear by the oasis in the desert. The twin moons were high in the night sky and their shadows danced among the trees. A soft wind welcomed Mel-e-gar as he materialised among them. His body added a brief display of light to the dimness and drops of water glistened like jewels on his silver grey skin. He adjusted his eyes to the gloom and using his water-time he searched the area. He was rewarded instantly by the soft sound of the Shakeilar that he had left behind. The sand near his dees began to swirl and slowly the Shakeilar revealed itself to the pleased welcome of

Mel-e-gar.

Mel-e-gar....You have returned.. I help? The familiar slow sound made him grin and he reached down and picked it up.

It glowed in his hands and Mel-e-gar joined with its water-time.

I need your help again.

He quickly outlined the plan and without hesitation the Shakeilar agreed, *I....Do much....For Grand-elder... It's Serliker's right...* He knew Serliker would love that. *Grand-elder! Well it was true but the respect and awe that the Shakeilar showed revealed the extreme loyalty they held for each other.* The quiet night was broken as he sang the song of transportation again. Holding the Shakeilar tightly he again appeared above the sea and as he transferred the Shakeilar to his mouth he plunged into the cold depths and swam down to Nual-e-gla. He passed easily through the barrier and then he opened his water-time to the Selahw. *Have you seen any yet?*

Without pausing its singing Nual-e-gla replied, *No, but I sense many are on their way.*

Good, I must leave you once more, replied Mel-e-gar and with a flick of his tail he dived down and passed through the barrier.

He swam through the cold waters until he felt the first warm currents. At more than a thousand dees down the temperature of the sea had risen to make it uncomfortable for Mel-e-gar but bearable. By using his sounds he could see the outline of the fissure more than ten thousand dees down. There was no way that he could swim any further as the pressure would crush him before he reached the ocean floor. He was amazed to find that it ran for more than two thousand klees, a gaping wound that spewed molten lava into the sea. No wonder the Keaverkack had left. The water was vaporising into turbulent eddies that fed the heat over an area many times its size, killing any creature that was pulled within its grasp, boiled alive.

The Shakeilar began to glow as Mel-e-gar fed the creative energy into it and with some sorrow he said farewell and released it from his beak. As it fell it began to expand and its surface threw off gushes of light that lit the darkness as it tumbled down towards the gaping maw. But even that light was soon consumed by the darkness. Mel-e-gar had to rely on using his sound to follow its passage down. The pull on his energies as the Shakeilar fed on him made him feel like his very life was draining from him. But when he felt that it was almost too much to bear, it broke contact. It had reached nine thousand dees and the last sound Mel-e-gar received was, *Do not grieve.....I do good here...*

Mel-e-gar waited anxiously for the yen when the Shakeilar would plunge into the fissure. He was humbled by the simplicity of its faith to do what was needed. His sounds saw the Shakeilar disappear and because he had delayed too long, the energy explosion that was created rapidly expanded towards him. He had to turn quickly to escape, but he was not quick enough and a wave of heat and water sent him tumbling beak over tail. The heat seared his flesh and Mel-e-gar cried out as the water sent him careening out of control. For one brief yen he saw the entire sea light up as if tay had come to the depths. But the darkness soon swept it away.

His body was buffeted about and he had no choice but to allow himself to be carried along. Eventually as the energy of the explosion died down he felt the water release its grip. He found he was not far from the surface of the ocean. He had waited awhile so his senses could reorganise. He swam quickly. His cry of relief as his beak broke the surface was cut short. The stars may have been welcoming in the night sky but Mel-e-gar's alarm pounded within his water-time when he saw where he had been thrown.

The sea was filled with Keaverkack, their great forms thrashing around not yet aware that they had a visitor among them. Mel-e-gar quickly scanned the area but there didn't seem to be any part that wasn't already infested. He plunged through the waves and tried to escape. But they had felt his vibrations and they rushed towards him. Mel-e-gar became confused as he searched for a way out. In his panic he forgot his watersong and he dashed this way and that. The Keaverkack seemed to grin at him and more than fifty of them soon had him surrounded. Their hunger was palpable and their delight filled the waters. Mel-e-gar imagined that he could smell blood and it took him a few yens to realise that he was indeed bleeding. The burns he had received had opened his flesh and the warm waters were making them weep.

The smell was driving the Keaverkack crazy but still they seemed to wait, maybe building themselves up to a peak so they could get the best from this impromptu feast. When his water-time told him that he was a fool, he stopped and he laughed at his own stupidity. The excitement of the yen had made him forget his watersong. Well he did have a lot to deal with on this tay! He cried his triumph at the Keaverkack and they sensing their prey was somehow about to escape rushed him. His song started but a high piercing sound broke his concentration and never hearing it before made him look at the Keaverkack in amazement. The sound built up and he felt it cut into his water-time. Being more proficient than some he easily deflected it and used enough energy to quickly form a thin barrier between him and the Keaverkack.

They went almost mad as he thwarted their hunger and they smashed into him and tried to tear into his body. Still able to move within the barrier he used his tail and beak to slap them from him. Buoyed by the success he battled with the Keaverkack. The siren still grew and it made his hold tenuous. It was starting to slip and now and then a Keaverkack broke enough of the barrier to make an attempt to bite him. The most he received were cuts as the teeth slid off his flesh as the barrier filled the gap.

Tiredness stole the strength from Mel-e-gar and he knew that there was not enough energy to transport him away. He had no choice but to swim for it and hope his sound would guide him back to Nual-e-gla and the safe protection of that barrier. He twisted and dived, turned circles and leapt from the sea as he fought a running battle, while his water-time had to cope with the raw sound of the siren. He soon became desperate which started to strip him of strength. His movements grew more tired and he could feel the blackness descending. But he kept at it, a battle that took him to the edge, and the precipice of the deathsong beckoned him. The wanting of that peace began to seduce him and the energy of his protective barrier sparkled and spat. The shimmering energy started to fade as he felt himself slide further down.

An image of Cual e lay entered his water time and she repeated her parting words, *Be true...Your Song can save you.....your song can save you...song...song....can save...You.. YOU!* Her sounds echoed though his water-time and he cried *that he had tried.* But she would not hear him and her sounds kept repeating their message. In his pain he shouted at her, *that she did not understand. He was trying but he was just too tired.*

But even that was torn from him as a Keaverkack sensing victory opened its great mouth and scooped Mel-e-gar from the water. The serrated teeth began to saw, trying to break through what it could only believe was a very tough dolphin, but in truth the shield was keeping enough of the teeth away. Mel-e-gar's strength was at its last ebb but then he made sense of her words. The power of the siren was now forgotten on his water-time but the power was the answer. *A song for a song*! The Keaverkack that held him grew more frustrated and it swam in circles as it tried to bash Mel-e-gar against its own kind. This enraged the other Keaverkack and soon fifty protagonists were tearing into each other in a wild frenzy.

Mel-e-gar tuned his song- well the best whistle he could come up with in the circumstances, slightly feeble but it was enough. He traced back along the paths of all the Keaverkack who were using their siren and found that it was much like an amplified water sound that his race used for finding their way in dark waters. This was enough to make him cry with joy and his sound joined with the Keaverkack and he turned their siren back on them with devastating results. They exploded in a shower of flesh and blood as their own siren was amplified fifty times. Mel-e-gar felt the Keaverkack that was holding him burst apart and he fell through the water stunned by the impact of the blast.

A few yens later found Mel-e-gar slowly swimming among the blood and gore. His water-time came slowly together and he was appalled by the devastation he had wrought. The only comfort he had was that now the dolphs as dolphins had a way to protect themselves in the future. It took him some time before he found Nual-e-gla and passed though the barrier to safety.

The Selahw held the limp form of Mel-e-gar to his side and used the water-time to ease Mel-e-gar's pain. Over the coming clars he helped Mel-e-gar to the surface to breath when it was needed and when Mel-e-gar felt better he told Nual-e-gla what had happened. The grief at the necessity for so much killing was shared and he told him that he did what was necessary for survival. Nual-e-gla knew that only time would help Mel-e-gar come to terms with what he had done.

Over the tay that followed Nual-e-gla used his sounds to penetrate the depth and reported what he saw. The Shakeilar was filling the chasm as it grew and it would soon seal the gap for good. Already the water was beginning to show signs of cooling but it would be many tays before it was complete. The Shakeilar was using the energy that it had received from Mel-e-gar to transform its mass. The price would mean its death as the transference would strip its identity and the rock would be just rock and nothing more. The Keaverkack were returning. Seduced by Nual-e-gla's song they came to feed on the originator. But the energy shield was far greater and it had no trouble in absorbing the sound of their siren.

By the seventh tay the Keaverkack gave up and finding their home was now habitable once more they left to feed on more easy prey. When Nual-e-gla judged the time was right it stopped its song and the dark depth was robbed of its beauty. The Selahw guided Mel-e-gar away and they swam to safer waters. The energy barrier died and they both broke the surface of the sea to meet the light of the tay. Mel-e-gar's injuries were now mostly healed, helped by the power of Nual-e-gla's water-time. He felt strong again and he knew that it was time to go home. Back to his mate and then a reunion with his friends. He was looking forward to seeing Ler-e-lea and Hil-e-gar. It would be his turn to surprise them. So it was with some joy that they dematerialised from the ocean.

* * *

THE RETURN

Celebrations had continued throughout Delikadove and Alk-e-lea had ordered the Beacons to be lit for the first time in generations to honour the occasion. These were large crystals that were imbedded along the coasts of the inhabited continents. Each had a dolph who was chosen to use its ability to keep the light bright within the heart of the crystal. When she had proposed it they had to search the library crystals for details on how this was to be accomplished. It was fairly straightforward. All the dolphs who were picked were to join in the same way as reading a normal crystal and a trigger inside would make the ignition. It was a spectacular sight to see. Every hundred klees a beacon burst with an orange light that would change to a light blue as darkness fell. Each beacon needed a small amount of energy from a dolph every twelfth clar to keep alight.

On the sixth tay Alk-e-lea was sitting by Ler-e-lea's bedside in the Healing building. It was situated on the outermost spiral. The single domed structure faced north and she had caused an opening to appear so that she could watch the lights dance in the night sky. A large part of the coast could be seen and a light breeze cooled her face as she watched whilst relating to the still form of her friend what she could see.

"You would love *this...*" Her voice caught and she stumbled on the words, "Everywhere! the sounds of laughter and singing can be heard. The relief that the *Keaverkack* have gone is so great that some say you can hear the celebrations coming from cities on the *northern continent*!!"

A feeble laugh escaped her lips and she turned and looked back at Ler-e-lea. The mound cradled her so completely that only her head was visible. The blue shimmer of the Shakeilar made shadows dance on the walls and sometimes the light would reflect from her unseeing eyes, making them glimmer a parody of life. Alk-e-lea went through the motion that had become something of a ritual. She leant over and moved her hand to see if the almost dead eyes would register. But like so many times before she failed to register any response.

The healers had tried all they could but nothing worked. None knew what the green shield that wrapped itself so completely around Ler-e-lea's mind was. At first they had believed it was a manifestation of her unwillingness to venture forth because of the shock of her partner's deathsong which had made her withdrawal complete. They had soon discovered that they were only partly right, for when they had compared it to the memory within Alk-e-lea's mind of the message and the pain she had received they found that whatever the green light represented it wasn't part of Ler-e-lea's mind or Alk-e-lea's. That left a mystery that could not be explained and with her position as Head of the Council Alk-e-lea ordered that for the time being that information should not be on general release. She had done such a good job that only five dolphs knew the details; herself and her partner and the three Healers that had attended Ler-e-lea.

With her mind going over the details she moved from the bedside and walked to the opening and was in time to see the nearest beacon flash off and on.

Her heart missed a beat as a cry of joy burst forth, “At last! *He has returned*!!” The signal she had asked for if any sign of Mel-e-gar was reported had come. The sadness was swept away as she ran from the room and without thinking signalled a door to open and sped out into the night.

A large crowd of dolphs had congregated on the crest of the hill that sloped down to the shore. They parted as Alk-e-lea ran through. She only stopped when she reached the front row and gasping for breath she looked at the sight that held the crowd enthralled.

The light of the beacon shone its welcome over the shore and for several klees out to sea. The waters shimmered and glowed as row after row of the Selahw broke through the surface. Their giant bodies cut great swathes and their flukes lifted from the water and slapped hard against the surface, sending great waves of water into the air. The sound rang out and the crowd roared with delight at the realisation that something wonderful was approaching. Leading them was the silver grey form of a dolphin who leapt and dived as it neared the shore.

Soon shouts of *Mel-e-gar!* came from the crowd and Alk-e-lea felt the energy of joy wash through her as the crowd’s shouts filled the night air.

From her right unnoticed at first came a dolph who put its arm around her waist and said, “*See my love*, he has indeed returned.”

She turned and looked at her mate; Bue-e-gar and they came together in a rush of limbs. Hugging each other close, she cried her relief with him and like younglings they broke from the crowd and ran down to the water’s edge to meet Mel-e-gar.

* * *

For several tays he had lain, held aloft by one of Cual-e-lay’s strong flippers, letting his tired and battered body recover some more before he returned home. Mel-e-gar’s water-time used the time to review the discussion he had with Serliker on the possibility of freeing the Selahw into the open seas of Delikadove. With the Keaverkack back where they belonged it hadn’t taken them long to pick the best place for them to make their home. The richest food source that would suit them was in the Hederlike sea, south of the Island of Tethilay. As Cual-e-lay was sharing his water-time she went over the information and passed it onto the rest. It was slightly strange for as each ripple went through him disclosing some more he heard it echoed by the sweet, warm song she sang to the others.

They would have stayed put if it wasn’t for Serliker’s desire to return to the world above but there were many who were curious to see what the seas above were like. The only problem that Mel-e-gar told them was whether they would be able to adapt to the fiery red light of Danetar. The exposure might be fatal as the different types of radiation had not penetrated their home in the cavern. But it was Serliker who solved that problem by revealing that the changes it had made to their ancestors made them capable of withstanding the over world’s radiation levels, maybe even better than the dolphs themselves. For a consideration it had to deal with in the beginning was that the rock of the cavern gave off high amounts of radioactivity, different admittedly but their cell structure would soon adapt to cope. Their self repairing mechanism was far superior to most creatures. The only problem Serliker could envision was a slight disorientation on seeing the vastness of the sky above the waters. But time would soon sort that out.

The tay came and the Selahw prepared to leave and Serliker found *itself* being picked up by Mel-e-gar and placed in his mouth. Now for the hard part for when *it* left, the cavern would lose its integrity and collapse upon itself. So Mel-e-gar would have to use his watersong to transport the entire herd of Selahw to a place fifty klees from the southern shore off the Arkelclared desert. This was something new for him to try and with Serliker's help he was shown the way for his song to be sung.

Cual-e-lay swam to his side after he had re-entered the cavern waters with Serliker now grasped tightly in his beak. The rest of the Selahw arranged themselves around Mel-e-gar in an ever increasing circle. When all were ready he began his greatest song. Cual-e-lay sent warm currents into his water-time and she stayed there as he sang, giving her strength and her love to him.

The light of the cavern flickered as the song began. Its yellow brightness dimmed then spluttered as the energy reached out to embrace the throng of Selahw. The cavern rumbled and groaned as he stepped up the tempo. Small rocks began to break away, showering them but as they hit the water, with some threatening to break over the backs of the Selahw, they touched the wall of energy and disappeared. The cavern was soon filled with a new light, overshadowing the old with its silver blue radiance. The song reached higher and higher tempos of energy and with a crash and a roar the water exploded around them. Great sheets leapt up as if they too wanted to be free. But just as they reached their highest point they fell back sending a colossal amount of water that showered down upon them. But they were held safe and still while all round, their home cried out its distress at being abandoned. With a shudder the walls gave in and an almost audible sigh could be heard as it all came crashing down. A battle commenced to see which would be victorious; rock or water. A new inland lake that would be open to the sky above or a colossus of rock that would see the light of a new tay.

For Mel-e-gar that was the last ripple in his water-time as the familiar pull took him and his companions to the sea of Roulisad. There was no witness to the explosions that erupted from the ocean in the middle of a cloud filled night. Plumes of water reached for the sky and like great cracks of thunder the ocean cried its birth pains. As each water plume disappeared a Selahw appeared and met a far larger world than they had ever known. The same pattern was repeated with only slight intervals between each, as a brotherling or parentling, sisterling or Grand-elder each cried its joy as their families were reunited in the ocean which was soon filled with the delightful songs of these great beasts.

Mel-e-gar, being the first with Cual-e-lay and Serliker, watched as each Selahw greeted him with a resounding *thwack* on the sea with their flukes.

The soft sound of his mate entered his water-time and she sounded, *Well, you have done much that the Selahw will be forever grateful. Many tales will be told about you in the coming seasons.* She stopped and tickled his side with a flipper, making Mel-e-gar laugh.

He nearly dropped Serliker who shouted to him, "*Watch it!*"

That only made Mel-e-gar laugh even more. With great difficulty he kept a hold on Serliker. He slid himself along her great side and stopped by her face and snuggled himself against her and he sounded, *You have made this journey more worthwhile than I could ever show....* While the rest of the Selahw played under the black velvet sky that revealed a few stars and many clouds. Mel-e-gar and Cual-e-lay swam away from them so he could show her his world.

Serliker kept quiet but *it* was making good use of the energy which flowed from them as they cavorted in the purple waters to get a greater view of *its* surroundings. *It* spied a *Kerg* flying home and sent a shaft of energy to intercept it. The energy found its mark and flowed into the sky-flyer with Serliker's essence quickly following suit but without taking control of the Kerg. It was unaware that it was carrying an extra passenger so there was no point in interfering as the Kerg was flying in the direction *it* wanted to go. It was enough for Serliker to use this new vantage point to get a wanderer of the sky's eye view.

Things had certainly changed. From the depth of *its* memory *it* realised that *its* old home continent had through continental shift drifted several hundred klees further west and now there were three other continents when there used to be only two. Well that is, above sea level, which by Serliker's reckoning had dropped by three or four hundred dees. Which alarmed *it*, because if it continued then within another 80 or more seasons Delikadove would be in trouble. As the Kerg flew over the equator and turned southeast, the light of the tay could be seen and this made Serliker lose *its* grip on the Kerg's energy field.

In an instant Serliker's essence was back in *its* hard shell. Spasms of shock swept through causing Mel-e-gar and Cual-e-lay to stop their cavorting in the sea and with one sound ask, *What's wrong*? as another spasm of horror shook Serliker.

They had to wait for *it* to calm down before *it* founds *its* voice.

I didn't realise...The images of Danetar you have shown me....

Its voice trailed off then and Mel-e-gar interjected, *What do you mean?*

Serliker's response was to cry out, *It's dying. Danetar is dying!*

Cual-e-lay was shocked by this and she turned to Mel-e-gar and sounded, *What does it speak of? How can the light that the Selahw have only dreamed of be dying?*

Now Mel-e-gar had not considered this possibility in all the changes that were happening and if Serliker was right then Delikadove would perish without the light of Danetar.

He used his water sound and responded. *We have noticed changes in Danetar and I have spoken that within a generation we will have to return to the seas. As each season passes the temperature rises making the land more inhospitable for the dolphs. But none have spoken that Danetar was dying!*

They both waited for Serliker to respond and finally *it* replied more coherently than before. *I should have seen this before now but my hunger to come back to live with the dolphs has blinded me... The image you have given me and all the sounds we have shared about the radiation of Danetar should have been enough but now that I have seen its red light I know that within a hundred seasons, maybe a few more Danetar will go into one final spasm that will engulf Delikadove and melt the ice on the outer planet of this system. After that it will collapse upon itself and become what we, the Shakeilar know as a white dwarf star. There is no more I can say. You will have to warn your kind.*

Mel-e-gar could feel Cual-e-lay's turmoil and even though in the depth of their waters they hurried to each other for comfort in the face of such helplessness the rest of his water-time boiled in desperation.

How could it be true?! Were they living at the end of times? His waters threw up different questions as he sought to understand what it really meant. But how could any creature accept that their home would end so soon. A whirlwind of emotion swept through his water-time as feelings of disbelief tried to make him reject the truth of Serliker's sound. *It made him know his loneliness that at different times he had felt because his watersong made him different and there were none like himself with whom he could share his fears and nightmares of troublesome water-times. Once more he was there, the weight of responsibility that burst into life compensating for his grief, changing numb feelings to quiet determination that even though all seemed lost he would continue with Edenlea and maybe one tay he would find a way to save his kind. It could only be this way for him and Mel-e-gar made a blindness to that inevitable deathsong of Delikadove. Even though no dream or song seemed enough to save his race he found comfort in the blackness that he had wiped his future clean. Open and waiting was his final conclusion.*

Part of his sounds passed to both Cual-e-lay and Serliker and when Mel-e-gar smiled they made no mention and allowed him a yen of peace. After swimming some distance Mel-e-gar quietly asked them both to keep what they knew to themselves. They both agreed as neither wanted to spoil the joy of the Selahw and they would leave it until Mel-e-gar had returned to his home to decide what to do next. Later he met up with Nual-e-gla, the Selahw who had helped him with the Keaverkack and arranged with him to lead the Selahw to the shore of Desilata. Keeping a sense of silence in his heart to see only that present tay.

It took them four tays to reach within ten klees of the shore and the Selahw made good use of the time to accustom their eyes to the light of Danetar. But it was night again when Mel-e-gar saw the light of the beacon. Over those few tays he, Cual-e-lay, and Serliker did share many sounds on the fate of Delikadove and had come to the conclusion that it would be best to share such knowledge only with the Head of the Council. Mel-e-gar believed this was still Gae-e-lea not yet being aware that Alk-e-lea had now taken that position. Maybe they would find a solution but until then there was no point in causing panic among the dolphs or the Selahw. With that settled Mel-e-gar led them towards the shore.

As he neared the beach he could see the waiting throng of dolphs and he called out for Cual-e-lay to ask the other Selahw to greet the dolphs with a display of fluke slapping. With the sound of flukes smashing down upon the ocean of Roulisad he leapt from the water and somersaulted through the air. When his tail touched the orange sand his form sparkled and changed to that of dolph. As he straightened up he found support from eager hands of two dolphs. Before his eyes had adjusted to the light of the beacon and not at first recognising who they were, he removed Serliker from his mouth and called out, "That must be you *Ler-e-lea*!"

With the light at their backs, casting them in shadow the tallest replied, "No, *I'm afraid not.* It is I, Alk-e-lea, and Bue-e-gar who welcome you back."

A note of sadness was mingled with the joy he heard in her voice. Mel-e-gar straightened and looked down and saw the wise eyes of Bue-e-gar and by his side Alk-e-lea stood graceful in the light of the beacon.

"It's good to be back," said Mel-e-gar and embraced them both. Almost as if a signal had been given, the dolphs on the hill ran down and they shouted and laughed his welcome home. Before he could find out what he had sensed in Alk-e-lea's words and before they could speak another word, especially about what they had seen him take from his mouth Mel-e-gar was swept along by the crowd across the beach.

Soon questions filled the air as they all began to ask, "*Why were you gone so long? What are those creatures out in the water? What happened to the Keaverkack?*"

This went on for some time but the roar of the crowd was soon to be broken when Cual-e-lay decided enough was enough and that her mate needed rescuing. She may have been half a klee from the shore and still joined with Mel-e-gar's water-time but she like the rest of the Selahw could easily hear the cacophony of questioning voices and minds. And none of them was pleased at the way Mel-e-gar was being treated.

Now Mel-e-gar didn't mind as he knew from the Council meeting he had been to before he had left that it was a normal reaction. But when he received her message in the stillness of his water-time he had to stop himself from laughing out loud, as her tone was indignant and her solution was to say the least, unique.

Cual-e-lay began to sing and the sound silenced the voices of the dolphs as the sound could also be heard within their minds. For them it was like reading a seeing crystal but what they saw and felt was sharper and sweeter as the song carried them along. Mel-e-gar watched as all the faces turned to look out to sea. The song told of his journey to the desert, his pain, frustration, battles, and discoveries that he had found below those barren wastes. For the first time more than a thousand dolphs shared his experiences as if they were their very own. The song changed and flowed as one after another, each Selahw took up the song. The dolphs cried and laughed together as Mel-e-gar's story took them through the caverns, to the finding of the bones, the Selahw and of course the indomitable Serliker. Like a fast flowing wave that crashed on the shore the sounds and sights filled all their hearts. The song cried out and they flew down to the depths of the northern seas, taking them to meet the Keaverkack and many who had not experienced these hungry creatures shook with fear, then cries of pain as they too joined the battle with Mel-e-gar. At last like a gentle winding river they followed him back towards the cavern and as the song returned to Cual-e-lay, she laid them down to a gentle rest.

The dolphs on the shore had the chance to see themselves through her eyes and first they were pleased but they felt shame that they had not given Mel-e-gar more space to breathe. Her gentle scolding, then a warm embrace of a welcome from her and the other Selahw. They were after all younglings together. At this point her song became a whisper and softly she let go.

Slowly eyes refocused and hearts began to beat once more. The stillness was broken as legs found that they had to sit down or fall down. So the multitude of dolphs sat upon the shore and together they quietly spoke their thoughts. Mel-e-gar walked among them and received many apologies which he waved away with a laugh and a warm smile. He found his way back to Alk-e-lea and Bue-e-gar who had also experienced the power of the Selahw.

"Now you know my story. Come let's sit down and you can tell me yours."

They could only stare at him and allow themselves to be led to the top of the hill, where they sat and allowed their minds to settle.

While they composed themselves Mel-e-gar sent his sound to Cual-e-lay, *You amaze me, I didn't know if you would be able to reach into their minds while they are in dolph form?*

She wrapped warm tentacles of love around his water-time and with a gentle laugh she replied, *I managed with you!* Before he could say that was because his water-time was better developed she interjected, *Yes I know what you are going to say but these dolphs are closer to forming a more open water-time than you have given them credit for!*

Her tone admonished him but he realised that she might be right. *Well maybe!*

That made them both laugh and Serliker who had remained in the background observing this added, *Yes, he can be too dismissive of his own kind. But I'm sure we will forgive him for that!*

It was enough for Mel-e-gar, and his water-time dissolved into a torrent of laughter at the audacity of a being who only a short time ago was the most blinded, thoughtless and self obsessed creature he had ever met!

Serliker's parting shot was to sound, *Me! Surely not... It* then gracefully retreated and allowed Cual-e-lay and Mel-e-gar some privacy.

Mel-e-gar was still laughing as he sounded, *I'm sure you will soon let me know if I begin to stray into that particular stream again.*

Yes, I will my great one! He laughed out loud at that and it made Alk-e-lea and Bue-e-gar look up from their private thoughts with puzzlement on their faces. Realising their puzzlement he shared with them the joke and for a yen smiles broke out on their faces.

But then Bue-e-gar said, "*Mel-e-gar* we have much to discuss but we have some *news for you...*"

His voice trailed off and Mel-e-gar's water-time sounded the alarm and he was about to say her name when Alk-e-lea said it for him. "It's about *Ler-e-lea.*" She paused and then said, "*and* Hil-e-gar."

It didn't take them long to tell what they knew and Mel-e-gar cried his concern into the night. It was Cual-e-lay who quickly sent her love and soothed his pain at the plight of Ler-e-lea. They may have been apart physically but the closeness they felt for each other while they shared water-time was by far the greater of the two. He sent his thanks and love back to her and told her to prepare the other Selahw to depart at first light. This would give him nearly twelve clars before Danetar would bring the dawn, time which he would spend with Ler-e-lea and perhaps he would be able to help her in some way.

Cual-e-lay broke contact and Mel-e-gar felt quite alone as he walked with Alk-e-lea and Bue-e-gar to the healing centre. They spoke softly about her condition and the fears that Ler-e-lea might have only a few tays left before her body would give up the fight for life.

Before he entered her room he asked the others to wait outside. He stepped through the opening and there before him snuggled in the enclosure of the sleeping compartment lay Ler-e-lea. Her face was a pale grey, the bones showing starkly beneath the tightly drawn skin. His heart fell to see her this way. He walked over and with an unconscious wave of the hand he caused an opening to appear in wall to allow in more light and a mound for him to sit upon by her side. Like Alk-e-lea earlier that evening, a soft breeze caressed him as he placed Serliker on the ledge by her side. *Its* light was dim and only a shimmer of shared concern touched his waters allowing him to concentrate on his friend. He reached out and stroked her face. It was so dry to his touch. From an opening in the wall which held a small pool of water he scooped some up and let it trickle over her face, gently massaging it in.

As he softened the skin he probed with his water-time and found the green barrier. Her eyes didn't show any signs of life but he could feel something respond. A flame of light sprang from his water-time and the area inside himself that had lain for so long blank and empty opened up and he knew what was needed. Somehow the gift, for that was what he perceived it to be, allowed him to pass easily through the barrier.

As his water-time flowed from him into her, a quiet voice whispered, *Welcome Mel-e-gar... Do what needs to be done.*

The flame that had ignited from the centre of his water-time began to warm Ler-e-lea's water-time. Her mind which had been closed for so long opened like a fiery flower with bright red petals that shimmered and glowed.

Her sounds travelled to meet him, *Mel-e-gar! Mel-e-gar! Is that you? I have been so alone.. Please take me home!* Her sound which for a yen was so bright fell silent, but not to oblivion, only to a gentle sleep.

When Mel-e-gar withdrew he found that Ler-e-lea's eyes were now closed and he found her hand wrapped tightly with his. He knew she would now recover but the loss of Hil-e-gar would weigh heavily upon her for some time to come. He had seen within the yen of her waters that the green barrier had separated Hil-e-gar's fate from hers and that somehow she had been saved. Mel-e-gar gently disentangled his hand and walked over to the opening. He saw the flow of dolphs as they returned to their homes and he could just make out Alk-e-lea and Bue-e-gar going out to meet them.

He reached out and made contact with their minds and told them the good news. They stopped and waved back their acknowledgement. He left the opening and sat back by Ler-e-lea's side waiting for her to awaken. He was joined by the warm waters of Cual-e-lay and they as one held Ler-e-lea's hand.

Whilst she dreamed of a green light that sparkled and shimmered, making a suggestion that a fine sleek dolphin watched over her.

* * *

5 S.E.

The white cliffs of still water glistened and sparkled, reflecting the orange light of the setting Solarn. A strong and cold wind blew from the north, chilling the air above the waves. The circle of dolphins swam lazily around Mel-e-gar, waiting for him to continue. He had ended his telling with a sad sigh that was now filling all the dolphins' water-time. With respect they stayed silent but many of the Elders had questions for him. The younglings of the school also had a full wave of questions and they were fit to burst when Mel-e-gar suddenly dived away from them. He cut through the water, his grey form silent as he swam away. They could only watch, open beaked as his body sparkled with blue fire. Then as if the very water swallowed him he disappeared from sight.

For a yen silence held sway but it broke as cries from young and Elders alike demanded, *Where has he gone? Why has he left like that? What is going on? How in all of Edenlea are we to get back to the warm waters of our home?!!* The sounds echoed in their water-time and above and below the waves as nearly a hundred dolphins cried their alarm at being abandoned in far colder waters than they were used to.

Only one dolphin remained quiet and she watched in disgust as her kind showed how shallow of spirit they could be. She watched as they all swam in circles. Even Mel-e-gar's family seemed to be disturbed by their Grand-elder's impromptu departure. At least they were not behaving as badly as the rest.

She gathered her water-time about her and as her anger built she channelled it up, shaping a giant wave and when she judged it right she screamed. The power of her anger was so great that its wave crashed through all their water-times. As they were still joined they all felt it smash into them at the same time. She laughed with glee as they tumbled through the water in so many different directions from the shock, causing her to move quickly as a rather large female came tumbling towards her. It wasn't a physical wave but the effect in their water-time was just as real. Deciding that it was better to follow through she cried, *You should be ashamed! Don't you listen? Have you not learnt anything??!!* She swam around them, slapping each with her flipper as she went.

She may have been a youngling but here in Edenlea the way was going to be different and she was going make sure they really understood that any dolphin had a right to speak when lea or gar saw such behaviour from others and they would have to listen. She watched as the dolphins righted themselves and their shame grew apparent to her water-time.

Taking hold of that she continued with her tirade, *You are no better than those dolphs that Cual-e-lay had to reprimand. There are things more important than our own desire for quick answers! It's like you didn't see, was he wasting his time?!* Her sound was tinged with sadness and the current of her anger which had flowed so strongly was now easing and without rancour she waited for her *Family* to reply.

At first no one responded and it was Mel-e-gar's sonling; Ser-e-gar who grinned at her and nodded his beak and sounded, *We should listen to this wise dolphin, for she has seen where we have not.*

He motioned for her to continue and a hot flush ran through her and now that she had calmed down it was slightly more difficult for her to continue. But bravely as all eyes looked at her with many nodding their approval she sounded, *I know that we seem to be left stranded here but I believe that we should all make good use of this opportunity to explore this region. After all our home is where Edenlea flows.*

This made them cheer and call out, "*Well Sounded Jux-e-lea! Well done!!*"

Now that she had done what needed to be done, she gave her tail a quick twist and she cut herself a path through the dark green waters to the surface. Closing down the channel to the others as her beak broke through, she breathed the cold sweet air. Solarn was gently lowering itself to kiss the horizon, making a great swathe of colour. The white clouds paraded themselves across the sky that was once blue now fired by orange, yellow and different shades of red. It was breathtaking, far more beautiful than in the southern waters.

Her water-time now calm was beginning to bubble with laughter as she realised that it was the first time that anyone had told an entire world of dolphins what was what.

She was still laughing when Ser-e-gar's beak broke through the waves and sounded, "You have the audacity and bravery of the youngling and we do thank you."

His eyes danced with good humour and Jux-e-lea replied almost shyly, "Thank you, but I only did what I felt was needed."

"You did indeed. Many of us were so deep within our waters as we lived the story of our past that my Elder's departure shocked us back to the present, when many were recovering from revelations that very few of us knew, especially the younglings as their knowledge was the most undernourished. But not you. You were the least surprised by Mel-e-gar's story." He looked closely into her green eyes and sounded, "He was right about *you*.. You are indeed like him..."

She returned his gaze with perplexity showing in her eyes, "What do you *mean*?" Her feelings were doing acrobatics and she wanted so much to know more of what Mel-e-gar had confided in his sonling.

Ser-e-gar swam closer and replied, "He told me that you had the same burning curiosity as himself and that one tay you would bring much needed wisdom to us all. My water-time tells me that this is that tay and it's only the beginning for you." He ended by smiling gently at her as she wrestled with her feelings for Mel-e-gar.

She couldn't find a suitable reply to his sound so she stayed silent. He stroked her side and replied for her, but within her water-time, *It is okay to feel the way you do for my fatherling but he has sounded his time is nearly over.* He could feel her sadness and deciding that she needed something to hold onto added, *Make good the time that is left for him.* He then turned from her and dived beneath the waves, leaving her to find her own way through the turmoiled waters of her heart.

With sad eyes she looked on as his tail disappeared beneath the waves, his last sounds going around and around, like an out of control whirlpool and her reply was, *How?!* when no one knew where he had gone and how could she get Mel-e-gar to see beyond her seasons for a short while to forget that their time would be brief. Her water-time lay heavy and cold as she turned her attention to the deepening twilight.

Soon the sky was filled with twinkling stars and somewhere out there was their old home. Which one, she didn't know and her heart cried out for Mel-e-gar and all that he must have lost when they had come here.

In her water-time she could see the grand cities of the dolphs and the great forms of the Selahw. She closed her eyes and her dreams for him welled up in her heart. Why couldn't there be more? Why couldn't she have been born in an earlier time so that she could be with him in those dark purple seas? She could feel his dolph hand entwined with hers as she re-lived the illusion of them both sitting upon that red hill. Her soul filled with hungry flames that burned through her, wishing so much for him to return and take her with him. *To be.. Some time to share, not much to ask,* but it seemed impossible as she rolled into an oncoming wave and buried herself in its wet embrace. Descending to rejoin the others another question burst forth, *Can a dolphin's heart break?*

They had taken her advice and had scattered, mostly in their family groups, feeding on the silvery fish that swarmed through Edenlea in a vast multitude. She could tell that they were settling down and taking some joy in exploring these northern depths. As she swam among them she spied Ser-e-gar and Car-e-lea with their three remaining younglings. They were grouped around Que-e-lea and Jer-e-lea. They were deep within their water-time as she swam closer. Ser-e-gar saw her and beckoned her to join them. A channel opened and she let her heavy water-time flow freely among them.

Que-e-lea helped to buoy her spirits by sounding, *We will find a way my dear. He may need you more now than ever before.*

Yes, joined in Ser-e-gar. *My fatherling is indeed in great pain and that could need a gentle heart such as yours. Be patient.*

Their comforting sounds helped Jux-e-lea and the warmth that they transmitted to her made her feel more hopeful and for a while she put her pain aside as they continued with their sounds on other matters.

Ser-e-gar and Car-e-lea brought her closer and she listened as Que-e-lea sounded, *We have been discussing what Mel-e-gar has told us these past jeanths and we have come to the conclusion that something else has been going on..*

Haw-e-gar interrupted, *As I have led the sounds of the other younglings on the reasons for no more secrecy, I have to admit that what has happened in the past may have been necessary.*

This surprised Ser-e-gar and he looked at his sonling with astonishment for his change of heart and then pride that his sonling was beginning to understand the wider implications of their ways. *Haw-e-gar, you continue to surprise me and....*

Before his fatherling could get carried away with the praise Haw-e-gar looked straight at him and with a certain amount of stubbornness sounded, *But I still believe we are right that much of the secrecy among our kind does far more damage*. He paused and added, *And I hold by that truth*. His water-time was solid as a rock and they knew he wouldn't give in on that.

Que-e-lea smiled at him and deciding it was time to move things on continued, *I agree and let's try and pierce some of this secrecy. We all know some of the past, and most of the Elders knew why we came here but not the whole truth. Only Mel-e-gar can tell us the rest. But what I find the most puzzling is how the past is being mirrored into the present.*

Yes! *Like an echo*, interjected Kel-e-lea, who had found much wonder in the stories, especially the Selahw and their songs.

Something like that, but let's go back over the events and try and piece things together, sounded Que-e-lea.

It was Zar-e-gar who voiced a secret troubling all the dolphins, particularly those around him now. *What about Tan-e-lea?* His sound broke into tears as the sadness he felt broke through. Turning his young pleading eyes to his fatherling, *What really happened to her?* The question hung in the silence as they all shared his grief and Ser-e-gar put a comforting flipper out to Zar-e-gar.

Who darted to his side and allowed his fatherling's water-time to embrace his hurt. *I cannot answer that..* And his own loss was mirrored in his sonling's eyes. All he could do was to turn to Que-e-lea and ask, *Did you believe the Rock's story for my daughterling's death?*

This wasn't the first time that she had been asked, for Mel-e-gar had questioned her at great length when she had returned from the island. At the time she hadn't seen any untruth in *the* Rock's explanation but over the intervening time something had begun to bother her about *it*. Taking the cue she had been given she replied to Ser-e-gar's plea, *Yes I do....But I believe it may have not told the whole truth.* She wrestled with her feelings and she opened her water-time to allow them again to experience what she had done in *the* Rock's domain. The essence passed quickly to them.

Car-e-lea gave all her feelings full reign as she tried to penetrate the entire image and with a deep sigh she allowed them to dissolve away into her water-time. Holding a feeling that she hadn't felt before and it was something very close to hope. For the effect which had been raised gave her an answer. *I know..* Her sound was a whisper and they held themselves silent as she continued, *There was a sadness to the Rock's voice which at first would seem normal.* Her sound became excited as the revelation began to sink in. *It was sad not because of Tan-e-lea's death as it would have us believe, but at what it was about to LOSE!!*

The last word came out as a deep cry and they were puzzled because they saw but didn't quite see what she saw. She looked at them and with exasperation in her sound and giving full force to her belief she cried at them, *Don't you see?! She wasn't dead when it told Que-e-lea!*

Ser-e-gar, hoping as much as she that she was right, still didn't get the full picture and replied anxiously, *You mean that she may be still alive?!*

Yes! Yes! she cried, her excitement washing through them.

Que-e-lea suddenly reached out in alarm and using her health sense pulled Car-e-lea's excitement down. *Be careful*, she warned. *You are endangering the one you carry. Your blood was moving too fast. The pressure will hurt the youngling. Try and stay calm.*

She used her adept water-time to feel her way through Car-e-lea's system, slowing down her heart beat and regulating her blood supply to the youngling which was only two jeanths from being born.

Car-e-lea felt herself calm down and she thanked Que-e-lea and quietly responded, *I have been foolish, but I know I am right..*

Now he knew where Haw-e-gar received his stubbornness from. Ser-e-gar breathed a sigh of relief that his mate was now okay and kissing her replied, *But it doesn't make any sense. The Rock didn't lie and if she our daughterling wasn't dead why hasn't she returned?*

Now Kel-e-lea had been following her motherling's stream and being free from any constraint on her level of excitement gave it all she had and cried, *I see! I see! Oh, my Motherling you could be right!!*

Que-e-lea, slightly annoyed at all these declarations of knowledge without any one getting to the point sounded, *Well, I'd rather you tell us than watch you jiggle about!*

With much delight Kel-e-lea told all, *It's to do with the mirror effect that was spoken of. Remember that Ler-e-lea entered the deathsong but didn't pass through and was held by that green light until our Grandfatherling freed her..* With triumph she declared, *That may have happened to Tan-e-lea!*

Her excitement was catching and even Zar-e-gar looked up from his fatherling's side with a new sparkle in his eyes.

Jux-e-lea seeing her point added, *And you believe the Rock was covering this up because it didn't believe anything could be done.*

Yes! replied Kel-e-lea with glee, *and our Grandfatherling may have come to the same conclusion and has gone to help her!*

Ser-e-gar seeing her logic sounded, *But if you are right, and I hope that you are my young one, why didn't he make the connection before?*

This dampened Kel-e-lea's spirit as she had no answer to that. Que-e-lea came to her rescue by sounding, *Maybe the fact that for the first time in more than eighty seasons he has begun to tell us the whole story and has had no reason to make the connection until totay.*

It would explain why he disappeared the way he did... replied Car-e-lea.

Her sounds seemed to ring truth in their hearts and Haw-e-gar concluded the stream for them all, *It would also give us another reason for why none of us felt her deathsong.* Before any could interrupt he added, *We have assumed that the Rock's words were the whole truth and as she was separated from us by being on un-water we wouldn't be able to feel her deathsong.*

They spent the following clars going over their reasoning and the more that they followed it, the greater the feeling of hope that burned brightly in their hearts. They rejoined the other dolphins and shared their feelings. The idea of the echo as Kel-e-lea called it took hold and they compared events, from Ser-e-gar and Car-e-lea's reference of the strange building and the voice of the crystal and Mel-e-gar's first encounter with *the* Rock, his subsequent trip to the cavern with Tan-e-lea's and Que-e-lea's adventure to the underground cavern on the island, right through to Ler-e-lea's strange encounter with the green light and hoping that somehow Tan-e-lea may have encountered the same and was still being held by the light. It helped many accept Mel-e-gar's departure and sympathy washed anew for him.

In all the excitement there was one water-time which found some of the reasoning slightly fragile and the more she looked at it the more vaporous it became. Ose-e-lea swam among them only allowing her pleasure to show, keeping any misgivings to herself. For she was the daughterling of the oldest dolphin among them when Mel-e-gar was away.

Her fatherling had made it to his seventy-third season the veul before and his name was Del-e-gar. He had been one of the first to be chosen, nearly forty-nine seasons before. It had been after he had encountered a strange dolph who had shown him another way to live. He had kept that secret even from his daughterling as that had been her motherling's wish. It had only been at Ose-e-lea's insistence that he had after Tan-e-lea's deathsong revealed his waters for her to see how she had begun and for her to understand the great loneliness of his water-time. After all her fatherling still loved that beautiful dolph and in the seasons since then it had kept his spirit warm to visit her in his dreams.

Ose-e-lea watched the others play and for a yen she caught her fatherling's eye, he nodded and shook his head negatively. It was not time to tell them that they may have an answer to the fate of Tan-e-lea and maybe it would never be right. She understood as being a motherling of four younglings she had some knowledge of Del-e-gar's feelings and those of Car-e-lea and Ser-e-gar. Part of her wished she could tell but it had to be from her fatherling's water-time, not hers. She trembled as she began to recall the complete sharing of waters, bringing a whirlpool of perspective that shifted as the images opened; tinged with Ose-e-lea's own sense of irony at the changes that had been wrought on her fatherling all those seasons ago.

* * *

ENCOUNTER

7225 S.N.

The forest covered an area of **9560** sq klees, blanketing the hills below the mountain range that split the western continent in half. There was only one main pass that enabled dolphs to travel from east to west or vise versa. In past ages it would have been blocked by the flakes of still water that would fall in the storms of winter, creating a white wall over a hundred dees high filling the pass completely. But that had changed since Danetar had expanded making a mean temperature over most of Delikadove of eighty degrees in the summer and seventy-three in winter. In the seasons that had passed since Mel-e-gar's return from the desert of Arkelclared things were getting worse. Large areas of the other three continents were turning to desert causing the dolphs to move their cities from the interior to the coasts. Mel-e-gar had begun his program for his semi-underwater cities twenty-eight seasons before. The first was created on the south-western shore of the northern continent. They say it's a marvel what he and the Shakeilar have managed to create and it was still growing, making it the largest city on Delikadove. His dream of Edenlea was well underway to becoming a reality but like many, Del-e-gar was concerned with other matters; like his forest. He thought of it as his, as he spent his time doing his best to stop the ravages of the hot weather from killing his home.

They called it the forest of ghosts, a place where creatures would go in but not always come out, including dolphs but not Del-e-gar for he knew every part, every secret, which he stored in crystals that he kept hidden in the heart of the forest and he was still only twenty-four seasons young. Now many would never believe his grand boast, that is if he ever boasted about it, but that was something he left to others- like Mel-e-gar, who he considered to be a braggart of the worst kind. If a dolph ever disliked another, this was he, even though he had never met, *The Great Mel-e-gar!*, as most dolphs now called him. For Del-e-gar matters had become worse when they had voted Mel-e-gar Head of the Council eighteen seasons before. The problem lay in the fact that while Mel-e-gar urged and most complied, many of the dolphs were preparing to leave the land- he was not. No, his love of Duorsilear (That was the name of the forest) was total and nothing and no one would ever make him leave. Again no one had but he thought that it was coming. He had a plan to take himself into the forest and live out his tays among the trees.

Now Del-e-gar was the last of a long line that stretched as far as records went, a family of dolphs who had for countless seasons lived and studied Duorsilear. He like his family before looked after the forest and took groups of dolphs among the trees, sharing with them his knowledge of the creatures that lived within its depths. He didn't mind that part of his duties, but he was glad that for the past six seasons the amount of dolphs that came were becoming fewer as each season had passed. Now only a trickle of them made the long journey from the city of Colisee on the Eastern shore. Colisee was the twin of Tueselaa which straddled the river below the forest on the lowland hills of the western seaboard, overlooking the Colertia Sea, the place where visitors would stay and where

Del-e-gar had his home. Not that he was there that much as he could be many jeanths away exploring.

It was the first tay of the new season that Del-e-gar awoke in his sleeping-chamber to start his latest venture. He was going to explore an area north-east of the city, a place that a distant ancestor had recorded in the crystals. That would tell him how the upper reaches of the forest were coping with the dry conditions. He wanted to update his knowledge and compare it with the old record. Although he might know all there was to know through the complete record of the crystals but the truth was that most were out of date and he needed to find out what was going on up there now. He might know the layout, the creatures and even types of trees and find his way home again but he had only explored a fraction of the great forest. He relied totally on the crystals, so much so that he sometimes forgot what he had found out and what his family had done in the past. But that was the way he was. Their knowledge was now his, so he made it his. Most of the dolphs of the city considered him to be a little strange but harmless enough. Now dolph society didn't produce many mavericks but like Mel-e-gar he was one. A comparison that would have horrified Del-e-gar if he had ever thought of it, but he didn't...

He stared at the ceiling and listened to the early morning calls of the Kerg, Makeilar, Twon, Cerser, and the brightly coloured Jewur, whose song always overshadowed the rest. The flyers of the sky world fascinated Del-e-gar and he had made many friends of them up in the forest. He stretched his legs and swung them over the edge of his sleeping mound. A broad smile spread across his face as he contemplated his next trek. He waved his hand and a circular mound rose from the floor. In the centre was a small crystal which he reached out and touched. Blue light began to radiate out and slowly a three dimensional image of the forest and mountains appeared. Slowly it registered his presence and he asked for a closer look at the upper reaches. Finally it pulsated twice and then it panned a view in front of him. He followed it, making himself familiar with the land marks. He could have done this by recalling the memory or reading a crystal by direct absorption, but this was a little invention of his own. He had changed the directional energies of the matrix inside the crystal and caused it to concentrate on a single point, using that to bounce off, radiating out of the crystal to place an image about four dees above itself. It wasn't that difficult and he wondered why it hadn't been done before.

If he had known that he had actually created a more primitive crystal he wouldn't have believed it. For his amazing invention was just like the first crystals created by the dolphs more than sixty million seasons before! The progression for a crystal to be able to pass information straight into the mind was a major leap forward for the dolph culture. But Del-e-gar who had lived all his young life being cut off from the main stream, was blissfully unaware of it.

Del-e-gar yawned and stretched to his full height of twelve dees, shaking the sleep from his limbs. With a wave of his hand the crystal withdrew the image and disappeared into the floor. It was another one of his little secrets and he delighted himself with the image of himself presenting his invention to the main Council and showing up Mel-e-gar. *Not that he would, he was not that kind of dolph!* After eating a good meal of Wunlaka (*a type of fish*) he picked up a small globe of Shakeilar from an opening in the wall and left his home.

It was on the outer edge of the city and he stepped straight out onto the blue grass of the lowland hills. Danetar was rising in the eastern sky, its red light radiating over the green and blue city, tingeing the domes with a purple hue. To his delight the grass was, in places waterlogged underdee which meant that for the first time in six jeanths it had rained heavily during the night. He enjoyed the feeling of water that oozed between his toes as he began his walk eastward. It wasn't long before he came to the edge of the forest, where he stopped and gazed up at the massive trees. These were some of the biggest that he had found, being more than three hundred dees high with a girth on average of ninety-four dees. For a yen he just stared and breathed the sweet smell of his forest after a storm. Small trickles of water flowed down the deeply ridged red/brown bark from the canopy of blue-green foliage that crowned the tree. Suddenly a Cerser flew down from the upper branches and landed neatly on Del-e-gạr's shoulder. It carefully folded its deep green wings and cooed its welcome.

He laughed in response and said, "Hello, my dear friend! Come to join me on this tay?"

The Cerser nodded its yellow and red beak, which curved downwards and nibbled his silver grey nose. Taking this for a *Yes* he reached up tickled its chest and with a chuckle concluded, "Good, let's be off then." And he strode forward with great confidence. His slim, finely chiselled face, that some might have said was rather weather beaten for one so young, wore a permanent grin as he made his way under the deepening shadows of Duorsilear.

He chatted amiably to the Cerser as they travelled among the trees, gradually turning north-east up a gentle incline. He was shielded from the early morning rays of Danetar by the broad canopy high above his head. It made his journey pleasantly cool and they seemed to lean forward as he passed, greeting him like an old friend. When it reached midtay he stopped and sat and leaned against one of the broad trunks, resting himself. The Cerser cooed and taking its cue from Del-e-gar it put its head under its wing and slept. He found himself dozing off and deciding that it was a good time for a sleep, he allowed his mind to drift away.

His dreams were gentle with images of his trees, tearing their roots out from the ground and walking with him through the cities. They talked and laughed with him as they startled the inhabitants as they wound their way among the streets, millions of trees jostling with each other to be near him, a familiar dream which warmed him each time it came. But then for the first time he heard a song of such beauty and depth that it carried him away on a cloud of joy. He didn't mind that he was being carried away from the crowd of trees. The sensation of well-being infused him and it was only when the song grew louder that he was startled enough to wake up with a jump.

The sound of the song was still playing its sweet tune in his mind as he rubbed his eyes and looked around him. His companion, the Cerser must have left, as his shoulder was now bereft of her presence. He thought that she must have gone back to feed her younglings in her nest, but normally she would have cooed loudly enough for him to awake. Something must have startled her was his conclusion. It took him a few yens to realise that dusk had fallen. There wasn't much light left to see by and as he never used his sound in the dark, (*It was not that well developed*), he found it difficult to see among the dark shadows. He was still holding his orb of Shakeilar, which he now raised into the air and made the silent command. Instantly a yellow light bathed him and chased the dark shadows away. It took only yens for his eyes to adjust and he looked around him. After re-orientating himself he continued with his journey.

It wasn't the first time that he had slept the tay away, as he found the ambience of the forest very restful. He looked on it as his reward for looking after them. With the light to find his way he made his way higher up ever steeper hills. All the while the song carried on playing in his mind. He did find it strange that the tune continued while he was awake but as he wasn't hearing it outside of himself he just thought that it must have been the echo of his dream and as it was so beautiful his mind was playing it back for him.

Soon he found himself running through the forest as the song carried him along. It was great fun as he seemed to grow stronger instead of growing weaker. The changing melody so absorbed his attention that he didn't think anything of it as he came to the upper reaches. He looked around and saw that many of the trees had either fallen down or were dying where they stood. He appraised the situation and reached out with his health sense and began to heal them. Soon new sap rose inside, causing the trees to shed the dead outer skin and branches began to blossom with new shoots. He laughed and sang, joining his song with the one in his mind, a duet which took him among countless trees of those high mountainous reaches, healing the sick and dying, faster than he had ever done before. It made him giddy and light, so happy that he accepted this miracle as the most natural progression of his inborn talent.

He danced and sang a night, a tay, a veul, a jeanth away. By the morning of the second tay on that second jeanth he came to the last tree, which had fallen crazily against two others. They seemed to be bracing their kindred, waiting perhaps for Del-e-gar to help. By this time he was convinced that he must be mad for no dolph, no matter how talented they were could ever do this. But the song played; the madness continued.

For one last time he reached out, his hands open and empty (*as he had dropped the Shakeilar long ago*), pure white energy sprang from him and pulled the tree upright. He then proceeded to caress and heal its wounds. By the time the tree had grown a healthy crown, the energy eased back and finally it died away. At that instant, his mind became lucid and the song fell away, taking notes of pure innocence like so many jewelled leaves to the ground. He saw what he had done and gave way to the shock and exhaustion that his body now registered. He crumpled and he fell into the supportive arms of a dolph that wore a corona of green fire.

She smiled and sang, *Sleep...*

His mind let go and he surrendered himself to the fading image of her smile.

As he awoke to the sounds of the sky-flyers, he at first thought it must have been a dream and he hadn't left his home in the city. But the warmth he was feeling throughout his flesh was not the same he received snuggled in a sleeping-chamber. He cautiously opened one eye and found himself looking into a face of a lea - that took his breath away.

He quickly closed his eye. *She can't be real! I must stop sleeping out like this. It's doing me no good at all!* he thought, berating himself.

But the warmth didn't leave and he could feel her warm breath upon his face. He longed for her to be real but still he held his eyes closely shut. Deciding something must be done he gathered his courage and quickly opened both eyes this time.

Yes, sure enough, she's still there, was his rapid thought. His mind raced and he closed his eyes again. Twice he did this and each time her beautiful face remained.

"Are you going to carry on *blinking* at me like that or are you going keep your eyes *open*?" she asked, laughing gently.

"*She speaks!*" he squeaked and blushed with embarrassment as his mind registered her voice and he opened his eyes. This time he kept them open and he just stared up at her, open mouthed.

Her green eyes and very compelling silver pupils appraised him. They seemed to be reading him as easily as he would read a crystal. He studied her face and found the gentle silver, grey domed head very appealing. A tinge of green seemed to flicker and it made small oval jewels sparkle in the early morning light. Her mouth wore an amused smile which made him curl his toes in delight.

He tried to move but she laid a firm but kind hand on his chest and said, "Be still, you are not yet ready to move."

She was right. His body felt warm but there was little strength in his limbs. He relaxed luxuriantly in her touch. He realised she was sitting down with his upper body laid across her lap. His legs were cushioned by the soft undergrowth of the forest and his head was cradled in the crook of her right arm.

He accepted his plight and said, "What do you intend to do with me..?"

She giggled and replied with a certain suggestiveness to her tone, "What *indeed*!!"

This made him blush even more. He had not given much thought to leas before and her reply was unexpected. *He didn't know what he could say or should say!* This avenue of thought persisted; after all he was sure that he was more than happy not to mate- that is until now. As the image formed in his mind she playfully ran a finger across his lips and leant over him and whispered, "*Naughty* dolph..."

This was getting too much. She had read him! How in all that is dolph did she do that?

The look of horror and surprise must have registered on his face for her expression changed and sympathy took hold. "I am sorry *Del-e-gar...*"

Del-e-gar! Del-e-gar! his mind repeated. *How did she know my name?!*

"Whoops!" was her reply. She stroked his forehead and replied. "I know your name because like many dolphs I can *join* my *mind* with *yours*. But you are one of those that have not learned."

This startled him even more and his mind raced with her words. *How could dolphs read minds? He had never heard of such things. It cannot be true.*

But she kept his gaze firmly held by hers and this time she sounded within his mind, *It's true. You have kept yourself away for far too long from your own kind..* She quickly changed that to, *our kind*, then carried on, *-and that has stopped you from finding a great many new and wonderful things.*

Her sound felt good to him and it seemed to ease away his concern. Which he knew he shouldn't let happen as his mind had always been right in the past. But that concern didn't materialise and he decided to forget the questions. All he wanted to do was to wallow in those green eyes. *Much more fun!*

She didn't seem to mind and allowed him his pleasure, which she seemed to enjoy. It seemed an eternity that they allowed their eyes to hold the gaze and it was like they melted into each other as time went on. She slowly guided him into her mind. That for him was like swimming in the cool waters of a giant lake. No, more like an ocean! His first encounter with water-time was a gentle experience. She allowed him to play and swim among her feelings. Many strange images shimmered on the edges, too far away to make out clearly so he let them be. He just enjoyed the sensation of so much freedom and gradually it began to seep into his mind, changing him in subtle ways, ways that would be seasons before he comprehended their full impact.

When he was more used to this fluid form of communication she began to sing for him. Once more he was lifted and embraced by a melody that made stars flash over the water and colours of many hues bathe him. *Arrh...! He would gladly pass into the Chisharnlay as long as he could listen to her sweet melody.* It made his heart cry out in ecstasy and the yearning for her took hold. So they loved and made themselves into one as their bodies joined with that special heat. When their passion was satisfied they returned and laid entwined, limb against limb, heart against heart, and slept the sleep of peace.

He awoke with the heat of Danetar upon his face and the smell of crushed leaves, giving a sweet perfume of the forest. It was so peaceful that his only desire was to stay snuggled among the leaves. Maybe it was the rustling sound he made as he made himself more comfortable or maybe it was the song of a Twon, singing its greeting to the morning. It could have been both because he jerked awake and sat up, causing the leaves he had been covered with to fly in all directions. *A dream? Maybe a dream within a dream? For he was sure that he must have asked that question...*

Her gentle musical laughter answered his demand, "You look so *funny*! A true creature of this forest."

It was enough for his breathing to ease and the wild flutter of his heart abate. Her humour caught him, making him look over his left shoulder. She was leaning against the tree, her arms stretched out against the great girth, her mischievous smiling face peeking around the tree. Her green eyes sparkled and danced at his wild expression. Her humour was infectious and he laughed his delight and threw a handful of leaves at her, which she easily dodged and he watched spellbound as she danced around the tree. While she was hidden by the trunk he sprang to his dees and brushed off the leaves that were clinging to his skin. Her laughter continued to kiss the early morning breeze and as she reappeared, she took his hand and pulled him through the forest. A dance that wound their way through the edges of the upper reaches.

She laughed her delight as he discovered his work of the previous tays. He reached out and touched newly grown bark and the strong vibrant beat of the trees told him all was well again. He was stunned at the magnitude of what was accomplished, which could only bring him joy. He stared opened mouthed in awe as he tried to take in all he saw.

The memory of those tays was blurred but he knew that from the northern heights to the southern range, the upper reaches had been either dead or dying from the harsh, hot winds that blew from the east. *How could he have done it? So much...To have healed klee after klee of devastation. True, he had the health sense to cure a tree if it had enough sap to feed the upper branches, but to bring back from the dead was impossible.* The scenes belied that fact and he allowed her to lead him among the fresh growths, trees restored that would have taken a thousand seasons to bring back.

His body felt the new life and swept any vestige of tiredness away from his limbs. There was so much to take in that he bade her to stop, "Let's sit here for awhile." Still holding her hand he pulled her down and they sat with their backs to a precipice. The trees seemed to have halted their advance up the mountainside about ten dees away from the edge. Which gave them shelter, as the upper foliage hung over them. Danetar had reached its zenith and the light filtered through the branches making dancing streams in the shadow of the trees.

The ground was covered in a fine purple moss that was extremely comfortable to sit on. It also helped to take some of the heat from the stone. He caught his breath and used the sight of the forest to calm himself down. She had draped an arm across his shoulders, massaging the tension away with her fingers. To help himself get his mind into some sort of order he asked her, "Do you know this place?"

With her head tilted slightly she looked at him and replied, "No.. Is it a good place?"

For some reason he felt surprised as it seemed she had brought him deliberately to this spot. "But I *thought...*"

Her other hand came up and touched his lips and with humour said, "I know little about this place. Do not see where there is nothing yet to see..."

He kissed her playful finger and looking up at her said, "Why did I know you would talk in riddles?"

Her mouth quivered as she repressed her amusement, which only made her more attractive. He saw amusement at his naivety and then a flicker of sadness touched her eyes. But before he could be certain she turned away and gestured with her hand, sweeping it in a wide arc to encompass the area where they sat. Her voice thick with emotion asked, "Tell me Del-e-gar. *Tell me* what this place means to you."

He swung himself round and with his legs dangling over the edge he motioned for her to follow suit. Clutching her hand tightly he gazed out and watched two Leujan who danced upon the warm currents of air high above the barren lowland hills that flowed down to the eastern coast. Their golden brown wings with tips of white would fold then open as they followed and circled about one another. Del-e-gar watched the mating flight of the sky wanderers and told her the story of the Yewanclas Precipice.

"Many seasons ago a distant ancestor of my family came to this place and she was named Yew-e-lea. The record she left behind in what I know as the first Crystal of Duorsilear told that she had been born in what was then the new city of Tueselaa in **2356** of the Cycle of Gooma. (*Which finished about 190,000 seasons ago.*) It tells that she went on the tay of her ninth season to explore the blue hills which led up to this mountain range. Which had been named after the Leujan, who nested on the tops of the small copse of trees which could not be seen most of the season because the clouds would obscure them from the observer..."

For a yen Del-e-gar paused, collecting his thoughts as a tide of anxiety made him spit out the next words. "Not as *now*! For the rains are infrequent and the clouds rarely come!!"

He had to shake himself and while she kept silent, the heat from her body warmed him and his attention turned to the Leujan.

The mating pair continued to swoop and dive, bringing their dance within a dee or two. Suddenly they broke away from each other and flew over their heads. The sound as they landed in the tree canopy above them moved Del-e-gar to motion in their direction and pronounced, "*They are the last pair..*"

He felt her eyes upon him but he didn't meet them. He didn't want her to see his eyes which were fighting to release their tears. Swallowing the lump in his throat he continued with his story. "It's ironic because on that tay Yew-e-lea sat here and watched a pair of Leujan and they too were the only pair nesting in the small copse of trees. She fell in love with their golden plumage and bright white collars around their necks. She tells they had a wing span of fourteen dees and mighty claws which they used to hunt the young of the Muala as they migrated from the lush pastures of the north-eastern plains down and across the continent, passing through the only gap in the mountains to spend the winter jeanths on the blue hills. But they too are now gone.

"We had for a short time, when I was a youngling of three seasons a dolph who came and followed the Muala, studying them and watching as they slowly succumbed when the eastern plains died."

He stopped and thought back to his first trip with that friendly dolph who showed him how to make friends with the Muala. It made him tighten his hold on her hand and she responded by squeezing, encouraging him to continue once more.

"His name was Jey-e-gar and he used to make me laugh with his tales of his early tays studying the Puga. But when he was mauled rather badly in the leg he turned his full attention to the Muala. *A safer pastime he used to say!* Maybe they still survive in other places...."

He fell silent and she softly asked, "What happened to *Jey-e-gar*?"

Del-e-gar laughed, breaking his heavy thoughts and replied, "The last time I saw him he was riding one of the Muala through the Gap. Maybe he still rides. I don't know but I only need to think of him riding those great beasts for it to make me smile fondly of those times."

Deciding that he would finish the story later he stood up and walked the few steps back to the line of trees and choosing the nearest he sat and gazed back at her

She seemed to glow under the light and for the first time he had a chance to study her. She smiled in response to his open expression of admiration and when she too stood up he watched her graceful figure almost flow towards him. She moved so silently, that with some shock he realised she must have stood seventeen dees. Again he saw the strange shimmer of green, as shafts of light struck her silver/grey form, making the muscles of her long legs ripple as she walked.

His love for her rose up as she glided to sit on her rounded hunches in front of him. She reached out and brought his hands to rest upon her thighs. With great silkiness in her voice she said "*Del-e-gar you must finish one story before bringing another into being.....*"

Her laughing eyes made him gulp in response and he allowed himself to be led, (*Well it was difficult to refuse!*) along that sensual path that when joined with her, turned dry dusty deserts into lush fertile forests. Each touch, movement of their bodies brought greater delight which made the bonding strengthen and when the stream had become a high waterfall, they tumbled over to crash among the great white water, swimming in their delirium of passion.

Later, he contemplated how happy; truly deliriously happy he was with being with such a wonderful lea. He raised himself on one elbow and this time he had the pleasure of watching her serenity of sleep. He didn't know how long he watched her but when dusk came his mind turned towards food and as it came to him that he no longer had the Shakeilar, he almost panicked. But as those thoughts flowed through he spied a small light rolling across the leaf strewn ground. He laughed with relief as it rolled to a stop by his dees. Then unbidden which surprised him, it opened and grew into a small dome. Red light flickered across its surface. Then an opening appeared which Del-e-gar quickly crawled into. The inside was hollowed out, giving enough room for him to sit comfortably near a raised dais that held a pile of steaming Wunlaka. It didn't take long for him to satisfy his hunger. *Leaving enough for... That was when he realised that he didn't know her name. Strange that he hadn't asked, then again maybe not for she had kept him much occupied!*

His thoughts were warm and he held them close. A strange fear disturbed him, braking those memories and it took a great deal of effort to shake the feeling off, determined that she would be with him for all time. That passion stoked his fires and again she surprised him when he suddenly felt her arms wrap around him.

She clung to him from behind and nestled her face into his neck and whispered, "I see you have found the Shakeilar.. And by the smell of cooked Wunlaka you have already satisfied your other *Hunger*!" She giggled as she emphasised the last word.

He blushed again and she carried on chuckling as she moved around and sat on the other side of the dais. He watched as the roof raised itself to allow for her extra height. When she was settled he offered her the Wunlaka, but she waved it aside. Again the Shakeilar responded and the food disappeared, smoothing out the floor, making more space for them. Then it became softer and flowed up creating two very comfortable seats around their forms.

When it finished Del-e-gar exclaimed, "How is it that my shelter responds before I signal it?" He found it quite perplexing. Her reply was soft but her eyes seemed to flash a silvery red. For a yen he fell into those eyes and was lost but he heard her words.

"You are my love, but you are blind when you speak; *MY*. This structure is alive and is a life form of great beauty and intelligence. It doesn't belong to you. It allows you to make use of it because it gains from the association. But it has its own desires.."

Each word seemed to burn into his mind and he cringed under her power. Maybe she saw the pain in his face because she broke the spell by gently kissing him and saying, "I mean you only love, but Delikadove is changing and you must change with it." This time her words were softer and reminded him that he had been apart from so much that his mind had become focused on a very narrow path.

He followed that for a short while but then something inside rebelled and he tried to fight the truth of her words. It only took a few yens but for Del-e-gar it seemed a lot longer. Two sides, the old fighting a fledgling of new water-time. It was almost a one sided battle and his stubbornness nearly triumphed. But like dangling from a precipice, he found the strength to hold on. A new form of light entered and he knew that his feelings for the lea was greater than the old and it filled his sense of water-time with love and a greater thirst for her as well as tomorrow.

So for the yen the old was banished to the edges, it wasn't transmuted as in time it would be, but stayed on the fringe waiting for things to change. The softness of the kiss made his sight withdraw from her and with a heavy sigh he said, "I'll be more careful in future what I say around you.." He managed to end it with a chuckle of wry humour, which made her relax with relief.

Later that night he told her the rest of the story of the forest of Duorsilear: "After watching the Leujan, Yew-e-lea turned her attention to the small copse of trees, which she named after her motherling and as she was a Watersinger she vowed to help the trees and the Leujan. In time she learned about the trees and she told that the name of an individual tree came to her in a dream; The Aiouqes. A strange name but it has held. In time she discovered that it was the blue grass which stopped the copse from expanding. How they had managed to come to grow in that one place seemed like a mystery which she had little hope of solving. It was many seasons before she found out the trees were here first and that in ages past they had covered most of the continent, including the eastern side. Why they disappeared in the first place, losing their domination, she didn't say...

"It was nearly thirty seasons later before she would act on the ideas she had as a youngling. For she as Watersinger had other duties that would take her all over Delikadove and where she quietly crafted her song so the Aiouqes would respond to her. Eventually she turned her back on the rest of dolph society and returned to the city of Tueselaa, where she mated with a dolph who shared her preference for all the creatures of the land.

"She had seven younglings who grew to help her and that began the lineage of the Guardians of the forest. She drove the blue grass back and began to seed the ground. Using her watersong she sped the process up and instead of taking five thousand seasons for an Aiouqes to reach maturity, she managed it in a season. By the time she passed into the deathsong (**2430 S.G.**) the forest covered 2,000 square klees and she made her younglings promise to carry on. As they never had the watersong they could only look after the forest and make sure the blue grass didn't dominate again. But one gift Yew-e-lea did pass on was the health sense; which could be used to cure any Aiouqes which succumbed to disease or damage.

"The Muala adapted and the Leujan flourished. By the beginning of our age; the cycle of the Neimas, the forest covered two thirds of this continent, on both sides of the Leujan mountain range. But we had to stop any further expansion because of new cities of the dolphs and the migration of the Muala. They made sure the forest stayed on the upper hills and left the lower plains alone.

"But now the forests are dying again not from the grass but from Danetar. My fatherling watched as the forest of the eastern side died back and we have only managed to hold on to the western side because the mountain range blocks half a tay's light. So it survives a while longer." He stopped and wiped the tears which had fallen unbidden as he talked.

"I knew that it would get much worse and when I saw that this side was now being affected, I would have been devastated if it hadn't been for the strange song which held me and I thought it was my own doing, that somehow I had managed to *cure.....them*!"

It was strange how love can also reflect resentment mixed with gratitude all at once. That made his next words harsher than he intended, "But then you know how..." His voice fell silent but the atmosphere between them was heavy as he awaited her reply.

She gestured with her hand and the red inner light of the shelter grew until Del-e-gar could see her face clearly. His heart sank as he took in her expression of misery. Slowly tears of silver, slowly rolled down her cheeks, forming droplets that were held for only a yen, suspended from her chin, then they fell. Silver pearls that splashed upon her knees. It was like time had slowed down so he would see the grief he had wrought upon her soul. Her eyes continued to stare at him, her lips slightly apart, as if the words she wanted to speak were frozen.

His heart seemed to twist inside; he so much wanted to take back his words. "I'm so *sorry.. I, didn't mean..*" he weakly cried.

She saved him from any more by holding up her hand and replying, "*Oh! Del-e-gar...* I only wanted to help you.. My song was a gift. I am sorry if it took more away from you than it gave...." She bowed her head and brought both hands up to her face and cried.

Great sobs of pain echoed around the chamber and Del-e-gar stared frozen not believing what he had wrought.

Her next words shook him. "I have done wrong. *I must leave you...*" She raised her head and her tear stained face made him lurch forward to hold her.

"No.. *Don't-"* he cried. But as his hands touched her the air shimmered and he fell forwards through empty air.

It couldn't be true..! he cried out in pain. His fingers clutched the empty air where she had sat. She couldn't go, was all he could think, but the shelter was now empty of her presence. His mind refused to believe his eyes. She had been sitting in front of him only yens ago. She couldn't just vanish.

"No! NO! NO.!!" he shouted and like a blind creature he scrambled around the shelter, hoping to find her. He searched and searched while he cried and ranted his pain into the confines of the shelter. Maybe she was outside waiting for him. All this and more cut through his mind and he clambered out of the shelter and stumbled into the dark. Now he was blind as the night gave no light to see by. But he tried and wildly ran and ran through the forest. Despair clutched his heart as he frequently knocked into trees, trying to find some trace of her.

He didn't know how long he searched, but he must have fallen once too often because he awoke, with the full light of tay shining upon him. His mind was muggy and as he sat up he looked down and saw dried blood caking his chest and arms. Dirt and bits of leaves covered the rest of him. He felt battered and bruised, inside as well as out. All he could think of was her, his beautiful lea. What had he done?!

His pain turned to anger and he screamed his sorrow, "*Come back to me! Please, I need you!!*" But no answer came, only the wind blew, empty and harsh against his face. He stumbled to his dees. Pain wracked his face as his bones protested. But slowly he made his way back to where he had left the shelter.

The tay passed and Del-e-gar finally returned to the precipice. His heart lurched as a wild thought came to him. Maybe she has changed her mind and returned. But there was no sign of the shelter and the ground where it had been was undisturbed. This tore him apart as it denied the events of the previous tay. *It would mean that maybe it had been a dream after all...*But his heart couldn't bear the thought and he continued with his search.

For seven tays he searched for any sign but the forest remained empty like his heart. Del-e-gar began to talk to himself, going over and over all that had happened. He grew more tired from lack of sleep and hunger. In the end some part of his mind remained lucid enough for him to tell him to go home; *To return another tay.*

For many tays he remained hiding inside his home. He ate when it was needed and sometimes he would go through some of the crystals that he kept at home. The time passed slowly, but he remained empty of any real desire to do anything. He stored her image in a crystal which he carried about his home talking to his memory of her. When he ventured out into the city, he passed other dolphs without seeing. He ignored any help that was offered and spoke to no one. This went on for more tays and by the end of the Jeanth he had withdrawn inside, slowly dying.

It was on a tay of a great storm that blew up from the west that pulled him from his home. The rain lashed the city and giant waves pounded the beaches. For some reason a part of him responded and he unlike other dolphs ventured out and made his way to the shore. The pure savagery tore into him, his body drenched by the rain and the wind seemed to scour him clean. Several times dolphs would appear at openings of their homes and beckon for him to take shelter. *But he just laughed at them, mad with delight.* Maybe it was his health sense which responded and took such joy from the storm. For at least his forest would do well with so much rain. He had never seen so many clouds, which hung like the black wings of the Kerg, taking Danetar's power and sheltering those below.

The wind grew stronger and it howled and roared around the city. Del-e-gar soon came to the beach and watched the waves surge up like a raised claw, then as if they saw their prey, lunge and tear chunks from the shore. By this time he was dancing and singing, allowing the wind to play with him. He twirled and sometimes he flew across the beach.

At times when his deehold was sure he would brace himself and raise his hands high above him and cry out, "*Lea! Lea! Sing your song..*" with a final cry, "*For **ME***!!!" Each time all his pent up grief would surge up, it was like he battled with the very elements to get her back.

He was sure, some time later, it was at the point the storm reached its height that his mind seemed to tear apart. Strange images flowed into the wind and rain, condensing into two forms, one of water and the other a grey stone that mirrored the flow of the wind. Each part fought a great battle for supremacy. The images wore his countenance and they grappled with very different styles. The fluid form tried to sweep the grey rock from its dees. But the other responded by tearing into, wrenching streams of water, breaking the fluid form of Del-e-gar apart. To and fro they fought. Sometimes one would seem to triumph but the other would find its way and tear back. An arm, a leg would disappear, then reappear. A mad dance that played out on the backdrop of an angry sky.

He felt it when the storm began to abate and his mind snapped back, tearing the image out of the sky. A flood of watery sense fell into him and he knew who had won. A brilliant light flashed into being, infusing him with a coolness that swept him up and brought him to himself. His mind settled as the wind died and only a gentle patter of rain was felt upon his body. When he finally looked around, his eyes saw clearly and a calmness replaced the pain that had dwelled for so long inside his heart and mind. He blinked away the rain and slowly a smile spread upon his face as he looked at the torn and battered beach. A lone Kerg cried out and flew across to dive into the sea. It reappeared with a large fish, that he suspected was a juicy Wunlaka, and flew high into the clearing sky.

He turned about and walked straight into her. His face buried itself into her chest, *purely on impact you understand!* He righted himself and thinking it was another dolph he had accidentally walked into, he exclaimed, "Oh *Sorry..*"

He stepped back and raised his eyes, but the green shimmer of her skin slowed his advance. He almost closed his eyes in fear that he was hallucinating again. But as his gaze slowly moved up, his heart took on a faster beat. His face flushed and his mind went into convulsions.

Could it really be?! When his eyes alighted upon her smiling face he sighed a sigh of relief that the whole of Delikadove must have heard, and he nearly fainted with the shock. But he steadied himself and with a cry of joy he leapt upon her. They fell backwards, landing on a handy dune of wet orange sand.

He had her just where he wanted her and his first word was, "*You!*" He didn't give her a chance to respond. He just followed it up with as many kisses as he could plant on her face and lips.

She laughed gaily at his antics but did not resist. It filled him with so much emotion that he laughed, then cried in her arms. They lay holding each other, allowing their love to reform.

She broke the silence and whispered, "*I heard you, and your water-time brought me back...*"

It was so good to hear her voice that he asked, "Will you sing for me once more..?" He waited, then it began, slowly at first and it filled his newly stabilised water-time and opened his heart. She sang and wrapped herself around him and as he clung to her soft and warm body the energy of her song took hold and grew in power. A green light sparkled into life and flowed about them. For him it seemed that they lifted from the sand and flew up into the sky, passing into a star filled black night. It filled him and great bouts of red flame bathed and caressed him. A lake of warm water flowed and ran with his heart as they passed swirling fountains of energy. The medley was sweet and after some time he felt the power slowly unwind. The crunch of leaves as their bodies rolled among the trees of his forest made him laugh and she joined his laughter with the last vestiges of her song.

When they came to a rest and Del-e-gar disentangled himself from her embrace he found they were back inside the welcoming heart of the shelter. But with one difference; a large crystal, that glowed with a bright flame burned in the centre.

He looked back at her and his water-time spoke under his own volition and it was a question he had to ask, *My beloved, what is your name?!*

He grinned at her and she grinned back, delight at his usage apparent upon her face.

She flowed into him and answered, *At last you ask the right question-* she teased then pronounced, *My dear Del-e-gar.. My name is Tan-e-lea.*

He roared his delight and cried, "Tan-e-lea! Tan-e-lea!"

She laughed and replied, "Yes that's what I said!"

They dissolved into a fit of laughter which shook the shelter and for the first time in his life Del-e-gar heard the Shakeilar inside his water-time, *Welcome...Dolph....You are much welcome here..*

His happiness at his first communication must have been infectious because Tan-e-lea pulled him down upon her and she giggled, "*I Welcome you to the power of water-time....*"

The following tays were glorious for them both as they shared their time among the forest. Together they helped stave off the ruinous effects of Danetar. Her care for the creatures and the Aiouqes delighted him and they spent many evenings walking and sharing ideas for the preservation of Duorsilear. She promised him that she would use her power of song to ensure it would not die away. He didn't question how she would accomplish this as his faith in her was complete. They made the shelter their home and the Shakeilar responded by growing in size and weaving itself around the group of trees near the precipice, a comfortable home that lit the evening sky with its red glow. Del-e-gar moved his crystals from their place in the heart of the forest and brought them to their home. She encouraged him to store the information that they contained into what he came to name: The Fire Crystal, imbedded on the dais that dominated the main room. Here they frequently ate their meals or played together in the pool that circled around it.

He never asked her where she or the crystal that carried the flame came from. His water-time did not want to be disturbed by the answers he might receive. That is the conclusion he came to in time but there simply was no desire to know. But not all was in the dark for she told him tales of the dolphs of many different times. His favourite was the tale of Xer-e-gar, who established the first sanctuary to Edenlea in the old time, during the cycle of Delikadove, where the name for their world was taken in the seasons that passed during those tays of firm establishment, on what she called; Un-water, a name he had not heard of before but he was to use it frequently in the seasons that followed.

Xer-e-gar's passionate belief that once more the Ddlphs would need the knowledge of their dolphin ancestors made him and his followers create a sanctuary in all of the main cities. Del-e-gar through Tan-e-lea's instruction began to understand Mel-e-gar's mission and the wisdom that the ancient Xer-e-gar had shown, no matter how much he had once loathed to believe that they should abandon their dolph ways to re-enter that watery domain. But his old self was now a passing memory and he knew that if they were to survive on Delikadove, it was the only way.

At times when they would talk on a still night, watching the stars in the sky outside their home, he sometimes saw a look of ancient times in her features. Her eyes would shine so bright as she told story after story that he felt she could have come from those times. But if that was true then her seasons were beyond count. His water-time always dismissed this fantasy and when he asked her how old she was, she would laugh gaily and say, "Del-e-gar, I am but an Elder of small seasons." It was never specific and in the end it was another part that was quickly confined to the depth of his water-time.

Their love grew and on a happy tay she announced that she would give birth to his first youngling. He was so excited that he danced through the forest announcing to all the creatures that he was to become a fatherling. His old friend the Cerser who would often visit, flew down from her perch to coo her delight for Del-e-gar. When he asked Tan-e-lea whether she would go to the city to get the help of a nursery motherling she would shake her head and refuse. For she was more than happy to give birth in the pool of their home. Which he quickly made sure was deep enough for her needs.

The Jeanths passed and her belly grew. He would often spend time talking to it, out of water as well as in. Tan-e-lea spent more and more time as a dolphin in the pool, getting herself ready for the first contractions. She told him all he would have to do to help. If she was too weak he would have to manoeuvre their youngling in position to suckle. Not that he had heard that was normally a problem, but she was concerned that he knew what was to come. So he learned at her side. Amidst talk of the birth she would continue with her stories and they would laugh and sing many times.

Finally the tay came. He had been out checking on some damage to a small group of trees near a crevasse three klees from their home when he received her call in his water-time. He stopped his healing and ran all the way. He enjoyed the ability to communicate while they were apart and this was a time when he knew how useful it was. An amazing thing this water-time. The wind was but a breeze that tay and Danetar didn't feel so harsh. The trees looked lush and healthy as the season was coming to its close. The wanderers of the sky that had migrated to the southern continent to escape the harshness of the long summer were returning to enjoy the cooler temperature of the short winter. This only lasted for three jeanths and they made the best of it for that short time. They were beginning their own preparations to nest and raise young. Their many calls filled the air and brought a welling up of happiness in Del-e-gar as he ran.

He almost dived through the opening which had quickly parted to allow him entry but he stopped short of the pool. The light inside the shelter was a gentle hue of green and red which he found instantly soothing. The *flame* in the crystal seemed brighter and it burned, giving its radiance that shimmered upon the water. He saw Tan-e-lea doing a slow turn. Her beak raised from the water gave a small cry. He dived in, his body sparkling brightly, adding its light, transforming him to the far sleeker dolphin form. He slid smoothly beneath the surface and swam to her side. He enjoyed seeing her underwater. It was amazing how large she was, even more so as she was heavy with youngling. He swam underneath her and turned himself so his beak was against hers and opened his water-time.

He encouraged her with small sounds and soothed the pain as each contraction rippled down her body, pushing the youngling further down. He eased himself down, allowing his flippers to feel each push as it came. Her water-time was full of images that mirrored what he saw as he came to the opening where he could see the first sign of their youngling. This went on for some time. Then suddenly she gave one last push and the youngling was free from her womb. Del-e-gar quickly guided their daughterling to take her first breath, then returned her to her motherling's nipple to suck. It was a bit of an illusion though as their daughterling was vibrant and strong. *After her first breath she needed no encouragement or help from Del-e-gar to feed!*

They had decided on her name after the fourth jeanth when they both knew it was going to be a lea. Her name was Ose-e-lea and she was a fine dolphin of five dees in length. Del-e-gar cried his delight into Tan-e-lea's water-time, *She is beautiful and takes after you...*

Thank you Del-e-gar.. You will make a fine fatherling.. Her sound was weak and he saw how tired she was. He sent energy to her to help and then sounded in delight, *We are parentlings!* They shared their joy and the fledging Ose-e-lea sent her own wave of satisfied water-time into theirs.

The three swam slowly around the pool, allowing Tan-e-lea and their youngling to gain energy to recover. Del-e-gar was so full of his happiness that if it hadn't been for the strong wave of sadness flowing from Tan-e-lea, his happiness would have been complete. He almost cried out as she beckoned for him to come and swim closer to her side. He had been keeping his eye on Ose-e-lea by swimming a little below her and he quickly responded and swam and joined his beak with hers. He moved so he could hold her with his flippers to her side, making sure he didn't disturb their youngling from feeding.

Tan-e-lea's sounds made his blood run cold... *I am sorry Del-e-gar but I must leave you now...*

He wasn't sure he had heard her correctly and he urgently sounded, *Tan-e-lea, what do you mean...? You can't leave me now!*

The panic was rising and his water-time returned him to that awful tay earlier that season when she had disappeared, seemingly never to return. Her sorrow filled him and she gently sounded, *I must leave.. I cannot stay in this place any longer.*

His water-time cried in pain and all he could manage was, *Why..?*

She wrapped his water-time with hers and he started to feel something slip away. Her sounds were becoming weaker, crying her own loss to him, *I wish there was another way, but my only love, you must leave this place. Take our daughterling to the nursery motherling they call Que-e-lea, of the city of Yengile on the northern continent. She will find a motherling with milk to nurse our daughterling.*

She stopped and he felt her send wave after wave of love, which slowly quietened his sorrow, enough so he would listen and remember all her sounds. Del-e-gar felt his heart grow numb and he began to see that this was indeed the time he secretly feared. He felt her flippers caress him and he made the decision to make the most of each emotion she made him feel, to enjoy her love and leave the mourning for a later time.

He was still subdued but he made a valiant effort to sound cheerful. *Tan-e-lea, I love you more than my own life but I will do as you ask. Tell me what else I must do.*

Her waters showed him how grateful she was for his sounds and she told him the rest, *I can only send you as far as Colisee. There you must send a message in your water-time.. To your old friend Jey-e-gar and -*

He still lives!? exclaimed Del-e-gar, *How can you know this??*

Just know that he does and be happy. When you meet him he will find a way for you to get to Yengile.

He found himself amazed once more by her knowledge and then something struck him and he exclaimed, *We must complete the birthing ritual!* His water-time showed his demand; the image of them throwing Ose-e-lea out of the pool to land on her dees to make sure she transformed into a dolph. The image she sent brought more sadness for Del-e-gar but it also had pleasure for their daughterling interwoven, creating a mixed blessing for him.

Her sounds confirmed it. *That is the old way. Our daughterling is the first to be a true youngling of Edenlea. She cannot change to dolph form and her younglings shall be the same. You must help her to adapt and make use of all that I have taught you and go and join Mel-e-gar.*

Now if a dolph had suggested that a season ago he would have laughed and fled the opposite way. But it showed the measure of change in him when he calmly accepted her council and replied, *You know I will do all I can for Ose-e-lea..*

Her water-time sounded her gladness and then he felt her begin to fade. It was like she was becoming a shadow in the water. A wispy green light flowed over her and the feeling of her body against his flippers began to withdraw. The sadness rose up and he tried to hang on but it didn't help.

In desperation he cried, *Tan-e-lea, I love you! Can there be one more song!?* His heart ached to dance among the trees once more and savour her embrace and her touch as they had on many occasions joined the fires of their love to be as one.

A single tear fell and splashed into his water-time. It created a series of ripples that sounded her final words, *My last gift for you Del-e-gar. Be true and remember I will always be in your heart if you need me....I love you...*

At the instant she disappeared from the water he and Ose-e-lea also vanished from the pool. The energy played her final song and it gave Del-e-gar a gift that he would hold close to him for the rest of his tays. He had that dance through the forest with Tan-e-lea and they glowed with green light as they twirled and laughed their way. She gave herself and they joined and loved each other. The energy crackled and roared, sending sparks, that transformed to green wanderers of the sky. Which flew so high that they joined the stars and shone their light upon the two dolphs who cried their love for each other.

Slowly the energy dissipated whilst Del-e-gar said his goodbye and as he kissed her sparkling form- he was torn away to splash into a wild purple sea. He could feel the residue of their dance die and he was left with the stormy waters off Colisee. He found his young daughterling whose water-time cried to be fed. He helped her to push her young beak above the tossing waves, holding her so she would not slip away. A fierce wind tore at the sea and Del-e-gar cried out, "*Goodbye Tan-e-lea!*"

He turned himself and headed for the shore. When he was within a klee he opened his water-time and sent it to the city, searching for a mind that he hoped was there. He saw the nine domes that were the mark of Colisee and dived through. It didn't take long. Soon he began to feel the edges of a water-time that was filled with the images of the Muala. His delight expounded from him and he made contact; *Jey-e-gar! Come quickly...*

The returning sound was surprised. *Del-e-gar! Is that really you?*

Yes. I need your help.. He showed his daughterling within his water-time and told Jey-e-gar that his mate had died, leaving Ose-e-lea without milk. *Please hurry!* Then he broke contact and waited in the turbulent sea.

It was strange because when he told Jey-e-gar that his mate had died, it was true for him, because he knew he would never see her again and his water-time had made the decision to keep the rest secret. Some things don't change and Del-e-gar had no desire to share the memory of Tan-e-lea, not even with his daughterling. All she would ever know was that her motherling was the most beautiful dolphin in all of Delikadove and that she had passed into the deathsong soon after giving birth to her. In time she would grow to accept her fatherling's reluctance to share sounds on the matter.

He didn't have to wait long. Jey-e-gar soon joined them and Del-e-gar warmly greeted his old friend. Within yens of his arrival he told Del-e-gar to make sure that Ose-e-lea stayed close. The reason was clear when the water bubbled with energy and he felt a powerful presence flood his water-time. The sound of Mel-e-gar joined him and he had just enough chance to take a last look at the continent that had been his home, before he felt the pull of the watersong, taking him to meet his destiny. Del-e-gar's last water-time before he materialised on the other side of Delikadove was of his forest. *Would he ever again see the trees that he had cared for and the place where he met a dolph that had stolen his heart....?*

* * *

The images of her fatherling and her youngling self fragmented and slowly slipped away. She felt tired and sad that she had not known her motherling and that the un-truth that her fatherling had chosen to tell for so long had stopped her from knowing the truth. But as she searched her heart she could not fault him as he did what he believed to be the best thing.

It was not until Que-e-lea had returned from the isle of un-water did he suspect that his Tan-e-lea and the grandling of Mel-e-gar were one and the same. How that may be so was something he and Ose-e-lea had discussed after he had told her about her motherling but neither could come up with an answer. All they knew and felt was that somehow it was so. The final irony for Ose-e-lea and something which her waters still found incredible was that it had been her fatherling's suggestion that two seasons before, Car-e-lea had named her new-born daughterling Tan-e-lea *in remembrance of his beloved mate!*

* * *

SENTINEL

5 S.E.

The flames filled the cavern with an orange and red light, which held the images of Del-e-gar, Ose-e-lea and Jey-e-gar being taken by Mel-e-gar's watersong. The last image of their safe arrival to the city of Yengile flickered once, then melted away. Slowly the flames responded to the emptiness by withdrawing into the crystals, causing the cavern to bring forth its natural blue light. *The* Rock remained still; gazing with sad eyes into the depth of the crystals. By using their power *it* had joined with Ose-e-lea's water-time to bring forth the images that the old knowledge had confirmed that Tan-e-lea was becoming the link which tied the old with the new.

It turned from the crystal array, sliding along the floor to the blue curtain of energy and passing through to the cavern which held the deep lagoon of water which the Sentinel had created for Tan-e-lea. The light from the outer cavern sparkled, dancing a private tune upon the otherwise undisturbed surface. Even *the* Rock was moved by the simple beauty that had an innate aura which mirrored *its* own calm acceptance of the fate which was yet to befall.

The Rock slid around the edge and looked upon *its* own reflection; *its* grey rocky features broke the spell which had held true for those few short yens. *Its* own reality shimmered back, giving *it* the image which had greeted Mel-e-gar all those seasons ago in the Sanctuary. So much had passed since those dark and deep water-times, but it was the future that now revealed a beckoning hand to *the* Rock. The urge to be about *its* new business called out, making *its* next task a hard one to fulfil but it had to be done before *it* could continue.

The image reflected in the water began to change. *The* Rock began to shrink in size, changing *its* mass. Then the surface began to flow as liquid as the lagoon, changing shape, creating, binding the molecules of *its* form into a round sphere. *It* watched the energy grow around itself. Sparks flew in all directions, some landing on *its* surface, bleeding into, making rivers of blue run over itself. Instead of the rather dull surface of rock *it* now shimmered with a sheen of blue and silver light which a dolph would recognise as the natural state for Shakeilar.

It now had the form which *it* held once before when *it* had sent one of *its* own younglings to the world of Delikadove. In fact they were almost identical, except *it* was of far greater size than Serliker had been. The image of *its* youngling entered *its* water-time. *It* had not seen Serliker since that tay on the world, which the inhabitants called Greathon IV in the constellation of Orion, when *it* had sent *its* youngling to Delikadove to spawn. *How things had changed.*

Serliker had called *it* the *Sentinel* but in the time that came after, the dolphs had named it *the Rock.* A difference which *it* had come to earn a great deal of respect for. The simplicity had made any need for grand titles obsolete. *Indeed things had certainly changed....*

In the beginning it had created the crystals that were embedded in the altar of Shakeilar taken from its own mass. For many seasons it had served well as a suitable front to speak with two voices and two identities. It had used the diversity of its creation with good effect when meeting with Mel-e-gar, showing him the task which he would follow throughout his life. But as all things with the passing of the seasons it had become more separated, evolving into something else. The advent of Tan-e-lea had triggered the final split, giving the flames new life. That was what it had meant by the fact that they were now truly eternal. For the part which had been keeping the crystal alive had been torn from itself, giving the identity of the Sentinel to the flames. It absorbed most of the knowledge of Delikadove and much that was beyond even that world. Which now left the Rock free from the responsibility of being, "The Sentinel." The Crystals would perform that role for the galaxy.

The Rock gave an audible sigh when the transformation was complete and *it* took time to enjoy being back in *its* original form. *It* hovered a few dees above the ground taking a last look at *its* refection then flew through the blue curtain absorbing the energy which had held the barrier in place. *The* Rock passed over the crystals, holding *itself* to one side. The Cavern looked much larger now that the barrier was down and *it* gave a satisfied sigh. It was almost time and *the* Rock waited patiently for the final task to commence, that would complete the work which had spanned two worlds.

The Rock had only a short time to wait and *it* felt the presence before *he* materialised within the cavern. The arrival of an old friend would be a welcoming way to end *its* time in this place.

The familiar silver sparkle of energy appeared a few dees away from the crystals, which responded by creating a column of flame reaching for the roof of the cavern. *The* Rock looked on with amusement as the Sentinel readied itself. It took only yens for Mel-e-gar to appear. He looked tired as his eyes surveyed the scene before him. *The* Rock waited for him to finish and then *it* said, "Welcome Mel-e-gar, we have awaited your arrival."

Mel-e-gar looked up at the spinning sphere and took a step back in surprise and exclaimed, "Serliker! Is that you?" His water-time was thrown into confusion as the last thing he had expected was to see Serliker.

"No Mel-e-gar, it is I, the one you have known as *The Rock* who greets you here."

"But *You*-"

"I know, this is what I was and now I am once more," interrupted *the* Rock. Then with much amusement in *its* voice *it* said, "You have much to learn *young* dolph!"

Mel-e-gar could feel the warmth that those familiar words conveyed and he smiled in response. He walked over to the crystal array and watched the flames dancing their way up to the ceiling.

He nodded his head and using his hand to gesture at the crystals he said, "I see that Que-e-lea's recall of events was accurate as far as this is concerned. But I feel that it is much stronger than before."

The Rock was impressed by Mel-e-gar's evaluation and making sure that *its* words could be felt as well as heard, *it* replied, "This my friend is *The Sentinel...*" Before Mel-e-gar could voice his obvious surprise at that, *the* Rock said it for him. "Yes, I know what Serliker told you all that time ago and at that time it was correct but things have changed.

Now the part which I once was is now alive inside those crystals, independent from myself to act in any way *it* sees fit."

That did surprise Mel-e-gar as he had always believed that whatever the crystals were, they were not part of *the* Rock. In fact he had not fully understood the workings but he had felt that *the* Rock used the Crystals for *its* own purpose, something separate and not really related. But *the* Rock's words had changed that perception and within his waters he felt the truth that not only himself but those who had come after, like Ser-e-gar and Car-e-lea had been talking to *the* Rock and not some unfathomable form which they all believed to have resided inside the Crystals! *So his previous understanding was wrong for the past but not so for the future?* Mel-e-gar felt the seasons heavy upon him as he tried to make sense of it in relation to all that had gone before.

The Rock felt his confused waters and caused the floor to create a place for him to sit upon and gave him food to eat while *it* answered Mel-e-gar's questions. Which were many. But the question he needed answering the most soon came.

"Mel-e-gar, the fate of Tan-e-lea as I told Que-e-lea was correct up to the point where she vanished from the waters of Edenlea but I felt that the rest could only be told to you when you discovered the connection between this time and the past."

For Mel-e-gar the connection was the green light and he realised that Tan-e-lea may have come in contact with the same force that had held Ler-e-lea. That was why he had left the other dolphins in such a hurry. For if that was true then maybe *the* Rock would tell him whether this was so. He felt *the* Rock's presence enter his water-time and like a gateway opening he found himself watching the drama unfold after Tan-e-lea had left Edenlea.

It stared at the empty waters in despair. What could have gone wrong? Did she have such little control that her own song consumed her? *The* Rock shifted *itself* from the water and entered *its* home on the island. When *it* appeared in the cavern the first thing *it* noticed was the flame of the crystals; it was much larger. But the thing which surprised *it* the most was the green tinge to the flames. *The* Rock recognised it as the same light that had appeared briefly when Tan-e-lea disappeared.

"*You*!!" *It* cried in anger and surprise, but even as the accusation left *it*, it didn't make sense. For the flame was part of *itself. How could it be involved? The* Rock calmed *itself* and changed *its* form so that *it* stood on two rocky legs and then created the appropriate appendages, like two hands, resting them on the crystals to take a more direct input into the flame.

It was true that *it* had found in past seasons that *it* was becoming further apart from what was held within those crystalline depths but *it* was still unprepared for the shock *it* received as *its* mind made contact. For instead of the familiar chime of *its* own self, a sound of power flowed through it and a voice which it had created but was now no longer under *the* Rock's control said:

I am. I The Sentinel. I have become your replacement in this place. You no longer Have dominance Here!

The Rock cried out and withdrew contact. *Its* arms and legs disappeared, returning *itself* to the more familiar rocky form.

It couldn't be true. Could it? *Its* mind questioned but there was no doubt that somehow the crystal had absorbed so much knowledge and identity of *the* Rock that *it* had become sentient, once whole now two parts. Then *it* realised how it could have happened. It was so simple. The process of fissionable fusion was used when enough energy was held within the cellular mass of the Shakeilar. The same way once long before, *The* Rock had spawned from *itself* many millions of Shakeilar, each as individual a life form as the original, a fission of mass to a fusion of energy to create a fission of form, so the final result did not deplete the true mass of the progenitor. A process like that would only happen once for the one chosen for the task. But somehow after so long splitting *itself* in two, using two identities *it* had set up the conditions that if held for long enough *it* would ultimately break apart.

The Rock was shaken from *its* waters by a loud clap of thunder that shook the chamber and the light of the flame exploded into the cavern. As it rolled towards *the* Rock, *it* used *its* energy to throw out an energy field to protect *itself.*

For a few yens *it* was bathed in flame but as quickly as it had appeared the flame vanished and then a voice came from the crystal, "Help Me....! Help Me finish it."

The flame was now only a faint glimmer in the heart of the crystals and *the* Rock realised that *it* had used up the store of energy and could not make any more. *It* would die if it wasn't replenished. Not only that but a perpetual cycle would have to be started to keep *it* alive, the same way most life forms could keep their bodies functioning for many seasons until the structure itself broke down. The deathsong as the dolph/ins called it. But the energy of the individual would carry on until it found a new structure to occupy or turn into something else entirely. In this case the crystals were not truly inhabited by a proper life form. The connection was broken when *the* Rock had made contact and the Identity that was being born had taken *the* Rock's other name of Sentinel.

The Rock changed *itself* again and made contact with the crystals. Inside a faint voice called out, *I am. I will Be.. Help her and She Help Me. I need Her song.*

So that was what *it* had been up to. *What have you done with her? Where is Tan-e-lea?!* asked *the* Rock.

The energy seemed weaker but *it* gave a reply. *She lies beyond this cavern. New place.. I create..* An image passed into *the* Rock's water-time and *it* saw the still body of Tan-e-lea. She was half in and half out of the water, part dolphin, part dolph. Stuck halfway.

The Rock parted from the crystals. *It* saw the wall of the cavern shimmer and change to a blue curtain of energy which parted as *it* entered a larger cavern which held a large lagoon of water.

Taking lessons from Serliker I should think, murmured *the* Rock and slid quickly to Tan-e-lea's side. She was unaware of her state and *it* knew that she would need great care to rebuild her.

Making a decision *it* opened *its* water-time and flowed back to the crystals, *It will take many tays for me to change her back if I can.* For a yen there was only silence but then faintly came the reply, *Use the Energy that is green...It is part of her...It s her song. I took it from her so I could help her to recover...Price I want is her to help me....* The voice died away.

The Rock seeing the truth in the sounds searched out the green light. When *it* made contact it was with a tone of pure sound that sounded of rain falling among the trees and of the creatures *it* knew as sky-flyers crying for food. It made *the* Rock cry with relief as *it* felt the power take hold of *it* and an exchange of energy took place.

All that was not of Tan-e-lea's form was held in that green light and she gave much needed energy to help replenish the Sentinel. Then it flowed through *the* Rock's water-time and passed back into Tan-e-lea. For many tays after *the* Rock healed the body of Tan-e-lea and to make sure that it would stabilise, *it* showed her how she could become a dolph as well. For her wish had been that and instead of fighting it *the* Rock created a new form. By the end of it she was far larger than before. Her new body was nearly eighteen dees in length while in dolph form and nearly thirty in dolphin. Using the knowledge of time and worlds gone before *the* Rock and the Sentinel increased her seasons so she would know how to handle and make use of her song to its fullest potential.

The images Mel-e-gar received broke up in his water-time bringing him back to the Cavern. *The* Rock was now hovering a few dees in front of him and he waited for the rest.

"It wasn't long after that Que-e-lea fell down the crevice and I healed her and told her only up to the point when Tan-e-lea had vanished from Edenlea. You must see why I did not tell the rest. For as you have already seen, the younglings of Edenlea cannot return to the land and the desire that Tan-e-lea held could not be released among them. She could not return..."

Mel-e-gar finished the fish and stood up, the mound he had been sitting on automatically disappearing and gave *the* Rock a hard long look before asking, "So where is *she now*?"

"Now the rest was out of my hands, so to speak. The Sentinel received her gift of life energy only after she was made aware that she couldn't return to the seas of Edenlea, not at this place in time. That was when the Sentinel told her that she could use her watersong to travel through time and she could finish our work in other places."

So that was to be the way of it. Somehow and it may have been the many seasons that Mel-e-gar had lived that he could no longer be surprised. His water-time made the connections between the tales of a green light that had appeared throughout stories of Delikadove. He now understood that it had been Tan-e-lea who had saved Ler-e-lea from the Keaverkack. *But it still didn't make sense. What need did the Rock have or the Sentinel for sending her back to Delikadove? What right!?*

His tiredness, the feeling of going on for too long and his grief at losing Tan-e-lea made him angry at *the* Rock and at the Sentinel. A low tone of black began to sound. He took a step towards the Shakeilar.

The Rock for the first time in *its* dealings with dolphs hesitated. The reaction of Mel-e-gar was unexpected. *It* spun backwards several dees. *Its* blue and silver light flashed in response as *it* felt Mel-e-gar raise the tone of his sound. *It* sent a probe but he looked like granite, hard and immovable in expression. His eyes were hooded and black with anger and pain.

No response in water-time, just an increasing wave of sound that *the* Rock wasn't sure *it* could contain. For the first time *the* Rock felt real fear for *its* own safety. Because if it came down to self preservation *it* didn't believe *it* could harm Mel-e-gar to a terminal end. Not just because of what *it* felt for the large dolph but also the future of too many were bound to this remarkable being.

The dark song built new notes and just when *the* Rock feared it was time to allow

Mel-e-gar to explode his wrath, a shimmer of light sprang up, its green vibrant tinge apparent and like a wave frozen in time it blocked Mel-e-gar's wrath as it exploded finally from him. His dark song, his own wave, but black of power instead of impacting and causing harm flowed smoothly into the green light. The cries of anguish from Mel-e-gar as he fell to his knees was the only thing that rocked the cavern echoing around. It was that sense of his grandling that allowed his song to end. The last note dissipated into the green light.

He had never felt so tired or so lost as those that he felt he had failed to save came crushing down, burying him. He had locked a great deal away, from the deathsongs of his parentlings to the deathsongs of an entire world. It was just too much. He had a breaking point after all.

The Rock hid *its* surprise well as Mel-e-gar's song faded and the green light disappeared. *It* moved swiftly forward and with a blue silver shower of light gave soothing sound to Mel-e-gar, "I.. *am*," and *it* nearly choked on the word, "*Sorry*! Forgive me. Sometimes I fail to see the burden others carry. My own sometimes blinds me. Understand that I cared a great deal for Tan-e-lea. I would not do anything that caused her harm."

It could have been that *the* Rock's attempt to sound sympathetic, which didn't really work, that made Mel-e-gar laugh, even though he did feel the truth in *the* Rock's sound for *its* feelings for Tan-e-lea.

The sound of laughter was so unexpected that *the* Rock suddenly became unstable in the air. With his usual deftness Mel-e-gar's hand shot out and saved *the* Rock from plummeting to the floor.

"You really are *something*," chuckled Mel-e-gar and climbed back to his dees while keeping a tight grip on *the* Rock.

"Let me *go*!" *it* cried indignantly. "Let me go *now*!!"

Mel-e-gar laughed again and opened his hand. *The* Rock didn't waste any time to fly quickly away and flashed an angry flash of blue and silver.

"Now don't you start," Mel-e-gar said good-naturedly. "One of us indulging ourselves is quite enough I believe." He looked away from *the* Rock and gave a sigh and added, "*I am sorry too*. It's unlike me to lash out like that." Then he couldn't help but smile again as he said, "You can really move when you want to, but I think you shouldn't practice any more complicated manoeuvres than up or down if I were you!"

That left *the* Rock speechless as *it* only managed a strangled sort of cry. It didn't last long as *it* finally managed to say, "I would have you know young Mel-e-gar that I..." Then *it* stopped, registered the fact he was teasing and said, "*Oh!*"

"It's all right Rock and it seems we should give thanks to a particularly fine dolph who managed to dissipate the force of my angry song. I don't like to imagine what might have happened if she hadn't intervened."

A presence that had stayed silent all this time declared, She told that she would leave something behind. She know that you hold great burdens Mel-e-gar. She understands your grief. You forget that time has given her own waters that pain. And that was the only comment the Sentinel would make. *It* stayed silent for the rest of Mel-e-gar's time in the cavern.

For a yen Mel-e-gar had hoped that he would see Tan-e-lea but maybe it would be enough that something of her had been there. *He did feel lighter but he knew that he should let the Rock finish and how could he blame them? They like he and now Tan-e-lea have their own problems and responsibilities that will always mean not always having the time or energy to give soothing words to help make the outcomes any easier to swallow. Sometimes the fish were just too big!*

The Rock having regained *its* equilibrium agreed and finished *its* explanation. That showed clearly that *the* Rock didn't instantly know everything.

"I had long forgotten those tales myself but the Sentinel had not. All I know is that *it* saw this and made the link when I brought Tan-e-lea back after I had first found her. *It* saw the truth and realised that not only for *itself* but also for *you* and the very existence of Edenlea was dependent on her travelling back through time and space to complete those tasks. A paradox had been created and she agreed when the Sentinel showed her on each occasion what she would have to fulfill. So I only know that she has completed and is completing each part that has helped you in particular to come to this point."

Mel-e-gar could only stare in wonder at *the* Rock and the heavy pall of grief lifted from Mel-e-gar's heart and with some amusement he gave his reply, "So she beat me after all!"

He laughed and laughed his joy with *the* Rock. After the laughter had died away Mel-e-gar was left to consider what he would do next. His water-time was filled with the remembrance of Tan-e-lea and over the next few tays, he and *the* Rock shared past times. Mel-e-gar soon understood how fully *the* Rock had been touched by Tan-e-lea, how *it* had shared *it's* loneliness with her and she had swept it away. *The* Rock had loved her as much as *it* was able, a new feeling and one that *it* would hold onto for all eternity.

Almost a veul later *the* Rock told Mel-e-gar that it was now ready to leave and when questioned by him, all it said was, "I have other stars to see and other planets to explore."

"I won't see you again, will I?" asked Mel-e-gar.

"No, it's time we parted. Go back to your family and live the rest of your life in *peace*.....and Mel-e-gar, you did have every right to feel angry."

Mel-e-gar bowed his head with thanks and respect.

The Rock launched *itself* straight up. The shiny sphere passed through the ceiling of the cavern with no more resistance than if the very mountain was made of air. A clean cut which made Mel-e-gar stand and look up the shaft which broke into the sky, which he saw was filled with stars and for a yen a flash of light streaked across, then was no more.

The cavern seemed empty and he turned to the Sentinel and said, "I must go back. Keep Tan-e-lea safe from harm for us all......" The flame of the crystal flared briefly for a yen in response but declined to sound. Mel-e-gar took it as an assurance and moved away from the crystal to walk into the cavern.

He stood silent for a few yens and remembered that Tan-e-lea was having all her inquisitive questions answered. "*Such a beautiful, sweet youngling*," he whispered. Then he began to sing. A song which held the cavern in fresh sparkling light and even the waters of the Sentinel were in awe as he sang a melody that told of the innocence of a dolphin called Tan-e-lea. Then as the energy built up, his form sparkling with renewed vigour, he vanished from the cavern.

7340 S.N.

A corona of green fire wrapped her in a protective cloak against the harsh wind which blew incessantly across the scorched plain below the Frelegar mountains. She stood looking out to sea, waiting for a sign that they still lived in the dark waters. She had walked among the dead cities of the dolphs, now long abandoned after the winds of fire had burnt the life from the Shakeilar and many of the dolphs that had lived long seasons on the southern half of the Continent. On the other side of the mountain range the City of Desilata was now also long abandoned, the place where her Grand-elder, Mel-e-gar had ventured from, many seasons before and found a way to rid the seas of Delikadove of the Keaverkack and where his friend Ler-e-lea had lain, waiting for him to return. But now all that was a distant water-time for she had ventured further along the stream of time to what would have been known if any had still lived as ***7340 S.N.****, only seventy-one seasons since Mel-e-gar had rescued those few dolphs that had survived the last Great Deathsong.*

Tan-e-lea walked down to the shore and started to walk over the hot sand. Without her watersong she would have died instantly as the oxygen of the planet was being sucked from the surface. Only in what was left of the seas could life possibly still survive. But she knew even that was short. The Sentinel had sent her to witness the final death throes of Delikadove and to rescue if they still lived, the Selahw. A remote possibility she knew but she wanted to try as she owed her Grand-elder that much. She had her own past water-times of the grandness of the Selahw and she knew why Mel-e-gar fell in love with one. She knew that Cual-e-lay was long gone but there must be some who had survived. She increased the protective energy as the temperature increased. The very seas were boiling. Great banks of steam rose up to the red sky. If it hadn't been for her use of sound she would not have been able to see anything at all.

Her trek took her westward and soon she could see the Island of Tethilay. It was now no more than a circular ring of red barren rock that seemed to bleed into the purple waters. It tore at her to see a place that had once born the weight of the last city that had been sanctuary for those dolphs that had fled into exile from the death and disease that had taken so many. It had risen in the shadow of the mountain that once seemed friend which became its slayer when the fire rain had burst forth to tear down the jewelled creation. She blinked back the tears that threatened and sang a low note and instantly she transported herself to what remained of the island.

For a few yens she had to scramble over the slippery rocks to find her balance. When she was firmly wedged between two large rocks, her legs dangling near the hot waters, she turned her sound to explore the depths. If they were not there then no creature, dolphin or otherwise would ever see their like again. Her water-time became desperate as she searched, changing position on the treacherous rocks to change her view. The purple waters were empty of even the smallest vestige of life. All her water-time could say was, *How could anything survive this?!*

The clars passed and still there was no sign. The tay was coming to an end, not that there was much difference as Danetar was now so large that its light bathed the entire surface. It was a giant orb of red light of which only half could be seen, blocking any real sky out with its fury.

She was about to give up when she spied a strange anomaly in the water. An area which covered about forty klees of where in ancient times would have been the coldest area of a planet; the southern pole. Her excitement rose as she realized that somehow it was cold enough to support life. Using the fullest range of her sound she explored the area, and indeed there was a great deal of life. As she scanned across the range she tuned herself to see with almost normal vision and she gasped with surprise, giggling in delight as she saw the protective walls that were transparent to her deep sight but visible when she tuned herself down. A huge bubble of Shakeilar enclosed the area. It was anchored to the sea floor by great lengths of twisted arms of the same substance and as she marvelled at the design a sound broke through and exclaimed, *Do you mind!*

Tan-e-lea cried with delight, recognising the sound of Mel-e-gar's old friend, whom she had met briefly once before. *Ahh! Serliker! You old fraud, it had to be you!*

Their water-times joined and each took delight in each other. She quickly shared with it her purpose and the instructions of the Sentinel.

You have arrived just in time my young dolph for the sea's heat is starting to fracture my surface. My charges would soon have entered the deathsong if you hadn't turned up.

We had better be quick then, replied Tan-e-lea. She quickly scanned the enclosure and saw nearly thirty Selahw swimming peacefully inside the bubble. Serliker had created much the same artificial enclosure as *it* had done before, below the Arkelclared Desert, but on a smaller scale. *Its* surface was indeed marked by small cracks which would have soon torn *it* apart, spilling the defenceless creatures into an instant death of the boiling sea.

First she transported herself inside the enclosure, changing her form to dolphin as she did so. Then when she was satisfied that she could enclose them with her song she began. The power was great. Energy of green fire blazed into life, wrapping itself round Serliker, who managed to keep *its* form as the song infused into *its* substance. The melody grew stronger and with a great cry they vanished from the sea, taking the last survivors of a dead world to the safety of a new world and a new time.

The transition took only yens but Serliker asked Tan-e-lea to pause so *it* and the Selahw could look from the vantage point of outer space at Delikadove. She slowed down the passing into the time stream so they could watch the death throes. Danetar had already swallowed the inner planets and it finally reached out and embraced Delikadove. The red tentacles of fire licked the surface, taking the last of the waters and the atmosphere. Their world seemed to shudder once as the tremendous forces inside the core burst forth cracking it open like a fallen Kerg egg, spilling rivers of red fire that sent chunks of flaming rock spinning into space. As Danetar withdrew, a few tentacles of fire remained taking a few last licks which pulled the planet apart giving birth to a ring of stone that would in later times be known as an asteroid belt.

She watched the spectacle as hot tears gave vent to her grief for the fate of Delikadove. She sounded her goodbye. She was soon joined by Serliker and the Selahw who sang a song of the last times, that had spanned for more than three hundred million seasons for the Dolph/ins and the much younger times of the Selahw.

As the last note died away she continued with the transition of her song and in a few perceived yens of time they were hanging over a new world. The orb of Serliker shared the orbit with a single moon. The sight of the blue watery globe suspended in the blackness of space took their breath away. Even Tan-e-lea who had seen it from this vantage point many times before shared with them their delight at seeing such beauty. In a real sense they had moved from the old to the new in an instant. It was only Tan-e-lea's suspension of the laws of time that allowed them to witness the death throes of Delikadove and their arrival at a new world. She broke the awed silence by declaring, *Welcome To Edenlea, our new home...*

* * *

71 S.E. (cycle of Edenlea)

He swam with strong strokes, laughing with his Grand-elder as they explored an area of Edenlea which was new to the dolphins. The light of Solarn was high in the sky, giving its gentle warmth to those below. They had travelled for many tays, going round the southern tip of the great western land mass of un-water. His Grand-elder was named Cas-e-lea and she wore her advancing seasons well. She looked fondly at Per-e-gar and nudged him with her flipper as they entered the new waters. She had explored a great deal of Edenlea and when she had reached her sixty sixth season she had promised the youngest of her grandlings that she would take him with her on her next venture. Per-e-gar had been thrilled and now she watched his eager beak take in all their surroundings, gasping at a sea which had no land in sight as they looked westward. She marvelled that he had managed to keep pace and was still undaunted after travelling for four jeanths.

Now that they had arrived she started to make a water map in her water-time of the best currents and most importantly of the best fish. It made her feel what her Grand-elder must have felt those long seasons ago when as the Legend goes: "*The Great Mel-e-gar brought them to safety on his mighty back and placed them in the warm embrace of Edenlea...*"

It still gave her a thrill that she was the youngling of his only sonling Ser-e-gar, who passed into deathsong some ten seasons ago. He had lived only a few jeanths after her motherling. She felt that he had no wish to continue beyond her time. Cas-e-lea watched as Per-e-gar played among a shoal of fish while those past water-times played inside her. She was the last of Mel-e-gar's Grandlings. Her brotherlings and sisterlings had passed on in the intervening seasons and she took solace in her grandling, who had the same playfulness and eagerness for exploring new places as she. A kindred water-time. He was only seven seasons young but he had proved he was a sturdy youngling on this trip.

Cas-e-lea flipped onto her back and floated on the surface, gazing at the clouds, dozing in the afternoon light. Suddenly a loud call of alarm broke her slumber and she flipped over and spying Per-e-gar some distance away swam towards him. He called not in alarm but in amazement and using both beak and flipper pointed towards the northern horizon. She followed his line of sight and she too was taken by surprise. For there suspended only for a yen hung a great silver, blue, and grey orb that shone with flecks of yellow light in the sky. As they watched open beaked it fell from the sky and a crack of thunder broke the silence of the afternoon as the orb plunged towards the sea. They cried in surprise as the water was hardly broken as it seemed to melt below the waves. She turned to Per-e-gar who had a thousand questions and exclaimed, "Now what in all of *Edenlea* was that?!!"

All they could do was to stare at the distant horizon and wonder....

* * *

She had chosen a part of Edenlea that was yet un-travelled by the dolphins, an Ocean that was the largest expanse of Edenlea on the other side of the Western continent. They passed swiftly through the centre of this sea and came to a stop several hundred dees below the surface. The green fire of her song died away and she sounded for Serliker to open the orb. She watched as *it* slowly unfolded the upper part which was nearest to the surface, while letting the pressure equalise with the outside.

The Selahw cried their joy and broke from the confines of the orb and quickly broke through the surface of Edenlea. Tan-e-lea waited for Serliker to contract *its* mass and when *it* had returned to *its* normal shape of a blue orb, she scooped *it* up in her beak and joined the great creatures in their raptures of delight at being free once more. Their great flukes slapped the surface sending showers of water into the air.

A Selahw named Reul-e-gla, broke from the rest and came to her and raised his flukes in a salute, sounding, *We have much to thank you for Tan-e-lea and you, Serliker. Your names will be added to our song and for all time we will sing this joyous rescue so all will know this time.*

She greeted him warmly in return and sounded, *You do us great Honour. May your tays be filled with everlasting peace.* She then waited for them to calm down. When they were ready she joined their water-times together and sounded, *We must leave you now but I shall return for a short time soon. But while we are gone you will need all the knowledge that will help you live in this place.*

In an instant she passed everything the Sentinel had given to her for them, hoping that it would be enough so that they could adapt to Edenlea. When she had finished she then sounded, *One more thing I will ask of you. There are dolphins in this place who have only legends to tell them of your existence. Please meet them and share your water-times...* She stopped, chuckled and continued, *There are two such dolphins who saw our descent. They are many tays from here but they will be the first you will meet. Be gentle with them..*

She sounded her goodbyes and sang her song to take Serliker to meet the Sentinel with whom she had shared the genesis of *its* creation. They passed from water to the depth of the chamber to which Tan-e-lea had not returned for more than sixty seasons in real time but was only twenty in her own. They materialised in darkness. Her green light cast shadows around them but disappeared as her fire died. Tan-e-lea had known *the* Rock had been due to leave soon after her own departure leaving the Sentinel to take *its* place so she had expected the same brightly lit cavern and not the darkness which greeted her.

She took Serliker from her mouth and held *it* up asking for light which *it* quickly gave, revealing under *its* blue radiance a cavern that was covered in dust and cobwebs hanging from the ceiling. Tan-e-lea gasped in surprise and quickly walked to where she knew the crystals to be. There were also rocks and pieces of broken Shakeilar covering the once pristine floor. There was no light from the crystals and her heart fell as she dusted the collection of grime from them. Under Serliker's light they shone dully and only *its* reflected light shone back.

Serliker broke the silence, "Well, a *right mess* this place is in..."

She gave *it* an irritated look and bayed *it* to silence. "What could have *happene*d?" Her anguish at the remains of the Sentinel made itself felt with Serliker, so *it* didn't reply but remained silent. *It* surveyed the chamber with her as she walked around the altar and made for what was once the chamber that had held her lagoon. There were great cracks along the wall and she found that she couldn't venture far. The waters were long gone, now filled with great boulders of rock and the cold lava of the volcano some distance above them. Her water-time tried to piece together what had happened. From the damage to the cavern she speculated that some time during her absence from the cavern the volcano had suffered an eruption. But she couldn't make sense of it as the power of the Sentinel should have been more than enough to cope with such an event. She wandered back and stared up at the ceiling and puzzled on how there was a neat round hole that allowed a glimmer of taylight to sneak through. Most of it was filled but the outline showed that once it must have let a lot more in.

While she puzzled over this Serliker decided to take matters upon *itself*. *It* flew from her grasp and landed neatly upon the raised dais. To Tan-e-lea's surprise *it* began to change the crystals.

Serliker used *its* water-time and searched the crystals for any remnants of what Tan-e-lea had called the Sentinel. *It* found the likeness to *its* old home rather disturbing but soothing all at the same time. For in truth Serliker missed *its* time locked away. *Less complicated!* Not that *it* really regretted joining with Mel-e-gar and experiencing all the adventures that had entailed, but somehow *it* felt that enough was enough and a few millennia of peace and quiet wouldn't go amiss.

It continued to wander among the dead crystals, finding nothing but emptiness. Serliker found the structure to *its* liking and moulding *itself* into their likeness flowed out to encompass the chamber. *It* passed under the startled dees of Tan-e-lea, and she watched as the rocks crumbled to dust. Then the dust disappeared, taking the cobwebs and hundreds of cracks around the room with it. Slowly the cavern began to shine once more, this time with a strong blue light with a silver hue. Delighted at the regeneration Tan-e-lea sounded her pleasure. At the last touch the crystals grew in size and flashed alive with a new fire, a beautiful blue flame which held her mesmerised.

Suddenly a deep voice bellowed forth into her water-time, *I am Back-*

Before *it* could finish Tan-e-lea cried out, *Sentinel!* Her eyes lit up in delight and a radiant smile was born upon her face. But then the voice shattered her hope. *Ah! Sorry Tan-e-lea, just joking*, sounded a rather sheepish Serliker.

And you should be.. cried Tan-e-lea, all hope disappearing from her. She slumped and Serliker grew a mound from the new floor and she sank gratefully into its embrace. After staring with blank eyes at the floor she raised her gaze and quietly sounded, *Is there no sign of the Sentinel?*

The light of crystals pulsated showing Serliker was still searching. Then *it* brightened with an orange flame. *Yes, I believe I have something... its* waters muttered almost to *itself*. Then an orange spinning ball burst from the crystals as Serliker exclaimed, *Yes, here it is!*

It hovered in the air, then descended slowly making *its* way to Tan-e-lea.

She opened her hand and *it* fell into her palm. *It* was heavy and as she turned *it* over, examining the surface, the orange light flickered and pulsated in her hands. Tentatively she opened her water-time and did what she knew her Elders had once done on Delikadove; read a seeing crystal.

Tan-e-lea found herself falling into the orange light, which changed as she came closer to the source. Time was stripped away and she found herself returning to the cavern, the way it looked when she last saw it, with one difference; there was a round shaft of light coming from the ceiling. It looked cleanly cut and the vision took a greater hold and she could not distinguish any difference from actually being there. But there was a difference for the sound of the Sentinel was far gentler than before and it seemed to come from a great distance. It caressed her water-time and the sights and sound of the Sentinel came upon her.

Welcome Tan-e-lea, I leave a message for you, in all that remains of my older self. I have judged that if you were successful in your last task upon Delikadove then sixty and more seasons will have passed. I am sorry that I am not there to welcome you home but.. Well I shall come to that later on.

The sound paused and allowed Tan-e-lea to compose herself to carry on reading the crystal. *It* seemed to judge when she was ready and the Sentinel continued, *Mel-e-gar came to us; the Rock and I told him of your fate. Your wisdom in leaving a responder to dark tones of his watersong was well placed. You did indeed understand his grief. He thanks you for what you have done.*

She was concerned that it had been necessary and was just glad that it had worked and her Grand-elder had come through what must have been a difficult time. She returned her attention back to the message;

Not all was told for we leave that last part for you. We have found a way for you to meet with him. But that again is for much later. When Mel-e-gar left I grew restless and it came upon me to venture from this cavern, to wander above and see the wonders of this new place you call Edenlea.

For the first time Tan-e-lea heard the Sentinel chuckle and *it* reminded her of *the* Rock. Then *it* continued, *I decided to hitch a ride. Unknown to him I shared space with Mel-e-gar, existing in the same space but at a different dimensional frequency. It was fascinating and it gives me a chance to allow you to share the last seasons of your Grand-elder and family.*

This brought delight for Tan-e-lea as she had wished that she could find out the rest of those times from Mel-e-gar's point of view. She knew the events, some she was part of but there was much she wished to know. *Its* sound seemed to respond to her water-time for the Sentinel then sounded, *I knew you would, so come, join and see....*

* * *

5 S.E.

His water-time mirrored the tranquillity of Edenlea as he slowly swam northwards. A great feeling of peace held him. Old feelings of responsibility in being the Elder of the dolphins slipped away, now that he knew Tan-e-lea was safe and was fulfilling her wish in being a dolph. The memory of *the* Rock made him smile at the fact that *it* had been wrong when long before *it* had sounded that Mel-e-gar was the last Watersinger of Delikadove. For in a real sense Tan-e-lea would witness the final times of their old home making her the last Watersinger.

He had chosen to materialise a hundred klees from where he had left his family and the other dolphins, now almost a jeanth ago, so that he could enjoy the silence and beauty of the cool waters, giving him time to decide what he was to tell them about Tan-e-lea. His water-time reviewed the past and as he began to feel the water-times of many dolphins he chose to tell the truth. For he knew the lesson that the younglings had to learn had been made. Their future was in Edenlea and not on un-water. Mel-e-gar had enough of secrecy and when he poked his beak above the waves on the fourth tay of his journey, seeing in the distance the forms of his dolphins playing under the light of Solarn he knew it would be for the best.

The waters were filled with a shoal of grey and silver fish, large enough to make a meal to satisfy his hunger. He fed greedily and enjoyed chasing and weaving about amidst the clamour of sound from his family as they spied his presence in the water. It was Zar-e-gar who met him. He was so intent on his prey, that he shot past Mel-e-gar and almost spun in the water as he turned sharply when he realised who it was.

Grand-elder! You have returned! he cried as he slid smoothly alongside Mel-e-gar and matched his pace.

The joy of his grandling's water-time infused into Mel-e-gar bringing wave after wave of the simple pleasure of being home. Slowly, allowing Zar-e-gar to release his feelings, Mel-e-gar eased himself from the embrace and sounded, *It's good to be home Zar-e-gar.*

Then Ser-e-gar and Car-e-lea were there, each taking turn in welcoming him home. Kel-e-lea and Haw-e-gar were just as boisterous in their welcome. Then Que-e-lea and Jer-e-lea came forward. In the outer waters he could feel the welcomes of the other dolphins and one in particular stood out, like a shining beacon; Jux-e-lea whose feelings were plain to see.

In spite of the clamour of different sounds, something gentle and warm came to rest inside his heart and slowly blossomed out to give Jux-e-lea her answer. Simply; *Yes*! It only lasted for a brief yen but he knew she was satisfied and for now he could turn his attention back to answer the many questions that needed to be answered.

Later that tay he had told them what he discovered in the cavern and to the astonished silence of his audience revealed the fate of Tan-e-lea. A wave of relief washed over him from his sonling and mate and the younglings cried their joy that she had survived after all. Mel-e-gar didn't know all the details of what she had accomplished but when Del-e-gar came forward with Ose-e-lea they learned much more! The exchange of times went on far into the following tay and when at last all were satisfied they split up into their family groups and continued to explore the northern waters of Edenlea.

On the fourth tay of his return Mel-e-gar gathered the dolphins around him and told them that he would return them to the southern waters. To the surprise of some, four of the families chose to stay behind. Each Grand-elder came in turn. They were the Del-e-gar, Ual-e-lea, Dwe-e-lea, and Kin-e-gar families, with the exception of Kin-e-gar's grandling Jux-e-lea who chose to go with Mel-e-gar and the remaining five families.

The only problem with splitting the group up came about when Que-e-lea added her sound to the discussion. *What about the leas who are heavy with unborn younglings? They will need a nursery motherling to help with the birth.* She looked to Mel-e-gar to give his answer.

But it was Jer-e-lea who answered for him, *I could go!* giving Que-e-lea a beseeching look. *I know enough to help them and we do have enough motherlings to help with the rest. I could learn as I go along.* Que-e-lea's water-time mulled over her request and while Jer-e-lea gave her best imploring look, she gave in and laughed, *Yes! Why not. I'm sure you will do fine.* The-relief could be felt by all as Jer-e-lea sounded her delight and flipped backwards in the water in joy.

Now that is settled, joined in Mel-e-gar. *We must arrange to meet up once a season, to share times together and any help that may be needed. Anyone have an idea on what part of the season this should be?* For a yen there was silence but then a youngling by the name of Sev-e-gar a brotherling to Jux-e-lea sounded, *Why don't we meet on the first tay of the new season?*

Good idea, replied Mel-e-gar. *That would make it the shortest tay for you in the north and the longest tay for us in the south.*

Then another, practical sound joined in. *I'm sorry to add this*, interjected Haw-e-gar, *but when you are gone there will not be a Watersinger to transport us here again.*

All eyes turned towards Mel-e-gar and a Grand-elder named Che-e-gar added, *He is right, Mel-e-gar. The journey would take more than six jeanths to complete. By the time we arrived back we would have missed a meeting.*

It was a good point and it wasn't lost on Mel-e-gar. He allowed his waters to sift through this and then gave his answer, *Yes, I agree. Sometimes I forget that my seasons are growing shorter. The solution I feel would be to make it once every sixth season and to alternate, so we of the southern seas come one season and you of the northern seas travel down to us the next season.*

There were murmurs of agreement from all sides. Then Ser-e-gar added his sound, *If that is to be so then we had better start to rename the cycle of the seasons.* He had sounded what some had felt before; it was time to change from the old cycle of S.N. as that was the old world's way.

Any suggestions? asked Mel-e-gar, throwing the question of naming the seasons out for any to answer.

Yes, I feel we should call it The Cycle of Mel-e-gar, answered Car-e-lea, who was swimming close to Que-e-lea and Ser-e-gar, as she was very heavy with her un-born youngling.

Mel-e-gar turned to her and sounded, *You do me Honour, but you would do me greater*

Honour if you would choose to name it: The Cycle of Edenlea.

Car-e-lea looked disappointed but she agreed his suggestion would be better. She liked the sound of it and from the movements coming from the young water-time of her un-born, she liked it too.

There were no dissenting sounds, rather the reverse as they happily agreed for it to become Seasons of Edenlea, dated back to their arrival which now made it the sixth jeanth of **5 S.E.** [**7273 S.N.**] Those who wanted to travel between groups at any time were welcome to do so but the next formal date would be **11 S.E.** when the northern group would travel south.

Mel-e-gar watched as the group divided and he waited for those families to say goodbye. It was at that yen that Haw-e-gar came to his parentlings and Mel-e-gar with a young lea.

He looked nervous as he made his sounds known. *Grand-elder, Fatherling and Motherling, I want to go with them.* It came out in a rush and he beckoned for the lea to come closer. Before they could reply he added, *I want you to meet Yen-e-lea. We want to be joined.*

Now this was a surprise for Mel-e-gar, but Car-e-lea smiled warmly and turning her attention to the lea she sounded, *Yes, you are the daughterling of Set-e-lea and Pan-e-gar, of the family of Ual-e-lea. You are welcome to our family.*

Then Ser-e-gar joined in, *Mel-e-gar I believe you had better do the joining of these two younglings.* He grinned at his fatherling as Mel-e-gar looked at them all in surprise.

He quickly recovered his composure and answered, *Well, Haw-e-gar, your parentlings agree. Shall we go and find your requested mate's parentlings and proceed with your Joining...?*

A look of relief spread over his face and he and Yen-e-lea grinned happily at each other and turned from them to find her family.

It left Mel-e-gar to sound, *Well he certainly kept that hidden!*

Which made Ser-e-gar and Car-e-lea laugh out loud, "Mel-e-gar!"

They then swam after their sonling and Mel-e-gar followed behind with Que-e-lea, Kel-e-lea, and Zar-e-gar. He joined his water-time with Que-e-lea and sounded, *Did you know about this?*

She smacked his side with her flipper and replied, *Mel-e-gar, you really do take the fish sometimes!* She turned and dived below him before he could return her smack.

He was left to mutter, *I can't know everything!*

For the last time the families of dolphins came together and with their beaks above the cool waters and as Solarn kissed the horizon, Haw-e-gar and Yen-e-lea came together beak to beak, both gazing with unconcealed pleasure into each other's eyes.

With their families in a circle around them Mel-e-gar began the Joining, "From *Star* to *Star*... From *Heart* to *Heart*... We are here to join these two younglings. Who will now be known as Elders." He smiled at them and then sounded within their waters, *Haw-e-gar repeat these sounds for your mate*; *I Haw-e-gar give you Yen-e-lea my love.*

With his eyes sparkling in the fading light, Haw-e-gar kissed Yen-e-lea and repeated, *I Haw-e-gar give you Yen-e-lea my love.*

Then Mel-e-gar turned to Yen-e-lea and sounded, *Now repeat these sounds for your mate; I Yen-e-lea give you Haw-e-gar my heart.*

She kissed Haw-e-gar and repeated, *I Yen-e-lea give you Haw-e-gar my heart.*

Now Mel-e-gar reached and touched each with his flipper and sounded, *You may sound your own wishes for each other.*

This was something Haw-e-gar had delved deep within his water-times, to come up with what he wanted to say to his Yen-e-lea.

He kissed her again and as he gazed longingly into her eyes he began, *I wish to warm you when you are cold, to touch and heal you when you feel pain. I am but a fish who gives to you my body to satisfy your hunger. May our love fill the stars and the waters of Edenlea be our home for ever more.....* He sighed as he finished.

She was so moved by his sounds she couldn't help but hug him tightly. The dolphins including Mel-e-gar called out their delight and when the happy sounds subsided they waited for Yen-e-lea to give Haw-e-gar her wishes.

She kissed Haw-e-gar and began, *I wish to give you hope when you are in despair, to make you feel we are one. I am your hunger that can satisfy you for all time. You are my love who loves me. Together we shall swim to the song of Edenlea.* Her sounds touched all their hearts and the cries of joy rang out once more.

The wind had picked up and as the first star could be seen in the twilight Mel-e-gar finished the joining by sounding, *You are the first to be joined in Edenlea. May your beginning show the rest the way to our new and bright future. You are now joined as one.*

His final words signalled the end and as Haw-e-gar kissed once more the rest of the dolphins rushed over and congratulated them. For a while the waters of Edenlea were awash with the thrashing forms as dolphin after dolphin, jumped, dived and generally enjoyed the yen of the joining.

When Haw-e-gar could escape the clutches of the joyful dolphins he swam over to Mel-e-gar and asked a question which all the younglings wanted an answer to but his joining had disrupted their chance. So he had agreed to go to Mel-e-gar to find out. *Ah Grand Elder, the younglings want to know when you are going to finish telling us the story? As we of the north will not be with you.*

Mel-e-gar had wondered how long it would be before someone asked that question and it came as no surprise this time that it would be Haw-e-gar who would ask.

He held his gaze with Haw-e-gar and joining his water-time, he quickly pulled the dolphins together to make his last pronouncement. *Haw-e-gar has asked when I will finish the story of Delikadove. Well as Del-e-gar should head the Council of the north and as he knows as much as I, he will tell those younglings in his charge.*

That surprised Del-e-gar and he made his way to the front and sounded, *I have not always agreed with you in times past but I salute your profound wisdom.*

Mel-e-gar roared with approval and sounded, *The same old Del-e-gar, don't change...* He was still laughing as he watched Del-e-gar wink back and gather his families around him, giving Mel-e-gar enough undisturbed water so he could make sure all his were grouped together.

The stars and moon were bright, bathing the waters with a silvery light, catching many an eye that had tears ready to fall as they waited for Mel-e-gar to begin his song.

They knew that it would be the last time any of them would see him again. They cried a last farewell as Mel-e-gar began taking their friends and some who were parting from families, away to the southern sea of Edenlea. The energy built up and Mel-e-gar sang a single note, quickly followed by a chorus of sound that took them from the northern waters.

The group gathered around Mel-e-gar had one last chance to wave goodbye before the power shifted them from the cold waters to the much warmer waters of the south. With cries from all they materialised in the midtay light of Solarn, south of the small continent where he had begun the telling of his story so many jeanths ago.

Mel-e-gar watched the families that had returned with him, play together in the early morning light on the third tay of returning to the southern waters. Zar-e-gar in particular was using his sense of play with the other younglings to show them how to harvest a shoal of fish, by creating a circle of bubbles to attract them. Then when they were in the middle he motioned for the younglings to dive in together, scooping up the fish in one go. It didn't go quite according to Zar-e-gar's plan for some of the younglings mistimed and scattered the shoal in all directions. Mel-e-gar chuckled as they scooted past in a furious race to make up for their blunder. The light that penetrated the waters created dazzling displays of colour as fish and dolphins become totally confused.

It wasn't long before Zar-e-gar left the younglings to it and catching Mel-e-gar's attention, swam over and sounded with good humour, *They will learn eventually when they get used to moving as one within the water-time.*

You have learned well. Your teacher would have been pleased that you are now passing that knowledge on, replied Mel-e-gar.

Yes, she taught me a great deal, he sounded, rather wistfully. His waters filled with the image of Vue-e-lea and his early tays learning by her side. Mel-e-gar seeing this sounded, *You miss her still..*

Zar-e-gar turned his sad eyes upon his Grand-elder and replied, *Yes, I do. There was no time to say farewell.* He then turned his enquiring beak to Mel-e-gar and asked, *Why didn't she come with us?*

His water-time seemed so sad that Mel-e-gar decided to take the opportunity and remarked, *There were many that couldn't come...But don't be sad, there is much I can tell you about her. If you wish to know?*

It was enough to make the very light of Solarn shine in his eyes and with great expectation sounded, *Oh! Yes!! Grand-elder, that would warm my water-time.*

Mel-e-gar was glad to see such light in his grandling and using his right flipper motioned for him to leave the others and to swim out to calmer waters. By using his water-time he gently led Zar-e-gar to join more completely and opened one of many pools that contained a tale of Delikadove. This one concerning a female dolph/in that was born on the twenty-ninth tay of the eleventh jeanth in:

7232 S.N.

On the southern shore where the mountains of Frelegar meet the sea of Hederlike stood the small city of Kerthiner. Its name came from the colony of Kerg which nested in the high cliffs to the east. Normally at this time of season they would have left to go north but like much on Delikadove, that had changed. When normally it would have been one of the coldest tays for that region it was one of the hottest and the Kerg had chosen to stay and rear another brood. So as Danetar baked the land three dolphs left the city. One was a young dolph by the name of Res-e-lea who was ready to give birth. Her mate Ion-e-gar wanted her to have the birthing in the pool of their home but she was insistent that they would do as dolphs had always done, that was to have her youngling in the purple waters. Now he wasn't alone in his feelings as the nursery motherling for the city, Nes-e-lea also advised that the heat of Danetar would be unbearable. But there is nothing more stubborn than a pregnant dolph and her will was more than a match for them both.

With one on each side she dived and changed in the waters. The sea was particularly heavy and great waves pounded the beach. With some trouble they made it past the surf line and headed for the shade of the cliffs. They nearly didn't make it as her pains were increasing in strength, but with an extreme effort she did. They could hear the calls of the Kerg filter through the waters as she gave birth to Vue-e-lea. Nes-e-lea and Ion-e-gar helped the new-born to take her first breath above the waves then to suckle on her motherling. When the feeding had taken place she was ready to be hurled from the sea in the ritual to make sure she could change to dolph. There was concern showing in all their water-times as in the past twenty seasons or more there were many being born who could only survive as dolphins. The change to dolph was becoming infrequent, which was making the prophecy of Edenlea a reality.

There was a small inlet between the cliffs, leading to an orange sandy cove. Res-e-lea watched anxiously as her mate and Nes-e-lea led the new-born Vue-e-lea. When they reached the first line of breaking waves they used their flippers to hurl her into the air. She spun in an arc and as her tail hit the beach a sparkling wave of energy engulfed her form, changing the dolphin to a dolph. Their cries of relief mingled with the Kerg as she stumbled on newly formed dees, then crumpled in a heap.

At that yen a shriek of a Kerg rose above the rest when a youngling chick fell from the cliff above and landed by Vue-e-lea's side. As the distressed Kerg flew above them, wheeling in a circle crying into the hot wind, they watched as Vue-e-lea slowly opened her eyes and peered at the chick which struggled in the sand by her side. The chick was in obvious pain from falling from such a height and Ion-e-gar expected it to succumb to the deathsong at any yen. But instead it crawled closer to Vue-e-lea and she seeing its pain slowly reached out with her hand and helped it to its pathetically weak dees. As she made contact with the downy feathers a small spark of silver energy jumped from her hand and embraced the young chick. Her parentlings watched amazed as the young creature settled down on her palm, still cloaked by the silver energy which revived the strength and straightened and healed young bones that had been shattered by the fall. Vue-e-lea's young face smiled as the chick called out and with a healthy waddle managed to jump the few dees to her head, where it settled down as she closed her eyes and fell asleep.

When Ion-e-gar had recovered from his astonishment he leapt from the sea and landed by her side. The youngling chick raised its immature wings and beak to warn him off. He couldn't help but smile at this display and respecting what his youngling had done for the Kerg he managed to lift her from the sand while the chick balanced on her cheek. When her head was cradled in the crook of his arm and her legs over the other arm, the chick slid down until it nestled under her chin. Calling out for Nes-e-lea to go home and fetch a travelling-shelter he walked along the inlet to a cave at the back. Res-e-lea still recovering from the birthing swam closer and waited until the nursery motherling returned.

Vue-e-lea stayed asleep for the rest of the tay and was lain in the shelter with the chick who had also chosen to sleep, and for some clars Ion-e-gar watched over them. The motherling of the chick had chosen to roost on the top of the yellow and orange dome of the shelter. When he had felt that it was safe to leave his new-born he carefully left, making sure he didn't disturb the adult. But the Kerg opened one large black eye, stared for a yen, then deciding he was okay closed it, ruffled its bright red feathers and went back to sleep, leaving him to go back to his mate and Nes-e-lea who was looking after her. Their sounds filled the now dark waters as they shared water-time, discussing their daughterling. It wasn't that remarkable that Vue-e-lea was going to be a Healer as for over ten generations on Res-e-lea's side each lea of the family had been, but it was astonishing that she had shown the capacity only yens after her birth.

The remarkable story of Vue-e-lea and the Kerg filled the sounds of the city for many jeanths to come and some dolphs who had studied the Kerg had come from all parts of Delikadove to watch their unique partnership grow. For most of the sixteen jeanths she was fed from her motherling and in between the youngling spent her time on the beach with the Kerg. Ion-e-gar had managed to coax the chick from his youngling's side and give it back to its own motherling. As if understanding the rapport between the two, the adult Kerg moved her nest to the cliffs nearest to the city, so her youngling could see Vue-e-lea every tay. By the time the chick was two jeanths old it had attained its adult feathers and was flying to her side. When Vue-e-lea was in dolph form it would perch on her shoulder and when in dolphin upon her beak.

The Kerg, who by this time she had named Kina, became her teacher and they could be seen often diving together then reappearing with a large fish in each beak. Their relationship grew so when Vue-e-lea showed a desire to become a teacher, her parentlings sent her to meet me in my city, so her talents could be passed on to the younglings who had been born only as dolphins, who lived in part with their parentlings in the underwater part of the city...

Mel-e-gar broke from sharing the story and as his water-time emptied from Zar-e-gar he swam for the surface, with his grandling following close behind. When their beaks broke through the sparkling green waters in the afternoon light, Zar-e-gar ignoring the look of preoccupation that held his Grand-elder sounded, *Thank you for telling me of Vue-e-lea's beginnings but isn't there more you can tell me?*

At first Mel-e-gar didn't respond, his waters feeling the sadness that had left so many behind but when he looked upon the eager beak of Zar-e-gar, he shook the feeling away and responded to the desire in the question by sounding, *Yes, I could but that will have to wait as I sense your Motherling is about to give birth to your sisterling!*

That fired delight in Zar-e-gar and he sounded, *Well what are we waiting for!* He turned and dived, making a straight line for where he had left his parentlings. Mel-e-gar laughed and followed quickly after his grandling.

When they arrived they found a circle of dolphins, securing the area around Car-e-lea and Ser-e-gar. Que-e-lea who was coming from another direction broke through and joined them. Mel-e-gar was pleased that the other dolphins had taken precautions against any Keeva who might wander too close. For the blood of the birthing could attract their attention but to a dolphin who was ready they were only a nuisance rather than a serious threat. His water-time quickly checked the area and was glad to find it was empty. He then turned his attention to Car-e-lea and added his water-time with hers in helping Que-e-lea and Ser-e-gar ease the birthing pains.

For the others the clars passed swiftly as each rhythmic contraction flowed through her form but Car-e-lea found that time seemed to have slowed and she could feel every movement with heightened sensitivity. She found the water-times of the others a help but she was totally aware of her unborn as slowly she pushed and pushed. The youngling's water-time was closely melded with hers and she checked on it just as Que-e-lea was assuring herself that everything was still all right. Then with an enormous cry she gave one final push and the youngling slipped from the comfort of Car-e-lea's water to the colder depths of Edenlea.

Que-e-lea was quick to help the youngling to the surface and Ser-e-gar whose water-time was bursting with emotion sounded his joy and joined his mate to have their first look at the youngling. Car-e-lea managed to turn and her sight was filled by the presence of her and making use for the first time of the name they had chosen cried, *Cas-e-lea! Cas-e-lea!*

The youngling turned her beak and bright green and grey eyes stared wildly as her young water-time cascaded into Car-e-lea. The others could only watch in joy as the proud parentlings kissed and nuzzled their new-born.

The only water-time that wasn't as joyful as the rest was Mel-e-gar's. It wasn't that his happiness was any less boundless but when Cas-e-lea broke free something broke inside him. A strange greyness to his water-time descended. He could feel the blood rush through him, making a strange dizziness that disrupted his sound. Slipping silently away, doing his best to be unnoticed he made for the surface. His body felt starved of air and a cry tore from his beak as another pain pierced his side. For one yen it felt as if the very light of Solarn had turned to the burning of Danetar, tormenting his water-time. Then the greyness turned blood red and he could feel a black wave washing over him. "Not *yet.......*" was his weak cry before the dark waters bore him away.

*   *   *

WATER - TIME

Tan-e-lea tore her water-time free from the Sentinel's as she shared Mel-e-gar's pain. Like him she couldn't believe it was that soon. She knew that he had entered the deathsong sometime in the last seventy seasons that had passed in Edenlea but because she had not lived in real time that length, it was hard for her to come to terms with. After all it had only been twenty *short* seasons for her since she had left him. With wild eyes she stared at the altar where Serliker's blue fire resided, hot tears washing her face.

Serliker sensing her distress poured the cool fire upon her. A wave of comfort came to her and slowly her distress at witnessing Mel-e-gar's deathsong receded. *It just couldn't be...* Her weak sounds brought another fresh wave of bitter tears, leaving Serliker little to do but watch and wait for her to give vent to her grief. It was something *it* had witnessed too many times in the last seasons on Delikadove and there was little *it* could do.

She still clutched the crystal and at first she didn't feel the pulsation that flowed from *its* depth.

But Serliker did and *it* had to break through rather roughly past her wall of grief and sounded, *Tan-e-lea, the Sentinel still calls. Maybe there is more, maybe hope? Its* sound was rather tentative for Serliker.

It was enough for Tan-e-lea to raise her head and she stared unblinking as she focused through the tears at the slow but insistent beat of the Sentinel. Taking her courage into her water-time she burst upon the scene that had started to be played out for her...

* * *

5 S.E.

As the pulsation of energy started to flow from the lifeless body of Mel-e-gar, the Sentinel used *its* own energy and smothered the pulse. *It* couldn't allow the dolphins to sense the beginning of the deathsong. *It* knew that in the clars that followed they might sense something was wrong and venture out to search for Mel-e-gar. *It* had to make sure that none would be successful. *It* carefully checked for leakage from the energy barrier and finding it secure *it* sent *its* sight out until *it* came to the dolphins. Seeing the celebrations continue undisturbed *it* watched for a few yens then withdrew.

When night fell the clouds were heavy and dark, obscuring any stars. Even the moon was unable to penetrate, only the occasional flash of lightning in the distance breaking through, dancing on the horizon. Many were resting on the surface and watched the display. The only sounds were the occasional murmurings as a dolphin settled for some sleep. Car-e-lea was joined by her family and it was only as Ser-e-gar joined them that Que-e-lea sounded, *Where is Mel-e-gar? I haven't seen him since the birthing.*

She didn't sound that concerned and the others could only reply that he had left soon after. Ser-e-gar took the precaution as he settled to sleep of searching his water-time, making sure that his fatherling was all right. But his search delivered nothing and he relaxed and closed his eyes to sleep.

The yens slipped by and with a start he opened his eyes and cried, "*Nothing*!" He was so startled that it hadn't registered before. There should have been a trace to show he was safe. But there was only emptiness as if his Fatherling had ceased to exist. While telling Que-e-lea and some of the others to stay with his mate and new-born he called out for the others to come quickly. Soon the area was filled with the urgent sounds as dolphins became aware that something was wrong. It wasn't long before they were surrounding Ser-e-gar.

He could feel a strange chill creep into their water-times as they, after using their sounds realized that Mel-e-gar was not within twenty klees of the area. The urgency grew as some sounded that maybe he had gone exploring but Ser-e-gar became convinced that his Elder was in trouble. He took charge and split them into groups of three. They were to fan out and search until they found something. They complied with no complaint, cutting through the waters in search of Mel-e-gar.

The night passed and by the time Solarn had risen to its zenith it brought a flow of heavy and sad water-times back to Ser-e-gar. Even Zar-e-gar and Kel-e-lea had been out searching, but they returned despondent, their silent sounds telling him that there was no trace.

It was only when they had all returned that one of the dolphins, an Elder named, Ban-e-lea remarked, *Has anyone seen Jux-e-lea?* For she realized that as far as she could tell she had not seen her the tay before either. One of the others replied, *Maybe Mel-e-gar and Jux-e-lea have gone for some peace and quiet...*

There was a ripple of laughter at that and even Ser-e-gar had to admit that it could have been a real possibility. But there was something nagging at his water-time and he couldn't keep the ripple still...that something was wrong. In the end he had to agree and advised them to wait for a few tays and if they had not returned then...Well he left the rest unspoken but they all knew what he meant. There was little chance of ever finding out if Mel-e-gar had passed into the deathsong or was floating helpless upon Edenlea. He knew that *She* took back very quickly any creature that was incapacitated for long.

Cas-e-lea was feeding contentedly as Ser-e-gar came and joined his water-time with Car-e-lea. *Where could they have gone?* he sounded.

She felt his concern and replied, *Maybe the others are right. They could have gone to share water-time together..* But even she wasn't convinced.

Ser-e-gar could only look bleakly at her and sound, *Maybe, but isn't it strange that I have lost contact with any sound of him...Or her for that matter?*

Car-e-lea tried to soothe him and asked, *How far did you search?*

He nuzzled her and replied, *We searched for a hundred klees. I had to restrain Kel-e-lea and Zar-e-gar from going any further. If Mel-e-gar had been hurt he should still be in the vicinity but you know how hopeless it is in such a large expanse of Edenlea.* He couldn't shake the feeling that they had missed *something*.... He was grateful when Car-e-lea used her body to warm him.

She felt a shiver pass through and sounded, *We can only hope...* He tried to take comfort in her sounds and as they swam near to the surface he watched the other dolphins play in the warm rays of Solarn. *If only I could be sure....*

As the Sentinel for the second time withdrew its sight, it felt the puzzlement of the dolphins and a wave of sympathy came upon it. But what it had planned could only be done one way. The motionless form of Mel-e-gar was quickly joined by the equally still form of Jux-e-lea. The Sentinel wrapped them in a blanket of energy and as the orange flame infused their bodies, a loud crackling broke the silence causing them to sparkle with the strange fire. It quickly consumed the forms and began to spin in the water. Faster it turned, sending shards of light in all directions. Then an explosion rocketed skyward as the Sentinel let go. Only a shadow of its former self remained with the ball of energy as it reached a point high in the sky before a final resounding explosion tore the fireball apart. A rain of fire rained down and sizzled to its death as each part plunged into Edenlea.

Ser-e-gar had just finished sharing his water-time with Car-e-lea when he saw a strange light explode in the distance. He called for her and as the other dolphins became aware, they too watched the fireball explode. For an instant the light of Solarn was overshadowed by the brilliance and many averted their eyes, but it penetrated and some experienced a temporary blindness as it washed through. Ser-e-gar blinked, trying to dislodge the afterimage from his eyes, trying desperately to see. For a yen he could have sworn that two fiery dolphin forms left the fireball as it disintegrated into a shower of fire. They seemed to fly into the air, changing into two large sky-flyers, that cried once and flew east disappearing into the large rain clouds that also seemed to have appeared from nowhere.

It wasn't long before it overshadowed the dolphins bringing a strong wind which scattered the remnants of fire until they too were gone. Over fifty dolphins dived for the calmer waters as rain pelted down. Only Ser-e-gar remained above as it blasted into his beak, stinging his eyes then turning to relief as it washed the shadow from him. He could see clearly now and he cried as a familiar touch sounded, *Farewell Ser-e-gar. Take care my youngling.*

The sounds with which he wanted to respond were stuck fast inside, causing his heart to burst with pain as he stared longingly into the grey light. He remained staring into the rain for some while, hoping there would be more but only the sound of the wind howled around him, tearing Edenlea into great waves. Finally he slipped from the storm above and descended to rejoin his family. But the calmness below tormented him as his fatherling's last sound echoed within.

It was Car-e-lea who rescued him. She swam to him, leaving Cas-e-lea with Que-e-lea and with the practised ease of many seasons slipped into his water-time and held his torment to her heart. Her sounds saw the truth of his vision and Mel-e-gar's last sounds passed to her.

It would take many tays for not only Ser-e-gar but the whole of dolphin kind to recover from the deathsong of Mel-e-gar and also of Jux-e-lea. She realised that somehow she had also suffered the same fate. It may have been the end of an era that had brought them to Edenlea but with much urging she persuaded Ser-e-gar to continue with Mel-e-gar's plan and take the Eldership, *to lead them into the future.*

6 S.E.

At the turning of the season the dolphins created six circles around Ser-e-gar, each one representing a season that had passed since they had arrived in Edenlea. With one sound they named him Grand-elder and thus the leadership of the Council of dolphins fell upon him. As the cheers filled the air and sea he turned to Zar-e-gar and sounded, *My sonling, you, I give a task. Go north and tell them of Mel-e-gar's fate.* He paused holding Zar-e-gar's wide eyes then sounded, *You have taught much to our younglings as once Vue-e-lea taught you. Now you must go and teach those northern younglings. When you are satisfied return to us, so your wise sounds can continue to help us reap the benefits of Edenlea.*

There were cries of agreement and Zar-e-gar who was completely overwhelmed by his fatherling's sounds found it hard to find his own. But when he did he anxiously asked, *Am I to go alone?*

Ser-e-gar smiled and replied, *No, young one, you may take two to keep you company.*

Zar-e-gar was a picture of relief as he turned and sounded for volunteers. There were many who wished to go, and choosing carefully, he chose; A Grand-elder named Fas-e-lea, and a youngling named Sol-e-lea, who much to his embarrassment quickly swam over and gave him a resounding kiss on his beak, much to the merriment of his fatherling and the others.

Ser-e-gar called out, *I see my son is indeed wise!* They all roared with laughter and Zar-e-gar had to put up with much teasing as the special meeting broke up.

On the following tay Zar-e-gar and his two companions were ready to leave. Ser-e-gar and what remained of his family joined in the farewells. They told him to pass warm water-time to Haw-e-gar and his mate and to make sure he collected many water-times in return, so they could learn how the *northern* dolphins fared. Much emotion was poured into Edenlea as they watched the three turn north. When they were no longer in sight Ser-e-gar and his family returned to the other dolphins.

It wasn't long before he and Car-e-lea were left alone to enjoy a few yens in private. She rubbed her beak with his and sounded, *I feel Mel-e-gar will look after them...*

Ser-e-gar stroked her side and sounded in reply, *His song will remain as long as there are dolphins who can see, hear and feel the essence of his water-time.*

* * *

At first the darkness was overwhelming, but as he continued to fall he allowed the deep blackness of it to swallow him. The pain which had stricken was now no longer tearing through him, only a sense of emptiness as the feelings which he knew slipped away. It was timeless as the void took him away from Edenlea. Random slivers of water-time conjured their own visions of his life. The mountains on Delikadove rushed towards him then disappeared into the void. The desert, images of Serliker, the Rock, the Selahw, and many of the dolphs and dolphins which he had known, all passed without comment or concern.

He had reached the point where the void held no questions or answers. It was like he had reached a communion with what he had done, no mysteries, for the seasons were only a beginning as well as the end.

It was only after the blackness stopped delivering its images did he begin to realise that he was waiting for something more. *Was there not more? A name came to him as the question brought a vague concern, a word? Chisharnlay...*Not only a word or a name but a concept of the deathsong, the place where dolphs and dolphins had played in bygone times. Where life transmutes to new patterns, new forms of existence. It had been accepted as fact that they did survive the disruption of the *song*. He had experienced his own contact when his parentlings had delivered their message and enabled him to say farewell long after their own passing.

But dolphs who had studied creative water-time had discovered that it was timeless, laws that existed in a new kind of water-time. To deliver all creatures in one Great deathsong, an instantaneous event for each world time. Where it was possible for all the old to meet as one, the end brought forth as it was in the beginning of all water-times....

The darkness was starting to change as the image of Chisharnlay passed through, bringing a grey light tinged with a red fire. He still puzzled over the question, only dimly aware that he was changing. The enigma brought back a discussion on Delikadove, when the Elders had asked, *Would the dolphs and dolphins of the old world still meet with those that travelled to the New Edenlea?*

Two worlds apart in space and time, a dilemma which had made many decide to forego the trip and meet the deathsong on Delikadove. To make sure that they would still meet with loved ones and not enter some limbo; confining them to an alien world's time of Chisharnlay. For him it had not mattered because somehow if it was true that they were separate it would give him a new adventure and that was enough for Mel-e-gar.

It was the red fire which was becoming brighter, chasing away what was left of the darkness and grey light that pulled his attention back. With a rush his water-time flowed through him, giving a crystal clear sight which also made him aware of the pain which had returned with a vengeance. The fire was now bright, reflecting the pain he felt inside, then as before. Blood could be tasted. Again it disappeared, leaving a feeling of well being which was at odds with what he had felt earlier. He began to search his water-time, trying to find the cause, but the fire only burned brighter. Suddenly there was a violent wrench, twisting him. Then for a yen it felt like he had burst apart. A vision of rain that burned with fire and the blackness returned, then changed making him sense blue skies, a wind which smelled of the saltiness of Edenlea and a patter of rain, gently falling.....

Was this Chisharnlay? he sounded as his body plunged into the warm waters. Only as he felt the strength of his flippers in the sea did he know that somehow he was back in Edenlea. A shoal of fish swam past and taking notice of the hunger that coursed through him he snatched one, enjoying the taste.

That was good... sounded Mel e gar, joy bursting forth. He felt the laughter play freely inside. Now he knew that it was not be his time for the deathsong. But when he made for the surface and poked his beak above the gentle green waves he received his first shock. For directly north there was a great expanse of un-water which stretched east and west as far as his eyes and sound could see.

Only a short distance away he could see the white froth of the waves breaking upon the shore. Yellow sand glistened and sparkled under the rays of Solarn. Judging by the position it was only a few clars into the morning. Beyond the shoreline a great forest could be seen and beyond that a range of mountains that, as he gazed upwards, stretched into the clouds. He could just see the whiteness of the peaks. Mel-e-gar was totally disorientated as turning round he looked south and was greeted only by more of Edenlea. He quickly searched his water-times for the images of Edenlea and un-water which he had seen when he had first arrived. Slowly the images passed as he tried to position himself and his heart fell when he came to one that matched the shoreline. He now knew that he was directly south of the great eastern continental mass, many thousands of klees away from his family. Somehow he had been transported half way round the world....

Well, he could soon correct that and proceeded to sing, but that was his next shock, for nothing happened. His watersong was gone. The confusion was now making him feel sick. *It couldn't be...His song must work!* He tried and tried but still nothing happened. *What was going on?* his water-time cried. Only the sound of the waves and the distant call of the many different sky-flyers answered him and for the first time he was helpless. For too many seasons he had relied on the watersong to get him out of situations, saving his life more than once. Now he was bereft of the only chance of returning home. He could swim but that would take more seasons than he believed still remained and he still didn't know why? Looking back at the pain he had felt he knew that it should have spelled the end but no, instead, somehow a strange twist of his watersong mixed with the beginnings of the deathsong had transported him here, healed but alone.

Many ripples passed though his water-times as he tried to answer his own questions but always they came up empty. It didn't make sense. After awhile he became tired of the whirlpool he had created. He chose to explore his new surroundings. In the past time he had only quickly scanned the area he was now in. He hadn't stopped before. Now he had the chance to do so. After eating a good meal of the rather large silver and red fish he headed for the beach to try and hope that he could still change to dolph. With the failure of his song he knew that there was a chance that he could fail and he just had to hope that this would work. If not he would be left stranded on the beach. It sent a wry chuckle through him as the image of Tan-e-lea came to him. She had once tried and look where that had left her. *There was no Watersinger to save him!*

He turned and headed further out, giving himself enough depth. When he was ready he dived and curved his body and burst through Edenlea, almost skimming the surface as he built up his speed. The water was hardly felt as he reached the surf line and with a tremendous leap, sailed through the air. Reaching the zenith point he let himself go and with a cry, that comes only from the foolish or the wise he somersaulted down. In the past, on Delikadove he could have pulled water vapour to shroud himself and change to dolph in mid-air. But without his song and as it didn't work on Edenlea anyway he had to wait until his silver, grey tail hit the yellow sand. With a burst of light the energy engulfed him, changing him. The transformation felt so good and two well formed dees sank deeply into the wet sand. He stayed on his haunches, letting his breathing settle. Slowly he raised his head and laughed his relief into the gentle breeze.

The roar of the waves behind him filled his sound and raising himself to his full height, he pressed his dees into the sand. Enjoying the sensation of water and sand oozing between his toes he began to walk along the shore. The confusion which had filled him passed as he just enjoyed the simple pleasure of exploring the beach. He came across many different shaped shells, which he picked up and examined. Their curled, smooth and twisted shape, with the shimmering colours reminded him of the crystals in Serliker's cavern and like those he placed them back with care upon the sand. They didn't have the same warmth or feeling of life but the cool hard touch was still pleasurable.

The variety was staggering and Mel-e-gar started to wish that his kind could have really explored the fruits that were held on un-water. Only a dolph would find it so attractive even though there were more than enough wonders of Edenlea to keep them fascinated and delighted for the countless seasons to come. It reminded him of that strange furry creature he had come across. The seed that would evolve into a race that if the Gateway Crystal had been correct about would some tay dominate un-water. *Would they find the same pleasure as he?* A question he knew he had little hope of answering. But he warmed himself with the feeling that if they did rise to sentience they could only treat their world with the love and respect that his kind had felt for Delikadove and the dolphins for Edenlea, despite the warning The Gateway Crystal gave that it could one tay be a threat to dolphin kind. He really couldn't see that happening and anyway the future was too uncertain to make such harsh judgements. Then he laughed, *A lot can happen in thirty-five million seasons!*

He spent the following tays exploring not only un-water but also Edenlea. The trees fascinated him, as being eighteen dees in height he was approaching the same height as the young ones along the top of the beach. They had a knarled and ridged trunk, bare of any branches all the way up. Only the crown had branches which hung down with what Mel-e-gar discerned were green oval fruit. On the ground below some had fallen, turning to a hairy shell of hard wood. Very strange indeed. He had to be careful as he walked among them as the small ones would dislodge their fruit if his hand strayed too close, making his dees quite sore. When he travelled further, the trees started to reach heights of thirty dees, allowing him some room without causing problems. But it did become more densely packed which meant without breaking them he had little chance of venturing further.

Fortunately later when he travelled a bit further along the beach he found hills which were thinly populated with the trees. The creatures were also fascinating; Large sky-flyers that were no longer capable of flying and very small four legged animals that reminded him of miniature Muala, without all the hair. There was one large hairless creature with a curved snout that reached up taking the small leaves from trees which were very different from the ones along the shore. It was grey skinned and had two teeth which curved over and under the lip. Very curious to watch. The further he travelled he found larger trees and sometimes expanses of green grass that had yellow, dappled coated beasts with great teeth which stalked the plains. One took one look at him and fled. He reasoned that his size helped dissuade the predators he met from enquiring too closely. But most of the creatures came to him, especially the different exotic coloured sky-flyers who would fly above or perch on his broad shoulders, enjoying his company.

He never ventured too far, only a tay's journey from the shore as he needed to return and feed upon the many fish of Edenlea. On the evening of a full moon he was just returning to another part of the beach when he spotted something lying on the water line, a dark shape which didn't move as he approached. As he came nearer the light of the moon burst from behind a cloud and lit the beach. He stopped dead in his tracks and stared in disbelief at the sight before him.

It couldn't be! he sounded, but when he made himself move closer he knew it wasn't his imagination.

Lighted by the rays of the moon was a dolph, lying face down near the waves, oblivious to Mel-e-gar's astonished gaze. What stood out the most were the black stripes which ran from the head, down its back to fork down the legs to the heels. He fell to his knees and with care he turned the dolph onto its back. Her face was serene in the light and her name came from him in a gasp, "*Jux-e-lea!!*"

He wasn't sure for how long he had just stared at her but when he made himself move he saw that the moon had shifted its position a klee or two across the sky.

What am I doing?! he sounded and gently picked her up from the shore, and with Jux-e-lea in his arms he walked up the beach and laid her down near the tree line. Her breathing was regular and she seemed fast asleep. It was only when Mel-e-gar went to place her hands upon her lap did he notice that she was clutching something tightly in her left hand. With care he turned her hand over and saw what she held. Her fingers obscured the symmetry but he could tell that *it* was a perfect sphere of red crystal that dimly pulsated in an easy rhythm.

Tentatively he placed his hand upon hers and was suddenly grasped by a vision of red fire that filled his water-time with a sound of the Sentinel, *Well met Mel-e-gar!*

The power was tremendous and he found that *it* gripped his water-time, allowing no response. Only the pounding of *its* sound could be heard, seen and felt.

You have questions dolph, but for now you will listen...This is all that is left of myself. What you saw in the cavern was my beginning as a true life form. As the Rock had sounded, I am the Sentinel but in times hence another will come and take my place for I was only the bridge and the fulfilment of a wish I have now invoked.

The power of the flame has taken, now you will be given. Long ago when you first met the Rock, it took from you four seasons and they were taken in exchange for the knowledge. But it also knew that in time you would have need of those. When you entered the deathsong I prevented the completion and took from Edenlea the one known as Jux-e-lea, using your song to change her. She wished, so I have given. We needed and we took; you needed we have given. The balance will be restored and now you may live your remaining seasons with Jux-e-lea. If, when she wakes she has changed her water-time and desires to return to her own time, it will be done. I, the Sentinel took your song away to make your four seasons stable and to remain sure.

Now you understand. Upon the winds I shall remain and circle this world until the very end of its time. Alone, but watching, and helpless to change.

For a yen the sound stopped and Mel-e-gar felt his water-time relax, but it was a brief respite for the Sentinel's sound snapped back;

You and Jux-e-lea have this place. Your time with your family is ended. They have felt your deathsong. Your part of Edenlea is beyond theirs to make sure you do not attempt to return. When I release your water-time, this sphere that holds the waters of you and your family will return to the one who holds it in the future. Mel-e-gar teach Jux-e-lea the best of your times. Enjoy your gift........

He gasped in surprise as his water-times sprang back into place. The sound had gone. Realising that he had closed his eyes he opened them and was in time to see the sphere glow brightly before *it* disappeared. Within a yen he felt her eyes upon him.

She reached up with her now empty hand and pulled him down. In a whisper she said, "*Hello Mel-e-gar.*"

Her eyes sparkled with delight as he returned her sound, "*Hello Jux-e-lea.*"

In that instant past concerns were swept away and with laughter sung gaily upon the night wind they found the softness of a well combined water-time.

* * *

71 S.E.

The image slowly faded away, bringing a satisfied smile to her face. She looked up from the crystal and sounded, "I am glad he was given a few seasons more. He deserved an extra water-time in peace."

Serliker responded with an affirmative spout of blue fire and sounded, "Didn't the Sentinel mention that there was a way for you to meet with Mel-e-gar?"

Tan-e-lea could feel the warmth of the crystal in her hands, still pulsating gently as she replied, "Yes, but *it* has not told me how just yet. There seems to be more to see, but for now I shall leave it. I can wait awhile longer. I am just happy that my Grand-elder could share his remaining time with such a lovely dolphin as Jux-e-lea." She then yawned, stretching her slim arms. "But for now I need to rest."

As if on cue Serliker's fire grew a little higher, bringing an energy wave rippling through the floor. Gradually a sleeping-chamber was formed in the place where her old pool had once been. Tan-e-lea marvelled at the changes Serliker was making to the cavern and still holding the crystal she walked over and lowered herself into the warm embrace of sleep. It was a measure of how tired she was to fall asleep so quickly. Serliker made the cover fall in place, wrapping her in the oval cocoon. *It* had chosen the essence of Edenlea, so her water-time would soothe her in her dreams.

After waking early the next tay, enjoying a hearty meal, she settled herself in the comfortable mound, near the dais and with Serliker's cool blue light bathing her she placed the fire crystal on her lap and allowed her water-time to meld as she had done the tay before. She could sense Serliker on the outer edge, a ripple of excitement passing through to her, as *it* waited for the images to commence. It made Tan-e-lea taste a familiar sensation and she chuckled quietly as the image of herself came to her, when in past time she had sounded her curiosity to Zar-e-gar and her Grand-elder. Yes, Serliker was much like a youngling, bursting with curiosity. It made it more so when Serliker with impatience sounded, *Go on. Get on with it. I want to see more!*

Together they swept into the red light and were taken to the edge of a blue sky where three dolphins could be seen below. They were swimming in perfect union northwards. Tan-e-lea and Serliker realised that the Sentinel must have stopped off a few times on the way back. As soon as that rippled through them they plunged down and found themselves sharing past water-time with Zar-e-gar, and his two companions.

* * *

6 S.E.

By the second jeanth, Fas-e-lea had told Zar-e-gar and Sol-e-lea that they should start to turn westward, so that they could make use of the north-east current that flowed along the western continent. They made no sound but just nodded their beaks and followed her with complete faith in her water-time. They were also more concerned with enjoying the warmth of the morning, which was a welcome change as they had passed through a heavy storm a few tays before. Zar-e-gar and Sol-e-lea continued with their game, while making sure they turned about after Fas-e-lea while they continued playing happily as they fished a large shoal.

Zar-e-gar found her company delightful as she seemed to share his fascination for the life that was a multitude in Edenlea. They were both approaching their eighth season and knew that in time they would make a joining, something they discussed often, going over the water-time they would share, with easy sounds that would make their young love more complete. He had marvelled on how easy it was to share with a lea and she didn't get in the way of him when he wanted to follow a fish. *Now that was important*! In all she would join in and for the first time he found his waters didn't ripple in annoyance. In fact he rather enjoyed it. He kept Fas-e-lea in sight as Sol-e-lea joined his acrobatics, matching pace perfectly.

His water-time had wondered what had made a Grand-elder want to leave her family and make the journey. So when they had given her a particular tasty fish to mark her fifty third season at the end of the third jeanth, he had made his curiosity known. Her answer was rather unexpected; she told them that in past tays on Delikadove she had helped Mel-e-gar, when as a young dolph she had discovered the answer to unravel *The Knowledge*, and with the help of many others they made it possible to travel to Edenlea. Ever since that time she was only happy when she could travel. So the chance to explore more of Edenlea was irresistible. But on *The Knowledge*, she wouldn't expand further and told them that when they arrived in the northern waters, they should ask Del-e-gar, as he could give a larger picture to fill their young water-times. Zar-e-gar had the feeling that she was playing with him, and it made him determined to find out...

The tays passed quickly to veuls, then jeanths. It was only when they had joined the current north did the temperature begin to drop. The fish changed and became larger. Great shoals would pass by. Zar-e-gar was delighted at the numbers and he made sure the others had their fill. He knew that the further north they went the more need they would have of an extra layer of fat. On the ninth Jeanth they spotted the waves of still water, like massive floating walls which made the light of Solarn glare back. Then at times the sky would be more heavily laiden with clouds, causing Solarn to become a shadow of itself, making the nights become longer. There was no sign of the northern dolphins and Fas-e-lea became more concerned as the tays passed. On a particularly cold night she stopped in the water and called for the two younglings to stay close and share water-time.

They descended several dees and the three stayed side by side. Zar-e-gar had the larger grey form of Fas-e-lea on his left and the smaller Sol-e-lea on his right. Like three waves their water-times came together. *What's wrong?* sounded Zar-e-gar, seeing how upset Fas-e-lea was becoming.

A strong ripple came in answer, *Where are they? I was sure that we should sight them by now.*

Sol-e-lea made her water-time respond as an idea occurred to her, *They may have gone further west. After all they may find the waters better nearer un-water.*

Yes! cried Zar-e-gar, *The shoals would be bigger and the waters safer*. He could understand as the season was far harsher than when Mel-e-gar had brought them here. They were not far from large floating packs of still water. He wouldn't have wanted to be trapped underneath its cold white surface. *How would you breathe?*

The images passed to Fas-e-lea and she understood their concern and was grateful for their sounds. Making a decision she finally replied, *You both may be right. It would be understandable if they have sought better waters. We will start right away.* With a flick of her tail she broke away and after getting her bearings she led them onward.

It took them more than six veuls to reach first sight of the un-water. With it brought the sounds of many dolphins. A cry of joy was released from them all as they made contact. A profusion of sound greeted them and it was not long before they were surrounded by welcoming dolphins. The familiar form of Haw-e-gar swept forward from the school. He rubbed his beak with Zar-e-gar and sounded, *Well, my brotherling, what brings you and your companions this far north?*

His water-time seemed far more relaxed than Zar-e-gar remembered. Great joy filled his sounds and he playfully slapped his brotherling. With great understatement he sounded, *Just visiting*

His brotherling laughed in delight and replied, *Come now, we must let you all rest. Then you can tell us what really brings you here*. He flipped tail over beak and led the three to the shallow waters only four klees from un-water.

The many sounds of happiness filled the waters in the large cove of un-water. Zar-e-gar was enjoying the company of old friends. Fas-e-lea joined up with Del-e-gar while Sol-e-lea rejoined her friend Yen-e-lea. The tay slipped to night and when the stars had filled the sky, a meeting was called. Giving the three travellers centre space around several circles of dolphins, Del e gar began:

We are here to welcome three dolphins from the southern sea... His sound was drowned out by the plethora of cheers. He had to wait until they fell silent. *But they bring with them sad news..* He had been filled in before the meeting by Fas-e-lea, who he nodded to make her sounds. She nodded her beak in return but motioned for Zar-e-gar to tell them the news.

For a second time he was the centre of attention which he would gladly have given away to have his Grand-elder back. All eyes and sounds were upon him. *I am sorry to tell...Mel-e-gar has passed into the deathsong....* His sound trailed off.

Many water-times went to Haw-e-gar. He just remained silent; he had been told before. The rest were stunned into silence. Zar-e-gar relayed his fatherling's sight of the rain of fire and Mel-e-gar's last sounds. There were many tears, but silently shed into water-times. Many didn't want to believe it but like the southern dolphins, they eventually accepted it.

Zar-e-gar looked towards Fas-e-lea and she again nodded for him to tell the rest. He was about to start when Kin-e-gar led his family forward, motioning them to stay in the front circle, before joining Zar-e-gar. *It's all right, I will tell them.*

There were puzzled glances at this and many began to murmur. Holding a flipper up for silence Kin-e-gar began, *My family has been told that Jux-e-lea..* His sound broke, but gathering his courage he renewed his sound, *That Jux-e-lea has also passed into the deathsong.*

This in many ways was more of a shock, while Mel-e-gar's passing was hard felt it was not completely unexpected as he was a very old dolphin, but Jux-e-lea was only just an Elder of sixteen seasons young.

The cries of sorrow filled the night and it was a while before Del-e-gar could make his sounds heard. *They brought us sad sounds but they do bring some joy.*

The dolphins grew silent with expectation, giving Zar-e-gar his sound to continue. *My motherling; Car-e-lea has given birth to a lea. They have named her Cas-e-lea and she is doing well.*

Now that was welcome news and the dolphins responded enthusiastically. Congratulations filled his water-time and he managed to bring a chuckle when he sounded, *Also I have come to teach you how to fish!*

Haw-e-gar came forward and remarked, *Well sounded my brotherling.*

Tears were transformed to sounds of joy and gradually the meeting broke up as Del-e-gar motioned them to part. When most had left he led the three with Haw-e-gar, who had been joined by Yen-e-lea, to break above the waves. Using his flipper he pointed to the shore and sounded, *You must wonder why we came so far west?* Before any could answer he added, *Well I shall tell you.. After Mel-e-gar had left us we explored for many klees. As the jeanths passed we found the waters colder and the shoals of fish had started to move further westward. But while some remained we stayed-.*

Del-e-gar stopped and a slight bitterness could be felt from his water-time. He noticed this and remarked, *I am sorry but we should have left the place sooner. By the fourth jeanth great floating islands of still water came from the north. One of the Elders proposed to investigate. I should not have let him but I too was curious. His name was Jyt-e-gar the mate of Ban-e-lea and he was gone for several tays. When he still had not returned I went to investigate. I found the still water to be treacherous, as it was easy to be trapped under the flows. On the second tay I heard his sound. He was crying for help. But I found it was impossible to continue further in Edenlea.*

Taking a chance I transformed myself to dolph form, landing upon the still water. I found it cold and hard in places and soft whiteness in others. Before I had walked many dees an explosion of sound knocked me off my dees. The power of the deathsong seemed to rattle the strange hard water. Then it began to split apart. I had to jump several times to escape falling in. Finally I made it to an area that had been torn apart. Edenlea was already becoming still and I watched as it hardened about the dead body of Jyt-e-gar. I reasoned that he must have been trapped and when he had no more air to breath below the still water, he had succumbed. I had to leave him there. My heart was filled with sorrow as I returned to the others. We left the area that tay and have not returned. Del-e-gar was morose with sad sound. He seemed to stare with expressionless eyes upon the waters.

Zar-e-gar feeling for him sounded, *You did what you could. We too saw the packs of still water. That was how we knew you must have ventured this way.*

Del-e-gar looked tired and his sad eyes turned to them and replied, *You saw when I did not...I am glad we have you here for the coming seasons.* With a twitch of his tail he dived, leaving them alone.

Haw-e-gar broke the silence. *He has not been the same since. The only time I saw joy in his water-time was when we first caught sight of the great forest upon un-water. He said it reminded him of home..*

The next tay Haw-e-gar took his brotherling to meet the new younglings that had been born. The first he met were the twins, which were a rare occurrence among the dolphins. They were born from Ban-e-lea, which added much to the sadness of the deathsong of Jyt-e-gar. He never saw his two younglings. They were now more than a season old and they stayed by their motherling's side when Zar-e-gar and Haw-e-gar came upon them. Ban-e-lea made them welcome and she introduced her twins; *The smallest is Mel-e-lea, but don't let her size fool you for her strength of tail is becoming well known.*

The youngling looked up from under her motherling's flipper and giggled. Using her flipper to stroke the other youngling Ban-e-lea introduced her, *Now Tor-e-lea, who is nearly twice the size of her sisterling and is much quieter but is learning to fish with great skill. I'm sure you will have fun with this one.*

The youngling wouldn't meet Zar-e-gar's gaze but he smiled and replied, *Your daughterlings are fine dolphins, Ban-e-lea. I look forward to teaching them both.*

With a wave of his flipper they parted, going to the next family. Zar-e-gar was much pleased when he saw Jer-e-lea and they quickly exchanged sounds. She was with a sleek dolphin named Cha-e-gar and it didn't take long to discover that they had joined during the season before. The next surprise was that Jer-e-lea was feeding her first born; Bue-e-gar. The youngling had her slim form but the eyes of his fatherling.

After mixing sounds Zar-e-gar found Cha-e-gar's sense of humour a delight and many sounds on fish were exchanged. It took Haw-e-gar to break the pair up to continue with seeing the new younglings.

Zar-e-gar's parting sound with his new friend, was to tell him that maybe it would be a good idea that Cha-e-gar should go find his Grand-elder, Del-e-gar and cheer him up. The dolphin readily agreed, thanking him for his concern and after giving Jer-e-lea a quick kiss, left to find his Grand-elder.

With her youngling close to her Jer-e-lea gently swam the dees to where three motherlings, side by side were each feeding a youngling. In turn she introduced them;

Firstly meet Gis-e-lea. Her youngling's name is Mul-e-gar she laughed and added, *because he always looks so serious. He must have very heavy water-time!*

The motherling laughed with Jer-e-lea and chuckled, *Yes, sometimes I feel he will become so heavy, he will plummet to the bottom of Edenlea!*

The others joined in, still laughing. Jer-e-lea introduced the next; *Here is Set-e-lea with her daughterling, Nas-e-lea. She tells everyone that her youngling does get enough to suckle and they reply, then why does she keep coming to us for more!?*

That brought more laughter. Set-e-lea who was a large dolphin, raised her flipper and rather nonchalant replied, *Well I was the same..* Even dolphins on the outer waters started to laugh at that.

Jer-e-lea had no need to introduce the final motherling as Zar-e-gar recognised her as Ose-e-lea, *This is her youngling, Eis-e-gar. He just sleeps!*

That brought a roar of appreciative laughter. Ose-e-lea's reply almost caused them to have convulsions, because they laughed so much. She yawned, flexing her body and sounded, *Yes, quite true...*

They were still laughing when Jer-e-lea told them she would meet with them again later. Zar-e-gar and Haw-e-gar spent the rest of the night feeding and sleeping. The next tay brought a brighter Solarn, but a chilled rain in the afternoon. He learnt that there had been three other joinings, Cha-e-gar's younger brotherling; Kan-e-gar had joined with Mat-e-lea, a daughterling of Set-e-lea, sisterling of Yen-e-lea, (Haw-e-gar's mate). Also Kan-e-gar's sisterling; Nen-e-lea had joined with Onn-e-gar, the eldest sonling of Ban-e-lea. Lastly the now eldest youngling of Gis-e-lea; For-e-gar, (After the perceived deathsong of Jux-e-lea), had joined with Las-e-lea, the eldest daughterling of Ban-e-lea.

He was pleased that a family still recovering from the deathsong of Jyt-e-gar had two joinings and two birthings in the last season. The whole school looked healthy and he was glad that the northern dolphins were fairing so well. They had tragedy but at least there were happy times among them. He knew that his fatherling would be pleased. It left him to muse that he had better begin the younglings' lessons. The sooner he had them trained the sooner he could return home.

To mark the entry to the seventh season, Del-e-gar called a special meeting. It was as Solarn was bringing the dawn and a fair breeze which welcomed the dolphins as they crowded round. They relaxed in the waters, their beaks above the surface. Many of the very young were still asleep or feeding but it didn't stop the ripple of anticipation from washing through them.

Zar-e-gar in particular was looking forward to this, as his brotherling had told him on the passing of the fifth season, six jeanths after coming north, Del-e-gar had opened his water-time to a story of Delikadove.

There was an early Legend that had dealt with a dolph named; Gam-e-lea who had lived during the cycle of Toomasel, three hundred thousand seasons ago on Delikadove. It told of her desire to become a Shika, a sky-flyer who only nested on the peaks of mountains. In those tays there were only four pairs, one for each mountain range on four of the continents. This desire was in dolph terms, totally- *Sky-happy*! But this didn't deter Gam-e-lea and she spent the rest of her tays trying to fulfil that aim. The story went on that she eventually convinced herself that she was indeed a Shika and she climbed a mountain of Bylinka and threw herself off. They say that she entered the deathsong with the derisive caws of the Shika as they watched her descent. The tale was a favourite among the dolphs and dolphins. According to Haw-e-gar, Del-e-gar told it so well making full use of his water-time that for some it made them laugh and for others, it made them cry their disappointment that she never succeeded!

Zar-e-gar could understand that as his time with Vue-e-lea had made him wish he could fly, as the Kerg. But he was never *sky-happy* enough to do other than dream of it. So with Sol-e-lea floating by his side, her gentle touch warming him, he waited with the rest for Del-e-gar to start.

When he perceived them to be ready he looked skyward and sounded, "We as dolphins of these northern waters look upon the new season with joy and a little sadness. Some of our family have gone. We know that there will always be times when the deathsong will *come*.." He paused then sounded, "This tay we remember Jyt-e-gar, Jux-e-lea, and of course, *Mel-e-gar*, who without his dream none of us would be here enjoying this tay."

For a yen his sound fell silent, allowing them to remember the ones they had lost. Helping the many rivers of water-time to flow towards the pool that Del-e-gar was creating, each sharing, bringing colour and life to a collective sea that allowed him to bring past tays to life. Deciding that all were ready he sounded, *Now it's time we share not only Mel-e-gar's seasons but all of those, Selahws, Shakeilar, dolph, and dolphin who brought together their wisdom, creating the events that led him to the final solution, that brought us to this, our New Edenlea....*

* * *

7182 S.N. (Continued..)

The first rays of dawn struck the edges of the opening, causing the blue light to shimmer with an orange hue. The night wind had dropped, leaving the air still. Mel-e-gar was at Ler-e-lea's side, hoping she might awaken but she remained asleep. Serliker was on a mound by the opening and *its* surface sparkled with the light of the new tay. *It* had remained silent over the clars that had passed allowing Mel-e-gar peace and quiet, deciding it was best to leave him alone.

Mel-e-gar had been grateful for *its* decision. Only when a Healer entered the room did Mel-e-gar look up from his vigil. His water-time flexed reaching out to Serliker, *I believe it's time we left her to their capable hands. There is nothing more I can do here. The Selahw will be growing impatient for me to lead them to their new home.*

Impatient, no, the Selahw would not know the meaning of that word. They have grown a different sense of time. A few clars of waiting would have been barely noticed. I am surprised that you have not realised that by now. What with your close relationship with Cual-e-lay, teased Serliker.

Very funny.. retorted Mel-e-gar, *I sometimes forget that they are not the same as us dolphs.*

The exchange of sound was un-perceived by the Healer, who with a wave of a hand opened the sleeping-chamber and examined Ler-e-lea. Mel-e-gar watched the strangely compelling movements of the dolph who kept his intense eyes focused on his patient. No sound passed his sombre lips, not once acknowledging their presence. The only discernible activity was the energy which was building up in the dolph's hands as he quickly passed them over Ler-e-lea's limbs. It was the first time that Mel-e-gar had watched a Healer at work and even Serliker watched fascinated. The dolph seemed to make a judgement and left the room without closing the sleeping-chamber.

Mel-e-gar was about to ask why, but decided that the Healer must have known what he was doing. It gave him a chance to see fully the state of his friend. Her body was very thin, and her skin was tightly drawn over the wasted muscles of her limbs, making her look very frail. His own health sense judged that it would take many jeanths for her to recover fully. It hurt him to see her this way and he wished there was more he could do for her. An idea struck him and turning to face Serliker, he asked within his water-time, *Is there anything you can do to help her?*

He could feel Serliker silently judge the situation before it gave *its* answer, *No, my young dolph. It would be better that she heals naturally. The time that will pass will help her to come to terms with the loss of Hil-e-gar. She needs that time.*

It was not the answer he had hoped for but he could understand the conclusion that Serliker had come to. *If that is the way, then so be it but I would ask you one task that you can perform for her.*

What would that be? replied Serliker.

Stay with her while I take the Selahw to the Sea of Hederlike. Keep me informed of her progress and if I have not returned by the time she awakes tell her that I will not be too long.

Serliker chuckled and replied, *That is not one but three things that you request of me!*

Its sounds caused Mel-e-gar to flick an annoyed ripple in *its* direction. Seeing this Serliker quickly added, *But I will do all that you have requested of me. Rest assured that she will be well cared for.*

That satisfied Mel-e-gar and after thanking Serliker he turned and leant over Ler-e-lea and kissed her goodbye. Taking one last look he bade farewell and strode from the room, along the winding corridors to the entrance that opened out to the outer edge of Desilata. As he walked across the open plain that rose to the brow of the hill, he opened his water-time and found the welcoming embrace of Cual-e-lay. Her sweet tones took away any last doubts that he held on leaving Ler-e-lea so soon. He was glad to have her warm waters mingling with his. He had missed her in the short time that had passed.

She had stayed joined with his water-time for the first two clars of his wait by Ler-e-lea's side but had to disengage to attend to matters concerning her fellow Selahw. The fact that he had missed her so quickly she found rather charming and only made her love for him even stronger.

When he crested the hill, the Selahw with Cual-e-lay at the head greeted him with an enthusiastic display of fluke slapping which he felt must have been heard for many klees around. With the strange duality of being joined with Cual-e-lay he experienced her joy as she caught sight of him running down the hill to the water's edge. With a great shout of pleasure he leapt into the air and dived smoothly into the sea. He angled his descent to bring him up just below her. He slid along her great form until he reached her head. Her large eye winked at him as he nuzzled his beak against her side. It felt so good to be back with her and they gave themselves a little time to enjoy being so close again before starting their journey.

After a brief discussion they chose to travel east, then south to the sea of Hederlike. Mel-e-gar had offered to transport them all there to save time but the Selahw had laughed and had sounded they would enjoy the journey. After all it would help them to become further accustomed to the strange waters. In the tays that followed Mel-e-gar spent his time telling them what had gone on in the seasons that had passed since their ancestors had left dolph society. They had many questions which he did his best to answer and they in turn answered his.

On the third tay he received sound from Serliker telling him that Ler-e-lea had awoken. By using Serliker he could share *its* senses, allowing him to see and speak with her. He could have joined directly with her but decided that it would be better to wait until her water-time was more stable. But if her water-time was up to it and she could reach the crystal, he would create a neutral water, enabling her to come to him. It would only take a little effort on her part, less dangerous than his plunging into her waters.

As Serliker made room for him, he felt his water flow into the crystal. It took a yen for him to orient himself and he saw her from a raised perspective. He realised that Serliker must have grown a pedestal some dees high to allow him to look down upon Ler-e-lea. The angle was off to her left and happiness filled him to see her eyes open. She couldn't move her head as the muscles were still too weak. He asked Serliker to cause an arm to grow from the pedestal. His view shifted until his was looking down directly above her head.

Her eyes widened a little as she focused on the ball of Shakeilar spinning above her. Serliker had made the bottom part of the arm which *it* was rested upon transparent so she could see *it* clearly. Her eyes widened even further as Mel-e-gar's sound came from the crystal. With a great deal of effort she gave a smile as his tones filled the chamber. "Do not be *alarmed* Ler-e-lea!"

She tried to answer but only a raw croak escaped her parted lips.

"No, do not try and speak. Try and reach out with your water-time to this crystal."

Mel-e-gar waited as she tried. Slowly and tentatively her water flowed towards the crystal. Feeling a little more confident she allowed her water to sink into the crystallised depths. He had created an orange island in the middle of a large lake of purple water, where she found herself gently materialising, standing fit and whole on the sandy surface. Mel-e-gar reached out and pulled her to him. They held each other close for a few yens, no need for sounds to tell each other how much their friendship meant to one another. They both blinked away tears as they parted and stood, enjoying the time. He could see the delight in her eyes as she surveyed the illusion he had created.

Finding she could now speak her sounds she blurted out, *It's wonderful Mel-e-gar!* and hugged him again.

Seeing that her water-time was far healthier than he would have believed possible he disentangled himself from her embrace and taking her hands in his sounded, *It's good to have you back Ler-e-lea. Your water-time has developed beyond my expectation.*

She looked up at her friend and replied, *All thanks to you Mel-e-gar, you are a good teacher.*

He smiled and sounded, *But I had a good pupil!* Seeing this exchange could get ridiculously out of hand they both laughed, agreeing that they had both travelled long rivers of water in the seasons that had passed.

They spent the rest of the time sharing the events that had passed since they had parted the many jeanths before. He had not been sure how much to tell but she urged him to continue until he had told it all. The only exception he made was to leave out the fact that he knew that Danetar would destroy Delikadove before a hundred seasons had passed, even though he knew that there never was such a thing as a, *good time*, to divulge that kind of information.

Instead he told her of Serliker, the Selahw and the way in which they had helped to allow the Keaverkack to return to their home waters.

This she was glad to hear but it brought forth her tears of grief at the loss of her Hil-e-gar.

Mel-e-gar did his best to give comfort to her and when she had exhausted her tears they sat upon the sand and shared the one puzzle that had saved her life and allowed him to rescue her from her coma.

The green light; what was it, and what did it mean? After much discussion they had to admit that they knew very little, except for one thing which Mel-e-gar found even more perplexing, adding to the mystery. That was Ler-e-lea's conviction that the green light had something to do with a dolphin, a strange and beautiful dolphin that reminded her of Mel-e-gar but was also very different. She could not explain it either, and unless they encountered it again it was unlikely to be resolved. A mystery it would more than likely have to remain.

Ler-e-lea's water-time was now tired and very full with all she had shared but she was glad that Mel-e-gar was safe and that he had found love with Cual-e-lay. On this she sounded, *I would like to meet her one tay soon. I am sure we will become good friends.*

I know she would like that, replied Mel-e-gar. Taking her hand and lifting her to her dees he added, *It's time to leave...*

Tired but thankful she allowed her water-time to retract and she slowly disappeared from the orange beach. *See you soon Mel-e-gar.*

Then she was gone. He caused the scene to withdraw, allowing himself to look down upon her from the crystal that was Serliker. Her eyes were now closed but a relaxed smile was upon her face. *Goodbye Ler-e-lea.* Then he let go, returning himself to Cual-e-lay in the purple sea.

It took more than a jeanth to complete the journey taking them into the next season. On the final tay Cual-e-lay and the Selahw gave a final thanks to Mel-e-gar and told him that if he ever needed their help he would only have to ask. The great creatures had honoured him far more than he believed he deserved.

Cual-e-lay made sure he was as close to her as possible and with soft sound revealed, *Mel-e-gar you have done more than you realise...You have added to the Selahw. Given new blood to our race and to yours....* Her sound trailed off in silence and she waited.

With startled fervour he cried, *You mean...You are carrying our unborn!* He was not sure that he had heard correctly but as she filled his water-times with laughter at his surprise he knew that he was going to be a *fatherling*!

His excitement exploded forth as the revelation sank in and with delight he cried his joy. With a tremendous surge he launched himself through the waves into the air giving loud cries as he somersaulted twice before plunging back into the water.

He sang a song and filled the sea with his happiness and when he had finished he was as a Selahw and together he and Cual-e-lay danced the ritual of the Unborn according to the tradition of the Selahw. A great dance that had them almost fused together from head to flukes as they leapt and cavorted through the waters, ending when they had as one mass launched from the water and pirouetted in the air, then to come smashing down, displacing the water in all directions. While this was happening the other Selahw had created a circle about them and beat out the tune of their song with their flukes upon the water.

When they finally came to a rest and calmed down, Cual-e-lay sounded, *Mel-e-gar would you choose the name of our unborn.* She liked it when he was transformed into an equal mass as she, and while he recovered his water-time to reply she stroked and caressed him.

His water saw a name clearly as he enjoyed her touch, *Star-e-lay!*

Ah! Mel-e-gar! I knew you would choose well. Our daughterling will have a fine name. She was indeed pleased and they announced to the Selahw the name of their unborn. Cual-e-lay told Mel-e-gar that Star-e-lay would be born sometime in the third jeanth of **7184 S.N.** Knowing that a lay's gestation period was almost four jeanths longer than a lea's made him realise that he had far longer to wait. Cual-e-lay found his anguish funny and she told him off for being silly. *After all it was no time at all...*

* * *

KNOWLEDGE

7184 S.N.

On the tenth tay of the new season Mel-e-gar travelled to Desilata to spend a few tays with Ler-e-lea in her home, mostly to check on her progress as she gradually relearned how to walk again. He had not visited for over a jeanth but had kept in touch via Serliker while he had spent most of the last season with Cual-e-lay as they waited for her to give birth. He had not been surprised when Ler-e-lea had asked to go home four jeanths before. However it was not without resistance from the Healers who felt she would be better served under their watchful eyes but she kept insisting until they made a compromise by allowing her to return, only if she agreed to have a Healer with her at all times. He found out later on a previous visit that she had chosen the one who was present when Mel-e-gar had first visited her over a season ago. The most difficult part for her was the loss of movement while in dolphin form. She had hoped that she might get some relief by being able to swim but the muscles of her tail had been affected, making her progress even slower. But she did have the companionship of the Healer. Even though he never talked, she found his silence and intense eyes rather comforting.

Danetar was high in the midtay sky, baking the city. Most of the inhabitants were within the cooler confines of their homes. So the city seemed rather deserted as he made his way to Ler-e-lea's. When he reached the inner circle the now familiar blue shimmer with flecks of red greeted him. Since Serliker had taken up residence *its* influence on the structure was very much apparent, making her home stand out among the uniform blue of the city. He passed his hand over a new red marker and an opening appeared. Stepping through he saw that she must have guests for there were openings to other rooms on both sides of the main entrance.

One thing that had not changed was the large pool which dominated the main room. The cool purple waters looked inviting as Mel-e-gar walked over and sat on the edge. Looking into the depth he could just make out two shadowy forms slowly moving along the bottom. Gradually they turned and made for the surface. Her beak broke through, giving a loud whistle of welcome to Mel-e-gar and she swam closer, resting her beak upon his thigh.

She looked really pleased with herself, her laughing eyes staring up at him. "*I am doing really well!*" she exclaimed, her light dancing voice filling the room. "Give me a few yens and I will join you."

She raised her beak and twisted with considerably more agility since the last time he had seen her and she made for the centre of the pool. The Healer by this time was swimming to the opposite side, gathering speed for a jump out of the water.

Mel-e-gar came to his dees to move back as the Healer leapt from the pool sending a shower of water over the walls and floor. This quickly disappeared as it was absorbed by the Shakeilar. There was a quick sparkle of white energy and the solemn face of the Healer turned his eyes towards Ler-e-lea.

Now Mel-e-gar was expecting what happened next so he took a few more paces back. When he had first seen what was about to happen he had been amazed with the ingenuity of it, because he had wondered how she could leave the pool if she couldn't swim fast enough to leap out. The waters of the pool suddenly dropped by two dees, to allow a raised mound, about four dees round, to grow from the bottom of the pool under Ler-e-lea as she stayed perfectly still in the position required. As the mound touched her the top broke open like a blossoming flower and wrapped itself around her middle. When that was complete the stem suddenly whipped back, plunging her beneath the pool only to release the tension loosening its grip as it whipped forward and freed her. Ler-e-lea flew through the air, across half the length of the pool to come down perfectly on her newly formed dees into the steadying hands of the Healer. She laughed with breathless excitement, "Let me do that *again*!" she joked.

Mel-e-gar was sure there was a gentler way of doing it but apparently the Healer had communicated to the Shakeilar what he desired and *it* had complied. He had to admit it did look exhilarating. It certainly made Ler-e-lea sparkle with delight.

In the short yens it took for him to walk over to them they were both dry, the water droplets taken from them almost instantly after they had been transformed back to dolph form. She did look much healthier. The muscles were regaining their fluidity. Only her left leg looked stiff as she slowly walked the few paces to Mel-e-gar into his welcoming arms. "It is good see you looking so well Ler-e-lea," he said, hugging her gently.

She looked up into his smiling face and replied, "I shall soon be back to my old self. The Healer has done much to help my recovery." They walked over to two mounds positioned around a raised dais that held a platter of steaming fish. Both ate heartily as they exchanged news. The Healer meanwhile had left the room, going into the next chamber, closing the opening behind him. As they relaxed Mel-e-gar said, "Has he spoken to you at all since his stay here?"

After quickly swallowing a morsel of fish she replied, "No, I have only just learned from the other Healers at the centre that he cannot speak." Her face was serious as she looked at Mel-e-gar. "Also he cannot hear and he cannot see..."

His surprise must have registered on his face for she added, "He is a *remarkable* dolph. Apparently he was born without those three senses but he has a well developed water-time which allows him to function much the way we do as dolphins while out of the water, the same way that you have learnt and the way you have taught me. But the most interesting thing is the way his water-time is. For without the other senses his view of the world is a strange place of dark shadowy forms, no colour but filled with a sound that can only be felt and not heard, rather like a series of vibrations." Her voice was filled with enthusiasm as she talked about her Healer.

Mel-e-gar was taken up by the idea as she continued to talk. "When he wants me to do something, you feel his intentions instantly, almost unconsciously-"

"Like the way dolphs have communicated with the Shakeilar these past ages!" interrupted Mel-e-gar.

"Yes! I knew you would understand. His relationship with the Shakeilar is very intimate; they are very similar. Serliker told me that when the need arises to awaken the Shakeilar he will be perfect for the job."

"I see that *it* has shared with you the idea of having to move and create new cites that encompass the sea as well as the land," replied Mel-e-gar.

The excitement was clear on her face as she answered, "*It* told me before *it* left. Serliker also wanted to make sure that I let you know about the Healer."

"Where is *Serliker*? I wondered why I did not sense *its* presence when I arrived."

She leaned forward, an intent expression upon her face, and replied, "You mean *it* didn't tell you?!"

"No, Serliker didn't." He laughed at her amazement and said, "Well are you *going* to tell me?"

Ler-e-lea was surprised that he took it so well which made Mel-e-gar laugh even more. "*It* doesn't tell me everything you know!"

Her face relaxed and replied, "Serliker left two tays ago with a Healer from the centre. *It* said that they would be gone for several jeanths to the city of *Ieulasayer.* I don't know why! All *it* said was that it was important."

She shrugged and raised her hands indicating she had nothing further to add. She relaxed into the mound as he leant forward and took another piece of fish. While he chewed, his water-time reviewed what she had told him. It was not much to go on. In the end he decided he would just have to wait and see as he could not afford to venture too far away from Cual-e-lay. He knew that if he went after Serliker he could get involved in something which would take him away for too long.

After they had finished eating, Ler-e-lea led Mel-e-gar into the next chamber where the Healer was sitting in a corner with a seeing crystal in his hands. There was no indication that his water-time had noticed them enter and Mel-e-gar who was curious as to how he managed to read a crystal that was filled with images found himself whispering to Ler-e-lea, "*How does he read it?*"

Ler-e-lea took his hand and whispered, "*You don't have to whisper!*"

She giggled as he said, "Yes, *sorry* I...*Well..*" His voice fell silent as he realised how foolish he must seem.

She laughed and said, "It's quite normal. Even I did it once when my parentlings came to stay, but you get used to it." Then she indicated the Healer, returning to the question of the crystal and answered, "He is not reading it. He is feeling it. From what I have learned he absorbs the emotions of images, giving him a fair idea of what is stored in the crystal."

He took one last look at the Healer and sat down by a table of Shakeilar. Ler-e-lea sat opposite, resting her hands on the smooth, shimmering surface.

"He really is remarkable.. Does he have a name?" he enquired.

She looked like she was swimming deep within her water-time before she answered, then with puzzlement in her voice replied, "That was the strangest thing about him. For all the time in the Centre none of the other Healers would tell me, saying that if the Healers wanted you to know then it was left up to them. I made my intention clear to him but he didn't respond, not until we had been here for more than two jeanths. Then out of the blue he came over when I was resting from a session of healing. Those intense eyes seemed to examine me intently for a yen; then his name just popped into my water-time: *Gre-e-gar*!

But why they keep such secrecy about it I don't know. Nor do I know why he decided to tell me."

Mel-e-gar could tell she was intrigued by her Healer. Deciding to copy her earlier gesture he shrugged and raised his hands and said, "Who *knows*!"

She narrowed her eyes and playfully swiped him across the table, which he easily dodged as she half menacingly said, "Mel-e-gar! Stop teasing!"

As she tried again he caught her hand, with laughter filling his voice replied, "I can see you have regained some of your strength, so I am sure that you will be able to find out for yourself."

"Hmmm *I bet...*" she retorted.

He decided to change the subject by asking, "I noticed you had more rooms than usual, expecting more guests?"

By the change of tact, she knew he wouldn't tell any more. Part of her wanted to ignore his question and not answer but she saw a way she could tease him. So with her most mischievous smile, she smoothly said, "Well, I believe you will just have to wait and see!"

He roared with laughter which was not the response she had desired and playfully he said, "Now the Ler-e-lea I have known is really back!"

She tried her best hurt look but then collapsed into a fit of giggles as they laughed together.

By the evening after exchanging the rest of their news, they were sitting by the pool when Ler-e-lea suddenly looked towards the main opening as it dissolved away revealing her mystery guests.

Mel-e-gar looked round and saw Wel-e-lea and a youngling standing in the entrance. They were both surprised and Ler-e-lea looked on with delight as her sisterling and Mel-e-gar called out their joy.

After much hugging, Wel-e-lea picked up the youngling and presented her sonling; Chm-e-gar. He looked shyly up at Mel-e-gar and deciding he liked what he saw reached out and clambered into his arms.

"I believe he *likes* you!" remarked Wel-e-lea, pleased that her sonling had taken to her old friend so quickly.

Mel-e-gar was a little overwhelmed but he grinned back as Chm-e-gar wrapped his small arms around his neck and snuggled his head against Mel-e-gar's chest.

He carried the youngling over to the pool with Wel-e-lea and Ler-e-lea following close behind. Chm-e-gar made it clear he wanted to go in, so Mel-e-gar took a firm hold of him, whispered something that made Chm-e-gar's eyes sparkle and threw the youngling into the air. Cries of delight filled the room as Chm-e-gar managed to somersault twice before straightening his young form as he disappeared beneath the surface.

Mel-e-gar cheered as the youngling came up and nodded his beak at him. Taking it as his cue he too dived in, filling the room with a dazzling display of energy as his form changed to dolphin. A tremendous splash of water was thrown up, soaking Ler-e-lea and Wel-e-lea. When he turned and looked above the water he saw them sitting and laughing as they shook the water off. The Shakeilar came to their rescue and quickly took the remaining water away.

Chm-e-gar found it very funny and his young beak bobbed up and down as his whole body shook with laughter. The two dolphins played together and Mel-e-gar found himself enjoying the simple games of a youngling. It made ripples of past tays he had shared with his friends.

Later, after Chm-e-gar, tired but happy was put in his sleeping-chamber for the night, Mel-e-gar, Wel-e-lea, and Ler-e-lea shared a light supper. It was almost like old times. If Jey-e-gar had been there it would have completed the picture. With that feeling running through his water-time Mel-e-gar asked, "How is *Jey-e-gar* these tays?"

It was Wel-e-lea who answered, "He left Nue-e-lea last season and ventured out on his own. The last I had heard he was making plans to go through the Gap on the western Continent. Apparently his idea is to see if the Puga and the Muala ever crossed the Gap themselves."

Then Ler-e-lea added, "Our brotherling seems to be devoting his life to those creatures."

Mel-e-gar could understand that, as they were fast disappearing from Delikadove. There were a few left on the eastern continent but most were to be found on the blue plains beneath the forest of Duorsilear. He was satisfied with their answers and turning his attention back to Wel-e-lea he said, "Your sonling is a fine dolph. Where is his fatherling?"

The question seemed to disturb Wel-e-lea for she lost her usual sure composure and reached out her hand for Ler-e-lea. Mel-e-gar was surprised at the response but after a yen Wel-e-lea turned back to Mel-e-gar and in a low, almost stilted voice replied, "Ran-e-gar has gone south to join the expedition to explore the seven cities in the Frelegar mountains....*I fear for him there..*"

His water-time quickly retrieved what he knew of the seven cities and as the knowledge came up he saw her concern. At the beginning of the cycle of the Neimas many dolphs saw the destruction of those gentle creatures as a warning to change their ways. A group formed a fellowship of dolphs. Their intention was to stay as dolphs and to leave the seas behind them. The full reasoning behind it was long since lost but he knew that at first the group was relatively small but over the seasons it began to grow. They had no real direction apart from not venturing into the seas until around **1209 S.N.** when a dolph came from a City of Malaroi on the southeast coast of the eastern continent. Her name was Xrl-e-lea and she began to bind them together. By **1230** she had enough followers to implement her ideas. Basically she wanted to establish a society away from the main stream so they could live fully without reminders of what they considered to be the old ways.

Now dolphs were free to follow any idea or philosophy they desired as long as no harm befell the rest of dolph society from their actions. The only concern that was raised in the Council at the time was that many of her followers were leading dolphs in their fields. Many were teachers of Science, Nature, Physics, Astronomy, and many others. After much discussion they decided there was not a lot they could do except to wish them well. The one tragedy seen by many observers of that part of dolph times was the loss of a brilliant student by the name of Pha-e-gar. It was said that after the disappearance of his teacher, a Healer by the name of Eil-e-lea, he became even more brilliant but more unstable.

For many it seemed strange that the disappearance of a Healer of Eil-e-lea's level wasn't further investigated. But then maybe they did and the record had been lost. *It had happened more than six thousand seasons before and not yestertay!*

There were rumours about Pha-e-gar, his strange behaviour and his extraordinary ideas. Some claimed he made progress in discovering ways for dolphs to create a device, using Shakeilar, that would give the power of flight. This in due course may have enabled dolphs to venture off Delikadove and explore the twin moons and maybe even further into space. But that knowledge disappeared with him.

Two further seasons passed before Xrl-e-lea led two thousand followers to the Frelegar mountains. For many tays after, mighty explosions rocked the mountain range. Because she had made an agreement with the Head of the Council that no dolph would venture within a hundred klees of the mountains, no one knew what was happening. Not until **1345 S.N.** did the Council organise an expedition to find out how their missing Elders were doing. There had been no communication for more than a hundred and twenty seasons. Ten dolphs left the city of Santiier, which was west of Desilata to travel south and discover the location of the descendants of Xrl-e-lea and her followers. They never returned. Speculation was rife throughout Delikadove that they had either died trying or had found the dolphs and joined them.

Over the following fifty seasons three more expeditions were sent out and they too failed to return. It was not long after that the mountains were declared to be dangerous and off limits to any dolphs, a decree that was only the second and so far the last of its kind on Delikadove. It was reinforced several seasons later when a dolph by the name of Oal-e-gar stumbled into a home in Desilata city, his face looking ravaged by a thousand fears and incapable of any speech. It was only when the Healers were called that they found out his story. His mind told about Seven cities that were in a valley in the middle of the mountains.

Oal-e-gar's mind told that his expedition, the last to go, found the settlement after finding a way around a giant wall of Shakeilar that blocked the only entrance. His party of eight dolphs were thrilled that they had found the place of the lost dolphs. When they had climbed high enough they managed to find a way over the mountain. The first sight they had of the seven cities filled them with astonishment. For the dolphs of Xrl-e-lea had blasted a valley out of the mountains, creating seven raised ledges which each held a city. They were joined by pathways of Shakeilar suspended above the valley floor. They realised that the greenness of the ground underneath must have grown long after the completion, as Giant trees had caused some of the paths to be pushed to one side. All the cities shone in the light of Danetar, sparkling and glimmering their welcome to Oal-e-gar's party. The magnificent structures towering into the sky, seemed almost to grab them from their precarious position, causing them to scramble their way down the craggy slope as fast as was possible into the valley.

They had expected some sort of welcome but none came, only the wind which howled around the structures as all was very much deserted. The cities may have shone with a semblance of life, but were lifeless of any dolph. After exploring for many jeanths they decided to return home. But on the tay they were due to leave they chose to have one last look around, each one choosing a city to explore, hoping to find some record of the inhabitants. Now as there were only seven cities and eight dolphs Oal-e-gar didn't see any reason to join the others and he stayed behind.

He waited and waited on the outer edge, sitting with his back to the giant wall. By nightfall he became worried for his companions. Choosing to wait until dawn to look for them he settled down to sleep. In the night he was awakened by screams which tore into his mind. There was such terror in the sounds that he lost his nerve and ran, scrambling the best he could up the mountain. He told how he ran with the screams ringing inside him for tays until he found Desilata. The Healers said Oal-e-gar's mind had been torn apart and it was only their skill in their use of water-time which allowed him to tell what had befallen him. Otherwise they might have never known. They had hoped to save him but he passed into the deathsong with a sigh of relief escaping his lips. The decree was reinforced and the seven cities fell into legend, which had held dolphs for thousands of seasons, until now.

The images fell from Mel-e-gar's water-time, his concern showing clearly on his face. He asked of them both, "Do you know the *Legend*?"

Wel-e-lea nodded her head, "Yes, Ran-e-gar told me when he heard they were going to send another expedition. He has reasoned that as six thousand seasons have passed since that time it should now be safe."

Ler-e-lea said she also knew as she put her arm around her sisterling and added, "I am sure he is right Wel-e-lea. After all the Council would never have sanctioned such a trip if they didn't believe it was safe."

Now Mel-e-gar should have expected that but he was surprised that Alk-e-lea as Head of the Council would have. He did not share that ripple but instead remarked, "Ler-e-lea is right. If you wish, I will go and see Alk-e-lea to find out more of the details."

Wel-e-lea looked up sharply at that and exclaimed, "But you *can't*. She and Bue-e-gar are heading the Expedition. They left *Santiier* yestertay. It took me and Chm-e-gar all tay to travel from there!"

Both he and Ler-e-lea looked at Wel-e-lea in astonishment. This was the first they had heard of it. They had assumed that it was a private expedition, sanctioned by the Council maybe, but as Alk-e-lea was going they and all Elders and Grand-elders should have been informed.

"*What is going on?*" they both exclaimed.

Wel-e-lea could only look at their confusion and shrug. At any other time it might have been funny.

Then Ler-e-lea, her face turning pale as the realisation hit her, gripped her sisterling's shoulder rather hard, her voice hoarse with a terrible feeling. "Wel-e-lea! You said they left from *Santiier*! But why use the old *name*?!!"

For a yen a look of confusion flickered across Wel-e-lea's face and she was about to answer when Mel-e-gar cried, "Of course! *Ieulasayer*! The name they gave it after Oal-e-gar returned. They wanted to obliterate any connection with the doomed expeditions from their city!"

Ler-e-lea then finished it for him, "And that is where Serliker and a Healer have gone. To join with them!"

At least they knew the reasons why Serliker left the way *it* did. Mel-e-gar quickly recapped, "So we know Alk-e-lea and Bue-e-gar are heading it with Serliker and a Healer, presumably to care for any injured, which may mean they know that they might find trouble. Add Ran-e-gar and you have yourself a small expedition. But why *Ran-e-gar*?"

Wel-e-lea who by this point was even more fearful for her mate stumbled on her words as she replied, "He has been studying the legend for many seasons. He knows all there is to know."

Well at least that made sense to Mel-e-gar. He and Ler-e-lea managed to calm Wel-e-lea down. They were sorry that they had alarmed her but it couldn't have been helped. It came as a shock to them both that Alk-elea would act outside the normal parameters of the Council. But he had one more thing to ask of Wel-e-lea, "Are there any more going?"

She wiped the tears from her eyes and gradually her normal demeanour returned as she replied, "Yes, a dolph by the name of Hia-e-lea. She specialises in surviving harsh conditions." She stopped, then making sure she held Mel-e-gar's gaze added, "There is one more thing you should know. When Ran-e-gar first told me I asked him if he was going to ask you to join them. His reply was no. They had decided that your involvement would alert the rest of Delikadove. They wanted to get in and out within a couple of jeanths at the most."

Mel-e-gar was not that surprised as he had been expecting something like that. Not that he would have gone as he didn't want to leave Cual-e-lay. He told them both that and they understood even though both of them wished he would. Ler-e-lea seeing how tired her sisterling was advised her to get some sleep. Mel-e-gar agreed and they all retired for the night. Gre-e-gar appeared in the entrance and helped Ler-e-lea to her sleeping-chamber. Mel-e-gar followed Wel-e-lea and as he turned to go into his own chamber he stopped her and said, "If it's any comfort I will I go after them if they have not returned by the birth of my youngling."

She smiled warmly, thanking him for his gesture and entered her room. Mel-e-gar was left alone and as the blue light began to dim he entered his room and climbed into his sleeping cocoon. The last ripple through his water-time as he fell asleep was that he just hoped Alk-e-lea and the others knew what they were doing. At least they had Serliker. *It should keep them out of trouble....*

* * *

The small party of dolphs left Ieulasayer as Mel-e-gar and his friends were settling down to sleep. Hia-e-lea led them through the darkness holding Serliker to light their way. They were all thankful for the coolness of the night as they trekked across the plains to the Frelegar mountains. Ran-e-gar brought up the rear, checking to make sure that no dolphs of the city were following. Alk-e-lea was talking to Bue-e-gar in a low voice as they followed Hia-e-lea's lead.

"Do you think it was wise not to include *Mel-e-gar* in this trip?" asked Alk-e-lea, still not sure of the wisdom of skulking out, keeping the whole thing secret.

Bue-e-gar looked up at his mate and replied, "My sweet one, you as Head of the Council made your decision based on Hia-e-lea's story. It made sense then as it does now. She made it clear that it would be a mistake for him to come."

Alk-e-lea had persuaded herself to believe that but she didn't feel comfortable with the whole situation, even though she could relate to the passion and urgency of Hia-e-lea's call. It was much the same when she somehow had felt Ler-e-lea's distress two seasons before. The power of the call had shaken her and whatever the green light was it certainly compelled action.

She looked down at Bue-e-gar, his face half in shadow. The light of Serliker was enough to pick out his sparkling eyes and comforting smile. There was not much that shook him and she was grateful that he had agreed to accompany her. "Well we shall soon find out how wise it was in the tays *to come...*" she remarked.

Bue-e-gar gave her a comforting squeeze as they both turned their attention to where they were going. The mountains were dark and gloomy. Shadows lurked on the horizon. It would be about ten tays before they reached the lowland hills that nestled at the base of the mountains. At least they knew where they were going. Not like past Expeditions who had very little to go on. They not only had the *Legend* but also an update that was much more recent.

It began several jeanths ago when Hia-e-lea started to have a series of strange dreams. Now she was a practical dolph who had spent the best part of her twenty-nine seasons learning survival techniques which satisfied her very practical mind. She had little time for what she considered to be the fragile and insubstantial ideas of *water-time*.

So the dreams which plagued her sleep were unusual and very disturbing. For tays she couldn't settle and her mate Tre-e-gar found her change of mood disquieting. It didn't help that she wouldn't talk about them and her frequent bouts of walking in her sleep didn't help matters. She had stopped taking younglings out on field trips, spending her time sitting, morosely searching her collection of crystals.

This went on for several veuls, until one night Hia-e-lea bolted upright in their sleeping-chamber and gave a piercing scream which shattered the quiet. Tre-e-gar quickly made the light of their home brighten and saw that his mate was shaking. Her eyes were vacant and her mouth twisted as another scream tore through her.

At that yen their daughterling, Ers-e-lea, who at three seasons young must have believed something terrible was happening, rushed into their room crying, "*Mamaling* what's wrong?!!"

Her distress at seeing her motherling this way tore at Tre-e-gar. He climbed from the sleeping-chamber and swept his daughterling into his arms. "It's all right young one. Your motherling just had a *bad dream*!" He climbed back in with Ers-e-lea still in his arms. Whatever was holding Hia-e-lea must have been spent for her eyes had lost their vacant look.

She looked around seeing them both staring at her, questions clear in their eyes. She didn't know what to say. The dream had left as quickly as it had appeared, leaving her worn out as if she had climbed several mountains. The stricken face of Ers-e-lea broke her silence and she reached out and cuddled her daughterling, "Don't *cry*, I'm all right."

Tre-e-gar gave her a worried look but decided to leave it until the morning. He motioned with his hand making the light dim to darkness and the three of them settled down to sleep.

After having their morning meal, and when Ers-e-lea had gone to see her friends he sat down near their pool with Hia-e-lea and tackled her about her dream during the night. "*I want to help*," he pleaded. "Why won't you *tell me*?"

She stared at the pool giving no indication that she had heard him but then she looked up. Her face looked tired and drawn. He had never seen her eyes look so haunted. She finally broke the heavy silence between them by saying, "I am *sorry* my love. But...I, just didn't know where to *start*.. It was so confusing. My mind feels different. *Oh*! It's just hard to *explain*!.."

Her frustration was apparent but Tre-e-gar persisted, "Try! *This cannot go on*..!"

She knew he was right but she just couldn't, as part of her didn't want to burden her mate with the visions that had been plaguing her sleep. The other part was afraid to. That somehow he might get pulled in, she didn't want that to happen. She loved him too much to take any chance that he might catch her madness. *No, she would find another way of dealing with it.* She reached out to Tre-e-gar and buried herself in his arms. "*Just hold me...*"

By the evening she had made up her mind. All three were out, just on the edge of the city, sitting on the dry, parched ground watching Danetar beginning to set. Tre-e-gar had noticed a change in his mate. She had been more relaxed, laughing and playing with their youngling, more like her old self. So it was with much surprise when she almost fell on him after chasing Ers-e-lea, landing heavily on her knees. Dark orange dust covered her legs and hands. She turned her lovely eyes on him and declared, "I am going away for a few tays... to Desilata."

It was so casually said that Tre-e-gar thought he had misheard. "*When?*" was all he could think of.

She laughed and said rather gaily, "*Tonight.*" His perplexed and dumbfounded expression was rather cute and she took hold of his face and kissed him deeply.

Well, his mind was in a state of shock; for tays she had been morose and sullen. Then they leave the city for a few clars and she is back to her cheeky self. He was not sure he could keep up with this, but she could certainly kiss!

They were both flushed as their lips parted. She sat on his lap and rubbed her cheek against his cheek and whispered, "It's good to be away from the city..."

Again, that surprised him for it was at her insistence that they had moved to Ieulasayer four seasons before. Ers-e-lea had been born in their home pool. (*As the sea was too far way.*) He gently took hold of her shoulders and moved her around so they were face to face. He gave her a quizzical look and said, "You are not *joking* are you?"

A shadow seemed to pass over her face and very slowly she replied, "No I am not..."

"But *Why*? You *loved it* here. You persuaded me that it was not only for your teaching but also any younglings we had, as they would grow up well here. What has changed?"

He was very perplexed by her change of mind. He had agreed with leaving the city of Malaroi as many dolphs had left now that Danetar had killed most of the life around the city. There was an idea to move the city west, maybe near Plesilea or Yengile. But that was seasons from happening as the Council had yet to sanction it.

Hia-e-lea had a fair idea what was running through his mind and she replied rather softly, "Since the dreams, I have found it uncomfortable being here.. *I need to get away*.."

"I see," he replied, "but why *Desilata*?"

She took a deep breath and answered, "I am going to see the *Healers* there." She held up her hand before he could question that. "I know we have a *Healing Centre* here but like I have already said I need to get away. I also know that I have never given much credence to *water-time*, but the dreams have made me aware that it could be my only hope of finding out what they mean."

Her passion was clear and he had to look away from the intensity of her gaze. As always she made sense, her logic infallible as ever. He knew there was no point in dissuading her, not that he would but sometimes he felt that he never really had any choice. She had made up her mind and was going. Turning back to look into her blue, grey eyes sparkling with the surety of someone who knows what they are going to do, he pulled her into his arms and with all the love he could muster declared, "Hia-e-lea you better get going.."

She held him tight and said, "Thank you. Take care of Ers-e-lea. I will be back *soon*."

She kissed him goodbye, picked up her ball of Shakeilar which she had brought with her to light her way and called out to her daughterling. Ers-e-lea came running over, breathless and covered in dust and Hia-e-lea quickly explained that she would be gone for a few tays.

There were a few tears but her youngling was getting used to her motherling disappearing every so often, so she was not that disturbed by the news. She gave her motherling the biggest hug she could manage and ran to Tre-e-gar.

They both watched her disappear into the dark night. Only the gleam from her crystal could be seen bobbing up and down, until that too disappeared from sight. He just hoped she found what she needed. With a heavy sigh he picked up Ers-e-lea and settled her on his shoulders. Giving her their crystal, she held it to light their way home.

Dawn was just breaking as she reached the outskirts of the city. It had taken her most of the night to walk the thirty klees from Ieulasayer to Desilata. She was tired but glad to see the shining blue domes of the spiral city. She had been here before many times, mostly to visit friends but this time she made straight for the healing centre, north-east of the city. Few dolphs were up and around at this time of the tay so she passed through un-noticed. Her first thought was to go to the city pool, which most cities had, to be of use for travellers passing through. But the closer she came to the Healing Centre the more determined she was to wait until she arrived there.

When she reached the outer rim, with the Centre in sight she balked, now not so sure. She found herself shaking, her mind going over and over what she was going to say. The building looked imposing, even a little threatening, but she slowly made herself walk the few paces to the entrance. A silver marker gleamed in the early morning light. Her fingers reached out, her hand hovering in front of the marker. Again her mind wracked with doubt. *What if she was going mad?* Her indecision crippled her mind. She didn't know how long she stood there shaking from head to dee but the decision was taken from her when an opening appeared, revealing a rather small pleasant dolph with silver eyes who reached out and took her hand.

His voice was gentle and warm, "*Welcome*, we have been *expecting* you." He pulled her through the opening.

She was startled by his words but she allowed herself to be led along a winding corridor to a large room that shone with silver and blue light. Most of the space was taken up by a pool which helped to draw her in.

If he had noticed her obvious confusion it didn't show as he softly talked to her. "You must be tired after your long walk. Come and swim and we shall share *water-time*. We knew you were coming. The Healers of your city knew of your distress. They told us to expect you and here you are."

She was still reeling from the fact that they knew she was coming. He startled her again when his soft tones said, "Yes, that is the power of the *water-time*, a blessing but also a curse. For we suffer the ills of our fellow dolphs."

His manner was so gentle and kind that she found it hard to believe he felt it was a curse. Before she could make any sound he led her to the edge of the pool and said, "Go on, dive in. I shall leave you now but I shall return later. There is food here if you wish it. The Shakeilar will respond as in your own home."

He let go of her hand and walked out. She stared after him thinking what a strange dolph but she liked his unassuming manner. The grime on her body felt heavy so she made up her mind and dived in, her form sparkling with energy as she changed to dolphin and enjoyed the refreshing cool waters for most of the tay.

In the evening the Healer returned and led her to another room, which was very different. The light was a soft orange glow that made her feel warm and safe as she stepped over the threshold. This time he stayed silent, a small smile on his face as he led her to the centre where a dome of orange and silver Shakeilar stood, much like a travelling-shelter but twice the size. Strange place for it she thought but when she passed through, she gasped with delight, for she had stepped onto a hill of yellow grass, sprinkled with trees with bright silver leaves. Red, blue and white flowers grew among them and as the perfume filled her she clapped her hands together and cried, "*It's Incredible!*"

A much smaller Danetar seemed to hang in the sky bathing her with gentle warmth. She turned back, expecting to find the opening but instead she only saw much more of the same. She was looking across a panorama of hills that swept across the landscape down to the sea. She slowly turned around taking in as much as she could. Her heart was fit to burst with the breathtaking beauty of it. To the south, white capped mountains stood majestic and regal against the orange sky and to the north a distant purple sea.

It was the smells and sensations that took her further and further into the scene. The more she absorbed the more she heard, like the many songs of the sky-flyers, cries and bleats of the distant Muala. She was no longer aware of whether the Healer was with her and she no longer cared. Like a youngling set free she ran across the hills, down one then up another, enjoying the sensation of soft grass under her dees, something she had rarely come across. Soon her mind convinced her that she could no longer be in the Healing Centre, that somehow she had passed through a gateway to another age. Even though she was being overwhelmed by the beauty of it her mind had registered that as Danetar was very small in comparison with what she knew, she must have been back in some part of Delikadove's past, a long time past to have such freshness and life all around her.

She was just weaving her way among a cluster of trees that wound their way between two hills to a valley below when she caught sight of a creature she knew to be extinct, or so she thought, for sitting on a solitary rock among deep purple flowers was a great hairy Neimas, whose startling blue eyes seemed to scan the sky as it sang a gentle song. She didn't understand but it made her want to laugh and cry all at the same time.

As she ran down the hillside, the Neimas must have heard her for it waved, beckoning with a great paw for her to join it. She stumbled down the last part and tripped, falling at the Neimas's dees. As she scrambled up she felt gentle paws lift her by the arms and placed her on its lap, all the while singing its song. Hia-e-lea felt no fear at the enormity of the creature, only joy at the touch of its silky fur on her skin. Feeling something underneath her, she laughed as she realised that it was a *He. Very much so.....*

The Neimas seemed to like her laughter and it began to make a booming tone which shook his chest and with his right paw patted her head. For a creature so strong he was surprisingly gentle, which had made them much sought after in past tays.

She sat following the Neimas's gaze as he watched the few white, fluffy clouds drift across the sky. A sweet breeze made his fur dance, stroking her skin. He broke a piece of rock and began to shape it with his paws. She watched fascinated as a yellow glow began to seep out, slowly spreading until it engulfed his paws. He was still singing and watching the sky but Hia-e-lea was held by the change that she could just see. Slowly the light died and with a nudge the Neimas indicated his paws, which he opened and there on his left was a piece of a cloud. That was what her ancient Elders would have called it and they were right, a cloud plucked from the sky.

Responding to his nudge she reached out and picked it up. The sensation was exquisite; it seemed to tingle with energy across her finger tips. But it was like holding nothing, because it was seemingly insubstantial. With great reverence she carefully put it in her mouth. That was her next surprise. Even though she might have seen images in the seeing crystal of dolphs eating this food it couldn't compare to the reality. It was like an explosion of colour which danced and played a wonderful tune upon her tongue. As it slipped down her throat she nearly passed out with the awesome feelings running through her. It was like an internally generated heat which massaged her from the inside out. It gave a glow which was unmatched by anything she had experienced before. And the stories were true; it was totally satisfying. She felt as if she wouldn't have to eat for a veul. She gave a contented sigh which made the Neimas laugh, his eyes looking at her with expectation. For a yen she was puzzled but then she remembered more of the Legend; *For after sharing their food it was the custom to lie together and share a story.*

Just as the Neimas began to lower her to lay with him among the purple flowers the light of Danetar was snuffed out, plunging them into darkness. Suddenly a flash of white light streaked across the black sky, making the Neimas cry a terrible roar of pain.

He let go of her and she fell to the ground. Shaken she looked up to see the dark shadow of the creature go racing after the fireball that was falling towards the mountains.

One yen she was on the ground; the next she was swimming in the purple seas. She was holding her beak above the waves as again she saw the light, but this time from a greater distance away. Her mind cried out as she realised she was too far away to help. She was a Watersinger and the city she could just see on the far shore; in the opposite direction of the light was her home and its name was Malaroi. Her whole being was in pain at the hopelessness of it all. She didn't know. She was too young to know how to make the jump to the Neimas' home. The only thing she could do was to use her water-time to find her friends.

The scene shifted and she shared with the Neimas' water-time as he made it back to his home in time to see the destruction that the fireball had wrought. The grey shadows of the Mountain were broken by hot fire which crackled and roared into the night. The smell of burning flesh filled his nostrils as he tried to put the flames out of a fallen Neimas. Hia-e-lea knew that it was his motherling and she cried with him. The area had been devastated by the fire, causing a side of the mountain to crash down, burning many of the Neimas. Those who escaped that, had been burned alive by the flames as the Meteor had exploded into a thousand fragments. A single tree burned, wood spitting and crackling as the wood splintered. The surviving Neimas called out for her to help but she didn't know how and she cursed her water-time for the hopelessness of having a power which she had such little understanding of. The Neimas must have been aware of her sharing his plight for he became angry and bellowed, screaming for her into the night.

It was just too much. She couldn't stand it any longer, so she tried to free herself from his mind and as if he wanted her to know what she had failed to do, he climbed up the rubble, crying at every limb that he saw poking through, but relentlessly he climbed higher. He knew he was the last and he wanted to join them. No Neimas could bear the solitariness of being without its own kind, so he climbed and climbed. When he reached the top he shook his paws at the sky and cried her name as he let go, falling through the darkness to join his bones with those of his loved ones. Hia-e-lea felt the impact and was swept up by a wave of darkness which had her screaming incessantly.

She was still screaming when she opened her eyes to be greeted by the sympathetic face of the Healer. "*It's all right, it's over now.*" He gave her a sip of water and soothingly said, "You have done well Hia-e-lea. We can make progress now. Sleep and be sure you are safe here." She was so grateful for his kindness that she quickly sank into a healing sleep.

When she awoke the next tay she found him still sitting by the sleeping-chamber. Looking up at the ceiling she saw the orange light of the room she had entered the tay before and at the far side of the sleeping-chamber she could see the dome of the shelter she walked into. *In that..What? Dream?* She was not sure at first but then she knew that it had been part of the dreams, the bad part anyway.

Again he knew what she was thinking and as he helped her out he asked, "Do you know the *Legend of the Seven Cities*?"

It sounded vaguely familiar to her so she said, "Sort of, wasn't that to do with Xrl-e-lea and the dolphs who followed her to the mountains of *Frelegar...*?"

As they walked out of the room back to the pool he told her the full story and after she had a long swim they sat together while he told her more about her dreams.

"The interesting part of your dreams is the fact that you have somehow linked to the past, beyond Xrl-e-lea's tay."

She looked puzzled at that and he said, "Hia-e-lea, you have shared a yen of time of a dolph who was alive when the Neimas race was destroyed. Now there are no records of the experience you have dreamed, so you couldn't have read it in any library crystal. But by sharing with you I know your dream was true and the name of the dolph has been confirmed-,"

She held up her hand to stop him and with a wry smile said, "But you just said there is no *record*- So how do you know that the character is real?"

The Healer softly laughed and replied, "Good point, if you let me finish I will tell you.."

"Fine..*please go on..*" she gestured encouragingly.

For a yen he felt slightly bemused as her gesture made a ripple that he had been treating her as a youngling. It turned to a splash of confirmation as he realized he had. Gathering his waters together he composed himself and then relaxed as he realized he was doing it again. It made him smile. She smiled back and they both felt a tangible shift in the atmosphere- almost like old friends.

"I was surprised to discover she was a Watersinger born **2724 S.G.** near the end of the age of the Gealasor. By checking with the other Healers I had this confirmed with the use of the crystal in the Council chambers, one of only two places that contain a list of all Watersingers born since records began. Whose access is restricted to the Head of the Council, the master Healer, and the Watersinger of any given period in time. It also contained some information about her.

"We now know she is the one who in **31 S.N.** began the movement which in time Xrl-e-lea took up. But what we didn't know until now is why. Your dream told us, she had a friendship with a Neimas, the first part of your dream. The second part saw her swimming off the coast where her home city of Malaroi was, which you know well as you were born there too. She was only eight seasons young and helpless to act.

"A strange series of events I admit, but you linked across time to her, so you experienced her pain when her water-time felt the implication of the fire ball and its destruction of those harmless creatures. The terror at being so young and unable because she had yet to learn the ability to use her song to move from one place to another, she blamed herself. She believed that she might have been able to transport them out before the Meteor hit. Maybe she might have but it was not to be. Her sharing of the last Neimas' deathsong broke her water-time. Being so young she could have been drawn into it. She might have preferred it if she had, but that again was not to be. What we did know is that she left her water-time and her watersong behind, never to use it again. She eventually died in **45 S.N.** ...."

He stopped, aware by the incredulity she radiated that the teacher-pupil atmosphere had once more been invoked. Like a youngling she stared at him in disbelief. He chuckled to himself. Maybe it's for the best, after all she was supposed to be so logical. He had just shifted the rules that made her feelings towards water-time clear- She had no time for it! He knew her dilemma. Did she accept what he said or was the alternative that her mind was breaking down? He knew what he would choose just as he knew in time what she would. After all her water-time was surprisingly well developed for one who, *Thought.*

After awhile her expression changed from that of disbelief to one of eagerness. She wanted to know more. No matter how ludicrous it might seem at first, *she needed to know!*

He felt the change, was pleased and said, "I do believe you are *ready* for another session."

He led her back to the orange room and when they came to the threshold of the strange shelter she stopped and asked, "What was the name of that *Watersinger*?" realising he had not told her.

He smiled one of his gentle smiles and replied, "Her name was *Isa-e-lea*."

He seemed to emphasise her name as if Hia-e-lea should know it. She was about to ask when he gave her a gentle push in the small of her back, sending her through. This time what greeted her was very different indeed.

It was early morning and Hia-e-lea was leaning against the side of a grey slab of rock, which jutted out from the mountain behind her. In front she was looking down at the place where five mountains came together. It was barren, just different shades of grey, which changed as Danetar rose higher. It was cold and she shivered as she made her choice. She knew that she was sharing a mind, or maybe a water-time would be more correct. It had no boundaries only greater horizons of movement which astounded her logical senses. Everything was fluid, nothing was impossible and she dared like none before. The very power of the water-time shook her and she was grateful for knowing that it couldn't reach her. She may have been seeing out of the dolph's eyes and shared the feelings *but it wasn't real, was it?* There was no time to contemplate that as she was taken up with the movements that flowed through the dolph she knew this time was Xrl-e-lea.

She seemed to have decided, turning around, making her way back up the incline. It took several clars before she reached the top. There were two more to climb and she reached the top of the final one late in the afternoon. Looking down she saw them. Hundreds of dolphs sitting, standing, waiting for her to return. There was a loud shout as one broke away from the rest and came running up to her. He was a tall dolph with black eyes in a long rather doubtful face. He smiled thinly and Hia-e-lea knew his name; Pha-e-gar. She smiled warmly at him, *but her water-time was thrashing with dislike at his stupid face.*

Now that came as a shock to Hia-e-lea as she felt Xrl-e-lea's dislike. She had never felt such a feeling in her life. It didn't seem right but there was little she could do but watch and try not to share Xrl-e-lea's feelings. It was difficult. As she looked around she could bare each mind, examine each thought, while they were oblivious to her power. Hia-e-lea retreated further allowing the full flow of Xrl-e-lea's water-time to take dominance.

Pha-e-gar may have been brilliant but his mind was easy to read, and he was only paying lip service to Xrl-e-lea, so clever but so stupid. She could read him so easily it was almost pitiful to see him pretend to fawn at her dees.

His words slipped through his lips like a whisper that chilled the bones, "*Have you found the place? We are ready to follow you!*"

He almost bowed to her and she could see the lie in his mind. *Yes only so far*. It was amusing. She reached out, put her hand on his shoulder and said, "Pha-e-gar you *honour me*." Turning to the rest she called out, "Be ready to move out in three tays."

The dolphs cheered and she had to hide the laughter which threatened to burst madly from her lips. Returning to Pha-e-gar, sweetness oozing from her, "Get them ready, wait for me *my love*."

He nodded and took her hand and replied, "*Of course my love...*" then turned away and shouted orders to make a permanent camp.

She watched as they set up the Shakeilar shelters around the base of the mountain range. By the late evening they had finished, and hundreds of lights filled the darkness, their radiance only broken when a dolph passed close, throwing his shadow into the night. Many could be seen walking amongst the shelters and the wind brought their voices as they chatted happily.

Fools, was her only comment.

Now it was time to start her task. She returned to the place she had found that morning. The stars were bright and the twin moons gave her plenty of light. Not that she needed it as her water-time gave her perfect vision in any darkness but the artist in her liked the backdrop of the silver and orange which threw the harsh sides of the rock into stark relief. Raising her hands she fixed the place in her water-time and began to sing. Her power was welded with precision as she blasted the rock away. The whole mountain range shook as she threw note after note impacting, shaping and changing, firstly to creating a valley then the rest. For three nights she laboured until seven ledges were formed in a perfect circle, each separate, raised a hundred dees above the valley floor, where she visualised a city to beat any gone before. A memorial to her pain.

Laughing wildly she turned north until she found the right spot, where two mountains met. Her final touch was to blast a circular pathway a thousand dees high and four hundred wide. The tremors were greater and even though she could feel them she was unperturbed, her song holding her upright as she moved deeper and deeper through the mountainside. Finally she was through and as she looked back at her work she was supremely pleased. It had worked, there was no rubble, only clean smooth rock, shaped the way she wanted by her watersong. In front of her there was a small valley which she knew any dolph would come through and a narrow pass through the mountains on the other side.

In her vision she could see them. For a yen she was taken by this picture of amazed explorers in the seasons to come. But then she felt the familiar touch of Pha-e-gar's mind, like a bad smell of a rotting Kerg. *No, that was an insult to those wonderful sky-flyers*. She could see, crawling across the recess of his mind that he had followed her, curious to see how she would put his knowledge into practice.

After all it had been he who told her how to create energy blasts from the Shakeilar. Not minding that the forceful use took all the life energy out, therefore killing it. His own insane wish to have the Shakeilar bound to his will. To her it was a joke and she knew he didn't love her. He may not admit it but Pha-e-gar was still bound to a lea named Eil-e-lea. Her deathsong had been the price he had paid for the Knowledge he sought. Even Xrl-e-lea didn't know all that had happened. His mind had been shattered by the experience, leaving just grey shadows instead of complete memory. The jumbled mix that had remained had by each season that had followed twisted his mind on a twisted path. But Xrl-e-lea didn't care as long as he served his purpose. It was his joining of the fellowship that had swayed so many dolphs to follow. So she mated with him. *Her mate!* It made her flesh creep.

He was still skulking behind her. She couldn't let on that she was aware of him as he had no intimation of who and what she really was. She stood there for a yen then turned round as by this point he had chosen to reveal himself and he clambered down to her. The words he was going to speak foremost in his mind. She cried out her joy and surprise and he almost purred like a Puga after having a good feed. "*My love*, you have done well with my device."

She laughed and replied, "All thanks to you my sweet one. *Your genius* is beyond compare." Her words were like a trigger and his whole mood changed, as she had expected.

His black eyes became darker and he hissed at her, pointing his finger at her, "You *Lie! Watersinger!!* You Our *Leader!!!*"

He spat each word, but she managed to keep her composure and playing with him she suddenly cried, "*Oh! Pha-e-gar! Forgive me! Long ago I-.*"

"Enough!" he screamed, "*You lie!*" He then opened his left hand revealing a small ball of blue and silver Shakeilar.

She could feel the pulsations as he prepared to use its energy against her. She felt sorry for the perversion that he had wrought and she vowed to let the life force of the Shakeilar go free as soon as this very insignificant dolph had played out his drama. Her next part was to fall to her knees and beg forgiveness from her mate, which she did and she could almost taste his perceived triumph over her. Her water-time felt it quite ridiculous *but still, it was entertaining.*

She quickly revealed the next part of her act, "*Please* let me go. Look, you have what you really wanted! A place for your cities and a whole new way of life for you to have *dominion* over!"

She used her eyes to good effect, pleading, begging. Then she did what she considered to be the best part; she screamed as loud as she could, shouting, "*Pleeese!* You have two thousand dolphs to be your servants!! Just let me *Go*!!!"

He looked down at her in complete disgust. Even he had not expected her to fall to these depths. *He was still stupid*, her water-time rippled. *He should have tried to finish me off by now*. His mind obviously had not made the connection that if she was a Watersinger then she had use of water-time, which meant she could read his mind.

Still he didn't. He just walked around her and then suddenly it popped into his mind like a water bubble which burst as he realised he was too late. His expression melted to one of misery, his confidence drowning in a rush of fear as she licked his mind with her water-time.

For a yen he seemed to show a burst of courage, raising his device as if to use it but she was tired of playing with him so she flexed and squeezed, his eyes nearly popping from his head as he felt her water-time flood into him, washing his life force into oblivion. She watched him crumple to the ground. Knowing the game was about to get very interesting indeed, she rushed over and cried, "*Darling don't leave me!*"

Xrl-e-lea had not missed the fact that her followers were beginning to follow the pass to her location. She waited for them and prepared for their minds. Before they arrived she took the crystal from Pha-e-gar's dead hand and whispered to it, "You will be the gateway." Then she threw it over her shoulder. In her water-time she saw the ball stop dead in the centre of her circular pass and rapidly expand, filling it nearly to the top. The blue wall of Shakeilar stopped expanding. It left a small gap only a few dees wide. The light of the two moons made the blue sparkle and dance, creating a dazzling display.

When they finally trooped through Xrl-e-lea was weeping for her dead mate, who they saw must have been killed by a loose boulder, which they could see she was draped over and he was buried under. There was just his hand sticking out. A gruesome sight for the dolphs but (*and Pha-e-gar would have been bitterly disappointed*) they soon forgot him and turned their attention to the wall the Shakeilar had created. While she let two dolphs cheer her up, she showed them how to pass through.

All they had to do was walk through it. Wherever one touched it an opening would appear, allowing them to pass. She enjoyed their delight especially the gasps of awe when they saw the valley beyond. What she did find highly amusing were the calls of many to make sure that one of the cities was named after Pha-e-gar, as it was his achievement in using Shakeilar that made it all possible. She let them have their dream and called for the seven specially chosen spheres of Shakeilar.

Dawn was fast approaching so she told them to hurry up. Seven dolphs came forward each holding a sphere, each a different colour. One by one she took them and threw them in the direction of a ledge. They flashed through the sky, and hovered, waiting until all were in position. Then as Danetar's light struck them they exploded with a rainbow of light, causing all the dolphs except Xrl-e-lea to look away.

She could feel and hear the Shakeilar talking to each other, changing their structure, converting energy from the air around them, converting it to matter, building, shaping until seven majestic cities towered into the sky. A glistening walkway joined them adding colour to the grey mountains. The dolphs cheered and danced their joy. They had arrived; they were home, a place where in peace they could become true dolphs.

Xrl-e-lea withdrew allowing them their yen of glory. It was not long before they raced each other to explore their new homes. They were not disappointed. Each one had all they would ever need: food, water, seeing crystals and libraries copied from all the cities of Delikadove, even some which had been lost to the main stream of dolph society.

It was at that yen Hia-e-lea became aware of herself again, still with Xrl-e-lea but more awake, like she had been submerged for awhile. She found her actions and the way she abused her power, nauseous. Pha-e-gar must have been mad to abuse the Shakeilar. It horrified her to think that dolphs since then had been sorry that he had left. She didn't want to contemplate what would have happened if he hadn't.

Suddenly the vision changed and she found herself sitting on a mound on a high platform, raised above a forum filled with dolphs. She could feel Xrl-e-lea's anger and she was plunged down to witness the next spectacle. There were shouts and cries from the dolphs gathered below Xrl-e-lea. She had ruled for seventy seasons. She looked old and tired to the young ones below and they were getting ready to announce her replacement. In all the seasons that had passed none had discovered that she was a Watersinger and they thought they could get rid of her. So unlike the old ways.

Her followers had changed. They ridiculed the old and infirmed. They had become creatures of a cold dark logic. If any did not perform at peak capacity they were quickly discarded. They threw them over the ledges, their bones to be picked clean by creatures that skulked and lived under the walkways. She laughed, a perfect society they called it. Foolish dolphs. None were over forty seasons in the forum. The term Grand-elder had been wiped away. It sickened Xrl-e-lea but she had proved that dolphs were a doomed race.

It was **1302 S.N.** or **70 S.P.** (*cycle of Pha-e-gar*) as the Elders now called the seasons. She had allowed them access to all the information he discovered and much more besides. They were ready to build their first Flyer. But she was now tired of her game and had decided to bring it to its natural conclusion.

The voices were becoming louder and suddenly a handful surged forward, their angry faces leering at her. She smiled and allowed them to pull her from her throne. They dragged her through and out of the city (*also named after Pha-e-gar*). As a crowd gathered they made ready to throw her over the edge.

She didn't resist and some grew fearful but others only became hungry for her blood. Two dolphs grabbed her and as they began swinging her between them, her bones creaked as they heaved her over the side.

She sang as she fell.

The cheers of the dolphs were broken as her song filled their minds and they saw their mistake. She welded her song well. It caught each mind and began to bind them together. Their logic broke under the pounding waves of her force, shattering the link to their bodies. None of the dolphs saw the change take place as she tumbled down. There were a hundred dees to fall before she hit the bottom and she didn't. The flesh became transparent. Her bones faded away and she became what she had been for more than a thousand seasons, a shadow of life that dwelt in her own torment for her perceived crime.

It had been at the time of her deathsong in ***45 S.N.*** *that she knew she had been mistaken. The anger she had felt then had taken shape of her last song all those seasons ago, sending her to the shadow world, to wander for countless eons of time. It was only when a motherling gave birth to a lea, who then entered the deathsong was Isa-e-lea able to cross the bridge and to take her place to be reborn as Xrl-e-lea.*

Then she began planning her revenge on the idea that dolphs should ever stay as dolphs. Maybe she had been a little sky-happy but she felt that her mission was to help her kind realise that their future was in the sea. It was safer to be dolphin. No land, no other creatures interfering with their lives. The only responsibility was to themselves. No need for Watersingers.

First she had as Isa-e-lea been driven that water-time was wrong because of the empathic nature of shared experience, the shared pain. Later it had twisted again as she to tried to find ways to punish her kind as the path to only dolph had included those like Pha-e-gar who would have involved them in even more pain than she could bear, the pain of those they wanted to dominate and of course that drive to the stars. She wasn't as mad to want all dolphs to die! Just to stay as dolphin and swim in peace and alone among their own kind in the sea.

That trickle of long forgotten waters faded as she rose above the towering cities, singing her final song. The dolphs below were lifeless. More than ten thousand dolphs entered the deathsong that tay and she was pleased. *She didn't want them all dead just those few!* She watched as a flock of Jewur began to circle over the cities, ready to feed on the warm flesh below. She wished them well as even her shadow began to fade and the feeling of the deathsong taking her to the realm of Chisharnlay came upon her. It was getting closer. She could almost touch the light. Her end had finally come. But then she felt something tug at the edges of her water-time and she cried with surprise as she suddenly found herself drawn back to the cities.

It couldn't be...! she cried, horror filling her. Her song began to tear from her waters. When it broke free she screamed. *No! NO!!! NOOO!!!!*

Not her song, *it wasn't fair.*

She had met her match, for the Shakeilar had chosen that they were not going to be abandoned. She would feed them. She had allowed the dolphs to do terrible wrongs against them. Many of them had been shattered by the legacy left by Pha-e-gar in experiments which shattered them apart. They had never been used this way *and they were not about to let her go! The one they blamed the most.* She would have to wait awhile longer before they let her enter *Chisharnlay*. She kept crying as she was drawn down, through the main dome where a short time ago she had sat upon her throne. She tried her best to fight it but the Shakeilar were too strong and when she saw what was waiting for her she gave one last terrible scream. It rang around the chamber as she was delivered into the confines of a large crystal that had taken the place of her throne. It was black with a scattering of silver and inside there was another crystal which she recognised as the one which Pha-e-gar had created and to her final horror his spirit was attached to it.

Welcome Back! My dearest...My loved one....

She found herself screaming as Pha-e-gar's sound filled her mind. She was gibbering uncontrollably as the Healer rocked her in his arms, "Hia-e-lea you are back. You are *safe* now." He could feel her body quiver with tremors that made him wonder how long her mind could withstand the pounding it was receiving. He knew there was more to come. He held her tight until the shaking subsided and she fell asleep. Using his water-time he pushed her a little deeper, making sure no dream would disturb her.

He walked out of the room and made his way to his private quarters. The cool blue interior helped to relax him as he sat by a huge bowl containing several hundred crystals of different colours and sizes which filled it to the brim. He reached out and picked up an orange crystal that he was using to store the dreams of Hia-e-lea.

Gradually he created a river to flow into the crystal, taking the latest information. With the intention set, it allowed the rest of his waters to mull over the dilemma which had raised itself inside. The last installment had confirmed his earlier suspicions that they were not dreams at all, but a series of transmissions through water-time, impacting and manifesting as a dream state. *If Hia-e-lea had been more aware of her own capacity for water-time she would have known from the beginning what she was dealing with and acted accordingly, instead of being driven half sky-happy!* He chose to wait until she had revealed the rest in the dream chamber, then she could be told. The transference came to an end and instead of returning it to the bowl he chose his next course and walked quickly out of his room, the crystal warm in his hand.

The afternoon light cast deep shadows as he made his way to the centre of the city. He passed several dolphs to whom he gave a quick smile and moved on, not wanting to stop until he was safely at his destination. His water-time was heavy as each ripple turned to waves of concern for the impact the Knowledge he was holding might have on dolph society. It would certainly change many minds and water-times as far as the likes of Pha-e-gar were concerned. *After all there were still some who admired him even after all the time that had passed. If they knew the truth would they feel the same?* He didn't like the feeling it gave him which was why he was hurrying to see Alk-e-lea. As Head of the Council she would know what to do.

He was almost running when he came to her home. Passing his hand quickly over the blue marker he was thankful when an opening appeared revealing the amused smile of Bue-e-gar. This quickly turned to a look of concern as he registered that it was not a social call by Yol-e-gar, who quickly explained that he had to see Alk-e-lea.

Bue-e-gar led the Healer through to the main room where Alk-e-lea sat, eating from a platter of fish.

"I'm sorry for this intrusion," explained Yol-e-gar, "but I have a matter of utmost *urgency* to discuss with you."

Through a mouthful of fish she waved him to sit down. Bue-e-gar was about to leave when Yol-e-gar added, "No, *please* stay, I would like you to hear what I have to say."

Bue-e-gar nodded his acquiescence and sat beside Alk-e-lea, and they waited expectantly for him to start.

Now that he had arrived he found himself quite nervous, "I...*Well* See for *yourself*," handing over the crystal to Alk-e-lea.

She studied it a yen and she began to read it but then she stopped almost immediately and looked up exclaiming, "This is a *dream crystal*! I am surprised at you. I cannot read this!"

In his hurry he had forgotten that she might refuse as Dream crystals were private and never allowed out of the Centre. "I know that," he explained, "but the circumstances are a little unusual. What you are holding is not strictly a Dream crystal. If you read it you will see what I mean."

Bue-e-gar looked at Alk-e-lea and remarked, "I don't believe Yol-e-gar is in the habit of breaking his own rules for no reason," his eagerness clear in his voice.

She smiled at him, "Bue-e-gar I know you want to read this but I don't like the idea of looking through someone's private dreams." She turned back to Yol-e-gar, her concern returning. "Before I do, tell me who these dreams belong to."

He had hoped she would just read the crystal as it would have made it easier to explain, but she was right. He had forgotten how cautious she could be at times. He gathered his water-time together and explained about Hia-e-lea and the bad dreams that had disturbed her over several jeanths.

It was enough and Alk-e-lea agreed. She relaxed herself, allowing her new sense of her own water-time to sink into the crystal. Her control was much better since her link with Ler-e-lea and the green light which had opened her mind to the beauty of the water-time. Gradually the visions swept through her and she saw what Hia-e-lea had dreamt. The power was nearly overwhelming and when it had finally finished her relief was tangible.

Bue-e-gar looked concerned as the crystal began to slip from her grasp. He quickly reached over and took it from her. She gave him a weak smile and said, "It's terrible, the images, what they did. Is it really true?"

She saw the sadness in Yol-e-gar's eyes as he slowly nodded his head. It was enough to make her feel really weak as her feelings went out in sympathy to Hia-e-lea. "What she must have suffered, dreaming that every night.." Her voice shook with thick emotion cloying at her throat, "*Now tell me the rest..*"

Before he did they gave Bue-e-gar the time to read the crystal. Its content moved him as much as it had done Alk-e-lea. When they were ready Yol-e-gar began: "Now you know why I felt it was important that you know, but that is not the main reason-,"

They both looked crestfallen at his words but didn't stop him, "-The images are being transmitted from the Frelegar mountains, repeated every three tays. Those in the crystal are only the first two tays. The next should come tonight."

Alk-e-lea and Bue-e-gar were stunned. Neither said a word. They were both reeling from the implication. If he was right and they had no reason to doubt his conclusion then someone or something had the power to transmit water-time over a distance that would be a hard task for even the best developed water-time, except for a Watersinger like Mel-e-gar. Then the truth struck; simultaneously they exclaimed, "*Xrl-e-lea!*"

His sadness could be heard in his voice as he replied, "Otherwise known as Isa-e-lea.."

Bue-e-gar finished it for him, "That means she has been there for the past six thousand seasons!"

"It seems that way," answered Yol-e-gar.

"But why *now*?" asked Alk-e-lea as she tried to come to terms with the idea of being trapped for such a long time.

"That is what I hope to find out and I want you both to return with me to the Centre. Maybe afterwards we can decide what needs to be done." He then stood up, took the crystal from Bue-e-gar and gave them his best smile, "Are you coming?"

When they entered the room where Hia-e-lea was relaxing in the pool, Yol-e-gar's water-time had returned to its relaxed state and he moved smoothly over and explained to her why Alk-e-lea and Bue-e-gar had joined them.

She was nervous at first but she found that his warm voice soothed any worries away. By nightfall she was ready, almost eager to enter the dream chamber. It felt good to have not only the Healer's company but also his two friends. She had seen Alk-e-lea once before at the Council chamber when Mel-e-gar had been sent to the Arkelclared desert. She had liked Alk-e-lea's manner then so having her there was no problem. Bue-e-gar she found sweet and charming as he made her laugh, making her feel she could tackle anything. She stood at the opening as the Healer said, "We shall be sharing with *you*.."

She stepped through into blackness. For a yen she thought she had lost her balance and was falling but then a faint light appeared and she saw she was walking down a long tunnel. There was a cool wind which promised sweet flowers and tall blossom filled trees. She was relaxed, no fear this time as she continued to walk closer to the light. Where she was she had no idea. There was no sense of time or urgency just a steady pace, getting closer and closer. At first the light seemed white but like a veil being lifted she saw it was a beautiful green, that spoke of life and love, transfusing her with health and she knew her mind was true and the dreams were only the last cry of someone who was alone and afraid. The light equalled redemption and forgiveness. She could feel hot tears well up inside as she reached out, wanting desperately to help the poor miserable creature that dwelled beyond the darkness.

Suddenly she was out of the tunnel under a hot blazing sky. A bitter wind blew across the pass where she had stood once before as Xrl-e-lea. She looked down at the broken rubble at her dees. That's when she noticed the boulder that Xrl-e-lea had used to cover Pha-e-gar. Out of curiosity she walked over and bent down to have a closer look. But there was no sign that he had ever been under it. Her mind reasoned that he must have turned to dust long ago. That was when she realized that she was in her time and not the past. It was a relief to know that she would not have to meet them again. *But why was she here?* There seemed little compulsion to do anything. She felt that she could just stay where she was. Then again she might as well look around.

The mountain side was no longer cleanly cut. There must have been a great deal of movement over the intervening seasons as the pass which the dolphs had come through was no longer there. But to the south the entrance that Xrl-e-lea had cut was still intact. The Shakeilar wall was the same, gleaming as new as if it had been put there only a yen ago. She walked over the rubble that had fallen in front of it and touched the surface. It felt warm and it rippled against her palm. She had expected it to be harder but instead it was soft and yielded as she pressed against it but sprang back when she released the pressure. For a while she clambered over the boulders trying different sections of the wall, and each time it was the same. Feeling more confidence she pressed harder and was surprised to find herself falling through, tumbling head over heals as she bounced over the rubble on the other side. Bruised and a little battered she came to her dees and looked around her.

The cities were as she remembered. They shone and sparkled under the hot light of Danetar. But instead of being something to admire the scene made her skin crawl as she remembered what she had witnessed. For they represented a pervasion, a way of life that was destructive and cruel. It made her ashamed to be a dolph. How some of her kind could have fallen to such depths still amazed and frightened her. The images of Xrl-e-lea being thrown over the edge filled her again, making her shudder, but she was determined to continue. Carefully she put her left foot, then her right on the walkway, not sure that it wouldn't suddenly collapse under her. Steadily she began to walk across. As she did so she looked over the edge and was surprised to see trees growing, fields of yellow and blue grasses, the twinkling of a stream caught by Danetar as it moved higher into the sky. Faintly she could hear the sounds of different creatures from the valley below. She stopped and moved to the edge and bent down to take a closer look. It was quite breathtaking; it made her wish there was a way down.

The Shakeilar rippled under her and it began to lower the walkway. She grabbed the side, trying to get hold but there was no need as it began to bend and fold itself, allowing her small portions at a time. Carefully she climbed down. When she reached the bottom the Shakeilar sprang back leaving her by a small stream that flowed across the valley floor and on through a small woodland. It reminded her of the place where she had met the Neimas, which brought her sadness. But she shook the feeling away, determined to enjoy exploring the valley. There seemed to be nothing to hurt her down here, creating feelings of a safe haven. When she looked above her she could see the walkway hanging like so many silvery strands in the sky. Each casting a thin shadow at her dees. How such life could still be here she didn't know but maybe it was the way the mountains sheltered the worst of Danetar's heat. It was much cooler and the air was sweet and moist. It was so peaceful, it seemed right that for all the dolphs that must have been thrown to their deaths that their bodies should bring forth such life.

Time passed, two, three tays came and went. She fed on fish from the stream and revelled in the coolness of the valley. One night as she lay under the stars, counting them, watching as some fell from the sky a shadow flickered out of the corner of her eye, making her spring to her dees. She looked around trying to find what had disturbed her peace. Only the shadows of the trees whispered back. Then again she saw it, this time closer, and she spun round hoping to catch sight of it. Again it eluded her. She smelt the breeze hoping to catch the spoor of the creature that was stalking her. A ripple of fear ran down her back as she felt eyes upon her.. Almost at once she felt its hot breath on the nape of her neck. She tensed, stricken still. The breathing sounded laboured, but there was no other smell except her own fear which filled her.

Remembering what she had been taught she unstiffened her limbs, sure the creature would hear a creak and pounce on her. Then she was relaxed enough to crumple to the ground. As her hands impacted with the grass she used them to spin herself sideways away from where she thought the shadow should be. Her breathing came fast as she landed several dees away from her original position. Taking a pause she looked around in the darkness. But there was nothing. She allowed herself to relax. As she did, the breath returned in the same place. She couldn't believe it. It must have paralleled her movements and come up behind her yet again. Deciding upon a more reckless course she spun on her heals to confront the creature and was met by.. Nothing. It had been too swift for her once again.

She crouched down trying to feel whether it had left any sign but there was no turned earth or blade of grass out of place. She started to panic and when the breath returned she nearly screamed, but more from frustration than fear. She kicked out as she spun round, hoping to catch it but it was no use. Every movement she made the shadow creature had anticipated. She was not sure how long she could go on like this. But it carried on for the rest of the night and when the first light of dawn banished the dark she almost cheered, hoping that if the creature stayed, at least she stood a chance of catching sight of it. Or maybe it would disappear back into the shadows.

She was so tired. She had scraped her hands and legs as she rolled, jumped and tried her best to find her antagonist. The morning was like the night, but worse because she thought that she should have been able to see it. Being chased by an invisible creature across the valley was not her idea of fun and her nerves were almost at breaking point. Suddenly she stopped as it came again, her mind almost laughing at the absurdity of it. It hadn't attacked her, just followed her, scared her, but that was only because she didn't know what it was. She had enough and sat on the grass. With a defiant cry she yelled, "You, whatever you are can *breathe on me* to your heart's content. But I am not moving from this *spot*!" Her voice echoed around the valley, repeating her words.

She waited as the breathing became faster, its heat warming her neck. Then she heard a low rumbling growl that almost made her jump up. But she remained firm and gritted her teeth as it became louder. Then it stopped. She had been expecting more to happen but nothing did. It was just gone. She slowly turned round... still nothing. Climbing to her dees she walked back to the stream to quench her thirst, expecting it to return at any time but it didn't. After she had drunk her fill of the cool waters she decided to see if she could leave the valley.

There was no way up the sheer sides so she returned to where she had come down originally and sent her intent to the Shakeilar, the way she would have done in her own home. It worked. The walk way swung down and crinkled as before, allowing her to climb back up. It was good to be out of the valley, even though the heat was almost unbearable. With that in mind she walked the rest of the way to the city directly opposite her. It was the largest and she remembered it was the one where Xrl-elea had lived. She was curious to see whether the crystal which had held her was still there. She felt safe in her conviction that the Shakeilar would not let anything harm her.

The city was filled with colour, which was dazzling as she passed through, along streets lined by hundreds of different shaped buildings. But the grandest of them all was at its centre where its multiple domes and spires pierced the sky. This, she remembered had been the Council chambers of Xrl-e-lea and her followers. She stopped by an arch that she knew was an opening. There was no marker but she touched the wall, and it dissolved under her hand. She passed through and it closed behind her. She stopped and tested to see if she could pass back, and it again dissolved away. Feeling secure that she could return she followed the corridor to the next arch. There were seven arches, each of which opened for her. Then she reached a blue and silver wall with a black marker. At this point she hesitated, not so sure she wanted to see what was on the other side. *Would the crystal still be there?* she wondered. Taking a deep breath she passed her hand over the marker. The wall rippled and disappeared, revealing the vast chambers beyond.

Tentatively, she walked in. The entrance closed swiftly behind her. Again she was unperturbed. The sight in front of her was even more overwhelming. There must have been hundreds of rows of sitting places around a high dais, which had the same stepped pattern she had used when climbing down to the valley. The high dome ceiling sparkled with millions of silver stars in a sea of purple. There were twisting columns which stretched up to the ceiling with streaks of yellow and blue almost swimming their way around. Finally her eyes came to rest on what had been the place of Xrl-e-lea's throne. She had been careful not to look before but now she had little choice as its black and silver light pulled her gaze. It must have had a circumference of a hundred dees. It was the largest crystal she had ever seen and she couldn't keep her eyes from it. Slowly she walked down the central aisle until she was near the base. Gradually she climbed the steps until she was standing close enough to touch it.

That is when a hungry growl broke the silence, and a harsh mocking breath breathed on her spine. She froze, her mind not believing that it had returned even as she knew it was playing with her. She heard as it sniggered, droplets of burning saliva dripping down her back. The pain was terrible and she thought she was going to faint but stopped it by fixing her eyes on the crystal. Her mind tried to reach inside, wanting to believe that if Xrl-e-lea was inside she would help her.

But her concentration was broken as she felt a hand burn into her shoulder and a whisper of sound which shattered the silence. "*Go on*, touch the crystal. *Break the bond that has held her....*"

A wave of nausea swept across her mind, making her gag. Its breathing increased and the pressure from the hand seemed to crush down on her. She stumbled, her hand reaching out...

A firm but commanding voice called to her, "Don't touch the *crystal*! It wants you too!"

The sound was like a breath of fresh air which gave her enough impetus to let her hand drop, diverting the momentum to her legs, falling to her knees. There was a cry of anger from behind her as the creature saw its actions thwarted.

Again the voice, so different from the putridness of the creature which still had its hand on her shoulder, commanded, "Leave this place! *You no longer belong!!*"

The creature howled, its cry defiant, "This i*s my City! You cannot do this!*"

It pressed down harder then she felt its other hand reach under her arm and with incredible strength it picked her up. She cried out in alarm and the creature howled its triumph. Even though she was held aloft she couldn't see what held her. Only a dark shadow suggested something actually was. She tried to find the owner of the other voice but she couldn't look behind her. Again, the creature squeezed her and her bones started to break as it tried to crush the life from her.

Suddenly she was thrown, and the blackness of the crystal came rushing towards her. She should have impacted instantly but a wall of green fire enveloped her, shifting her to one side. She was transported as if time was reversing. Everything went black and she found herself sitting, her back and arm twisted, broken by the power of the creature, her eyes burnt away.

But she could hear the roar of pain that filled the chamber, "You cannot be! *Watersinger*!! They should not have allowed it!"

The roar turned to pitiful sobs as the other voice returned. Hia-e-lea could tell it was a lea's voice that commanded the creature. "You have dwelled too long beneath the cities. *Everything changes...!*" Her voice changed becoming kinder, "*Ah..! You poor creature*, you have become your own *nightmare*. Let me heal your pain."

There came a tremendous shriek, "*Noooo*! You are not *Eil-e-lea*! Only her, it was only ever her!" His terror was ringing around, becoming fainter and fainter until she could no longer hear it. Even though she couldn't see, she knew he was gone.

She felt so tired and wanted to sleep. But a gentle hand stroked her face and touched where her eyes had been, bringing brightness and a glaring light that made her heart lurch as she blinked and cried, "*I can see*!"

Everything was blurred. Then gradually it all came into focus. She saw she was sitting against the entrance of the Council chamber and there kneeling by her side was a dolph who glowed with green fire..

She must have passed out for she awoke, feeling refreshed to the sound of singing. It was a gentle but sad song which made Hia-e-lea think again of the Neimas. The sound stirred her to sit up and she saw the lea, sitting by the black crystal watching her.

The dolph stopped her song and said, "I am glad to see you have awakened. I am sorry that I took your sight but it was better that you did not see the creature that held you. I have done the best I can with your other injuries but you will have a scar on your shoulder, which in time should fade."

She seemed to flow towards Hia-e-lea, not walk and the corona of fire sparkled as the lea came and helped her up. It was strange because she could see the lea's hand holding hers but she didn't feel warm flesh, only a light tingle which tickled the palm of her hand. Her mind raced with questions but she didn't know where to start.

The dolph smiled kindly. Light laughter filled the room and Hia-elea allowed herself to be led to two mounds. She sat as the dolph sat and finding her voice at last stated, "I thought it was the creature that burnt my eyes!"

The strange eyes of the dolph studied her before she replied, "I had to make sure. You were not ready so I did what I must."

Hia-e-lea could only accept her answer, knowing there was nothing she could do even if she didn't. Her mind left it and turned to something she could ask, "*Who are you?*"

"*A friend.*"

The enigmatic answer only filled Hia-e-lea with more curiosity, so she pressed, "Don't you have a name?"

The dolph's smile grew wider and she softly answered, "Yes, but my name is of no importance. But if you like you can call me, *Watersinger*. Will you be happy with that?"

Hia-e-lea could feel the humour radiate from the dolph as she replied, "I see I will not get any more from you, so I will call you Watersinger." Her mind told her she was being played with but kindly, not with malice. She returned the Watersinger's gaze trying to find an answer to why this dolph should be here in the first place. She was grateful, as she knew that whatever the creature was it would have surely killed her.

Then something changed inside her and she found herself falling into a giant green lake. There was no splash or sound as she slipped into the strange domain, her mind somehow knowing that she had broken through to the Watersinger's water-time.

Welcome Hia-e-lea, you have found your way here at last. I have been waiting for you.

The tone was different, stronger somehow but still gentle and musical. She didn't feel alone in the lake, more like being held close in a motherling's arms.

There was momentary confusion because she wasn't sure how she was supposed to answer. It was met by gentle laughter and the voice intoned, *Feel it. Give me your sound in water-time.*

But she didn't have a water-time, as she had never believed in it. There was more laughter and Hia-e-lea nearly cried in frustration. *How could she answer? It didn't make sense.* She was tempted to leap out but the voice stopped her by repeating every thought she just had. This startled Hia-e-lea. *Now what was going on?* But then it dawned on her, *Of course, I have a water-time, my dreams!!*

The Watersinger then added her sound, *At last! You understand.*

Nearly.. admitted Hia-e-lea, knowing she didn't fully.

It was given to her when the dolph explained, *Your dreams are a part of water-time, the place we all go to see new places, experiences, loves and much more. But it is only part of the greater sea that is water-time. All dolphs have this. They just forget, so it falls down and lies waiting for them.*

Isa-e-lea was one who first denied then used her own power in confusion which created Xrl-e-lea. Even then she tried to swim the other way and was placed into that crystal with the remains of her mate Pha-e-gar, who she used, then threw away.

At that point Hia-e-lea felt she had to interrupt, *He was not much good himself. He deserved his fate.*

There was a sigh that rippled the surface of the lake, building into waves which buffeted Hia-e-lea. Then the sound came, *Ah! No, poor Pha-e-gar! He was in pain for a long time, his lost love, his guilt, his nightmare. No, no creature deserves to be further exiled, tormented, joined with the thousands of others, who were also victims to their own pain.*

For the first time she saw the shadow that had chased her and she now could see it was Pha-e-gar, shaped grotesquely, with the shattered lives of those Xrl-e-lea killed so many seasons ago. Even she had to admit he had certainly suffered for any wrong he may have committed. It raised a question for her so she sounded, getting more used to water-time, *But I saw him killed seventy seasons before the others.*

It was not that simple, replied the Watersinger, *for his water-time was a fragile thing which sought the safety of the Shakeilar. Pha-e-gar infused into the Entrance crystal. His addiction to knowing more and more had tied him to it when he could have been free of it long ago.*

He stayed awhile before gradually moving, watching her, knowing that the Shakeilar was going to trap her. He was ready when they put her in the crystal. He believed he had won, but the Shakeilar trapped him there too. They fought for a thousand, two thousand seasons before he managed to call the ones held by her watersong, bound together to wander the empty cities. The only reason he escaped was because the Shakeilar were losing energy and they were dying so they allowed him to join with the others then cast him down to the valley below.

The ripple of sound ended, allowing Hia-e-lea to absorb the pictures into her water-time.

It was like a tragic game that should never have been played. The idea that the creature was a mixture of all those poor fools who had tried to kill Xrl-e-lea made her water-time shudder once more. *They must have been tearing into each other all that time*, sounded Hia-e-lea.

When you arrived they saw their chance. They played with you for amusement then attached themselves, so you would be unaware. You see when you tried to rid yourself of it, you couldn't. It never left you. It only fell silent, whilst it clung to your life energy. The Shakeilar couldn't tell the difference. Your mind was the perfect block for them and they hid waiting.

When you came into this chamber they saw their chance once more to have their revenge on Xrl-e-lea. They had done it many times before but each time they failed. Pha-e-gar, who is the guiding light for the rest, knew he needed to have someone of living flesh to touch the crystal under their own volition.

He always managed to get them to the threshold, but just as they are about to, he whispers to them urging them on. Which frightens them and they try and escape. It's his own impatience, and none would ever move fast enough for him, so he smashes them against the crystal trying to force the mangled body through. When that fails he takes it and throws it into the valley, to satisfy the ones he carries. The poor unfortunate dolph who he has just killed gets trapped with them, their identity submerged under Pha-e-gar's. He had a long wait before you came along. The wave ended, its implication clear.

Hia-e-lea remembered the old stories that the Healer had told her about the Expeditions and how they all disappeared. Now she knew what had happened to them and she nearly went the same way. Her gratitude for the Watersinger flowed out, thanking her again. She then sounded, *But why are you here? Is there more to this than you have told me?*

Now a larger wave flowed towards her and upon the wave of sadness came the Watersinger's reply, *I am here to warn you, to show you what lies in wait for you.*

Hia-e-lea was now confused. She believed she had already travelled there, forgetting that she was dreaming her dream.

The reply came, *No, this realm is your dream world and I have shown you the dangers. That is all I can do until you come to me. I have attached myself to Xrl-e-lea's call, for she is the one who needs you to free her and to banish Pha-e-gar and his followers. But her need is not true and she would have taken your form and re-entered your world to destroy it.*

But what about Mel-e-gar? Surely he can stop her! She wasn't liking the way the sounds were turning, even though she knew in her heart that the Watersinger was right.

The dolph sent calming waves and sounded, *No two Watersingers can ever come in direct contact. It's to do with the song. If she began before him, his song would be absorbed by hers. Because in reality there is only one. While I stay here she cannot retrieve hers. If I leave she may free herself as the Shakeilar is not as you have seen. That is her vision, to fool you. They are all dying. Her life force cannot sustain them much longer and when they fall she will be free. But as soon as she leaves she will have to bind herself with Pha-e-gar so she can use him one last time, to enable her to transport to Mel-e-gar's location and take his place.*

Then the ripple changed to one of pleading. *Hia-e-lea you must come and heal this place. Bring those that can shape and renew the Shakeilar, another to heal Xrl-e-lea, and three to share the burden of broken water-times.*

The Watersinger's sounds were more like tears as they rippled to Hia-e-lea. She was about to ask more when the light of the pool began to fade and a whisper sounded, *They have already been chosen. Come quickly.*

They had been confined to their shelters for three tays as the storm blew across the plains below the hills of the Frelegar mountains. The rain lashed the three shelters which were huddled together as the ground around them greedily soaked up the much needed water. From the hills old rivers were reborn, quickly filling the dry beds, snaking their way across the plains, eventually finding their way back to the sea. For a time the many dormant seeds would sprout forth, covering large areas with blankets of purple, yellow and red grasses. Multitudes of different flowers would blossom and the creatures which had fled to the cooler confines of the mountains would come down to feed upon the riches until Danetar returned to burn the land once more.

These thoughts filled Alk-e-lea and Bue-e-gar as they watched the first splashes of colour already sprouting from the refreshed land, through the transparent wall of their shelter. Both were pleased that the heavy rains had returned, even though it had meant a delay, which Hia-e-lea had bemoaned, her impatience shining fiercely from her eyes when the rains had first come down. But it was she who had told them that they would have to stop because of the dangers caused by the flooding, and the chance of landslides, even though she had made it clear that if she was alone she would have kept going. Alk-e-lea had made sure that Yol-e-gar should keep a close eye on Hia-e-lea just in case she did decide to go for it alone.

The shelters had been moulded together allowing movement from one to another without having to step out into the rain, but still keeping three separate rooms. Ran-e-gar was sharing with Serliker, while Hia-e-lea and Yol-e-gar shared the second, leaving the third for Alk-e-lea and Bue-e-gar. They kept the same routine of sleeping during the tay and being awake at night, making it more comfortable to walk in the cool night air rather than being burned during the tay. Alk-e-lea knew that it would be at least two more tays before they could move on. By watching the purple grey clouds that blocked the orange sphere of Danetar, she could tell the wind was beginning to ease. She watched awhile longer then turned to Bue-e-gar who had made the same decision and passed his hand across the transparency returning the wall to its normal opaqueness. The deep yellow light of the Shakeilar flared up, compensating for the withdrawal of the natural light from outside.

He sat down by the small bowl in the centre of the room, his bones creaking as he made himself comfortable. He gave a small gasp as a twinge of pain shot across his chest. Fortunately it didn't last.

Alk-e-lea seeing his discomfort sat beside him, her face filled with concern. "Are you *all right*?"

He sighed heavily, "I am fine, just my many seasons catching up with me."

She was not convinced but decided not to press him whilst making a mental note to ask the Healer to take a look at her mate when night returned. Instead she made him lie down, as she joined him. The sleeping-chamber arose from the floor, enclosing them both in the soft contours. The light dimmed to darkness. For a while she lay listening to his heavy breathing as he descended into sleep, whilst her mind played in water-time.

She was concerned that the journey was taking its toll on Bue-e-gar. She had known that his health was not too good before they had left and the dreams of Hia-e-lea had shaken them all. The very fact that dolphs had killed dolphs was hard to accept as the very thought repulsed them. In all the long seasons of the dolphs there had never been any indication that any would contemplate such an act. It had been her mate who had anguished over it until he had asked for a dolph named Ran-e-gar to be included. Bue-e-gar knew that out of the dolphs who studied past time Ran-e-gar was the one that knew the most about the beginning of the cycle of the Neimas. Hia-e-lea had voiced her concern that as Ran-e-gar was mated with Wel-e-lea, a close friend of Mel-e-gar, they were taking a risk that he would find out what was going on. But after much discussion with Yol-e-gar they finally agreed it was a risk worth taking.

Bue-e-gar had spent the tays before they left talking with Ran-e-gar about those past times. To his dismay Ran-e-gar had told him that he believed that dolph society had been on the verge of a new age, which in time may have produced the same society that Xrl-e-lea had created in the mountains. It seemed hardly credible but Ran-e-gar insisted that all the elements had been there; the desire to stay as dolphs and to leave the very concept of dolphin and water-times far behind. The Healers had become the only ones who still treasured the use of water-time and in time they too may have been removed.

It had been Pha-e-gar who had the ideas of changing the use of Shakeilar, not only for sky-flyers, but also in using the energy for healing, creating crystals from a single Shakeilar and separating them so as to isolate the energy, forcing it to be used in one direction. When it had been drained it would be thrown away. The comparison Ran-e-gar had used was if a dolph took a another dolph and while still alive, slowly tore chunks from it, sucking the juice from each part. It was enough to tell them what an agonising death the Shakeilar would have suffered. They had questioned him further when they realised that if Pha-e-gar had made the practice acceptable then eventually the Shakeilar race would have died out. But Ran-e-gar had laughed rather grimly and told them Pha-e-gar had found a way around this; he could force them to reproduce. How he had found out about such a trigger and been able to force it without the Shakeilar resisting, Ran-e-gar didn't know, but he was sure that Pha-e-gar had found a way.

It had all lain heavily upon Bue-e-gar. His many seasons had been disillusioned that the dolphs could have been capable of any cruelty. But Ran-e-gar came to his rescue when he told him and the others that the Leader of the Council at the time had been aware of

Pha-e-gar's plans and he allowed enough freedom for the dolphs who liked the new ideas to come forward. When it was out in the open he was going to find a way to cut what he considered to be a disease of mind out of dolph society. Before any plan was formulated Xrl-e-lea had come to him and asked to be given permission to take her followers to the Frelegar mountains. This was the best he could hope for so he agreed. If the leader had been opposed to the growth of dolph *Mind* it would have fuelled it and made it harder for any action to be taken to remove it in one go. As it turned out Xrl-e-lea did his job for him and when the Leader had asked whether Xrl-e-lea would be taking Pha-e-gar, she had smiled and said, "*I shall become his mate*," laughing as she left his chambers.

It was successful in removing the ideas of Domination of *Mind* from dolph society. But still *water-time*, over the many seasons was left further behind. Only each new Watersinger, with the help of the Healers kept the idea alive. The sanctuaries of the Old Edenlea were hardly ever visited and many were turned into Healing Centres, which also helped to keep the dream alive. It was enough to balance the growth of *Mind*, making sure it never again produced the perversion of *Dark Logic* above all else; to just take and never replenish. Ran-e-gar had emphasised that if *Mind* had taken precedence then dolphs now would have lost any chance to return to water-time. He even felt that they would have destroyed themselves eventually, pointing out that when Xrl-e-lea had killed the dolphs they were already fragmented by their own deeds. Killing the Grand-elders and going on to make sure none grew into those Elder seasons had broken the continuity from one generation to the next. They were destroying the very wisdom that could have saved them. As the Grand-elders, if they had been allowed to live, may have discovered Xrl-e-lea's secret and maybe removed the threat before it could have born its devastating fruit.

With the dreams of Hia-e-lea added to the background information that Ran-e-gar provided it helped to view those tays as a lesson which must never be forgotten. Bue-e-gar had been grateful for Ran-e-gar's words which did ease his feeling of despair about the whole business. When they made their plans for leaving it had been at Ran-e-gar's urging that Yol-e-gar should go and ask Serliker to accompany them as he felt that *it* would be best suited to freeing the other Shakeilar from their bonds with Xrl-e-lea and Pha-e-gar.

When Ran-e-gar returned to Ieulasayer to tell Wel-e-lea, they had agreed to meet him there in two tays. While he was gone the rest of them had gathered together in the Healing Centre to make final plans. It was then that Yol-e-gar had expressed some concern over Bue-e-gar's health. But with normal stubbornness he had insisted he was going and if he was due to enter the deathsong, then he would rather be with Alk-elea than die alone. She remembered clearly the feeling it had given her when she considered that for his great age he could still display a youthful exuberance for adventure even at the risk of his life. These thoughts eased into the fluid sound of her own water-time and feeling suddenly afraid for her mate she cuddled against his warm body, giving him her strength as he slept.

They waited an extra tay after the storm to allow Danetar to dry the earth once more. By the evening the travelling-shelters had resumed their normal compact size and with Hia-e-lea leading once more they made their way over the hills to the mountains. As they drew closer their minds were filled with the image of the Watersinger. Alk-e-lea had pondered the most over the last part of Hia-e-lea's dream as she felt she knew this strange dolph. The possibility that she might meet the dolph who had contacted her when Ler-e-lea was in trouble excited her. When she had first seen the dolph she had felt Mel-e-gar would have wanted to see who was the originator of the green light that had saved his friend. But even though she understood the reasons why Mel-e-gar couldn't meet her she still wanted him to be with her and the others. She had to satisfy herself with the knowledge that Mel-e-gar could be told on their return.

Serliker's light cast their shadows into the darkness of the mountains. *It* became brighter, illuminating the area for the dolphs. They had found a way that should, if Hia-e-lea was correct, deliver them onto the pass where Pha-e-gar had been killed. They had to stop many times as they climbed up as Bue-e-gar found it increasingly hard to keep the pace. Yol-e-gar had looked him over with his healing sense but there was little he could do except give him bursts of strength to keep him going. Many times they had to divert because of recent rock falls, and rivers of water slowed their progress even more.

Only Hia-e-lea seemed unperturbed by each setback as she radiated unswerving determination. Her strength pulled the others together and by the end of the night they had reached a ragged slope of scree which gave way under them, sending them tumbling down.

Alk-e-lea tried to slow Bue-e-gar's descent but even with Ran-e-gar's help they couldn't stop him. As the scree slipped further, they lost hold of him.

It looked like he would slough into Hia-e-lea. But she used the further momentum to launch herself in the air. She somersaulted once, her dees regaining contact on the bottom of the scree slope. She jumped once more and landed safely beyond a small boulder.

Unfortunately Bue-e-gar was not so lucky and his prostrate form smacked into the boulder with a sickening crack. Alk-e-lea and Ran-e-gar reached the bottom with only minor scratches and bruises. Yol-e-gar had thrown his weight sideways so he wouldn't hit the boulder. Coming to his dees he scrambled over the scree and bent down over the still body of Bue-e-gar.

Danetar was slowly rising giving him more light to see the extent of Bue-e-gar's injuries. His hand came away, sticky with hot blood. His water-time told him that the fracture was deep, putting pressure on the brain. Carefully he used his healing and eased the pressure, closing the fracture. The damage was not extensive but it had caused strain on Bue-e-gar's already weak heart. He could mend torn tissue but the regeneration of old and worn out muscle was beyond his power. The rhythm was irregular but he did manage to slow it down and for awhile he restored the balance of the chambers. The blood supply became more regular and Yol-e-gar had to hope it was enough. By the time he withdrew he found Alk-e-lea's imploring gaze boring into him. "He needs to rest for a tay, then maybe he will recover."

She knew the truth of his words and with Ran-e-gar's help they lifted Bue-e-gar and when Hia-e-lea had caused her shelter to grow they placed him inside.

It was only later when they looked about them that they recognised that they had made it to the pass. It had altered drastically. Before it was about thirty dees wide; now it was only twenty. Most of it was filled with rocks and boulders. Falling scree from the slopes of the two mountains had changed it completely.

Hia-e-lea saw that the Watersinger had spoken truly when she said that the images Xrl-e-lea had sent about the condition of the pass were false. There was only room for her shelter, so the others decided to get what rest they could by taking turns with Bue-e-gar.

Alk-e-lea was already inside washing the blood and grime from her mate's head, with the water provided by the shelter.

The three remaining dolphs silently stood at what remained of the wall of Shakeilar, which for seasons had barred the way to the valley. It was only by using Serliker's light did they see the extent of the decay that had come about, for most was still in shadow. Great chunks of the wall were missing. Thousand of cracks ran into these open wounds that cried of past pain. Hia-e-lea felt Serliker's torment at seeing one of *its* own kind reduced so.

Its voice spoke the anger, "*Look*! What *your kind* have done!"

None could rebut his words. Hia-e-lea reached out with her free hand and touched the surface. Unlike before in her dream the surface did not yield. It was cold and hard. She gave a gentle push. All of them jumped back in alarm as the wall lost its hold and came crashing down. A cloud of dust filled the entrance, making them choke and splutter.

Serliker cried out, trying to send energy to restore the Shakeilar, but only a thin layer of dust remained. The storm had delayed them too long. They were too late to save this one.

Afterwards Hia-e-lea tried to get Serliker to talk but *it* had withdrawn. Only a dull grey light permutated *its* surface. Even using her water-time she couldn't get *it* to respond. In the end she gave up and placed *it* on a boulder, not liking the harsh coolness *it* radiated into her hand. She rejoined the others, sitting in the shade of a nearby overhang.

"Is Serliker still refusing to talk?" asked Yol-e-gar.

"*It's* completely withdrawn. I don't know what to do, other than to leave *it* alone," she replied rather mournfully.

"Serliker will recover. *It* must be a shock to find one of *its* own this way," added Ran-e-gar.

She nodded her agreement and said, "We better decide whether we three go on now or wait until Bue-e-gar awakes. Alk-e-lea isn't going to leave him alone here and Serliker is no help at the yen."

Yol-e-gar coughed some more dust from his lungs before replying, "We have to wait until all of us are ready. Your dream told us that we all have something to do when we reach the cities."

"Yes, I know but the more we delay the worse it's going to get," she replied rather shortly.

"The best we can do is to rest and proceed in the morning," interjected Ran-e-gar, "and hopefully Bue-e-gar and Serliker will be ready."

Yol-e-gar gave him a grateful look and said, "Ran-e-gar's right, we will need all our wits about us when we confront whatever remains there."

Hia-e-lea knew they were right and she settled for taking the first watch. She positioned herself in the entrance, sitting beyond the layer of dust that was all that remained of the wall. Whilst she sat looking into the blackness, she tried using her water-time to penetrate the gloom. It didn't take long for her to become quite adept at finding the contours of the tunnel. Gradually moving her sound further along she could not find any obstruction. It was a curious way of seeing and soon she was confident enough to declare to herself at least the way for them was clear. With normal sight only a small spark of light broke the darkness which she now was sure indicated that the other end was still open.

As Danetar descended she was about to take her rest when from the corner of her eye a glimmer of light flickered. At first she thought it was Serliker but when she turned to her right the light shone from the corner of the entrance. Puzzled she walked over and crouched down. To her disbelief she saw what it was. A small round globe of blue and silver crystal was half buried in a small crevice in the ground. Excitement filled her as she pried it out. The welcoming glow beat a rhythm upon her palm. It held her mesmerised for a yen before realisation filled her and she rushed back to the others, particularly Serliker.

The others including Alk-e-lea quickly surrounded her to see her find. Darkness was descending rapidly and the blue light shone brighter as more of the natural light dissipated. Serliker was still on the boulder where she had left *it*. No sounds were spoken as they all knew what she held. With smiles on all faces they nodded to each other and walked over to Serliker. Hia-e-lea carefully placed the much smaller crystal by *its* side. Almost immediately the darker blue light of Serliker burst forth. With Yol-e-gar and Hia-e-lea's help the other two also joined with Serliker's water-time.

I did not sense your presence. I only saw the empty shell of your past existence, stated Serliker.

Slowly a sound came from the blue sphere, *I... Have... Been....Alone... My...Kindred....Need your help.*

As the ripple of sound permeated their collective waters, Yol-e-gar suddenly gasped in surprise, *You were a healing crystal!* Then recall of Hia-e-lea's dream gave him the answer. *You worked with Eil-e-lea but then how did Pha-e-gar manage to use you?*

The sphere's sound became more fluid as *it* shared but sadness flowed forth as *it* answered, *You knew of Eil-e-lea's disappearance and the dreams gave you what Pha-e-gar and then Xrl-e-lea came to believe; that Pha-e-gar's actions sent her to the deathsong.* There was a pause of sound as the sphere considered *its* waters.

It was not his action but hers that caused the tragedy. A ripple of surprise greeted that sound but *it* continued, *She tried and did heal what they both conceived to be a dead or dormant Shakeilar. With my energy and her design of water I was joined with the Crystal.... It* stopped again; *it* became puzzled but sounded resigned as *it* added, *My waters must have fragmented over time, for some of the images have been lost for all I can reveal is the fusion worked but there was a backlash of energy that somehow blew Eil-e-lea's waters and so her life away. I know that I was bound to the other Shakeilar, and my will was subverted by whatever was held within the Crystal.*

There was confusion and shock from all waters but it was Ran-e-gar who broke the silence. *Then are you saying it was not Pha-e-gar who abused you but the Shakeilar crystal that you healed?*

Yes and no.. was *its* reply.

Serliker saw the truth of the Crystal's sound. *We know Pha-e-gar found knowledge that allowed him to do many things and the picture is clear that the Shakeilar crystal that they helped gave him answers. He then must have used that knowledge to abuse the Shakeilar.*

It would seem that the Crystal did not consider that Pha-e-gar was unfit for the knowledge it gave but it had been restored so it must have been grateful for its new life, answered the Sphere.

So as he came out of the joining he used that information to make the other Shakeilar bind with you, joined in Hia-e-lea.

Yes it could be. There are many empty and dry places in my waters but I feel that the Shakeilar would have kept me bound to it in any case. All I can add is it was desperate to make sure no other knew its nature. Even Pha-e-gar's memory was adjusted so he would forget that there was more to his new Crystal than it appeared. It was enough for his hunger that he had final control over the energy within.

Didn't do him much good though, commented Alk-e-lea.

Only the silence of sadness met those final sounds.

Serliker now understood a great deal more and *it* was just for now happy that the crystal sphere had survived after all. *It* thanked Hia-e-lea for finding the Shakeilar.

She didn't respond to Serliker as she was bothered by the fact the Crystal she was now sharing water-time with was the same as the one that had been inside the larger crystal which held the spirits of Pha-e-gar and Xrl-e-lea.

Before the ripple disturbed her further the sphere answered her enquiry, *Dolph.. You saw only shadow of my form as we used the image to hold Xrl-e-lea. An illusion which surrendered her will to us.*

At least that made things clearer to Hia-e-lea and the others who had also wondered how *it* could have been in two places at once.

All of them remarked later how well balanced the Shakeilar was, considering the awful things Pha-e-gar and his minions had done to *it*. It gave them new hope that the other Shakeilar were still holding on.

In the morning Bue-e-gar surprised them with appearing at the entrance of the shelter looking fit and well. He laughed to see such surprise. "*I may be old* but I can still show you younglings a thing or two!"

Alk-e-lea stood by his side and she could only shrug as she didn't know how either. The first she knew was when he awoke her and proceeded to make her feel very much aware that he was much better. Yol-e-gar insisted on checking him out but could find nothing wrong with him. Even his heart was normal. *Indeed he could have been a dolph of thirty seasons instead of seventy-five!* Not even a scar disturbed the smooth contours of his grey head.

Only Bue-e-gar knew the truth but he was not about to upset his mate and his friends with the true reason for his apparent recovery. He just made sure not only did he enjoy it but also his loved one. When they were ready he stood in the front, with Hia-e-lea on one side and Alk-e-lea on the other, and together with the others closely following on behind, they entered the tunnel. Serliker and the sphere held by Hia-e-lea shone their way. The blackness opened up revealing that even Xrl-e-lea's tunnel was cracked and scarred with gashes that disturbed the once unblemished surface. Small rivulets of water ran down the walls into pools which they had to splash through. Gradually the distant point of light grew bigger until they could just see the domes of a city in the distance. They shielded their eyes as they came out of the gloom, allowing time for their eyes to adjust to the harsh light of Danetar.

The seven cities no longer shone. Most of the domes had fallen in on themselves. The walkways were splintered. Far below the once lush valley that Hia-e-lea had seen was a barren waste land, scorched by Danetar and she cried to see it so. They stood stunned to see such devastation. The pride of Xrl-e-lea was now only a ruin. The wind blew across the entrance bringing only the taste of death.

Again Bue-e-gar surprised them by turning to Yol-e-gar and quietly saying, "Now it's your time to heal the Shakeilar."

Serliker added *its* sound, "I will help you Yol-e-gar. Take hold of me and together we shall see what can be done."

Hia-e-lea was surprised but handed over Serliker. Yol-e-gar's silver eyes were wide with the enormity of what he had been asked. But resolutely he moved to the edge of the ledge where they all stood and with Serliker held tightly in his grasp he bent down and touched the surface of a small piece of the walkway which was hanging limply over the precipice. Opening his water-time with Serliker he found the health sense amplified making it easy for him to visualise the Shakeilar as it was in Hia-e-lea's dream. His body stiffened as the energy coursed through him, melding into the crystal surface giving new life to the old. Gradually the walkway began to shimmer and sparkle. With a thousand cries filling his mind he felt the other strands respond and reach out to him. Colour filled his vision. Blood rushed to his head. Dizziness made him sway but he stayed firm. At Serliker's urging he released the energy and toppled over.

Bue-e-gar saw his predicament and lunged forward, stopping him from falling over the edge. The strength of the dolph was enormous as Yol-e-gar was lifted and moved to the entrance where he was laid down. Serliker slipped from his hand and Bue-e-gar snatched the sphere up and passed *it* back to Hia-e-lea.

Slowly strength returned to Yol-e-gar and he was able to walk back to join the others. They were staring at his handiwork and Bue-e-gar's broad smile told him he had done well. The walkways were restored. Even the cities looked better. But he knew that there needed to be a lot more energy infused into them. The city directly opposite was the only one that looked restored. The spires and domes were filling out as they watched. The process continued until *it* once more overshadowed the rest with *its* magnificence.

Hia-e-lea found herself once more in the centre of their attention and with a warm smile from Bue-e-gar she took the lead and led them across the walkways. Her mind filled with the vision of her dream, turning it to water-time, gave her the awareness that Pha-e-gar's shadow lurked ahead, waiting for them.

When they had walked halfway across the apparition materialised in front of them, an enormous grey shadow that was filled with half glimpsed faces of tormented dolphs. Only the twisted face of Pha-e-gar had any real solidity and it raised two arms that were no more than wispy trails of shadow that only suggested more malevolence.

Only Ran-e-gar baulked at the apparition and his mind screamed at the terror he saw in front of him. It was enough for Pha-e-gar and he lunged forward.

But Hia-e-lea raised her hand at the creature which had tormented her. She held no fear now. Even the memory of its hot breath could not shake her and with the commanding voice of one who knew her own fears she faced them and proclaimed, "*Leave him.* It's time to end this *Pha-e-gar*!" The shadow of the creature wavered, hovering still as it gazed down at Hia-e-lea. A flicker of fear crossed over the face and the other insubstantial shadows of the other dolphs shrank away from her presence.

Then its voice not only filled all their minds but also echoed off the mountainside, even though its wailing voice was directed at Hia-e-lea, "*You know me youngling?*" the voice rasped and droplets of saliva spat at her.

She didn't waver, knowing that a shadow could not harm her if she did not allow it. "We have met in my dreams and I have come to help you." Her words were quietly and softly spoken.

The shadow retracted another pace. Pha-e-gar's countenance suddenly snarled and it cried, "*You*! Yes, you are the one she was calling!" It gave a ghastly laugh and added, "But youngling, you have to pass me first!"

For a yen she hesitated not liking the implication but then the reassuring presence in her dream told her she could pass in safety, if the others only gave warmth and love to the creature. This passed swiftly among them.

Ran-e-gar did his best to overcome his fear and Bue-e-gar came to his rescue and reached back and pulled him closer. "Do not be afraid. They cannot harm you."

Hia-e-lea let Bue-e-gar look after Ran-e-gar and with the strong presence of her friends now facing the creature she stepped forwards. There was a tremendous shriek and the creature attempted to smother them. Not with any real physical presence but with the weight of such appalling misery that they found themselves slipping and Hia-e-lea cried out, "*Hold firm!*"

They responded to her call, but they were still slipping back. The blue and silver light of their new friend flared up, showering the shadow. Pha-e-gar cried out, his tortured eyes blinking in pain, the confusion apparent, and it was enough for him to break off his attack. A mournful cry escaped his lips, "You cannot be here!" Then he shifted from despair to anger and pointing at the crystal he spat, "You killed her! *You killed my Eil-e-lea*!"

A swirl of black shadow formed, and before any could react Pha-e-gar swiped at the sphere. But he had forgotten his nature. He was just shadow and even though he tried he couldn't gain hold. Hia-e-lea's hand kept hold. Even the freezing cold which came with each swipe didn't disturb her grip. She just felt increasingly sad as Pha-e-gar howled louder and louder. It had stopped pushing them with its pain and they all gave one great heave and the shadow was flung back. With a cry of impotent rage Pha-e-gar retreated.

They were surprised to find that they had been shifted to the edge of the walkway. They had been only yens from being pushed over the edge to join with the many bones below. Fortunately the creature was now fast fading out of sight, its shrieks filling the morning air. Quickly they made their way back to the centre of the walkway.

Ran-e-gar had been shaken but not broken and they allowed him the luxury of a few yens to gather his strength so they could continue.

The walk through the city was made in silence, all eyes peeled for any sign of the creature. It had occurred to them that their escape was too easy and the final confrontation would come when they entered the main chamber. The outside appearance was deceiving as much of the inner city was falling apart. Homes lining the unnaturally straight streets had roofs missing and entrance ways had crumbled in. But the light of the Shakeilar could be seen trying to restore the damage. Yol-e-gar and Serliker's energy was still working. The further they moved in the more damage they saw. Streets were filled with rubble of cracked and broken crystal. They found their way around these obstructions, sometimes having to backtrack to find the way to the main entrance. Finally as night began to descend they found the first arch. This was open and there were puddles of water with moss starting to grow on the walls and floor. As they passed through they found each arch open and more signs that the elements were slowly eroding the city. Only the main arch had its entrance closed and the black marker reflected the light of Serliker. They paused waiting for Hia-e-lea to proceed.

She had stopped because she could feel the malevolence of Pha-e-gar waiting on the other side. There was no feeling of Xrl-e-lea or of the Watersinger. Hia-e-lea turned to Alk-e-lea and said, "I'm not sure I can." Her confidence was beginning to wane.

Alk-e-lea could feel and see the consternation in Hia-e-lea's eyes and knew that if it was not for Bue-e-gar's comforting presence she would have fled as fast as her legs could carry her. "We all understand but we have to go on. There is too much at stake."

Her words were cut short by a loud crack of Shakeilar being broken apart. The entrance way was suddenly torn away, revealing the hideous features of Pha-e-gar. The darkness only added to his presence and he in his domain was now very substantial in form, no longer just shadow. Before any could react warped arms pulled them into the chamber.

Serliker and the sphere were torn from Hia-e-lea, and flung across the room. Through the suffocating cloak of despair they heard the sounds of the two spheres impacting against a far wall.

Serliker, making use of being so close to *its* kin, poured hot vibrant energy into the chamber. Light exploded around them as *it* did *its* work and the creature let go and used its arms to wrap the cloak of shadow around itself to hide from the glare, crying with pain, "Take it way! *Take it away!*"

From their various positions around it they watched the shadow grow smaller until only the shade that was Pha-e-gar was remaining. It howled at them but was not inclined to do anything more.

Bue-e-gar was the first to pick himself up from the central isle and look around. Serliker's power was fast restoring the chamber. The raised dais was reforming and the only thing which seemed undisturbed was the giant black and silver crystal that started to pulsate like a steady heart beat. He tasted fear of the growing presence inside the crystal and he knew that they were about to tackle the will of Xrl-e-lea.

Across the room Hia-e-lea saw where he looked and she gasped in surprise as a form began to superimpose itself over the crystal.

Alk-e-lea, Yol-e-gar, and Ran-e-gar had silently moved down the centre isle and stood with Bue-e-gar, all watching the apparition. None of them could move any further. They were held suspended.

Only Hia-e-lea was free to act. She quickly checked on Pha-e-gar but even he and his minions were silent. A frozen scream upon his tortured face told her that Serliker had awakened Xrl-e-lea and given her power to act.

The deadly silence was broken by sweet smooth sounds of Xrl-e-lea as her features took form. “Well done *my dear*. Thank you for coming to *my rescue*.”

Hia-e-lea tried to ignore the words as she desperately sent her water-time to Serliker, pleading for *its* aid, *Help me! Withdraw your power!*

A wall of grey shadow came down. *Naughty little dolph. It is under my will now!*

The sounds tore into her water-time taking any hope that remained away. She tried a final plea in another direction. *Watersinger help us! Plea-*

But she was cut short by the insidious sounds from Xrl-e-lea, *Ah! How sad! Your little friend is no longer here. She left because she was bored with waiting so long.*

She tried her best to fight, knowing the sounds were false. The Watersinger would not abandon her, but soon her mind and water-time became still as Xrl-e-lea’s will dominated.

“Your *Watersinger*!” spitting the words into the silent chamber, “Was wrong when she tried to pervert my message to you. For Pha-e-gar has been under my command these many seasons. I won that battle long ago and he and his cronies have led victims not to open my prison but to feed me their life energy. He has even ventured to other places and snatched the odd dolph and brought them back for me! I gave her the story she told you and she unwittingly ensured your arrival here. Even Serliker has become mine to command. You see I needed, not just one mind but two that were more water-time than mind to free me. The seasons have been long but I waited until your kind returned to the old ways!” The laughter which roared forth was almost hysterical as she continued to taunt Hia-e-lea, “*Water-time! water-time!*”

Hia-e-lea found herself moving across the room, closer to the dais. What was left of her own will had fled to the deepest part of herself. It began gradually, her water-time slipping from her and only partly aware that the Healer had also been moved into position beside the giant crystal. Her arms moved in unison with his and slowly she reached out. She screamed, knowing that Xrl-e-lea was making her do what Pha-e-gar had tried to do, to touch the crystal and free Xrl-e-lea from her prison. It was over quickly, their water-times flooding into the sphere, joining with Xrl-e-lea.

For a yen, Hia-e-lea and Yol-e-gar were aware of each other but before they could sound their own distress at having failed, they fell into a nightmare of continuing horror.

The cry of exultation was hideous to hear as she fused her water-time together, replenished and whole once more. The crystal exploded into energy which she also absorbed, restoring her body. No longer a shadow she felt warm blood in her veins and a strong heart beat with excitement as she picked up the almost lifeless dolphs and threw them to Pha-e-gar, whilst releasing her hold over him to allow him to feast on the remains of Hia-e-lea and Yol-e-gar.

He fed greedily consuming their warm bodies. Soon their tortured features could be seen under the cloak of shadow, silent screams twisting their faces. Pha-e-gar slobbered his thanks and she sent him away. Before he skulked out of the chamber, he turned hungry eyes on the three remaining dolphs, still frozen by her will.

“No, I have plans for these! Soon you will have all Delikadove to feed on. Now go!”

He began to fade through the now restored entrance, muttering curses but then stopped once more, his eyes swiftly scanning the chamber, his hunger forgotten as he searched the room.

“*What is it?* What do you hunger for now Pha-e-gar?”

"There it is; *there it lays!*" shouted Pha-e-gar in triumph.

Seeing where he was now fixated on, she spied the blue shimmer of a small crystal. With a flick of her hand the sphere was instantly brought to her grasp. Turning to Pha-e-gar, "This is what you want *my dear*," she taunted, holding the crystal out to him.

"No! *Yes*!" he cried in pain and anger. For a yen an image of Eil-e-lea flickered before him. Lying curled up, her death apparent and he remembered his screams of anguish as he had left the shelter those countless tays ago. The newly reformed crystal had been gripped feverishly in his hand and he had stared unbelievingly at the final crushing blow.

His tree, his golden branched haven had been torn, a great open wound, where the trunk had split in two. It was still standing tall in part, but a third of the trunk had been blasted away, scattered in great chunks upon the ground. The shelter had stood there, an island in that sea of devastation. To his eyes it taunted him and he had run screaming and screaming from his ruined valley.

Picking his thoughts from him, she could almost feel pity for him. No, he was just a pathetic fool but she would give him this, well in a way. "*Pha-e-gar!*" she called. He blinked away the past and stared expectantly at her. "Here you are *my dearest*!" mocked Xrl-e-lea and crushed the sphere to dust. There was a weak flicker of light as the fine dust slipped through her fingers. She raised her hand and threw the rest at him.

He raised his head as the blue silver flakes showered over him, his eyes wide in shock. He could only whimper as the last flakes came to rest on his twisted face and he knew it was finally coming to an end. There was nothing left and with her terrible laughing scorn ringing inside him he fled the chamber.

Serliker slowly rolled behind a pillar behind the dais, leaving an image of *itself* behind. *It* was sorry that Hia-e-lea and Yol-e-gar had to be sacrificed but *it* knew that it was the only way to bring it all to an end. The anger *it* felt at the death of the Sphere so recently revived was kept tightly under control, *its* water-time hidden as *it* silently entered the pillar, fusing *itself* into the Shakeilar, spreading out changing *its* mass, replacing the old with *its* new healthier substance. The very core of the city was discreetly moving aside, using some of Serliker's power to transfer *its* consciousness out of the city, along the walkways to the next city, each time joining with the water-times of each Shakeilar until all seven were ready for Serliker's signal. By keeping the same colour and symmetry *it* had become not just one but all seven cities including the walkways.

If Xrl-e-lea noticed the subtle change she showed no awareness of it. To Serliker she was busy keeping her will fixed on the other dolphs while her body settled down, making sure the energy had transformed completely into flesh. It made *its* water-time shudder to see her take delight in being so alive, without a hint of pity for the lives she had so casually snuffed out. Now all *it* had to do was wait until she made the next move.

She crossed the dais like a black wave, searching the fragments of crystal for the sphere which held her watersong. Without it she would not be complete and even though she might enslave dolphs without it she knew that she was vulnerable to Mel-e-gar. The image of the dolph swam in her water-time, taken from Hia-e-lea, taunting her with the fate that might be in store if he became aware of her existence. She used her dees to scatter the fragments, becoming more desperate as she saw that it was no longer there. A snarl tore from her as she kicked over more of the fragments on the dais. A silver glimmer caught her attention as the pieces scattered. Bending down she swept away more to reveal a tiny crystal that shone with pure silver light. Her cry of triumph rang out and for a yen her will slipped, allowing Bue-e-gar to take a step forward. She crowed as she carefully picked up the sphere. It was the size of a small seed. It was no wonder she had missed it. She placed it on her palm and opened her water-time to fuse with her song.

She was oblivious to Bue-e-gar's silent approach. Barely noticeable, a low humming whispered around the chamber.

Her cry of triumph turned to anger, then frustration as her water-time entered the sphere and found her song was fading away. The more she tried to sweep it up the more insubstantial it became while the humming changed tempo and Bue-e-gar had a dee on the first step of the dais. She couldn't believe she was to be cheated when she was so close. Xrl-e-lea tried again but the silver sphere gave a small pop and crumbled into fine silvery dust.

How could this be?! her water-time screamed. Then she became aware of a presence standing very close behind her. She swung round as she came to her dees and gasps of surprise and fear escaped her lips.

Bue-e-gar stood relaxed, staring up at the visage of Xrl-e-lea, smiling as he continued to hum a faint tune.

"*How?!!*" she exclaimed her eyes wide at the apparent ease with which Bue-e-gar stared up at her. He didn't answer, just continued to smile, as if he had just met an old friend. It made her recoil and she stepped away. He stepped forwards and she stepped further back. Her water-time writhed with incomprehension as she tried to understand how a mere dolph, an old one at that had broken her hold over him. Struggling to keep control she tested her will and found it still held the other two dolphs. A glimmer of glee sparkled inside as she warned, "*Stop Dolph* or I'll tear the life from your companions!"

Bue-e-gar's smile grew wider and the tune changed tempo, making the air sparkle with faint silver light that teased her. She stumbled backwards as her water-time screamed in panic when she saw that he held her song. "*Impossible!* You are not a *Watersinger*!!" Her voice was shrill as she watched the silver light expand towards her. She flinched as it started to envelope her.

Her fear suddenly broke, and her anger began to rise as the determination not to be thwarted took hold. With a sweep of water-time she sent it out to crush Alk-e-lea and Ran-e-gar. It made contact and with a swipe took their life from them. They crumpled to the floor of the dais while she cried her delight. The bodies smouldered as the energy engulfed the flesh.

From the entrance Pha-e-gar swept through, his cloak wide and consuming as he rushed to feed on the remains. He gurgled and spluttered his hunger upon the blackened bodies. As the cloak descended he gave a savage cry and consumed them.

Her fear lifted and she stretched to her full height, now glaring with savage ire at Bue-e-gar. But still his pose was unchanged and the tune changed once more. She found his unperturbed expression infuriating and she swung her arm to crush him. Her hand passed through the silver light, reaching for him. Her hand never reached him for the light flared up and she cried in pain, withdrawing from the silver fire that now cloaked him. To her horror her hand and lower arm had faded to shadow. She could still feel her hand but it had no substance.

Pha-e-gar heard her cry and swept across the chamber to the dais. The tormented faces of Alk-e-lea and Ran-e-gar had joined the rest and he flew over Bue-e-gar to face him, using the visage of his friends to taunt him.

If it was possible Bue-e-gar's smile grew wider and a barely audible sound of tutting could be heard in the background of the tune which continued to play.

Pha-e-gar glared at him and turning to Xrl-e-lea growled, "Is there *nothing* this dolph cares for? We kill his friends and he does nothing! *What kind of creature is this?*" pointing a boney finger at Bue-e-gar.

She ignored his question and waved her vaporous lower arm in front of Pha-e-gar's face. "Look what he has done!!"

He looked up at her as if she was stupid and rasped, "Use the power that is in this place!" indicating the chamber.

Puzzlement flickered across her face, then a smile of glee swept her misery away. She knew what he was referring to and the image of her transition from her prison took hold. "*Yes! the Shakeilar!*" She turned and swept her eyes across the room until she spied the sphere of Serliker. With a cry she used her water-time to break *its* energy to recreate her arm. But water-time passed through and she found she could not take hold. Then she saw that *it* was only an illusion. "*It's gone!*" was her mournful cry.

Serliker heard her and acted. The chamber shimmered and began to flow like a great blue wave. Pha-e-gar and Xrl-e-lea stared in disbelief as the walls rushed towards them. Both cowered as the wave crashed down, but instead of impacting against them it passed through and like so much water flowed away. When they dared to look up, a midnight sky greeted them and a cold wind blew across the grey empty ledge where they stood.

The city was gone and looking wildly about them they saw the other cities including the walkways melt into nothingness. The only things visible were seven shining spheres that were piled neatly at the entrance of the tunnel Xrl-e-lea had once created. Now exposed to the elements, with all their power stripped from them they stood helplessly staring at the smiling countenance of Bue-e-gar.

To Xrl-e-lea's despair her body also began to melt away and slowly she changed, her screams echoing around the mountainside as she returned to the shadow she had been. Then in the air above them Serliker materialised, a flaming ball of blue fire that bathed the ledge. The light passed through Xrl-e-lea and Pha-e-gar, making them look even more insubstantial. *Its* clear tones sealed their fate. "The time has come Watersinger.."

Bue-e-gar's calm face nodded his agreement and then the shades witnessed the transformation as he revealed his true nature. Slowly green light permeated through his grey skin, changing the silver light. The tune that he had been humming fell silent and a clarity of breathtaking beauty filled the night as another song took over.

Gradually Bue-e-gar's face grew limp. His face showed the tiredness but a certain amount of relief was clear in his eyes as the Watersinger moved out, forming into a glorious green body that showed the mark of a tall, slim lea. Her eyes flashed green, red, and silver in a continuous cycle as she surveyed the cringing forms of Xrl-e-lea and Pha-e-gar. Her voice was sweet upon the wind which only made them cower even more. "*It's time to go home..* But first we must restore what has been broken."

Pha-e-gar was first to feel the power of her song. His shadow grew wider, until the thousands of faces of his victims could be seen clearly. Their features were no longer tortured but calm as they welcomed her release. One by one they detached, whittling Pha-e-gar down, until only his pathetic morose shadow remained. Thousands of dolphs, each just a shadow filled the ledge. Serliker's light expanded to included them all. Then the Watersinger sang four notes in quick succession.

From the crowd flowed four dolphs; Alk-e-lea, Ran-e-gar, Hia-e-lea, and Yol-e-gar. They came to her and she indicated for them to watch what was going to happen to the rest of the dolphs.

Thousands of murmurs rippled across the crowd as she began to sing. Her song filled the shades and Yol-e-gar and Ran-e-gar found themselves among the dolphs again. Their water-time fused together as they walked among them healing the pain, creating fresh water-time that transformed the thoughts of the dolphs until they understood their own past, freeing them finally from their physical bonds.

In the centre of the group a large swirling mist appeared. White light flashed from it. As it expanded the dolphs who had been touched by Yol-e-gar and Ran-e-gar stepped through. All water-times sounded with expectation, "*Chisharnlay!*"

The path was clear and they were free to continue with their life journey. Even Xrl-e-lea and Pha-e-gar could not help but stare in wonder as the once victims found their hearts' desire and travelled onwards into the mist. By the time the last dolph had passed through, they turned imploring eyes to the Watersinger, wanting release from their own torment. But she raised her hand and the gateway flicked once then disappeared from sight.

Bue-e-gar and the others had expected to pass through themselves and they cried their surprise to the Watersinger. Her water-time eased their concern and slipping her water-time to Ran-e-gar once more she told him what he must do. To the others she indicated Pha-e-gar and said, "*Watch..*"

Ran-e-gar filled his water-time with images of the past and stood in front of the imploring gaze of Pha-e-gar. He found he could touch the dolph. He hugged Pha-e-gar and opened the power to embrace the dolph he held.

The mind of Pha-e-gar began to change as the past came flooding back. Each turn he had made was brought into stark relief. His guilt over the death of his teacher. Each subsequent wrong made him cry but Ran-e-gar showed him that he was part of a great cycle of water-time that had created his life to be an instrument that had meaning. He had the chance to grasp the understanding and make all that had gone before worthwhile. Layer after layer was sloughed off, changing Pha-e-gar until he was but a youngling once again. Ran-e-gar knew that it had come to an end and he opened his eyes and stared down at the new-born cradled in his arms. The swirling light reappeared and Ran-e-gar stepped through into light.

His friends could just hear his faint farewell and waited their turn. Now the Watersinger turned to Xrl-e-lea who had shifted a few dees closer to the swirling mist. She looked hungry and for a yen they believed she would pass through but she stayed just by the rim. A look of panic filled her eyes and the Watersinger made another gesture and raised her eyes to the stars and called. The sound was so highly pitched that it passed from the dolphs' hearing. She stayed open mouthed for several more yens. Then she relaxed and smiled at Xrl-e-lea and whispered, "Come.."

Xrl-e-lea looked at the Watersinger in puzzlement and stepped forwards but her attention was snatched away as a ball of orange light shot out from the mist. Her water-time was flung back and she fell to her knees at the image of the meteor that had torn the heart out of a youngling named Isa-e-lea.

The past crashed inside and she saw herself and the Neimas, who had become her friend playing among the trees of an ancient woodland. She again felt his strength as he picked her up and together they ran across the lush plains to his home, where they shared pieces of a cloud and told stories that made them laugh until tears came. Again she wept bitter tears for that lost time. The revenge on her own kind was a youngling's hurt for not being able to do all that she wished; to be an Elder with the power to stop disasters from happening. That had been her wish but how things had become so twisted. Hurt wracked her body again and she called out for the Neimas.

A passage of grief properly expressed can bring greater life to blossom forth and Xrl-e-lea opened her eyes to see her friend towering over her. Like her he was shadow, but shadows can touch and he lifted her from her knees, roaring his pleasure at finding her again. The other dolphs found lumps of emotion filling their vaporous throats. Even the Watersinger had tears form in the corner of her eyes as they watched Xrl-e-lea change whilst she was held by the Neimas. She became smaller and her features melted and changed to what she was truly.

A youngling named Isa-e-lea waved to them as she balanced on the Neimas' shoulders and they turned and walked into the light which rapidly contracted until it too disappeared.

Only the light of Serliker and the Watersinger lit the night. She turned to the three remaining dolphs and said, "I must go. Now that they have passed to Chisharnlay, I can no longer stay."

Together they exclaimed their surprise at seeing that their way to Chisharnlay was closed. "*What was going to happen to them? Would they pass through too?*"

The Watersinger laughed and waved as she began to fade from sight. She did answer but with actions not words.

*   *   *

CRYSTAL

He awoke with a start and rubbed his eyes as the dim blue light filled his vision. The shelter seemed larger as he looked around. He shook the dream from his water-time, hoping that when they did get to the mountains that it wasn't going to be that bad. Bue-e-gar was still disorientated and he sat up and looked to his side. Alk-e-lea was soundly asleep. He stroked across her shoulders and nearly decided to stay with her but now that he was awake he walked over to the wall and waved his hand. He hoped the rain had stopped but when he looked out he almost shouted in surprise. For the ground looked dry as if no water had ever quenched its thirst. Also he saw the hills were now in the far distance when he had been sure they had camped by them several tays ago. They should have still been there. Danetar was approaching the zenith point, indicating midtay. Bue-e-gar, now totally disorientated, played with the notion of waking Alk-e-lea but first he had to check by going outside.

Stepping out onto the ground he looked in all directions. To the south the hills and mountains, but his next surprise was that they were west of Ieulasayer and could only be ten klees away as he could just make out the glimmer of the domes in the distance. Then he saw there were only two shelters instead of the usual three. An image from his dream of Ran-e-gar entering the mist filled him and he knew that somehow it was no dream. Stunned by the realisation he opened the second shelter and found Hia-e-lea and Yol-e-gar asleep in their respective sleeping-chambers. But in the centre of the room was the blue light of Serliker resting on a pile of multicoloured crystals. He counted them. *They were the final proof that he was indeed very much awake and of course alive!* He sat down staring at the crystals and a ripple ruefully sounded, *Now I do feel my age!*

He sat musing over the crystals for quite a while until he felt a warm hand on his shoulder and a clear stream of water-time flowed into him, *How are you feeling Bue-e-gar? We wondered how long you would sleep for.*

He blended his waters with hers and sounded, *I am fine Hia-e-lea, but a little confused.*

She chuckled, *It is not surprising, all of us have been through a lot these past tays.* Her ripple changed course and sounded, *I see your water-time is as clear as ours and as deep.*

With a lurch of his water-time he saw what she meant which made him exclaim with amazement, "*Water-time!*"

The wave crashed down, creating wider ripples as he felt the clarity of his own water, liking the feeling it gave him as he knew that somehow he now possessed the capacity of a full water-time. The question rose from the depth and splashed into Hia-e-lea, *Would you please explain how this is possible?*

It brought further chuckles from her waters and bubbles of explanation burst, revealing what he had missed.

A parting gift from the Watersinger, is how Serliker put it. But I can see that you believed what we experienced was a dream but when you saw only two shelters and the seven crystals you admitted that it was not a dream.

He sent a ripple of confirmation while her water continued, *The rest of us remember the Watersinger leaving and the next thing we were aware of was waking here two tays ago. None of us know how we were turned from the deathsong or more precisely the gateway of Chisharnlay and restored to our lives. When the shock had abated we questioned Serliker but all it would say was that we were never really dead. It said that it was something to do with time and we should not worry, just accept that we had survived. That brought our attention to the fact you were still asleep and that Ran-e-gar had not come back with us. Serliker explained that you needed rest as you were recovering from your fall still-.*

Now protest burst forth in Bue-e-gar as he interrupted her. *But I had already recovered!* he sounded, rather indignantly, *and I can clearly see myself with you all at the end. I may have been dead but I felt fine!*

Waves of laughter met his indignation and she sounded, *But your body was never there, only your mind.*

Excuse me?!

More laughter came from Hia-e-lea at his bemusement but she explained further, *According to Serliker, the Watersinger created a resemblance of you to put your mind and her water-time in. Your body was held invisible to us and in a frozen state until she could return you, so none of us would be aware that you were not you!*

Her mirth grew even more as his water-time exploded with hundreds of bubbles of incredulity.

You may find this funny but I don't! he exclaimed. Then his waters suddenly calmed as he recalled what had happened the night before they entered the city. *So that is how I managed it...*

Hia-e-lea's waters nearly ruptured with glee as she teased, *That's what Alk-e-lea said. But don't worry, Serliker told us that the Watersinger was busy communicating with it when you and Alk-e-lea were otherwise occupied...Well we believe so....*

She left the rest unsounded but Bue-e-gar's waters slowly began to bubble with amusement as he appreciated what Hia-e-lea was inferring. A gale of laughter blew across his water-time and he and Hia-e-lea laughed until tears poured forth and both found themselves hugging themselves, fit to burst. Their laughter woke Yol-e-gar and he joined them. When they explained what was so funny he added his mirth and for awhile peals of joy rang around the shelter

When tears were wiped from their eyes Bue-e-gar was told the rest by Hia-e-lea and Yol-e-gar. There was further joy when they revealed again the knowledge gained from Serliker that Ran-e-gar had only passed through to Chisharnlay to help Pha-e-gar's return. After the transition he was rejoined with his body. But instead of returning with them he was transported to the home of Ler-e-lea where his mate was staying. The Watersinger knew that Wel-e-lea had felt something when he entered the mist. So that she would not worry she made sure he could be there to explain what had happened. This came as a great relief to Bue-e-gar.

The greatest puzzlement to them all was that none could recall clearly what the Watersinger looked like. The only image was of a dolph who they knew was a lea but no detail of feature was clear except for the colours, a green light mixed with an infusion of red and silver. If Serliker recalled, *it* never let on but just agreed with their description.

They knew that when they returned to Ieulasayer and Desilata the dolphs would be trying to figure that one out for seasons to come. Especially Mel-e-gar, as another Watersinger in their midst's raised many questions of what should have been an impossibility.

Later when Alk-e-lea joined them in the shelter Serliker added *its* water-time and brought their attention to the seven crystals. *These Shakeilar wish to return with us and to be put in the care of Mel-e-gar, it* stated.

Hia-e-lea asked, *Haven't they had enough of us dolphs?* Her sounds were mirrored by the others.

Serliker responded, *I know but they do not blame all dolphs for the wrongs of a few. After all they can only survive with your kind. They want to make sure water-times return and they see Mel-e-gar's revival of those times with all dolphs as their only hope. But now that all of you, with the exception of Yol-e-gar whose water-time was already well developed, have had yours revealed to you and with Alk-e-lea as Head of the Council, the changes to come will produce greater fruit...*

It fell silent but they knew *it* had more to tell. But Serliker seemed to hesitate and Yol-e-gar broke in, *Is there something that you have not told us?*

A sigh slipped into their water-time as Serliker sounded, *We do have a problem which the Watersinger left us*. It sounded ominous and a chill of apprehension was felt as Serliker gave a greater sigh and sounded, *There are seven crystals but one of them is not the same...*

The shelter suddenly glowed with a green and blue light as a crystal at the bottom moved from the pile and rolled off the mound. Hia-e-lea caught it as Serliker added, *This is Pha-e-gar's Crystal, how it would have looked to him if the healing sphere hadn't been covering it.*

They had all forgotten about that Crystal and the feeling of foreboding grew as the image of Pha-e-gar's shadow seemed to shimmer before them. Serliker allowed them time to calm but then insisted, *Allow all water-times to flow into the Crystal and tell me what it says.*

Nervous eyes looked at each other, as they waited for one of them to do as they had been bidden. The Crystal changed to a deep rich brown, then grey, yellow and settled on a rich blue green which seemed to flow towards them, refreshing their waters. They tingled with excitement as in one motion they dived together into its depths and heard these sounds:
If Logic = Mind and water-time = Feelings. Can Logic = water-time?

Before they answered, Serliker warned them, *The answer is not a simple yes or no. You have to know the truth of the answer. I dared not, as the Shakeilar's conscientiousness has knowledge which has been absorbed from Pha-e-gar and vise versa.*

What I can tell you is that as a youngling he raised this question. His logic denied any possibility of an answer other than a negative. Water-time was obsolete to him. He was trying to find a way that would help his cause to a full logic mind set. But his own sense of water, no matter how much denied had made him very afraid that he was wrong. Because he couldn't resolve it the equation began to haunt him. It drove him almost mad in frustration and he tried to wipe that question from all possibility. His tragic friendship with Eil-e-lea and the results from the healing of this Crystal compounded this desire. But it did give him answers. We know he learnt the ways that allowed him to vindicate his dark logic and his subsequent actions as he went on to abuse the Shakeilar and the very essence of water-time. But what else is lurking in its depth?

It was a question that was haunting them all. What that answer might be made them all pull back. Then Alk-e-lea asked, *Didn't the healing sphere give any hint?*

No, unfortunately not. Xrl-e-lea killed our friend before any answers or even how we should approach this Crystal.

Serliker's reminder of the sphere's demise left all feeling numb with renewed grief.

After a yen Hia-e-lea sounded, *Do we dare try and answer such a question?*

Their waters became even more quiet as they contemplated what needed to be done. It seemed a long time before Bue-e-gar broke the deadlock and sounded, *If the Watersinger wanted us to have access now then surely she would have revealed the answer to us..*

They could only stare silently at him, allowing their waters to swim around the dilemma which Bue-e-gar's statement raised. None could come up with a worthy answer and after further exchanges of sound they decided to leave it until they returned to Desilata to allow Mel-e-gar and the Council of dolphs to make the final decision. Hia-e-lea put the Crystal back with the others and as the light faded from the shelter they prepared to go home.

* * *

The special meeting of the Council was to be convened on the sixth tay of the third jeanth, allowing Mel-e-gar to spend a few more tays with his mate and his new-born, Star-e-lay. Their youngling was doing well; she was over twenty dees in length, not much smaller than Mel-e-gar. She was a light grey with the beak of a dolphin but the body of a Selahw. Also her tail was more dolphin which made her lines in the water look strangely curved. The other Selahw took her strangeness for a sign of good waters and welcomed the youngling eagerly into their song. They spent the night beating her birthing with their flukes. All remarked on how well named she was for on each side of her dorsal fin were two white splashes which looked much like two stars.

A message was quickly sent to Mel-e-gar about the meeting. He had known that Alk-e-lea and the others had returned since Wel-e-lea had sent a message that Ran-e-gar had suddenly appeared in her room at Ler-e-lea's home. If it hadn't been for the birthing he would have met the others but there was nothing more important than seeing his daughterling safely born. Even though ten tays had now passed he was reluctant to leave Cual-e-lay and Star-e-lay but his mate urged him to go as their youngling was doing well. All she did ask was that he wouldn't be away too long. With his promise given he swam through the purple waters, bringing his song forth. With a flicker of light he disappeared from the depths of Hederlike and reappeared in dolph form on the outskirts of Desilata.

By the time he reached the spiral street, Danetar was mid-sky and barely visible through the thick blanket of dark orange and black clouds that were speeding in from the east. Somehow it was appropriate as he joined the eager throng that wound their way to the Council chambers. The excitement was tangible in the air, mirrored by the flashes of energy lighting the distant underside of the storm front. The weather seemed to be breaking all the rules as the temperature dropped by the time he had managed to navigate his way to the entrance. It was such an abrupt change that it made him pause. A roll of thunder broke above and flashes of light grew stronger. The temperature should have been going up not down with such a heavy front and he just escaped as a sheet of rain fell from the sky, bringing frozen chunks of ice which bounced off several dolphs before they had time to scurry for cover. He stood under the arch and watched as the domes along the spiral began to flow together, creating an arching cover above, gradually blocking the rain and ice from view. Someone must have given the signal.

There were cries of relief from the dolphs as the Shakeilar's light grew stronger, illuminating with strong blue swaths of colour the entire spiral. It was impressive. He had heard of it, but this was the first time he had seen it in action. Now he knew why they had designed it in a spiral. He imagined it must look much like a shell of a sea creature from a sky-flyer's point of view.

Turning from the arch he walked through the corridors to the chamber beyond. Most of the dolphs were dry by the time they made it in and he stopped again at the main entrance as the seats filled. On the dais he could just make out the faces of Alk-e-lea, Bue-e-gar and three others which he knew must have been Yol-e-gar, Hia-e-lea, and Ran-e-gar. On the raised part of the dais he saw several crystals sparkling with different colours. He counted seven and to one side another who he knew was Serliker. Deciding not to make contact he stepped to one side and waited as the throng became a trickle until finally all that had made it from the other continents as well as the local cities settled in their seats.

His water-time flickered back to the last time he had seen so many dolphs in this place and wondered what kind of reception those on the dais were going to receive. Especially Alk-e-lea as she had broken council rules by going off and not consulting the inner chamber to which Mel-e-gar also belonged, even if it had been an honorary position since he was as yet too young to be among the Grand-elders. Strictly speaking so was Alk-e-lea but as the Head of the Council of all of Delikadove she was normally the only one outside those rules of restriction. The normal minimum age limit was fifty seasons and over for admittance to that inner sanctum.

Choosing the last vacant seat by the entrance Mel-e-gar sat down and waited as the sounds of more than twenty thousand dolphs gradually died down. Alk-e-lea broke away from the others and strode to rest her hands on the raised part of the dais which held the seven crystals and she began to speak, "*My friends*, we have grave news to tell...."

Her voice was strong and sure as she proceeded to tell the waiting dolphs about the events that had passed since Hia-e-lea's dream to the confrontation with Xrl-e-lea and the mysterious Watersinger.

He listened intently as the story unfolded while the dolphs reeled under the impact of her story. Many times in the clars that followed her narrative was broken by cries from the floor as the members of the inner chamber showed their displeasure at her actions. But by the time she had explained the reasons a heavy silence descended, only broken by murmurings which Mel-e-gar could just make out as, "*Watersingers! Shakeilar and dreams!!*"

It was not much longer before Alk-e-lea came to the matter of the Crystal holding the enigmatic question and several dolphs were invited to try their minds at answering it. But none succeeded. Finally she looked to Mel-e-gar and he felt her water-time, urging him to come forward.

The revelation of another Watersinger and that *she* was also the one connected to Ler-e-lea swirled inside as he walked slowly to the dais. Even the knowledge of what Xrl-e-lea and Pha-e-gar had done had not impacted as much as that. He had felt that the following of such logic for its own sake was a mistake, but understandable because of the way dolph society had been leaving behind water-time. He had known enough not to be surprised by that part of the story. The taking of life though had shaken him and that mixed with the "*Watersinger's*" use of Chisharnlay caused greater whirlpools of confusion.

They only fell away when Alk-e-lea spoke softly, "Mel-e-gar try the Crystal. The Watersinger told Serliker that all seven are to be put in your care but we need to know if you can access that Knowledge."

He could only nod his acceptance as he plunged his waters and met; If Logic = Mind and water-time = Feelings. Can Logic = water-time? The sounds seemed to burn their impression with watery flame as he knew that he had failed. He felt he should know and for a yen he was sure he heard a voice say, *Once...*

As he raised his head, withdrawing from the Crystal he felt Alk-e-lea's hand on him, knowing he had failed. Her waters met his, *We were hoping.. But maybe in time someone will know the answer and unlock the Knowledge that Pha-e-gar discovered.*

Hmmm...Did the Watersinger place the question in the Crystal? he questioned and before she could answer he made another ripple indicating her water-time, *And this?*

Serliker now believes she activated the defence mechanism of the Crystal which produces the question when probed by a water-time and yes, she is responsible for my water-time, not only myself but also Hia-e-lea, Ran-e-gar, and Bue-e-gar. Yol-e-gar believes that he has been endowed with a greater perception. We have, after all been at the gates of Chisharnlay and Ran-e-gar not only passed through but returned, even though he cannot remember what happened on the other side of that gate. She helped us all, and we as a race have much to be grateful for as I and the others believe she has allowed our kind to learn much that we have buried for too long.

The waters rippled and broke away as he answered, *Yes and maybe more than we can imagine.*

There was not a lot the inner chamber could do about Alk-e-lea's misdemeanour as Mel-e-gar's exclusion had been imperative to the success of laying Xrl-e-lea's story to rest. The legacy of Pha-e-gar would impact dolph society to make the move back to the seas more urgent than ever. The way Danetar was changing only added to the decision for Mel-e-gar's research to continue. At that meeting he asked them to push forward with teaching the younglings the ways of water-time, with the use of the Healers in the forefront much to Yol-e-gar's pleasure. Hia-e-lea and the others heartily approved this as they gathered up the crystals and with Serliker's agreement *it* turned *itself* into a bowl so Mel-e-gar could carry them to his home in Plesilea.

With the exception of the seventh as the Grand-elders ruled that it should stay in the chambers of Desilata for the immediate future to allow others to come forward and try to answer the riddle. But also and this was most important was to make sure that if it was opened then the exploration of that Knowledge would be under strict conditions. They had to make sure that if the darker knowledge still existed then they would have to decide their next course of action. Mel-e-gar and those of Alk-e-lea's expedition made that very clear to the rest of the Grand-elders. Another Pha-e-gar they didn't need!

It was while swimming with Star-e-lay, showing her a few tricks with Cual-e-lay that Alk-e-lea's water-time, urgently called him to Desilata. There was great sadness behind the call and he quickly passed his intentions to his mate as he vanished from the sea and returned to Desilata.

It had been seven jeanths since the meeting and all the crystals were now at his home with Serliker, where he split his time with his family. There had been increasing fears expressed about the Crystal and it was decided that Mel-e-gar should take over the supervision. It was felt that a Watersinger would be best placed to deal with the Crystal when the time came that it gave up its secrets.

He didn't like to leave so abruptly but Cual-e-lay always sounded on how much she enjoyed sharing his waters as he travelled all over Delikadove, passing what she saw to the rest of the Selahw as they treasured each story and added it to their great song.

By the time he had run from the outskirts to Alk-e-lea and Bue-e-gar's home he knew with a heavy feeling that something was wrong with Bue-e-gar. His hand shook as he passed it in front of the marker and as the opening appeared he stepped through into Alk-e-lea's waiting arms. A great wave of sorrow crashed through his water-time as she hugged her tears to his breast.

"It's *Bue-e-gar...*" were her only sounds but feeling Mel-e-gar's strength she led him to the room directly opposite. Nestled among the folds of his sleeping-chamber by the pool lay Bue-e-gar, his eyes closed, his breathing ragged and very slow. Quickly Mel-e-gar used his water-time to appraise his condition and saw that the old dolph's heart was beating erratically, getting slower as Mel-e-gar stood over him.

Bue-e-gar's eyelids flickered open as he sensed Mel-e-gar's presence. His mouth opened but no sound came forth. Then a rush of water-time flowed into Mel-e-gar's and while the body may have been incapable the dolph's water-time was clear and warm as he sounded, *I'm glad you have come Mel-e-gar. Don't worry, there is nothing you can do. Yol-e-gar has been and he could do no more.*

But maybe.. Mel-e-gar sounded, but with a flick of his water Bue-e-gar silenced him. *No.. it's time I was going. Do you realise I should have passed into the deathsong on that mountain. She gave me these extra tays and I am satisfied. In my last tays I have found the beauty and truth behind the water-time..* A chuckle bubbled forth in his waters as he added, *I even know the answer to the riddle!*

Mel-e-gar almost asked but he somehow knew that the answer would be meaningless as his own understanding would be missing.

Bue-e-gar broke the ripple by sounding, *You are wise Mel-e-gar but be patient. There will be one who will know...* The sound changed and he added, *Leave me to my love...Goodbye Mel-e-gar....*

Alk-e-lea added her waters as he withdrew and watched as Alk-e-lea closed her eyes on fresh tears as she shared her last water-times with her mate. The breathing slowed until he gave a sigh which filled the room. Bue-e-gar's expression was soft and peaceful. Slowly the energy began to build as the deathsong took hold. Alk-e-lea let go of the limp hand, raised herself to her dees, and moved back.

From the sides of the sleeping-chamber, the two halves of the cover snapped into place enclosing the body of Bue-e-gar. Alk-e-lea buried her face into Mel-e-gar's chest as the chamber shimmered then broke open. The folds of the chamber rested as before, waiting for its next occupant. The emptiness seemed greater. No trace of Bue-e-gar was left. His deathsong was complete.

* * *

7197 S.N.

Nearly fourteen seasons passed before Mel-e-gar was finally able to unite his song with the power of the Crystal, the one out of the seven which held the enigmatic Question. It wasn't to answer that question but instead to create a city and free the Shakeilar from its burden of knowledge.

From the depth of his water-time the design of the city burst forth, carried on the wave of his song, melding with the sphere of Shakeilar at his dees. An explosion of colour swept around him, across the bay, covering the red grass of the plain with light, expanding to meet the shore, slipping under the surf of the purple waters, descending down to cover for several klees over the sea bed. Several domes blossomed under the water creating the first of the homes for those dolphs that were willing to bring their younglings up as dolphins. This enabled the Elders to have the unique experience of being as dolphs while under the water, allowing them to guide their younglings in the transition without being apart.

When an area of nine klees, in nine spiral arms were complete the blanket of colour began to pulsate with each changing rhythm of his song. A thousand bubbles of light burst forth, shimmering as they changed, expanding, reaching for the sky as complex spiralled domes were born. In his water-time he followed the essence of the Shakeilar as its joy created what Mel-e-gar wanted. The city edge, near the shore raised itself by several dees in places. Then platforms of rippling Shakeilar grew from the edge, out over the sea, raised by several dees above the waters. Satisfied, he turned his song to what on this tay would be the final addition. The beat grew deeper as his creative force began to weave a column of light that blossomed forth from the centre of the city, creating nine domes that would be the new Council chambers.

On the outskirts of the city he could just hear the roar of approval from the hundreds of dolphs that had congregated there the previous tay to watch him and the Shakeilar create the first city to be of the sea as well as the land. The ultimate expression of their own duality, which he knew would also be the last major creation of dolph society. He had plans for six more, which was not only his own desire but also that of those Shakeilar that were brought back with Hia-e-lea. It had been at their urging over the seasons that had passed since their return that they wanted to be part of dolph society again and the ideas for the new cities had been born from that mutual desire. He allowed those waters to pass from him and sang his last note. In his water-time he saw the blue and green light flare once then die down to a gentle glow as the Crystal sparkled into existence on the dais in the centre of the Council chamber.

His water-time mused on the fact that his watersong could work so well and so closely with the Shakeilar as in past tays it would have been impossible to sing without causing them much pain. But that was what made the seven spheres so different from the normal Shakeilar. Their existence with the power of Xrl-e-lea had not only taught them to shield themselves from any harmful aspects of the watersong but also they needed the close proximity of a Watersinger for their continued survival. This had made the creation of the city in a tay instead of a jeanth or more as the library crystals had informed him was likely.

He had searched for any knowledge on how in past times the cities had come about. It had been more than two thousand seasons since the last city had been created on Delikadove. It had come as no surprise to discover that it had fallen to the Healers to take it in turns. Sometimes as many as fifty would pour their waters into a sphere of Shakeilar, tay after tay as it responded to the creative energy and the matrix of the design to slowly grow a city. In the records he had seen that the last one had been in **5910 S.N.** the city of Seuma, east of the Bylinkan mountains. He had travelled there the previous season to see what differences there were, if any with past designs. It straddled the river of Swenerly, which was now no more than a trickle, but the walkways connecting the two halves of the city had given him the idea for launch platforms to the underwater part of his own design. It had taken the best part of thirteen seasons to formulate plans for the final shape and with Serliker's urging he had chosen the bay which his parentlings had named after him.

Mel-e-gar walked through the city, occasionally touching the sides of the homes as he passed by, feeling the vibrant warmth flow into him from the Shakeilar thanking him for what he had done.

Well, we did it, he corrected, *despite the fact that they said it couldn't be done.*

A chuckle rippled his waters as he saw the image of Alk-e-lea's incredulous face when he had explained at a meeting of the Council, a few seasons before, that he proposed the separation of the Knowledge of Pha-e-gar and the message left by the Watersinger from the water-time of the Shakeilar. It had been suffering under the burden, unknown even to Serliker because the question of, If Logic = Mind and water-time = Feelings. Can Logic = water-time? had blocked any access to the Shakeilar's identity.

It had only been through Mel-e-gar's close association with the Crystal over the intervening seasons that he discovered a way around it to the personality beneath, bringing the pain which it suffered to the surface and when they shared water-time, they both saw a way in which the creation of the city could also allow the separation of the two aspects. So they had worked on it until to the satisfaction of both, the plan could go ahead.

He almost ran the rest of the way, excitement building up inside as he passed through the entrance of the Council chambers. He barely noticed the thrilled faces of the dolphs that were now pouring into the city to investigate the marvel which they had watched in awe on the outer plains. He slowed to a walk as he approached the dais and reaching out he picked up the green, blue sphere and opened his water-time to access it;

If Logic = Mind and water-time = Feelings. Can Logic = water-time? greeted him and he laughed out loud, "*Yes*! It has worked perfectly." His joy echoed around the chamber. At least now any who wished to could come and try to answer the question without any more harm to the Shakeilar. His waters passed back to those first jeanths after its return when it had been open to all the Elders and Grand-elders, who found they were unable to answer the question.

Gently he placed it back on the dais. A pang of regret filled his heart as he looked into its soft depth. It was a pity that he had not been able to answer it. For some instinct told him that answers lay beneath that question which might help all of Delikadove. He also knew that the darkness the others feared didn't exist. For he believed the Knowledge Pha-e-gar used was in itself harmless unless acted upon. And that sense of importance for their future on Delikadove persisted. In his waters rippled Bue-e-gar's last sounds making Mel-e-gar say to the emptiness, "*Maybe some tay..*"

* * *

7231 S.N.

Jan-e-gar stood among a sea of prostrate dolphs in their sleeping-chambers, or as one of the Elders had named them, Death-chambers in the converted Council hall. As he was looking around, with the low moans and the occasional cry of pain filling his waters, it was hard to imagine that once in this place so many important events had happened. He was not even born when his Grand-elder, Ran-e-gar returned with the others and the crystals but if he tried he could just picture them on the now vacant dais. His water-time rippled as the stories that he was told passed through. For a yen better times eased his own pain.

He was brought back when a dolph shouted, "Don't just stand there *Jan-e-gar*! Bring the crystals over here!!"

He was jolted back to the grim reality when he saw the stern silvery eyes of Yol-e-gar's impatience bearing down on him as the dolph strode through the chamber intent on relieving Jan-e-gar of the two crystals that he realized were throbbing in his hands.

He found his voice, "*I'm sorry*, I-" His words lapsed to silence as he hurried to the Healer and handed them over.

The silver eyes of Yol-e-gar softened, much to Jan-e-gar's relief as the Healer quietly sounded, "I know it's hard but we cannot afford any wasted time here."

Jan-e-gar dropped his gaze, no longer able to keep eye contact as a wave of shame passed through him.

But it soon slipped away and he became almost spellbound as he watched Yol-e-gar tend to his patient. His hands were still quick as they moved over the sores that oozed green and yellow pus making it hard to tell whether the poor dolph was lea or gar. Yol-e-gar's skill made it look easy as the sores dried up and slowly the healthy grey skin was restored. An amazing transformation in the dolph who Jan-e-gar could now tell was a youngling lea of about seven seasons.

Her eyes flickered open and she managed to breathe her words, "*Thank you..*"

The Healer dropped his hand to her forehead and the eyelids dropped as he with great gentleness declared, "Sleep."

A mound grew from the floor as Yol-e-gar's body shook from his exhaustion and he gratefully sat down to rest. His weariness seemed to grow as he indicated for Jan-e-gar to sit down for a yen. The floor responded and he joined the Healer.

Yol-e-gar seemed to study him before speaking and the tiredness was even more apparent as he slowly remarked, "We may lose this battle..."

The eyes grew distant and Jan-e-gar was not sure the Healer was strictly speaking to him.

"I have passed this way for eighty-six seasons and I am tired. My health sense allows me to heal most of those dolphs I can get to. But there are just too many..."

He stopped again and the eyes refocused on the young dolph, lying, now peaceful in her sleep. "If it had not been for her I would be like the rest of the Healers, only able to ease their pain but not take the disease from their bodies."

Jan-e-gar was puzzled by this and he was about to open his mouth to speak when Yol-e-gar raised his weary eyes and explained, "No, not her.. *The Watersinger*. She gave me more than I knew those long seasons ago. I am sure your Grand-elders would have told you about those times...But I am not enough. We have lost four hundred thousand in the last two seasons. Most of the old cities have been abandoned because the Shakeilar have somehow also been afflicted and are dying too...But then you know all this." The dolph shook his head and added, "Don't take any notice. I have a tendency to ramble these tays."

What could he say to the old dolph? Jan-e-gar felt helpless and only wanted to leave the harsh sick smells and the sight and sound of his race slowly dying. He sprang to his dees, the feeling to run as far away as possible becoming almost overwhelming.

He felt Yol-e-gar's shaking hand grasp his and say, "Go young one, leave Desilata and return to the city of Melegarn. *This is no place for you..*"

The Healer's words pounded waves of grief inside him as he ran from the chamber and into the low blue light of the covered streets. Hot tears blinded him as he ran smack into a dolph, whose gentle hands stopped him in his tracks. Blinking the tears away he looked up into the strong vibrant eyes of Mel-e-gar.

"Steady there.. *It's all right.*"

The Grand-elder read his hurt and Jan-e-gar allowed himself to be held as he poured out the shame he felt at not being strong enough to cope with the death that now haunted Desilata.

Mel-e-gar's waters caressed his pain away and with water-time told Jan-e-gar to go home and wait for him to return. Then under the protectiveness of his song he would take Jan-e-gar to his city.

He watched until the young dolph was out of sight. His waters could still feel the residue of pain that Jan-e-gar transmitted to him. It was understandable that the dolph had enough. Wel-e-lea's grandling may have passed twenty-two seasons but like many older than he, they had broken under the strain of witnessing so much death. It was even harder if you lost most of your family as well.

His waters flicked back to the first season when the disease struck, wiping out whole families in two to three tays. It had taken Yol-e-gar's best effort to heal any at first but his ability increased as that first season came to an end. He knew the Healer was frustrated by being unable to teach the knowledge to any of the other Healers. They had to be grateful that he himself had the power. Even though the strain was terrible, Mel-e-gar was surprised that Yol-e-gar had kept going for so long.

That was where he was heading and he quickened his pace as he passed through into the old chamber. Every time he visited, the smell struck him first. It made his stomach cry in protest but it passed as he wound his way to Yol-e-gar who was bent over another dolph.

Those who were awake and strong enough called out his name and it seemed to brighten the atmosphere as those dolphs saw hope in the presence of the Head of the Council walking among them. He raised his hand in acknowledgement and smiled warmly at those eyes he held with a warm glance.

Yol-e-gar stood up and the weariness cleared from his brow as Mel-e-gar clasped his hands in welcome. The Healer motioned to the dolphs and remarked, “Your presence here is most welcome. They all look forward to your visits.”

“I visit as often as I can and Yol-e-gar, my old friend, I have good news.”

His words made the dolphs eyes brighten and he tightened his grip on Mel-e-gar and with hope in his voice asked, “Is it coming to an end?!”

“Come, I have an announcement to make.”

He led Yol-e-gar to the empty dais and declared, “My friends the disease is beginning to pass-.”

Those who were able managed a few weak calls of cheer and Mel-e-gar waited until quiet was restored. “There have been no new cases for two veuls and the signs look good for it staying that way.”

He paused, his voice softer and finished with, “I know for some here that this news will be little comfort but I hope the rest of you will give thanks to Yol-e-gar and the Healers who have staved off a more terrible fate.”

There were many who gave thanks and though many more would pass into the deathsong most would recover to see brighter tays. Mel-e-gar and Yol-e-gar stepped down from the dais and with a motion of his hand indicated for the Healer to follow him to a side chamber. As they passed through, dolphs held out hands and gradually smiles lit up their faces as hope filled the room.

When they were seated under the soft blue light of the much smaller chamber, that used to be used by the Council for meeting those individuals who wanted a private audience with a member of the Council, Yol-e-gar sighed with relief and said, “I’m glad it’s coming to an end..” For the first time he felt himself relaxing and allowed the curves of his seat to ease his weary bones.

Mel-e-gar waited then with sadness said, “Yes, *but too late for some..*”

The pain of his own loss filled him and Yol-e-gar feeling this added, “I know, I heard, it’s been a jeanth since your loss. *I am sorry Mel-e-gar..*”

The wound of his water-time was still raw and open as the waters returned him to their pain as they succumbed to the disease. It was terrible. He had been in Yengile, helping the movement of younglings who were free from the disease to his city when Cual-e-lay’s cry swept through him and he had to leave Que-e-lea and her helpers to finish the travelling. When he materialised in the Hederlike Sea he knew that she was dying and their youngling too. The other Selahw had losses in the beginning but that was only in the first few jeanths, then no more, so it came as a surprise when it struck Cual-e-lay and Star-e-lay, nearly two seasons later.

The Selahw had been holding them up so they could breathe easily, their bodies covered in blisters that made him cry out and he swam underneath, so he could be between them. Her waters filled him and she sounded, *My love, our time is ending...You have given me much that has made my life complete- No! Don't!* she cried as his tears splashed into her waters, *Hold your tears my love. We will always be as one and our daughterling will pass with me to Chisharnlay....I love you...*

Her sound had fallen silent and a small cry came from Star-e-lay as his daughterling who being so weak just managed to sound, *Fatherling!* before she joined his mate.

"*Mel-e-gar! Mel-e-gar!* Are you all right!" shouted Yol-e-gar as he shook him, making the tears that had filled Mel-e-gar's eyes splash on the Healer's hands. It was enough to break the waters and it cleared for him to see the anguished face of Yol-e-gar staring intently at him.

"I am all right.. *It's just so fresh..* We have all lost so many." For them both it made faces of friends be recalled; Ler-e-lea and Wel-e-lea who died in the first tays, Alk-e-lea and Ran-e-gar at the end of that season, and many more.

They sat in silence in private waters before Yol-e-gar asked, "How is Del-e-gar doing in Yengile?"

The question brought a weak smile to Mel-e-gar's face as he answered, "That dolph has done well. When I brought him and his daughterling from Colisee with Jey-e-gar I would not have believed the help he was to give us."

"To believe a Healer of the Aiouqes would be so good at healing Dolphs!" interjected Yol-e-gar.

It brought a chuckle to Mel-e-gar, his waters recalling that tay six seasons ago when his old friend Jey-e-gar had contacted him with the most unusual news, a young fatherling with his daughterling newly born calling for help amidst a violent storm and the motherling nowhere in sight.

There had been a strange aura of mystery about them which in the intervening seasons he had never penetrated. *The biggest one was why Ose-e-lea, the newly born could not change to dolph*? The only answer that was ever suggested, was maybe she was a sign that a bigger change than the last was yet to come.

When the disease first appeared and the first hundred were in the Council chamber at Yengile and while being immersed in the cleaning of the victims' pus filled sores, that Del-e-gar had quipped to Mel-e-gar; "*Maybe I should have stayed with the Aiouqes!*"

At the time he had dismissed it as Del-e-gar's ironic sense of humour amidst the first dead and dying but when he had met with him and received the good news that there had been no new cases, Del-e-gar had admitted that if it had not been for his daughterling's uniqueness, he would have returned to his forest, but then he had laughed and said, "*But that would have been the actions of another dolph!*"

He had again been puzzled by the abrupt shift of mood of his friend but dismissed it as normal for Del-e-gar! He chuckled again and knew whatever motivated his friend he would be eternally grateful that Del-e-gar had stayed. Not only for his healing but also because from the yen of Ose-e-lea's arrival she became a symbol of Edenlea and it helped to persuade those parentlings who had at first refused to go to Melegarn city with their younglings to do so. Now of course those who did also owed Del-e-gar as there had been no deaths among those younglings.

The ripple of water-time trickled away, returning him to Yol-e-gar and he reminded the Healer how Del-e-gar had offered his services.

"At the beginning of the outbreak he came to me and asked to help. As we needed all the help we could get I took him to the cases in Yengile and he seemed to know what to do.

He said, "*Dolphs were much like the Aiouqes!*" I asked him to explain but he smiled and said, "*We all have our secrets Mel-e-gar!*" And we never spoke of it again. As you know he proved successful, but even he couldn't manage them all, not after the cases grew from hundreds to thousands in the first few veuls."

Yol-e-gar's face became haunted as he agreed and said, "There were just too many and there were some that even I could not heal."

"It was the same for Del-e-gar," remarked Mel-e-gar, "But he said that he sensed that the worst was over. That was several veuls ago and he has been proved right. Like I said, no new cases these past two.."

Yol-e-gar nodded his head and added, "It's the same here but I believed it was just a lull in the storm. It shows how tired I must be.."

Four jeanths later the healing centres of Yengile and Desilata were empty of sick and dying. There had been no new cases and the disease had gone as quickly as it had come. The final death toll had been six hundred thousand, a fifth of the population of Delikadove, the greatest among the Grand-elders and the least among the Elders and the younglings. Afterwards it was discovered that those born after **7222 S.N.** *who had been afflicted by the Great Change, which stripped them from being able to turn to dolphin form at will, had no losses at all. When it was discussed during a meeting at the Council chamber in Melegarn city all surviving Grand-elders agreed that maybe the disease was nature's way of giving a further push back to the sea. It helped to make sense of such loss whether it was right or not. It gave comfort which helped dolph society pick up the pieces.*

"One of the saddest parts of that time was the abandonment of so many cities; *Desilata, Ieulasayer* on the southern continent; *Tueselaa, Colisee, Gothina* on the western; *Yengile, Kelfa, Tynaina, and Zylasayer* on the northern. Both Del-e-gar and Yol-e-gar had tried to save the Shakeilars but there was nothing that helped. I and Serliker tried but again it was hopeless and we had no choice but leave. It made Melegarn city expand two fold and the demand for a new city grew. So that the displacement of dolphs would not be too great I, with the help of two of the remaining six Shakeilar created a city on the southern shore, looking over the Hederlike sea, which we called Alkelbuan, at my request to honour Alk-e-lea and Bue-e-gar. The other was south-west off Tueselaa which became known as Aiouqanlay at Del-e-gar's behest for his trees," narrated Mel-e-gar. He paused and pulled his waters together before putting the final piece of information into the dais crystal in the Council chamber.

"Lastly as all dolphs born after **7222 S.N.**-" when a youngling entered the quiet chamber. He held up his hand before she could speak and continued, "-suffer from the involuntarily change to dolphin form when enough water, as in rain storms fall on them, all cities are now permanently covered, the design taken from the city of Desilata. Finish-*Store*."

Mel-e-gar placed the crystal back on the dais where it was quickly absorbed. Turning from his position he looked down at the lea and asked, "Hello, what can I do for you?"

"I.." She stopped and looked down at the floor, then took a deep breath and blurted out, "*What's that?*" pointing to the green and blue sphere on the dais.

Her deep blue eyes flashed brightly as he chuckled and answered, "That my young one is the *Knowledge Crystal!*" He then stepped down from the dais and took a seat on the first row near her as she stood staring into its depth. She seemed totally absorbed and he studied her. She was only about five dees and he guessed maybe nine seasons young, still a youngling and they were not permitted in the chambers.

He wondered what had brought her all the way from the underwater part of the city, when she turned and declared, "Why is the sea *blue*?"

Her puzzlement filled her open face and her question made no sense. "What do you mean? You must know that the seas are purple and not blue."

Even though he was sitting she still had to crane her neck to stare fully into his eyes and with great indignation replied, "I know *that! Silly old dolph!*"

He was quite taken aback by her manner but her inference made him laugh. *Silly old dolph!* he repeated in his waters. He liked that. It made a change from the usual respectful manner he was treated with these tays. His laughter grew louder the more indignant she became and she was about to turn away when he put out his hand and said, "I am sorry but your approach made such a change."

He took her hand and climbed back onto the dais. Her head only came up to his thigh so he picked her up and sat her on the raised part of the dais beside the Crystal.

She gave him an appreciative smile and softly remarked, "It's a bit too tall for me."

He chuckled in agreement and asked, "Before we go back to your blue sea, tell me your name."

"*Fas-e-lea!* and what is yours?" she replied.

"My name is *Mel-e-gar*.." He had to stop her jumping down in shock and she looked like she was about to burst into tears which unsettled him but he had to admit was pretty normal among the younglings. "It's all right," he said trying to calm her down.

"But.. *But*.. You...Are.. *him*!!" she spluttered, her body shaking.

He couldn't stop himself and he tried to stifle a giggle but as he failed, laughter burst forth. Her face changed as she watched him and gradually her manner lightened until she was laughing with him.

When they had finished he gestured with his hand and with great warmth asked, "Tell me about the blue sea?"

Fas-e-lea grinned at him and declared, "In the Crystal! *It's in there*."

Her words sent a shiver through him and he could feel his heart quicken as he looked at her then back at the Crystal. *Could it be..?* his waters rippled. The excitement built and slowly he asked her, "Did you see the question?"

"Pardon?" looking even more puzzled, not understanding the implication of his question and she confirmed it by adding, "It's a lovely blue, with white clouds and lots of strange sounds."

He clasped her startled face in his hands and cried, "*You've done it!!*" Seeing her confusion he dropped his hands and explained, "We have waited forty-seven seasons for a dolph to answer it and....You walk in here and just do it!"

His water-time was eager to plunge into the Crystal and making sure Fas-e-lea was not left out said, "Wait one yen and I will just see if it is still open."

She looked at him as if he was stupid and opened her mouth to say something but decided not to and waited for him to finish whatever he was going to do.

It was as if a hunger had awoken inside him and he trembled as he placed his hands on the Crystal and was greeted by;

ACCESS GRANTED... INFORMATION RETRIEVAL COMMENCES IN TEN SECONDS...9-

He broke the connection, his waters reeling, *She has done it, somehow.* Then it struck him, *Of course! If the question is displayed then you have already failed. The answer is instinctive!* he sounded to himself. His waters mulled over the information given, *Strange way and what do-* SECONDS, *mean?!* He mulled it over then shouted out loud, which almost made Fas-e-lea fall off the dais, "*YENS!*"

He took hold of the Crystal and lifting Fas-e-lea with his other hand sat both of them down on the lower dais and placed the Crystal in between them. "Now join your water-time and we shall go and see these blue waters of yours."

His excitement was contagious and she beamed at him as they dived together into the green and blue depths...

Again he was greeted by the stilted sounds. When it came to zero a great sea of water appeared, which looked blue-green. It was getting further away and as the image shrank to an orb hanging in the blackness of space, the seas looked pale blue with layers of white cloud over it. Their waters burst in awe at the beauty of its shining presence. Then more sounds began.

SEVENTH COLONY PLANET....MASS 5.98 X 10^{21} TONNES.... SURFACE AREA 5.1 x 10^{8} SQ KM..... DISTANCE FROM STAR NAMED SOL... 149,600,000 KM.... THIRD PLANET OF TEN.... ADDITIONAL UPDATE: OLD COLONY ON PLANET FIVE.... DESTROYED BY FLUCTUATIONS IN GRAVITATIONAL FIELDS OF PLANET SIX AND SEVEN OF THIS SYSTEM.... NOW ASTEROID BELT.... RESULT NOW NINE PLANETARY BODIES AROUND SOL: ADDITION: THIRD PLANET HAS ONE MOON... END SEQUENCE... MORE INFORMATION AT REQUEST... WAITING... WAITING...

Mel-e-gar could understand most of the sounds and KM seemed to be kleos but a strange way of sounding it. *Is this what Pha-e-gar discovered- A gateway to another world?!!* In the background of their waters the voice kept repeating and deciding that there would be plenty of time to answer those questions later, sounded to Fas-e-lea, *Should we go on?*

Yes! Yes! her water-time rippled and he responded to the sounds, *More information.*

ON LINE SEQUENCE START UP...EXAMINATION OF CELL STRUCTURE...SUITABLE FOR THIS COLONY....OXYGEN/NITROGEN ATMOSPHERE...GRAVITATIONAL FIELDS WITHIN ACCEPTED LIMITS.. WATERSINGER REGISTERED.. ACCESS IS NOW GRANTED.... IS TRANSFERENCE REQUESTED?

The meaning of those last sounds were clear, and Mel-e-gar hesitated in going any further with a youngling in tow. She felt his ripple and urged him on. *All right but I better*

check to see if we can come back again!
Almost instantly the response came.

OPTIONS: PLEASE CHOOSE:
(1) TRANSFERENCE OF water-time ONLY:
(2) TOTAL BODY TRANSFER:
WARNING! CHOICE TWO - ONE WAY ONLY!!

The choice was clear. They could visit only through water-time but deep down Mel-e-gar knew that at long last his answer to the question of the survival of his race was now assured. The secret that only he and Serliker knew could come out in the open. With a flick of his waters he chose the first option and together they went to explore what Mel-e-gar had already named *Edenlea*..

* * *

DELIKADOVE

7 S.E.

He picked his way through the trees, bending double to navigate his way past the low branches. Sometimes he stopped and brushed the dark brown bark with his hands, feeling the life that pulsated, reminding him of past tays long ago. The trees were very different from the Aiouqes he had cared for but the deep, rich green foliage helped him satisfy his longing to be back in his old home. The forest floor was damp underdee and the soft spongy surface squelched water as he walked, reflecting in his waters those lost times. He travelled deeper losing himself among the shadows, a desire that made his heart ache. He conjured up an image of her face, her green aura illuminating her lithe form as she ran through the tortured ways of his water-time. His path was purposeful in its intent and he allowed enough of his senses to return to the present to see that he had made it to his destination.

The clearing was a hundred dees wide and in the middle was a solitary tree, different from the rest, with light green and yellow foliage, with upswept branches that made an upside down tear with its shape. Del-e-gar let out a low moan as he walked over, bending down so his head wouldn't disturb the lower branches. He twisted round and carefully lowered himself so he could lean back against the tree. The trunk creaked as he adjusted himself. Even sitting he could reach up and easily touch the branches. When he first walked among the trees he first believed that they were young trees as most were only of fifty dees but he soon realised that they were not like the Aiouqes and would not reach those great heights. He had to adjust to moving amongst them as at first he felt that he could all too easily break such fragile looking branches if he accidentally brushed against them. Over the seasons that had followed their arrival in the northern waters, he had spent a great deal of time among them and grew to know and love them as he had those Aiouqes he had once cared for. This always conjured her up and his love could run free as he recalled their passion among the trees.

As he held her beauty once again a trickle of water flowed around bringing the sound of their youngling who had asked many times why he had not mated again. He had always answered that his love for her motherling was too strong and that he had no desire to share with any other. He knew others had mated again when losing a mate, like Mel-e-gar who after many seasons had found the love of Sye-e-lea but only then to lose her in a resurgence of the deathsong that had previously taken Cual-e-lay and Star-e-lay which was a tragedy. Del-e-gar had not known how Mel-e-gar had withstood such losses. But then he had never dared to love again so it was hard for him to understand why Mel-e-gar had. No, his waters held only her green visage and the bond was as strong now as it was then. The trickle flowed away taking any doubt he may have had, allowing the fullness of his love to flow freely and as in so many past times he re-lived that season of his youth when his life had changed so dramatically.

* * *

Jer-e-lea watched as her youngling played with his friends, her waters returning to the story of Bue-e-gar who she had named her sonling after. She wondered what he would have made of Edenlea and laughed as she knew he would have loved it. She had not known him as he was already part of the legend of the old ways when she had been born, but with Del-e-gar's telling she had come to feel a closeness with that old dolph. Indeed all the dolphins who had not known the fullness of those past waters had sounded on how close they had felt to their past. It had helped them understand where they had come from and also made the wonder of Edenlea more precious.

It had been a veul since he had finished the telling, deciding that as most had been there at the time of the last seasons of Delikadove, it did not need to be told. He had made the other Grand-elders answer any questions and it was enough for now but she knew that there was much that even those who had been younglings at the time did not know. She had not pressed it but had discussed it at length with Cha-e-gar, leaving her curiosity unsatisfied and that was why as Solarn advanced steadily bringing a fresh cool tay she had decided to seek out Del-e-gar.

Her course followed the shore line south, round the cove to the line of jagged rocks, showered in white spray as wave after wave crashed over them. Following the directions given by Fas-e-lea she rounded the rocks to the yellow beach on the other side. By using her sound she checked the depth then turned her beak towards the shore. Gradually she picked up her speed and almost skimming the waters she swam towards the beach. On the back of a wave she leaped upwards, spinning her form round so that her tail was in position. As it touched the sand her body sparkled and changed. She steadied herself as a wave of dizziness tried to take her balance. Slowly her senses cleared and she advanced up the beach to the tree line. Part of her waters had not been sure it would still work as it had been many seasons since she had last changed to dolph form.

It had been on Delikadove and she had been only three seasons young when she had been told by her parentlings and Mel-e-gar that she would no longer need it when they moved to live in the Hederlike sea. Her water-time brought back the sense of loss as her young self had tried to come to terms with that announcement. In time she found there was no need for it and her Elders had been correct. Even after coming to Edenlea she had not had the desire until now when the very past called her name.

It took her some while to feel comfortable being out of the water but as she walked through the trees she began to understand why the Grand-elders still spent part of their tay on un-water. The sights and sounds of the forest were delightful. The sensations of damp leaves underdee and the calls of so many types of sky-flyers made her forget why she was there in the first place. It was only when the outer fringe of her sight caught a flash of grey that she turned from her heading and broke through the trees into a clearing. She saw what had caught her attention before her. Del-e-gar was leaning, looking relaxed against a tree, marking the sense of loneliness she felt seeing the tree standing alone in the centre. She walked across the green grass not sure how she should announce herself as Del-e-gar gave no indication that he was aware of her. His eyes were closed and a small smile was upon his lips as if he was seeing, in his waters, something that amused him.

Jer-e-lea was held by the scene. The rustle of leaves and the faint calls in the background made it so peaceful. Deciding she had better wait until he woke she walked a few dees closer and sat in front of him spending the time studying his face. There was no mark to tell his age as she knew from past images of him that his face had always looked rather weather-beaten but there was an aura of long seasons about him, tinged with a feeling of sadness and loss. Her waters were following this course when his eyes opened and with great softness said, "*Hello Jer-e-lea..*"

His voice startled her slightly and as she looked into his eyes the aura she felt grew stronger. She knew like the rest why he always looked so haunted but being with him as dolphs made the pain seem greater and wave after wave radiated from him making her feel slightly sick and the pit of her stomach ached. She tried to shake it off and was surprised when Del-e-gar leaned forward and touched her forehead. A tingle of energy ran from his fingers through her, taking the sensation of nausea away.

"I'm sorry, but you caught me dwelling on *past tays*." His eyes softened and as Jer-e-lea opened her mouth to speak he explained, "It's all right. Your waters just amplified how I was feeling when I lost my mate. But I also see that your body is still settling in its dolph form."

That she could feel to be true and she waited until she felt sure of what she wanted to say, then explained why she had come looking for him. "Fas-e-lea told me you would be here and I felt it would be better for me to ask you here rather than in Edenlea."

A shadow of tiredness crossed his face and with heaviness he replied, "I knew one of you would want me to tell the rest but I had not expected it to be you." He shrugged as if resigning himself to the course that had been decided by her presence and added, "But then again maybe it's right that the *last one* of our race should question so."

His words made a shiver run down her spine, hearing it put that way. She had not dwelled on that since she was a youngling when in that season on Delikadove their race knew that there would be no more born with the ability to be dolph, something she had to keep secret from her own younger brotherlings and sisterlings as well as the rest of the younglings born after her. Only her elder sisterling knew her secret. It had been Mel-e-gar who had made the connection when after **7247 S.N.** leas began to give birth to dolphins. The ability to change to dolph had been removed by the effect of the deathsong that had decimated Delikadove. The only exception of course was Ose-e-lea who they now knew was the daughterling of Tan-e-lea, which explained why she had been born as a dolphin, forever unable to be a dolph many seasons before the Great Change came about. It gave Jer-e-lea a strange sense of kinship with Ose-e-lea as her own birth in **7262 S.N.** had also caused *quite a fuss...*

"You could put it like *that*!" broke in Del-e-gar.

His remark scattered her waters and she looked at him perplexed by the wry humour that now filled him. "What is so funny about that?" she asked.

Her question seemed to strip the humour away and his eyes grew dark as he answered, "No, it's not funny. It was just hearing your naivety that makes my amusement more ironic than humorous. Look, you like most of the younglings had little idea what was going on, except what Mel-e-gar told you when the last families resided in the semi-underwater city of Starnay. But your birth at that time created a great deal more than, quite a fuss!" He sighed and then sounded, "The best way to tell you is the way of water-time and you will see what I mean for yourself."

She nodded and anticipation filled her as he motioned for her to lie down beside him. When she was comfortable she felt his water-time pour into her. Like a great wave she was taken back to Delikadove to witness the final trauma of their race through the eyes of *Mel-e-gar....*

7262 S.N.

For the first time he found the Council chamber oppressive. Only the cool green and blue light from the Crystal of Edenlea (*Changed from the Crystal of Pha-e-gar after its opening the seasons before*) gave him any pleasure. He used it to steady his angry waters as more of the Grand-elders cried for him to leave. He did not respond to their calls but stayed silent letting their anger wash over him. For a yen he felt the tiredness of his age weigh heavily in his water-time. He was only a few jeanths from reaching his hundredth season, outliving almost all his friends. *But still there were Del-e-gar, Que-e-lea, and Fas-e-lea which made him give thanks for such good water-times.*

The stream widened as he readied his argument to counter their foolish claim, seeing once more the innocent eyes of Fas-e-lea when they had returned from their first of many trips to the world of Edenlea. She knew without realising the full importance of their discovery whilst her Elders tried to dismiss the Crystal as a legacy of corruption of Pha-e-gar. Not believing when he told them that Pha-e-gar had only brushed the surface never being able to go any further because he was not a Watersinger and his frustration and fear of water-time turned him into the individual he became.

But the inner Council had rejected Mel-e-gar's explanation and when he had told them that Danetar was going through a cycle of expansion and collapse, that would finally explode to swallow their world, they listened but most were not convinced and then at the end of **7260 S.N.** Danetar began to retract bringing a massive change for the better. The rains returned and Mel-e-gar only just held onto being Head of the Council. He had checked with Serliker, who had returned to the Selahw when the disease had returned for the second time to recreate in the Hederlike Sea the conditions of *its* old underground home. It had told Mel-e-gar that the retraction marked the beginning of the final phase and for many seasons to come would fluctuate in ten season cycles until finally on one cycle of expansion it would not stop and a Super Nova would occur. That information he relayed to the Council but it was rejected. Now he was again trying to defend himself even though he knew he was now to lose.

He looked at the few faces and the irony of the situation was felt deeply. The last deathsong had swept through the population killing so many that when it ended at the beginning of the season they were down to forty thousand individuals. All but a handful were under sixty seasons. *Now these last hundred Grand-elders were situated around him in the mostly empty chamber telling him he was wrong*! There were eight Grand-elders who supported him and had requested that they should come with him to the meeting but he declined their kind offer as he was happier if they stayed in the City of Starnay with their families. He hoped that the Council would listen but deep down he knew it spelled the end of his tenure as Head of the Council and he felt a certain amount of relief that it was coming to an end.

His waters returned him back to when the disease first appeared and then to the aftermath when they believed that they had beaten it. For thirty eight seasons it seemed that this was indeed so but it returned with a vengeance in **7253 S.N.** It lasted for a season and a half and wiped half the population away. Losing his beloved Sye-e-lea had nearly broken him and it was only his sonling's strength that had kept him going. They had no Yol-e-gar that time as he was long gone which left the burden of healing to Del-e-gar who did his best but it was impossible for one dolph to heal a planet. So on its third return in **7260 S.N.** little could be done but to hope it would die away. It did only after he had put total quarantine on the last pockets of the population. It only lasted a season but it took four of the remaining six cities he and the Shakeilar had created. The last two inhabited cities were the city of Melegarn and the last to be created after the first births of the dolphs who were not dolphs but dolphin was the shining city of Starnay on the isle of Tethilay. This was named after his daughterling and now held the hope for a new time within its bright walls.

It helped him gather his strength to try and get the last Grand-elders to listen to him. He silenced the calls with a glare at each one and exclaimed, "*You must listen*, her birth is not a sign that our race is turning back to *dolph*!"

"You are wrong, *Mel-e-gar*! She is the hope we have waited for. Her birth and change to dolph shows that we are recovering. She is the beginning!" The dolph who challenged Mel-e-gar strode from his seat and stood at the base of the dais glaring up at him.

For a yen his name escaped him but then it came. "Han-e-gar, I understand but even if it was so, our world is still dying! We must go forward rather than back!!"

The eyes of Han-e-gar flashed angrily and he pointed at Mel-e-gar and turned his head and spoke to the other Elders and called, "He must *Go*! I believe it is his own desire for that!" indicating the Crystal, "Which is wrong! The deathsongs that have struck our race these past seasons are the result of those crystals being brought back from the Frelegar mountains. *They should have been destroyed!!*"

Some of the others cried their agreement but a few stayed silent until a lea stood up and challenged Han-e-gar, "No you cannot blame Mel-e-gar for that. It was his predecessor who made that mistake!"

"Lay-e-lea! How can you sound so?! I tell you he must go!" replied Han-e-gar.

She looked up at Mel-e-gar and he saw the pity that was clear in her eyes but she said no more and returned to her seat. Mel-e-gar felt the hopelessness of his task. Even he had to admit that Jer-e-lea's birth two tays ago had amazed him but his instinct told him that she would be the last to be born of dolph kind.

She was a spasm of genetics creating one more before it died away for good. Dolphs were obsolete on this world and dolphins would only survive while the seas could support life which would not be for much longer. The level had reduced dramatically in the last forty seasons and there were less fish to be found. But for him there was a pattern because the disease had reduced them enough so a few could survive on those remaining fish. The dolphs in the Council chamber would not live much longer and with a heavy heart he made his decision to pick up the Crystal and said, "You will not listen so I have no choice but to leave you to whatever fate awaits you. If you change your sounds you are welcome to join me at Starnay."

The anger of Han-e-gar exploded at Mel-e-gar and he declared, "You and those of that city are forbidden to venture into this city or any part of the mainland! I will take the leadership of the Council and we shall survive!"

Mel-e-gar shook his head at Han-e-gar, and left the chamber. As he strode out he could feel the dolph's eyes burn into his back. With a sigh of relief he passed into the corridor and made his way to the shore where he stood on one of the platforms he had used so often to dive into the sea and he looked back at his city. The lights glowed strongly and for a yen he could believe he was back to happier times, when his only problem was to check on a certain Nursery Motherling who made him laugh when they had first met. He smiled into the darkness of the night and flipped himself into the air, doing a back flip as he changed to dolphin and sang his song to return to Starnay.

7268 S.N.

Mel-e-gar had spent the seasons after that last Council meeting with his family and continued the preparations for the time when they had to leave their home. The Selahw were often in his waters and he spent much time sharing his sound with those gentle creatures. Their wisdom was a continuous source of joy which he and his old friend Serliker spent many a dark night going over. At such times Serliker always managed to lighten his burden with *its* unique brand of humour, especially when they recounted their experience under the desert of Arkelclared.

It was on a such a tay, returning from one such meeting that Mel-e-gar swam swiftly through the purple waters to the Isle of Tethilay that he made a decision to ask a question to the Crystal that had been bothering him for some time.

His waters were diverted as the isle came into view. The ocean seemed to give the illusion that the Isle of Tethilay was riding the waves. For a yen he nearly decided to go to his home on the isle straight away when he changed his waters and turned east to follow the southern shore to see how his family and the other dolphins were doing.

It was not a particularly large island, only thirty klees from its northern tip to the southern shore and sixty three wide but it always made his waters feel the comfort of home. It was dominated by the volcano that had lain dormant for many thousands of seasons. On the whole it was fairly barren except for the nesting Kerg which still cried their calls from their nests on the eastern side.

When he was about a klee from the southern shore he slowed his pace as he caught sight of Zar-e-gar fishing with his teacher, Vue-e-lea. He may have been only two seasons young but his grandling had a certain flair which his teacher made good use of. The purple waters broke apart as the two dolphins leaped forth, spraying Mel-e-gar and inviting him to give chase, which he did with ease and for a while he enjoyed the antics. When Zar-e-gar broke away and his course began to take him further north, Mel-e-gar gave a nod of his beak to which Vue-e-lea responded and carefully guided the youngling south.

It was something which happened often when some of the younglings strayed too far north. Some had questioned why they couldn't go north and were simply told that it was not safe. Very little was told to them. None with the exception of Jer-e-lea knew that dolphins had once had the ability to transform to dolph and Mel-e-gar made sure that none ever found out. It was important that they know only dolphin ways as when they were ready they would travel to Edenlea. He spent many nights telling them of their new home and that the purple waters were changing which would in time make it barren of fish. He never told them the truth as scaring them with tales of Danetar exploding seemed pointless.

Keeping them around the southern shore had worked well for fourteen seasons ever since it had begun at the end of the second deathsong. The idea had grown until those that agreed with Mel-e-gar's choice to have a nursery guided by Que-e-lea accepted that it was best to bring up those younglings without any mention of dolphs. The Grand-elders and Elders spent only short periods of time in Starnay and as each season passed had become more adept themselves in being dolphin. Having a volcano in the middle of the island, blocking any view of the north shore and its city helped a great deal and this had been his reason for choosing it in the first place.

Seeing that all was well he left the school and swam further east until enough distance was covered for Mel-e-gar to sing his song and reappear in his home in the middle of the city. The room was in darkness as he sparkled into existence by the small mound where a solitary crystal was at rest. The room sensed his presence and an orange light grew in strength banishing the gloom. It was fashioned much like his past homes but vacant of any pool which was obsolete now that he spent more time in the Hederlike Sea. Dotted around the room were many crystals that reflected the orange light causing a dance of colour that made the emptiness more welcoming. Choosing a seat by the central crystal, he sat and opened his waters to the welcoming flow of what were now familiar images of the blue planet.

It made his entire being tingle with excitement as he surveyed the giant seas that were so vast as to be almost overwhelming. The two largest land masses were incidental but his dolph side took pleasure at seeing such richness of life. There were forests that made Duorsilear look like a small copse of trees as they covered great areas. The only difference that Del-e-gar had pointed out was that even though there were giant trees of a sort they individually were still smaller and somewhat less majestic than the Aiouqes. It had made his old friend cry as it was enough to remind him of his loss.

There were reports of Duorsilear's final destruction the season before when great earth tremors were felt. When they had been able to verify this they discovered that the mountain range had been torn apart and the life of the Aiouqes swept away by the eruption of the earth. There were only a few stumps sticking up among the rubble of a devastated continent. The remains of the old cities, long abandoned were crushed to dust and some totally buried. It had been hard for Del-e-gar as he had kept crying that his mate had promised to save them. Which had made little sense to Mel-e-gar as his friend had never really spoken about his long dead mate. As the sadness came back he diverted the stream by changing focus to concentrate on the seas. Again there was more life in so many strange forms that made him long to travel in body to this new place, but he had to wait until the younglings were ready.

As he pondered the images he recalled the conversation that he had with Serliker about life on other planets and in particular, sentient life forms. For Serliker had access to some of the knowledge *its* progenitor had carried, namely *the* Rock who had shared with *it* stories of strange beings inhabiting the many worlds in their galaxy. Each time *it* always turned back to the question of *Edenlea* and whether or not a sentient race inhabited that domain. But there were no answers as Serliker was unfamiliar with that world even though since the disappearance of *the* Rock and the city of Beslika that his sonling and mate had witnessed in **7255 S.N.**, Mel-e-gar had wondered whether *it* had left to go to the new planet.

He did not know why, but something told him that he would not be surprised if that was so. He had given that answer to Ser-e-gar and Car-e-lea to help explain why *the* Rock had chosen to speak to them when they had explored the old Sanctuary.

It not only brought back fond waters of their bewilderment which didn't totally go, even after he had given them his explanation but also times of sadness that seemed to cast its grey shadow over those times.

One in particular was Car-e-lea's sadness at the deathsong of her fatherling, Jan-e-gar who with five others, which included two very old friends of Mel-e-gar had been buried when the ruins of the city they had been exploring had collapsed. They had managed to recover four of the bodies but unfortunately they never found Jey-e-gar and Ler-e-lea's old healer Gre-e-gar. He had never fully understood why two very old dolphs would risk their lives that way. He gave a heavy sigh and allowed the stream to trickle away.

There was one thing that their deaths and *the* Rock's disappearance had given him- the determination to continue with the movement towards Edenlea, not only for himself but in a way to honour not only those that had gone the way of the deathsong but also those friends who had continued to support him when many of his contemporaries could only scorn his ideas.

Now at long last they were on the threshold and in a few more jeanths they would pass through the gate. The stream swung back returning him once more to the question of sentient life. In the thirty-six seasons since Fas-e-lea's innocence had opened the Crystal he had not dared ask that question, taking only the response that as it was open by definition of *Colony* status that it was suitable. But now he had to know for sure. It would end all his plans if the answer was positive and he would have to try and accept that his race was destined for extinction. *Even though his waters would strive to alter that course, he knew he could not beat a Super Nova!*

Opening his waters he asked, *Is there Sentient life on the blue planet?*

WORKING......

There was a stillness in his waters that waited for the cold tones of the Crystal to respond. Instead of answering him it gave him three options to choose from.

ANALYSIS AS FOLLOWS...

PAST.

PRESENT.

FUTURE.

PLEASE CHOOSE...

He had expected a straight answer, but it intrigued him to find out so he answered, *Give full analysis of all three starting with,* PAST *and follow through.* In the time he had spent with the Crystal he had become used to its strange sounds that were so unlike the Shakeilar he had known. Even though he had separated the conscious part of the Crystal when they had created Melegarn city, it puzzled him where the knowledge really originated from as he doubted Pha-e-gar could have been the source of such strange sounds. That had been one question he had asked and had been told, ACCESS TO THAT INFORMATION IS DENIED!

It had been the only time when he had felt a vibration of emotion which sounded like soft laughter. It only made him wonder even more. The low hum in the background of his waters made him return his attention to the repeated tones of:

WAITING.....WAITING.....

Realising he had made the Crystal wait he replied, *Please continue..*

The image of the seas vanished to be replaced by a scene of a hot humid planet filled with even stranger vegetation and great beasts that flew, swam, and hunted other equally massive creatures. Oddly enough the range of light yellows to deep oranges and great cloud formations were not unlike Delikadove even though the rest was totally different. The picture changed making him focus on smaller, more agile creatures that came into view. They bounded over the swamps on their hind legs, balanced by thick tails and waving their small arms with sharp claws.

These they used proficiently, cutting into flesh, tearing chunks out of the struggling creature they had caught as they swarmed over it, devouring it with amazing speed. They seemed organised and their dark green and brown skins were splattered with blood from their prey. It didn't take them long before they quickly disappeared through the giant fronds across the marshes to firmer land where they divided the residue of the meat with the ones who had waited for their return.

Mel-e-gar saw many young skip around the dees of the adults, swishing their tails as they fed on scraps that fell unbidden from the dripping bundles of flesh. He watched as they spread out and after feeding lay in the sun and slept.

Mel-e-gar was startled when from the corner of the scene, high in the orange sky a great light blossomed to be followed by a sound that shook him to his bones, startling the creatures out of their slumber and to charge around in panic as the light grew larger. He could just make out a corona of flame as the scene shifted and it was as if he was flung from the surface into outer space. After his senses had settled he saw the light impact the planet, sending up a great dark cloud that quickly covered the world. Then it moved and it really was a strange sight to see a planet rock on its axis, then tilt one way, shifting its orbit.

The tones of the Crystal filled him as it explained:

BY CONVERTING SPATIAL AND TIME VECTORS GIVES LOCAL TIME AS THIRTY MILLION SEASONS AGO..... METEORITE IMPACT ON COLONY PLANET SEVEN.... RESULT.... ORBITING SHIFT FROM SOL WITH AXIS SHIFT.... REDUCTION OF SURFACE TEMPERATURE BY TEN DEGREES....DESTROYED NINE TENTHS OF ALL LIFE....INCLUDING REPTILIAN RACE ADVANCING TO FULL SENTIENCE.......-

Stop! he cried as the full impact made itself felt within his water-time. A whole race as well as most of the creatures destroyed numbed him and he felt the loss as it made him even more aware how close they were themselves to that fate. When the ripples had calmed he enquired of the Crystal, *Were there no survivors?!!*

NO...

The answer hurt, especially as it was so final but wanting to know more he asked, *What does,* "REPTILIAN" *mean?*

WARM AND COLD BLOODED SPECIES..... SURFACE ABSORPTION OF HEAT BY DIRECT USE OF LIGHT FROM SOL.... VARIOUS SPECIES SURVIVED AND STILL LIVE ON PLANET.... BUT LINEAGE OF SENTIENCE NO LONGER VIABLE...

So they died from lack of sunlight... he mused. It was not a question but the Crystal took it as such.

PREMATURE ICE AGE.... LASTED ONE HUNDRED TWENTY THOUSAND SEASONS... MASS MUTATION IN VIRAL ORGANISMS..... VARIOUS DISEASE WIPE-OUTS.... ONLY A FEW REPTILIAN SPECIES IN SOUTHERN HEMISPHERE SURVIVED...

Do you have a name for those creatures that had been advancing towards sentience?

BIPEDAL SPECIES....DOLPH-OID....-

He interrupted the Crystal, puzzled by the Crystal's explanations especially with, *Dolph-oid!,* and enquired, *Please explain answer... More fully.*

SPECIES...UPRIGHT..USE OF HIND LEGS FOR MOVEMENT OVER LAND SURFACE.... DOLPH-OID MEANS...DOLPH-LIKE... CONTINUATION OF PREVIOUS ANSWER NOW GIVEN.... NAME NOT TRANSLATABLE.....

It was a pity as he would have liked to have known what they had called themselves and the Crystal's answer of Dolph-oid made it easier to understand when he indicated for *it* to continue with present and future. At first believing that it must be a negative, its answer surprised him again.

PLANET NOW VIABLE.... COMPLETE DIVERGENCE OF WARM BLOODED LIFE FORMS NOW PRESENT.... LAND AND AIR COMPLETE AT THIS TIME.... ONLY OXYGEN TRANSFERENCE FROM SEA WATER CREATURES INHABIT OCEANS... ONLY ONE SPECIES OF LAND BASED CREATURE VIABLE FOR FUTURE SENTIENCE... FULL SCAN NOW GIVEN....

The view of the planet he requested now came into view and he found himself plunging down into a deeply forested area. When he came to rest he was surrounded by trees and deep foliage that was wet and the air thick with moisture. There were many cries and calls of creatures that seemed to surround him. Flashes of creatures came and went, so many that he couldn't keep up. His vision started to blur when a small furry creature crawled along a nearby branch and stopped. Its tail was wrapped tightly around the limb and two large eyes, that were dark as night blinked curiously at him. One forelimb with five tiny fingers clutched a small red fruit. It moved it to its mouth and bit into the flesh. Mel-e-gar was mesmerised by the creature as he watched the creature consume the fruit. It was so tiny that it would have barely filled up his own hand. He was about to ask for more information about it when the Crystal's sound replaced the image and he was again looking at the planet from the vantage of space.

DIVERGENCE OF SPECIES HAS CAPACITY FOR SENTIENCE....... FINAL FORM... DOLPH-OID...

How long before sentience reached?

WORKING.....

FULL SENTIENT STATE THIRTY-FIVE MILLION SEASONS..

It amazed him the Crystal could be so precise and it followed that he had to ask his final question, *Would our presence on the planet interfere with that species?*

COMPLETE ANALYSIS GIVEN.....

SPECIES UNABLE TO INHABIT SEAS.... DOLPHIN OCCUPATION THEREFORE VIABLE... NO IMPACT ON DOLPH-OID SPECIES....-

Then it did a strange thing and to Mel-e-gar it seemed to hesitate before completing its answer.

....*FUTURE* VIABILITY OF DOLPHIN RACE QUESTIONABLE....

Now that didn't make sense if they would not interfere with the youngling race why would dolphins be at risk?! His query flowed along the stream and its impact on the Crystal brought this answer:

EXPLOITATION OF LAND, SEA, AND AIR BY DOLPH-OID RACE CONFIRMED..... IMPACT ON DOLPHIN DIVERGENCE ALSO CONFIRMED....

Exploitation! What does that mean? frustrated by the use of such an unfamiliar term.

CONSUME...TO FEED ON...TO TAKE...TO DESTROY...TO CHANGE...FOR SPECIES OWN USE WHILE RISKING ALL OTHER LIFE FORMS ON PLANET...

But that is...! he exploded, trying to find the sounds he needed. His water-time whirled in many confused and angry pools but then something of his own race came along a cold stream and he wondered if some part of Pha-e-gar had been left behind in the Crystal's make up after all. *Or was this part of the Knowledge that Pha-e-gar made use of?* As *its* answer sounded much like the, *Thoughts*, that Hia-e-lea had encountered when she and his friends had confronted him and Xrl-e-lea in the mountains. *Would another species fulfil the logical path that they had tried to complete and would the dolph-oid species also self destruct??*

His query was answered.

DOLPH-OID SPECIES DOMINATION CONFIRMED.... ALL SENTIENT RACES RISK THEIR OWN SELF DESTRUCTION ON THE PATHWAY OF SENTIENCE.... OUTCOME UNKNOWN AT THIS TIME...... PROBLEM OF DOLPHIN SURVIVABILITY IN EDENLEA HAS ALREADY BEEN PUT IN MOTION....

How can that be?! cried Mel-e-gar.

ACCESS DENIED...

The finality of that statement tore into Mel-e-gar and he had no way of navigating around that particular storm in his waters. The only hope he could take was that whatever the Crystal was keeping from him it knew more about the future than he, and maybe given the vastness of time involved, their race might find a way to communicate with the prospective dominant race themselves. *After all, if sentient, the race should be able to understand...*

He knew enough to proceed but just to make sure he asked, *Can I proceed with transference of dolphins?*

TRANSFERENCE OF DOLPHIN COLONY CAN PROCEED.... it confirmed.

Mel-e-gar was about to break contact when he was sure he felt a slight rumble in the outer range of his water-time and he was startled when the Crystal gave out a high pitched sound.

DANGER! DISTURBANCE IN YOUR LOCALITY.... SEISMIC ACTIVITY... *DISENGAGE!* it screamed at him.

Suddenly he was knocked from his seat. His waters ripped from the Crystal as he saw the room tilt and cries of dolphs filled him. He rolled across the room and smacked into the wall. The light of the chamber fluctuated as he tried to come to his dees. The room and floor lurched again and he stumbled back to the mound and with a swipe of his hand gathered the Crystal up. It pulsated, flashing green and blue as he made his way to the opening that almost poured into the street. He looked up and saw an angry red haze covering the volcano and with a sickening surety, knew that it was erupting. The waters of so many dolphs pounded inside him, tearing and crying their panic as the city began to shake violently. Several times he was knocked from his dees and he barely kept grip of the Crystal. Thousands of dolphs were fleeing north, emptying from their homes in wild abandonment. Some stopped and helped those that had fallen while others just kept running.

Then another tremor shook the city and he fell as a rain of fire fell from the sky. As the enclosure which normally would have covered the city was now open hot lava fell, burning those running for the sea. On impulse he brought his song to play and tried to create a cover to help the others. The screams made it hard to focus his song but he saw from his awkward vantage point his energy field spread outwards and upwards taking the fire from those below. While the ground continued to shake he tried to make his way, almost crawling while he sang. He could have saved himself but he could only have taken a few hundred dolphs with him and even then he was not sure that it would work with that many.

By the time he had stumbled to the edge he was brought up sharply to a halt as the earth screamed and tore the ground away. A chasm tore apart the Shakeilar and its screams filled his waters as it tried to bridge the gap to save the dolphs. But the stress of the land moving under it was too much and when a river of hot steaming lava broke over the crest of the hill the Shakeilar lost its structural integrity and began to withdraw. Mel-e-gar rolled away onto open ground as he knew that any caught as it retracted its mass would be crushed.

The waters of the city cried its grief as buildings melted away and with a tremendous rush the lava broke through bearing down on Mel-e-gar as he lay prostrate by the chasm that blocked the way to the sea. With desperation he crawled further along the edge, torn between holding the energy barrier up and saving his own life by transporting himself out.

Then another violent wrench made the land bulge upwards and for a yen he lay, his legs dangling over the edge of the chasm. The heat struck him and he cried in pain and sang his song. He was only just in time as lava swept over him. For a yen he was covered in lava and from inside that red glowing heat his energy protected him as he made the final note and vanished from its embrace.

He acted quickly as he reappeared above the sea, transferring the Crystal, that somehow he had managed to keep a grip of, to his mouth and pulled enough vapour from the ocean to change in mid-air. Even the sea was warm as he plunged into its depth, curving his dive to reach for the surface. His beak bobbed above the waves as he witnessed the destruction of the island. The volcano had blown sideways. Even from his viewpoint two klees north of the island he saw the great swath of red lava pouring relentlessly into the sea. Great billowing clouds of steam erupted as hot lava impacted on the water's edge. Overhead, the clouds had darkened the sky so night seemed to have fallen prematurely and when the sea shifted, dragging him away from the isle he saw part of the island break apart almost totally destroying the volcano. He felt the next change and transported again as the sea changed direction and was swept up in a tidal wave of immense proportion.

With the instinct of a survivor he reappeared among the school of dolphins in the southern sea, northeast of Tethilay, and whilst startled beaks began to cry their surprise he opened his song to do what he had failed to do in Starnay and with an explosion of sound gathered them up and dematerialised with them.

In the tays that followed Mel-e-gar led the survivors to the southern shore of Arkelclared, where they rested as they grieved for lost friends. While the younglings remained unaware of the disaster of Starnay they were told that their home in the Hederlike Sea was being shaken by increasing tremors that had made it impossible for them to remain. Their main concern was to find enough fish to feed the nine families that Mel-e-gar's song had saved. This task he entrusted to Zar-e-gar who quickly led them to a shoal heading east. They followed it as they fed but his grandling soon pointed out that they would have to travel even greater distance to find more.

On a night when a great storm ravaged the sea, Mel-e-gar called for the Grand-elders to come together. They dived deep to avoid the tumultuous waters and curved a stream away from the main group. With the compliance of the Elders who were enough to keep the younglings together, Mel-e-gar transported the Grand-elders back to the Hederlike Sea to see what remained of the isle. When the dolphins materialised their first sight was the dark outline of Tethilay. He had expected to see the glow of the Volcano but there was not much left of the island. Investigating further he and the others leaped from the sea to land on the now cold rocky surface. It was only when the nine dolphs stood surveying the devastation did they see the numerous bodies that were half buried in the now solid lava streams.

There were too many to count. The arms, legs, and the stricken faces of some appeared to grow like tortured flowers from the grey surface. The light of the Crystal that Mel-e-gar held aloft picked out more as the group stumbled around trying to see if any survived. There were no sounds that seemed appropriate to declare their shock at seeing so many that had failed to escape. The fissure that Mel-e-gar had nearly fallen into was now filled with cold lava. Carefully they picked their way south and all stopped sharply when they came to the dark shadow that loomed over them. Mel-e-gar moved closer allowing the light to reveal the frozen wave of lava that had been fused by the impact of the tidal wave that must have swept across the island destroying the main cone and somehow the impact had left this monument to its passing.

On closer examination Mel-e-gar's blood froze as he saw the many grey faces of dolphs who must have been caught in the act of fleeing. They jutted out of the face of the wave solidified as they ran. Some were like those jutting from the ground, just the odd limb whilst others showed bodies half in and half out. It was grotesque and Mel-e-gar could only stare in bleak silence as he recognised faces of friends.

It was Dwe-e-lea who pulled him away, her tears sparkling in the light as she almost dragged him from the terrible scene. Part of him was not there, somehow seeing those he had failed had frozen his waters. He did not respond to her as she spoke to him and he would have stayed that way if a shout from Kin-e-gar had not broken the spell.

"I have found one *alive*!"

To Mel-e-gar's right the light skimmed the hunched form of Kin-e-gar as he called for them to come over. Moving in a panic he stumbled and was only saved by Del-e-gar's quick actions. "Careful *my friend*.."

With the dolph's help he made it to Kin-e-gar and a moan of anguish broke his silence as he saw the partially buried form of Vue-e-lea. He fell down by her side and saw the burns covering her upper torso, disfiguring her face, but she was recognisable. Her breathing was ragged and her eyes closed as if in sleep. Blinking away his tears, he summoned his water-time and flowed into hers. In the centre was a small glow which quickly began to fade as he moved closer.

As he came into contact her sounds met his and she whispered, *Mel-e-gar...I knew you would come. Tell Zar-e-gar to keep fishing....* Then silence as she slipped away. He felt the pulse of the deathsong and withdrew. Sitting back on his haunches his hand upon her head, he felt her parting and turned his face to the others and sounded, "*She has gone...*"

It was hard for them to leave her like that but there was nothing more they could do. Seeing so many bodies was something new for them all, as the deathsong within the confines of Shakeilar had meant the last energy of the form turned to consume the flesh and absorbed it.

It had been the reason that the Shakeilar had also died from the disease. The act of absorption had meant that the virus was able to mutate to attack the crystalline structure. It had only been after the last wave that the Healers with Del-e-gar's help had come to that conclusion but it had been far too late.

The burden of so much death lay heavy upon Mel-e-gar as they made their way back to the sea. His waters tried to come to terms with it, but he seemed to flounder as he stared blindly across the land. Out of the corner of his left eye a silver light seemed to sparkle but when he turned round it had disappeared. "*Did you see it?*" he asked.

"See *what* Mel-e-gar?" replied Del-e-gar at his side.

He pointed in the direction they had left Vue-e-lea and with anguish tearing at him he answered, "I- Saw a *light*.." His voice fell silent as they looked on. None of them had seen the light and as he turned his back on the devastated land he looked helplessly at the sea.

"Maybe it was a falling star that caught your eye.." offered Fas-e-lea. He could only silently nod his head in agreement. His friends seeing his distress poured their water-times into his and a wave of support picked him up and in one sound said, *It is time we made use of the Crystal. We can no longer stay on Delikadove...We need you Mel-e-gar to help us through this time.*

Yes... he sighed and as their waters flowed away he saw clearly what he had to do. As the light bathed them he turned to Fas-e-lea and said, "I would like you to return with me to *Melegarn* and help persuade the Council to come with us." Then to the others he added, "The rest of you I will return to the school to wait until we return, hopefully with more dolphs." With those sounds spoken he found his strength and as they agreed he dived into the sea.

The angry disc of Danetar was breaking above the horizon when Mel-e-gar and Fas-e-lea leapt from the ocean onto the raised platform at the edge of the city. They had expected to have been met by some dolphs but all was quiet. They looked at each other, a wave of foreboding passing between them as they began to walk into the main part of the city. He had expected to see the cover in place but all was open to the deep orange glow of Danetar. The further they walked the more apprehensive they became. There was no sign of anyone, and several times they called out but only silence greeted them. Taking the turning between two of the high domed buildings, they entered the main Council chamber. Still there was nothing, not even light from the Shakeilar and once more he had to employ the Crystal to light their way. When finally they came to the closed opening of the chamber a shiver ran through him. Normally the entrance would be open if the Council was not in session. A ripple ran through his waters as he passed his hand over the marker. Expecting the entrance to open he was startled as it remained closed.

Fas-e-lea turned to Mel-e-gar and offered in a whisper, "Maybe they are in a closed meeting."

He would have agreed as sometimes when the inner Council met they would make sure no dolph who was not invited could share in the discussion, but the lack of light and warmth in the city made it all wrong.

"Maybe you should try as they have banished me from this city," he answered, hoping that was the reason.

She walked over to the marker and tried but again nothing happened. She looked at Mel-e-gar and exclaimed, "This cannot be! *What is going on?!*" Her voice rose and the panic was clear in her voice.

He put out his hand and rested it on her shoulder and squeezed as he comforted Fas-e-lea. "Well there is another way round this." He smiled and she grinned back and for a yen they shared a stream of past water-time when she had once dared to enter the chamber without permission. His smile turned rather grim and with a single note the entrance shattered.

She laughed rather nervously and said, "Well that is *one way*."

"Mmmm, but that *should not* have happened," murmured Mel-e-gar.

Together they stepped through and were hit by an awful smell. They shrank back as the light showed them hundreds, maybe even thousands of rotting bodies. They were strewn everywhere, many draped over seats, others laying where they fell in the aisles.

After carefully stepping over the bodies they reached the centre dais and Mel-e-gar activated the large crystal that had replaced the one he held. To make sure Fas-e-lea was not left to just stare at the carnage he encouraged her to join his waters and together they found the last message of the Council.

An image of a weak dolph swam into view and both saw it was Han-e-gar, the dolph who had exiled Mel-e-gar and those that followed him. His sounds brought only more anguish to their already tired hearts.

I as Head of the Council leave this last message that hopefully some dolph will find.... We are dying.. The waters turned bad over the last jeanths and even though we have sent out many to find clean waters they have all returned with tales of dried river beds and the water they did find was also unfit to drink. That was our first problem, then the fish started to die and countless numbers were washed ashore. Our younglings are dying and there seems nothing to do. The Council met and advised us to contact Mel-e-gar at Starnay. But what could he do! Can he make bad water good, put fish in the seas. No, I believe not.

I had another consideration; if he and others like him came, we may consign them to the same fate. Even though I and the Council disagree with Mel-e-gar's outlandish dreams, I would not wish any of this upon him.

The image changed and Han-e-gar reappeared looking deathly ill but his sounds were strong.

The Council has called upon me to call on Mel-e-gar but I fear it is too late. We have sent two dolphs to travel the great distance to Starnay.

Another shimmer and this time a different dolph appeared, a lea who neither of them knew. Her face was covered in sores and blood oozed slowly from those on her forehead. Her sound was filled with sorrow as she completed the final message.

Two tays ago we lost Han-e-gar. I have been chosen to give this final report. There has been no sound from Mel-e-gar and the City of Starnay. The dolphs we have sent have failed to return. We do not know what has befallen them. Have they stayed at Starnay, or did they never make it? We cannot answer these questions. Late yestertay an explosion was heard from the south and a great light shines on that horizon. Those that can still walk could not tell whether it came from the southern continent or the Isle of Tethilay. Maybe we have seen the destruction of Starnay. We just do not know...We have no hope left..

I have one last thing to add. Mel-e-gar, if you still live forgive us. We should have listened to your wise sounds. I have one wish and that is that you and your followers have already made it to your Edenlea...

She stopped and coughed as fresh blood ran from her chin. But a sparkle lit her eyes as she finished with, *If you have then I really am talking to myself.*

As the image faded the crystal crumbled to dust and a low tremor ran across the dais. Mel-e-gar looked around in alarm as the chamber began to vibrate. Grabbing Fas-e-lea's hand he pulled her and shouted, "*Run!*" She looked shocked as her waters were still recovering from the dead lea's message so she was slow to respond. But Mel-e-gar pulled her firmly and together they ran across the room, jumping over bodies as they strove to escape the chamber. The vibration increased as they made it to the entrance and as the light bobbed up and down in Mel-e-gar's hand they saw cracks running across the walls. The floor buckled and with a burst of speed they made it out to the main street. The buildings around them began to fall.

Unlike Starnay the Shakeilar was already long dead and the release of the energy that had been kept for the message caused the city structure to fall apart. Soon they were having to dodge shards of crystal as they made it to the shore. Without stopping and still holding her hand he leaped into the air and as the resounding crash bellowed through the air their forms sparkled and changed slipping into the ocean.

They didn't change course until they were several klees from the mainland. As their beaks broke through the waves they were in time to see the shoreline erupt and for a klee, into the ocean. The underwater part of the city was blown into the air, to fall as soft dust that was caught by the updraft which blew it north.

It really is all over.. his waters whispered. The sight of his city being now only dust severed the last connection with Delikadove. A race that had lived in happiness and peace for countless seasons had fallen and only the fragment that was in his charge could possibly begin again. The stream of his waters missed the rhythmic pulse of the Crystal in his beak and it was Fas-e-lea who flicked her waters, exclaiming, *Look!*

With a swirl his waters re-orientated his sound enabling him to see the changing colours that flitted across the surface; blue, white, and red. It kept repeating as they both watched intrigued by the spectacle. Then a sound filled their waters;

HE HAS GONE.... TERMINATION OF LIFE FORM....... SADNESS IS FELT.... LOSS IS GREAT....

It was the first time he had ever known the Crystal to sound spontaneously and the emotion was very lea, as if the Crystal was a lea that cried for her lost mate. He had separated the Shakeilar consciousness and so there should not have been such a response. Very strange because he had searched to see if there was another hidden in the intricate matrix of the Crystal but he had found nothing. The other times when there had been a suggestion of emotion he had put it down to some last echo of the Shakeilar's old self. It also puzzled Mel-e-gar why it should refer to the city as *he*. In all the dealings with Shakeilar none had ever expressed a sense of he or she. Even though to him *the* Rock and Serliker seemed all gar, but the race was asexual so it did not make much sense.

While he pondered this the colours faded and the Crystal reverted back to green and blue. Leaving this new mystery for the yen he took one last look then dived down and sang the note to shift them across to join the others.

Deciding to give them time to absorb the news of Melegarn and for the realisation that there were no more to come he chose the following tay to announce the news. With Ser-e-gar and Car-e-lea on each side they led the families within a hundred dees of the shore of Arkelclared.

Before he initiated the Gateway he joined his waters one last time with the Crystal. A flow of red, blue, and white light shimmered then died to the normal blue green, only the second time he had seen the bright colours before the normal tones. He asked, *Are you a life form? Are you Shakeilar?*

The answer was simple. ACCESS DENIED....*AND NO!*

Mel-e-gar froze. A shiver ran through him. *It was an answer. Then what he was dealing with was something other than the life force of the Shakeilar but what?* He knew he would never know. Maybe it was one secret that he should let go. Part of him didn't really want to know for certain as the use of the Gateway was going to leave it stranded at the bottom of the ocean on a dead planet.

Truly hoping that it was just the echo of whoever fixed the matrix of the Crystal he broke away from the group and did what he had to do. He descended to the bottom of the ocean and dropped the Crystal. It rolled a few dees and came to rest among the scattered pebbles. Responding with its usual coolness it sounded:

WORKING....

ON LINE SEQUENCE COMPLETE....
INITIATE POWER SOURCE...

Taking that as his cue he began to sing. The song's power flowed into the Crystal, causing it to expand rapidly. Thousands of colours brought brilliance to the sea and he could hear the sounds of those behind him cry with awe as the Crystal stretched into an oval disc, from the bottom to the surface of the sea. Then the voice added to his song:

TRANSFERENCE READY....
POSITION DOLPHINS WITHIN POWER SOURCE...

Everything else now forgotten but the task in hand, Mel-e-gar reached out. With love and excitement filling his song he wrapped the dolphins within his grasp and together they passed through into a new world.

7269 S.N. (1 S.E.)

It had been a beautiful first season in their new home. All found the blue, green waters refreshing and even though they found the higher oxygen content caused strange sensations it did not take long for all to adjust and feel at home. Mel-e-gar shared his sounds with the eight Grand-elders and none were sorry they had come. Edenlea renewed them all washing away past hurts and past grief. The very task of surviving when they only numbered fifty-six was a tremendous undertaking which gave new purpose in their elder seasons. Already six of the Elder leas were carrying un-borns, including his sonling's mate Car-e-lea.

As the newly named Solarn sank below the horizon Mel-e-gar swam to join his family. Car-e-lea was chasing Ser-e-gar, who was on the tail of Haw-e-gar, doing several loops in the water laughing gaily as each tugged the tail of the one in front. While he watched, a stream of past times flowed in and he saw his *own* play with his first youngling Star-e-lay and his mate Cual-e-lay. He felt sure they would be pleased, and as the image changed he saw his other mate Sye-e-lea and their own delight at the birth of Ser-e-gar. There were so many seasons to count, all leading to this, a new tay. The only tremor in his waters at this point was seeing a vision of Serliker who with the remaining Selahw he had left behind. Even though he knew it was not possible to transfer the four hundred remaining Selahw he still wished it had been possible. He missed their gentle wisdom, their great fluke dances and the sound of such wonderful songs.

His waters flowed back to Serliker and the sounds he had been left with on the tay before the destruction of Starnay.

Mel-e-gar! You will soon have to go. My young one, you will travel across space and time in an instant of song, to Edenlea. That is your ultimate destiny, so do not weep tears for us.

He had responded with, *But you and the Selahw will die here!*

Serliker had laughed at that and admonished the dolphin, *I die here! Ha! I survived mostly alone for millennia upon millennia, and I will live until the last star fades in this universe!*

He couldn't help but laugh at Serliker's tenacity.

That is better young dolph. I have sent a call to the matrix of Sentinels and it may take a few seasons but I can keep the Selahw alive until then. They know and trust me as you might say only as a youngling can of its parentling.

He could not argue with that and replied, *Serliker, I will miss our shared sounds and maybe somewhere, most likely in Chisharnlay we will meet again.*

Maybe, I hope so too. One thing more, do not leave it much longer. Farewell Mel-e-gar, you have much to learn!

He could still hear Serliker laughing as he poked his beak above the waves and watched Solarn melt into the sea. The fresh salty breeze caressed him as stars began to appear. His yen of solitude was broken by Car-e-lea who joined his vigil and sounded, *Do you know which star is Danetar?*

His water flowed a sad ripple, *No, the Crystal showed me the star map of this system and our old world revolves around a star not visible from here.*

It would have been nice to have shown my un-born Tan-e-lea where we had come from... she solemnly replied.

The sound sparkled in his waters and with a smile he sounded, *That is a good name for your un-born...*

Car-e-lea laughed and sounded, *Yes, it was Del-e-gar who suggested the name and Ser-e-gar and I readily agreed. A beautiful name for our daughterling.*

Small drops of light scattered the image, leaving Jer-e-lea breathless with all she had seen. The flickering shadows around the tree masked Del-e-gar's expression but her sounds sensed his weary breathing. At last the story had been completed and as she turned onto her side she saw a shimmer of phosphorous green energy alight upon the old dolph and from some great distance she heard the sounds of comfort from a spectre of his past.

My love, take your rest...

It left a warm glow inside her. She watched the light expand and as if space itself was twisted swept Del-e-gar away. She took her leave and even though she was happy for him it did not stop the tears that rolled down her cheeks, each holding an image of those that never made it to Edenlea.

* * *

With a tilt of his golden brown wings, he turned south under the clear star filled sky. The silver orb of the moon showed him his way and her embrace kept his flight sure, passing over mountains and the silver blue sparkling rivers that twisted their way through tree filled valleys. He was no longer the weary dolph who had seen too much and lost his heart but a strong vibrant Leujan, a symbol of her promise that made his curved beak open and cry with the wind as his eyes blinked in surprise as his flight descended to a mountain range that was shaped like one of his great wings. Instead of feathers there were trees that called him and he returned the call, "*Aiouqes!*"

He swooped down and as he twisted to land on the crown of one of the trees his form changed. His wings folded and disappeared. The contours of his body ran fluid. With a cry of exaltation he slipped easily into the waiting Aiouqes and as one, stood proud and tall overlooking a valley filled with old friends.

The green mist swirled around him as he waited. His arms that were now branches felt her touch and her gentle laughter kissed his heart. Slowly his waters changed, running down the trunk, his awareness feeling the hunger of roots in warm soil. Leaves that danced with rain and the one who had been Del-e-gar felt his true peace. *He was home at last..*

* * *

71 S.E.

There was a dull ache within her waters as time split apart allowing her to return to her waiting body within the cavern. The sound of Serliker greeted her as the red crystal faded from her grasp.

"Welcome back. Your impromptu departure down the time line caught me unawares. But I can tell from your water-time that you have kept your promise."

She turned, smiled and answered, "I did and I did not.."

It flashed *its* light in confusion, "*Tan-e-lea*.. Only I talk in riddles! Explain!!"

Casting back *its* often used sound, she laughed gaily, "You have much to learn *young Serliker*!" For a yen the lights went into a spasm of colour until she calmed *it*, "Be still and I will explain." When the lights settled, she began walking round Serliker and revealed her own puzzlement. "I wanted to show Del-e-gar that our love was still strong and even though time separated us I had not forgotten him. When his deathsong began I chose to give him a gift and I transported him to reside within an Aiouqes. She paused, took a deep breath and explained, "*I did not save the Aiouqes on Delikadove*..."

"But how, as they now exist here on this planet? I presumed you must have brought them here," interjected Serliker.

"No," she said slowly as she considered the implication. "I found that they were already here. Maybe they are native to this planet but I sense that may not be so."

Its waters conjured an image of *the* Rock. "*Maybe it* brought them here," Serliker offered.

"Whatever the reason it made it easy for me to give Del-e-gar what he most desired...."

"A fine gift," agreed Serliker. *Its* light warmed her and as she let go of Del-e-gar's image she moved over and rested her hands on *its* smooth roundness. With a change of stream she softly sounded, "Now I must keep one last promise."

"Agreed," responded Serliker and gave her the time line for her to approach. Her body slumped as her waters departed. *It* caused the cavern floor to rise and wrap itself around her and with one swift motion laid her gently down.

9 S.E.

They played in the refracted light streams that made the water dance under the warmth of Solarn. Mel-e-gar chased Jux-e-lea and their two younglings through Edenlea, twisting this way and that, continuing the game, enjoying a fish, quickly snatched as they followed the current. His attention was caught by a sudden movement and he gasped in surprise as a green cloud changed the water ahead. Jux-e-lea cried her surprise as she too saw what lay ahead and as their water-time came together the single sound struck, *Tan-e-lea!*

Their game was forgotten as they swiftly used their flippers to urge their younglings to swim between them. Ien-e-lea and Kor-e-gar, the black markings reflecting the green light stared wide eyed at the apparition. As they had no knowledge of Tan-e-lea they could not understand what the cloud of green water meant. But they were not unaware of the change in their parentlings, of the rising joy that was spreading like a current from them.

Quicker than the eye can see the green water enveloped them and her sound filled all:

Hello Mel-e-gar, Jux-e-lea, Ien-e-lea and Kor-e-gar. It's time...

The younglings did not understand but their parentlings knew and Jux-e-lea's cry of joy turned to fear. Even though she knew it had to happen sometime she had hoped that they could have more time.

His water-time held her close as Tan-e-lea's own sadness sounded, *I know*.. In response her light infused into them and Mel-e-gar passed onto his family all that had happened in Edenlea since he and Jux-elea had been taken from the other dolphins.

He knew that Tan-e-lea had not arrived to take him away, only to help his family after he had gone. He allowed the sights and sound of the images to flow into him and as each passed he felt the tug of the deathsong take hold. Unlike the last time when the Sentinel had restored his missing seasons he felt no pain, just warmth and love of those around him, past and present.

His love for Jux-e-lea caught her in a light that made her see the truth of the time and she wept again but the young waters of their younglings breathed her a song which Tan-e-lea sang and as the waters flashed she managed to reach and kiss Mel-e-gar before they were parted.

Ien-e-lea and Kor-e-gar cried as they saw their fatherling fade but Jux-e-lea held them as they saw the water fill with stars.

Then it seemed to fold. Then a rush of cool water enveloped them. As they came through they were greeted by cries of surprise as dolphins from all directions swept towards them. Only when she saw her motherling come rushing towards her did Jux-e-lea know where she was. Holding her younglings close she allowed the warm waters of her motherling to embrace her, crying delight that she was home.

Tan-e-lea watched from the clouds as the dolphins filled Edenlea and the sky with joy. As Jux-e-lea and her family swam among them she whispered farewell and returned to where she had left Mel-e-gar. The deathsong had been completed and his still body was now shaded by the overhanging branches at the top of the beach. Her vaporous form glided down and lovingly wrapped him in her green embrace. Her last task was to fulfil the message of the Sentinel. Time flowed forward and the shore changed and trees died away. The land and sea came together; mountains moved. When she felt it was right, and the earth was deep she laid the body of Mel-e-gar in his final resting place. He was dolph and the rock he lay in kept his form true. Then she changed, bringing new energy into play. An orb of light pulsated; blue, white, and red as the Knowledge of a race was placed in his hand.

Only when the last trace of Tan-e-lea had departed did the light grow even stronger, filling the small cave that held Mel-e-gar's body. Her light blinked in rapid succession as she stirred herself awake. *At least she was home at last. Now all Tawny had to do was wait. And Tawny was good at waiting..... She would wait for his bones to fossilise and they would and this time she would warn herself. No more mistakes. This time when she digs up the overgrown fossil she would destroy the Crystal!* So a young lady of very human stock wouldn't get trapped in the paradox of time! She allowed her light to fade and as the darkness returned she called out defiantly, "***Chyserona!!*** *The cycle will be broken!*"

EPILOGUE

71 S.E.

She had spent a few tays with the Selahw, helping them in their discovery of Edenlea. She joined in with their songs of past times and she told them of Mel-e-gar's final seasons with Jux-e-lea and their two younglings. The great creatures beat the time of his last song with their flukes and as always the story would continue.

When the two dolphins who had seen their descent from the sky drew nearer, Tan-e-lea bade the Selahw a final farewell and returned to her home on the island.

A veul later found Tan-e-lea sitting on the beach, staring at the expanse of Edenlea as she idly heaped cool wet sand over her thighs and dees. Her water-time was deep, sending pools of images to the surface of all that had happened. She was no longer that innocent youngling who would have passed into the deathsong if it had not been for the Rock's intervention. But she had lost her family even though she was happy that the power of her watersong had been used to travel through many waves, helping her race to fulfil their destiny in coming to Edenlea. It still had meant that she could no longer interact with them. She was unique, a dolph among dolphins.

That had been explained to her. She had been sent over sixty seasons into what would have been her own future to be apart. Her parentlings, brotherlings and sisterlings were now shadows. Only their offspring lived in Edenlea and those who could have changed to dolph were also gone, leaving a pure line of dolphins for the future. So she could not return as the line of Watersingers had been ended with the dolphins and as she was the last of all that was once of Delikadove even though she had been born of Edenlea, she had to be left behind. She was not sure what was going to happen to her and the very ripple of being alone for the rest of her tays made her shiver with a wave of sadness.

She could not help the tears that started to fall, her hands almost blindly picking up more sand to cover her legs when a shout disturbed her melancholy haze.

"Look at what you are doing!"

"*Oh! Sorry* Serliker!" She made to brush the sand away when *it* began to spin out of the mound that she made, sending the fine yellow sand in all directions. When *its* smooth surface was restored *it* hovered a few dees above her while she started to laugh her gloom away.

Its lights flashed a cycle of colour as she wiped her tears and giggled at the indignity that flowed from *it*. Seeing that Solarn was about to set she held her laughter at bay and remarked, "It is late and we might as well return to the cavern."

"You cannot change the subject so easily young dolph! What in all *Edenlea* made you bury me?!"

It obviously was not going to let it drop so as she brushed the rest of the sand from her legs, climbing to her dees she held out her hand and said, "It was not on purpose *Serliker*! My waters were otherwise engaged."

Her explanation made *its* lights flutter and *it* took notice of the aura of sadness that she still felt because *it* replied, "Well next time be *more careful.*" *It* paused then added, "And Tan-e-lea, you are not *alone*."

After Serliker settled in the palm of her hand, she stroked *its* surface. Her actions made orange colour that warmed her as she nodded and said, "I know I have you for company *but I miss them...*"

Its sympathy rose and softly *it* said, "There is no going back, only forward..."

Its sounds were so like Mel-e-gar that she brought her hand up, so her eyes were level with *its* smooth surface, and with some suspicion asked, "Serliker, why did you say it *quite like that*?"

She felt Serliker's waters retract as if being caught out by *its* slip made *it* unsure, but then *it* returned with boldness, "I felt hearing Mel-e-gar's sounds would make you remember that the future could hold many surprises."

She agreed with that and as she made her way along the shore, taking pleasure in the breeze that cooled the heat of the tay away, she waited allowing the silence to speak. Tan-e-lea knew *it* was keeping something from her and because *it* sensed her suspicions in the silence Serliker explained,

"Tan-e-lea," *it* slowly began, "I have allowed you this rest this past veul-"

"You have *what*!" She interrupted, annoyed at the arrogance of *its* sounds. She was deciding whether she would toss Serliker into Edenlea to teach *it* some manners or whether to really bury *it*, when *it* lifted from her hand in alarm and moved several dees away from her. *Its* lights flashed wildly and as if taking some delight from the panic she had caused she made to snatch *it* from the air.

"Tan-e-lea, *do not be hasty*. I was only *saying*,-"

It dodged her hand as she again interrupted Serliker, "I know what you were saying! That is why I am going to *bury you so deep* it will take you a *season to escape*!"

Serliker flew higher, responding to her anger and pleaded, "All right, I will re-phrase my sounds."

She eyed him suspiciously and dropped her hands and said, "Well, go on then."

Serliker dropped from *its* position, but still kept a healthy distance from her when *it* explained, "I am trying to tell you that you have a greater and more dangerous task ahead."

She groaned at *its* sounds, her waters still tired from all she been through. But her curiosity surfaced as she asked, "*All right* Serliker tell me more."

She readied her song, green energy enveloping her form as she waited for Serliker to tell her the last part of her impending voyage. What *it* had shown her on the beach, before they had returned to the brightly lit cavern, had excited her and dismayed her all at once. Any fears of a future, living out her tays alone with Serliker had been swept away by the vision. Her energy flowed cleanly through her as she turned her silver, green eyes on Serliker and with humour said, "And there I was believing it was all over, that I had finished my task."

A wave of blue and red light swirled around Serliker as *it* responded, "I wanted you to have some time to rest before revealing the rest. *Its* light increased as *it* added, "Now are you ready?"

She smiled and said, "*Yes Serliker.*"

The cavern's blue lit walls reflected the combined energy of Tan-e-lea and Serliker.

EPILOGUE

The green and silver running into red and the blue, sending a shower of sparks as her song twisted her sense of time.

Only as she melted away did she catch *its* last words, "*Remember young one we will meet again when I have become thousands...*"

A frozen blast of air hit Tan-e-lea, scattering her energy as she fell several dees onto hard frozen earth, that turned out to be a slope of a mountain. With a cry she slid down, falling headlong into a pile of wet flakes of still water. For a yen she was dazed. Then as her sight caught the glaring whiteness all around she shook herself free and sat up to find herself staring down into the dark black eyes of a hairy creature that grunted and stepped back. It was short, no more than three to four dees high, resembling a knarled stump of a tree and held in its hairy hand, a long, shining white object that it raised over its head as it screamed into the frozen tay.

She shrank from its cry but then almost laughed with relief as she realised that her song had worked well once again. If it had not been for her knowledge of the still water that she had named, *Sloona* in one of her more uneventful tays she would have been surprised to have seen so much all around her. She shook the rest of the sloona off herself as she stood up, making the creature cry with alarm as she towered over it.

Being four times its size obviously made the creature nervous but it held its ground. Waving the object it held, it made guttural sounds that she took for a challenge. Well, she was not sure what to do next but she was glad that it had been so easy to find them. She opened her hands and said, "Hello Dolph-oid, I-"

But her greeting to the creature was cut short because it screamed and ran, covering the sides of its head as if in pain. She watched its fast disappearing back, stunned that her sounds should have such an impact. She stood staring open-mouthed for some while. But her waters ran a stream, *What strange creatures these dolph-oid are. This is going to be harder than I first believed.*

Deciding to follow she began her trek through the white wilderness muttering under her breath, "*I should have buried Serliker deep while I had the chance..*"

* * *

Every hundred thousand seasons or so the Guardianship of the Shakeilar race convene. The Sentinels from all over the galaxy come together to give a progress report to the highest law of their kind. Remarkably enough this was one occasion that the Guardian, appointed more than six hundred million seasons ago, was going to be late. Its name was Chyserona and it was busy below the main chamber which bore a great resemblance to the chambers in the cities on a small planet that had recently been destroyed by a super nova. One difference was that it was deep inside the bowels of an asteroid that the Shakeilar race had turned into a space faring vessel which cruised the galaxy making impromptu calls on worlds already colonised by their race. As the Sentinels responded to the call they quickly made contact, creating a string of spheres which attached themselves to the central cavern, passing through the surface of the asteroid with very little resistance from its iron and nickel surface.

It carefully took note as each Shakeilar joined together, the hum of their many sounds filling the chamber above as they awaited *its* appearance. The only reason that the chamber existed was that Chyserona could indulge *itself* in whatever manner *it* pleased in the comfort of *its* temporary home. It was always temporary since unlike past Guardians who spent more time in the asteroid making the other Sentinels do all the work, *it* liked to get out and about to basically interfere as much as possible, as some of *its* kind had noted on more than one occasion. But Chyserona preferred to see it as keeping the sounds of the Galaxy in harmony.

A blue light grew in strength as Chyserona prepared *its* surprise to the Sentinels. *This is going to cause quite a stir*, *it* thought as the energy wrapped round the four still forms began to rise, passing through the ceiling to the now impatient sounds above.

Every sound fell silent as the four forms hidden by Chyserona's energy appeared in the bowl of the chamber. More than a hundred Sentinel senses gazed in wonder, wondering what their Leader was up to.

When the energy dissipated revealing what lay underneath, bedlam broke loose and the chamber vibrated with the astonished and angry sounds of a hundred irate Sentinels.........

LINEAGE OF

EDENLEA DOLPHIN FAMILIES

[Correct as of 4 S.E.]

Family One

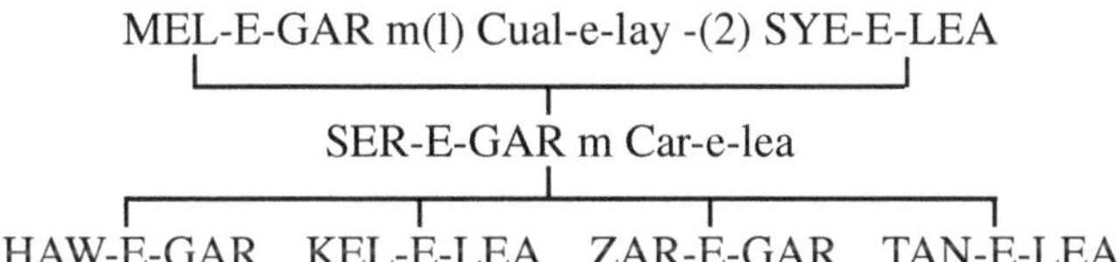

Family Two

ELY-E-LEA m Dag-e-gar (Sisterling-QUE-E-LEA)

PEL-E-LEA m Dal-e-gar

ILY-E-LEA JER-E-LEA SAG-E-LEA TEG-E-GAR TES-E-LEA

Family Three

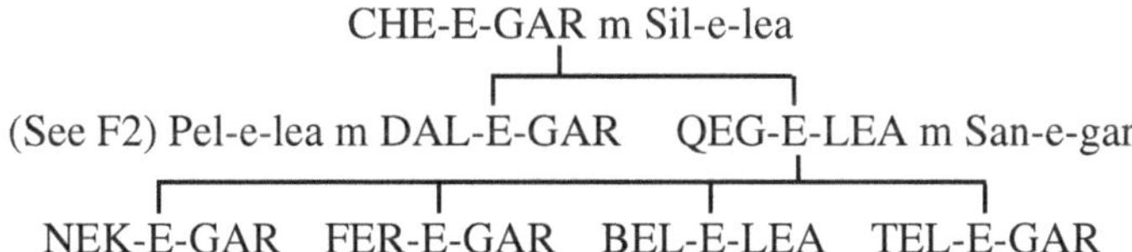

Family Four

FAS-E-LEA m Chi-e-gar

TAG-E-LEA m Gel-e-gar

LEA-E-LEA TEY-E-LEA REA-E-GAR

Family Five

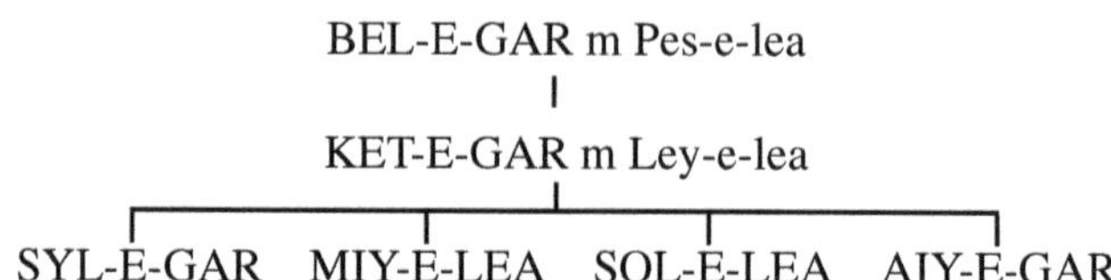

Family Six

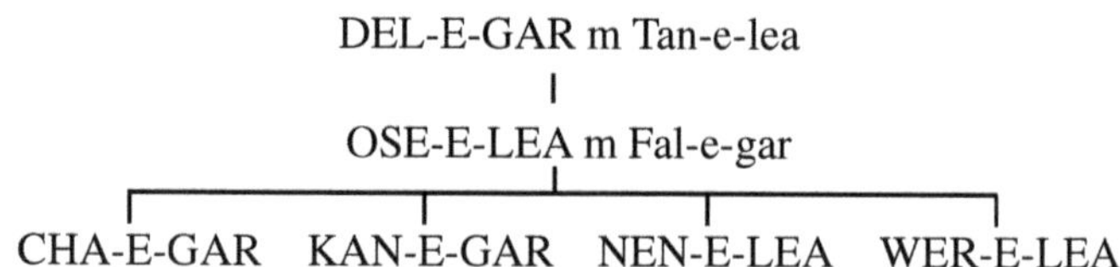

Family Seven

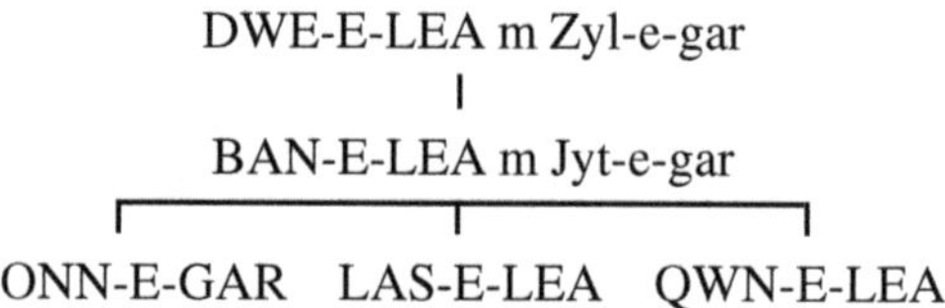

Family Eight

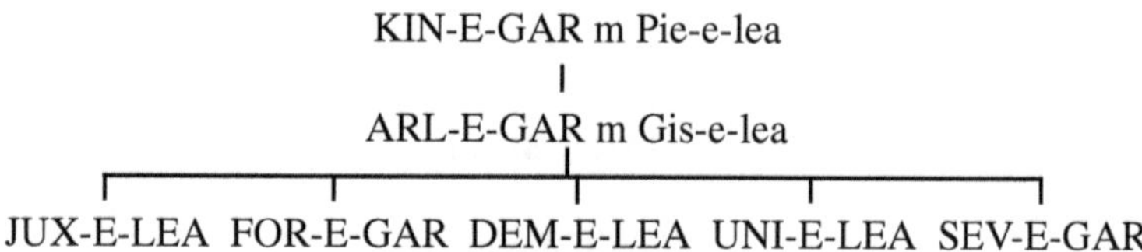

Family Nine

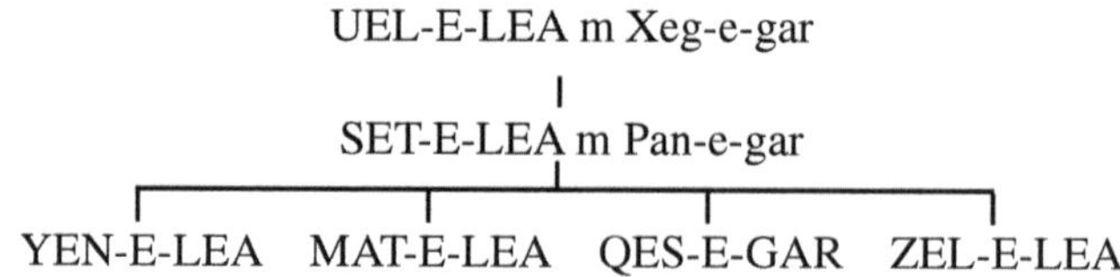

GLOSSARY

Aiouqes: Name given to individual trees of the forest of *Duorsilear*; were massive coniferous trees with a crowned canopy of blue-green foliage, had soft deeply ridged red-brown bark.

Aiouqanlay, city of: Situated south-west on the western continent: Established **7231** S.N. After the Great Deathsong of **7229** to **7231** S.N. Named after the *Aiouqes* of the western continent.

Aiy-e-gar: Sonling of *Ket-e-gar* and *Ley-e-lea*(**4**): Grandling of *Bel-e-gar*: Born **3** S.E.

Alk-e-lea: Mate of *Bue-e-gar*: Became Head of the Council during the deathsong of the *Keaverkack* in **7182**: Held position until **7222**: Friend of *Mel-e-gar*: Born **7147** S.N. Died **7229** S.N.

Alkelbuan, city of: Situated on the south coast of the southern continent: Established in **7231** S.N. Named after *Alk-e-lea (Head of the Council of all Dolphs from* **7182** to **7222** S.N.) and her mate *Bue-e-gar*.

Arkelclared, desert of: The Eastern continent but since ancient times has only been known by its name: Uninhabitable by Dolphs.

Arl-e-gar: Sonling of *Kin-e-gar* and *Pie-e-lea*: Mate of *Gis-e-lea*: Fatherling of *Jux-e-lea*: *For-e-gar*: *Dem-e-lea*: *Uni-e-lea*: *Sev-e-gar*: *Mul-e-gar*: Born **7234** S.N.

Ban-e-lea: Daughterling of *Dwe-e-lea* and *Zyl-e-gar*: Mate of *Jyt-e-gar*: Grandling of *Dwe-e-lea*: Motherling of *Onn-e-gar*: *Las-e-lea*: *Qwn-e-lea*: *Mel-e-lea*: *Tor-e-lea*: born **7233** S.N.

Beacons: Large crystals embedded along the coasts on *Delikadove*.

Bel-e-gar: Grand-elder: Mate of *Pes-e-lea*: Fatherling of *Ket-e-gar*: Grand-elder of *Syl-e-gar*: *Miy-e-lea*: *Sol-e-lea*: *Aiy-e-gar*: Born **7209** S.N.

Bel-e-lea: Friend of *Car-e-lea* on *Delikadove* [*No relation to Bel-e-lea* (**2**)].

Bel-e-lea(2): Daughterling of *Qeg-e-lea* and *San-e-gar*(**3**): Grandling of *Che-e-gar*: Born **7266** S.N.

Beslika, city of: A ruin on a hill looking over the city of *Plesilea*.

Brotherling: Brother.

Bue-e-gar: Mate of *Alk-e-lea*: Friend of *Mel-e-gar*: Born **7109** S.N. [*No relation to later Bue-e-gar* (**2**)]: Died **7184** S.N.

Bue-e-gar(2): Sonling of *Cha-e-gar* and *Jer-e-lea*: Grandling of *Ose-e-lea* and *Fal-e-gar*: Great Grandling of *Del-e-gar*: Born **6** S.E.

Bylinkan, mountains of: On the Northern continent of *Delikadove*.

Calader: Tree: Only found in the desert of *Arkelclared* of *Delikadove*.

Car-e-lea: Daughterling of *Jun-e-gar* and *Tus-e-lea*: Grandling of *Chm-e-gar* and *Lon-e-lea*: Mate of *Ser-e-gar*: Motherling of; (*See Ser-e-gar*]: Born **7243** S.N. Died **61** S.E.

Cas-e-lea: Daughterling of *Ser-e-gar* and *Car-e-lea*(**5**): Grandling of *Mel-e-gar*: Mate of *Zac-e-gar*: Motherling to *Mas-e-gar* and Grand-elder to *Per-e-gar*: Born **5** S.E.

Celsen, age of: Cycle of seasons that lasted for nineteen thousand and fifty five seasons: Ended at the commencement of the cycle of *Gealasor*.

Cerser: Type of bird on *Delikadove*: Found only in the forest of *Duorsilear*.

Cha-e-gar: Sonling of *Ose-e-lea* and *Fal-e-gar*(**1**): Mate of *Jer-e-lea*: Grandling of *Del-e-gar*: Fatherling to *Bue-e-gar* [*Not to be confused with Bue-e-gar born **7109** S.N.*]: Born **7256** S.N.

Che-e-gar: Grand-elder: mate of *Sil-e-lea*: Fatherling of *Qeg-e-lea*(**1**): *Dal-e-gar*(**2**) Grand-elder of (**1**)*Nek-e-gar*: *Fer-e-gar*: *Bel-e-lea*: *Tel-e-gar*: (**2**)*Ily-e-lea*: *Jer-e-lea*: *Sag-e-lea*: *Teg-e-gar*: *Tes-e-lea*: Born **7213** S.N.

Chi-e-gar: Mate of *Fas-e-lea*: Fatherling of *Tag-e-lea*: Grand-elder of [*See Fas-e-lea*]: Born **7222** S.N. Died **7260** S.N.

Chisharnlay: Concept of the deathsong: Afterlife.

Chm-e-gar: Sonling of *Wel-e-lea* and *Ran-e-gar*(**1**): Grandling of *Cla-e-lea* and *Kin-e-gar*: Mate of *Lon-e-lea*: Fatherling of *Jan-e-gar*: Grand-elder of *Car-e-lea*: Born **7183** S.N. Died **7256** S.N.

Chy-e-lea: Head of the Council on *Delikadove* from **18097** S.C. to **19054** S.C.: Predecessor to *Gei-e-gar.*

Chyserona: True name of *The Rock*: Also titled as *Sentinel: Guardian.*

Cla-e-lea: Motherling of *Wel-e-lea*: *Ler-e-lea*: *Jey-e-gar*: mate of Kin-e-gar: Grand-elder of *Chm-e-gar*: Great Grand-elder of *Jan-e-gar*: Great Great Grand-elder of: *Car-e-lea*: Born **7140** S.N. Died **7212** S.N.

Clar(s): Hour(s)

Colertia: Sea of: The great sea between the western continent and the continent of the *Arkelclared* desert.

Colisee, city of: On the west coast of the western continent on *Delikadove*: Abandoned during the Great Deathsong of **7229** to **7231** S.N.

Council: Held by Dolphs for special discussions and occasions: Each City had its own chamber: But central location of higher councils placed where the holder of the High Elder lived or primely worked.

Crystal the: also known as the *Crystal of Pha-e-gar*: *Crystal of Edenlea*: Origin Unknown.

Cual-e-lay: A female Selahw who befriended *Mel-e-gar* and later became his first mate: Motherling of *Star-e-lay.*

Dag-e-gar: Sonling of *Ers-e-lea* and *Pon-e-gar*: (**1**)Mate of *Ely-e-lea*: Brotherling of *Que-e-lea*: Grand-elder of [*See Ely-e-lea*]: Born **7205** S.N. Died **7259** S.N.

Dal-e-gar: Sonling of *Che-e-gar* and *Sil-e-lea*(**1**): Mate of *Pel-e-lea*: Fatherling of [*See Pel-e-lea*]: Born **7232** S.N.

Danetar: The sun of *Delikadove.*

Deathsong: To Die; Death; Dead.

Dee(s): Foot, feet.

Del-e-gar: A Grand-elder: Mate of *Tan-e-lea*: Fatherling to *Ose-e-lea*: Grand-elder of *Cha-e-gar*: *Kan-e-gar*: *Nen-e-gar: Wer-e-lea: Eis-e-gar*: Guardian of the forest of *Duorsilear*: Born **7200** S.N. Died **7** S.E.

Delikadove: Home world of Dolph/ins.

Dem-e-lea: Daughterling of *Arl-e-gar* and *Gis-e-lea*(**3**): Grandling of *Kin-e-gar*: Born **7264** S.N.

Desilata, city of: On the northern coast of the southern continent of *Delikadove*: Abandoned after the Great Deathsong of **7229** to **7231** S.N.

Dolph(s): Dolphin(s) that have transformed from the water to the land.
Duors: Highest mountain on the western continent.
Duorsilear, mountain range of: On the western continent:
Duorsilear, forest of: On the western continent: Looked after by a Guardian.
Dwe-e-lea: Grand-elder: Mate of *Zyl-e-gar*: Motherling of *Ban-e-lea*: Grand-elder of *Onn-e-gar*: *Las-e-lea*: *Qwn-e-lea: Mel-e-lea: Tor-e-lea* [*Not to be confused with Tor-e-lea, motherling of Mel-e-gar*]: Born **7207** S.N.
Eaarklisade: Northern sea on *Delikadove.*
Edenlea: All of the sea: Firstly used by the Dolphins of ages past, then revived by *Mel-e-gar*. Also used in term of Cycle of Seasons; S.E.
Eil-e-lea: Healer: Friend and Teacher to *Pha-e-gar*: Born **1180** S.N. Died **1215** S.N.?
Eis-e-gar: Sonling of *Ose-e-lea* and *Fal-e-gar*(**5**): Grandling of *Del-e-gar*: Born **6** S.E.
Elder: Parent, Mother, Father: used by Grand-elders, Elders and Younglings: Also used after a Dolphin has passed its **14**th Season: Can vary: Mark of respect.
Elderlings: Plural of Elders.
Ely-e-lea: Grand-elder: Mate of *Dag-e-gar*: Motherling of *Pel-e-lea*: Grand-elder of *Ily-e-lea*: *Jer-e-lea*: *Sag-e-lea*: *Teg-e-gar*: *Tes-e-lea*: Born **7202** S.N.
Ers-e-lea: Daughterling of *Hia-e-lea* and *Tre-e-gar*(**1**): Mate of *Pon-e-gar*: Motherling of *Dag-e-gar* and *Que-e-lea*: Grand-elder of *Pel-e-lea*: Born **7180** S.N. Died **7262** S.N.
Fal-e-gar: Mate of *Ose-e-lea*: Fatherling of [*See Ose-e-lea*]: Born **7229** S.N.
Far-see: To use the Watersong to explore great distances.
Fas-e-lea: Grand-elder: Mate of *Chi-e-gar*: Motherling of *Tag-e-lea*: Grand-elder of *Lea-e-lea: Tey-e-lea: Rea-e-gar*: Born **7221** S.N.
Fatherling: Father.
Fer-e-gar: Sonling of *Qeg-e-lea* and *San-e-gar*(**2**): Grandling of *Che-e-gar*: Helper of *Que-e-lea*: Born **7263** S.N.
For-e-gar: Sonling of *Arl-e-gar* and *Gis-e-lea*(**2**): Mate of *Las-e-lea*: Grandling of *Kin-e-gar*: Born **7260** S.N.
Frelegar, mountains of: That divide the southern continent on *Delikadove*.
Gae-e-lea: Head of the Council before *Alk-e-lea*.
Galdane: Horseshoe crab of *Edenlea.*
Gam-e-lea: Ancient Dolph who lived in the Cycle of *Toomasel*.
Gar: Male: used by Dolph/ins
Geallea, sea of: Between the North and west continents on *Delikadove*. Later known as the First *Edenlea* by *Mel-e-gar*.
Gealasor, age of: A cycle of seasons **10,000** seasons ago: Lasted for **2731** seasons: Ended with the beginning of the cycle of the *Neimas*.
Gei-e-gar: Guardian of *Duorsilear*: Head of the Council in the last season of *Celsen* over ten thousand seasons ago on *Delikadove*.
Gel-e-gar: Mate of *Tag-e-lea*: Fatherling of [*See Tag-e-lea*]: Born **7241** S.N.
Gis-e-lea: Mate of *Arl-e-gar*: Motherling of [*See Arl-e-gar*]: Born **7237** S.N.
Gla: Male: used by the *Selahw*.
Gooma, age of: Lasted for **4,000** seasons: Ended **190,000** seasons ago.
Gothina, city of: Situated south-west of the city of *Colisee* on the western Continent.

Grand-elder: Grand Parent, also Grand Mother, Grand Father: A term used by Grand-elders, Elders and Younglings: Also for all Dolph/ins who have passed their **60**th season: Can vary: Mark of Respect.

Gre-e-gar: Healer: who attended *Ler-e-lea*: Born **7160** S.N. Died **7255** S.N.?

Greathon IV: A planet in the constellation of *Orion.*

Guardian: A *Shakeilar* who co-ordinates the affairs of the *Sentinel*s as their leader: Who calls a meeting every hundred thousand seasons or whenever an emergency situation arises.

Haldom: Type of crab.

Haw-e-gar: Sonling of *Ser-e-gar* and *Car-e-lea*(**1**): Grandling of *Mel-e-gar* : Mate of *Yen-e-lea*: Born **7260** S.N.

Healer: A Dolph who cares for the sick: They must show an adeptness of use of the healing energy: Similar to the use of *Water-time*.

Healing, centre of: A building in each city used by the *Healers* to tend the sick: They are also the places where apprentice healers are trained.

Hederlike, sea of: The purple southern sea on *Delikadove*.

Hia-e-lea: Mate of *Tre-e-gar*: Motherling of *Ers-e-lea*: Grand-elder of *Que-e-lea* and *Dag-e-gar*: Student of Survival in harsh conditions: Born **7154** S.N. Died **7229** S.N.

Hil-e-gar: Mate of *Ler-e-lea*: Born **7164** S.N. Died **7182** S.N.

Ien-e-lea: Daughterling of *Mel-e-gar* and *Jux-e-lea*(**2**): Born **8** S.E.

Ieulasayer, city of: On the southern continent, west of *Desilata*: Once known as *Santiier*: Changed **1398** S.N.: abandoned during the Great Deathsong of **7229** to **7231** S.N.

Ily-e-lea: Daughterling of *Pel-e-lea and Dal-e-gar*(**1**): Grandling of *Ely-e-lea*: Born **7261** S.N.

Ion-e-gar: Mate of *Res-e-lea*: Fatherling to *Vue-e-lea*.

Isa-e-lea: Watersinger: founder of the movement to become only Dolphs: To leave *Water-time* behind and embrace The *Mind* = Logic: Born **2724** S.G. Died **45** S.N.

Jan-e-gar: Sonling of *Chm-e-gar* and *Lon-e-lea*(**1**): Grandling of *Wel-e-lea* and *Ran-e-gar*: Mate of *Tas-e-lea*: Fatherling of *Car-e-lea*: Explorer of the Old ways: Born **7209** S.N. Died **7255** S.N.

Jeanth(s): Month(s).

Jedikar: One of the twin moons of *Delikadove*.

Jer-e-lea: Daughterling of *Pel-e-lea* and *Dal-e-gar*(**2**): Mate of *Cha-e-gar*: Motherling of *Bue-e-gar* [*Not to be confused with Bue-e-gar born **7109** S.N.*]: apprentice Nursery Motherling: Born **7262** S.N.

Jeralea, river of: On the Northern continent on *Delikadove*.

Jewur: Type of bird on *Delikadove*.

Jey-e-gar: Sonling of *Cla-e-lea* and *Kin-e-gar*(**3**): Friend of *Mel-e-gar*: Student of the *Puga* and the *Muala*: Born **7169** S.N. Died **7255** S.N.?

Joining: The ritual for declaration of love: To be mated.

Jux-e-lea: Daughterling of *Arl-e-gar* and *Gis-e-lea*(**1**): Grandling of *Kin-e-gar*: Mate of *Mel-e-gar*: Motherling of Ien-e-lea and Kor-e-gar: Born **7258** S.N.

Juxelayer: A star seen in the southern hemisphere on *Delikadove*.

Jyt-e-gar: Mate of *Ban-e-lea*: Fatherling of [See *Ban-e-lea*]: Born **7236** S.N. Died **5** S.E.

Kalan, age of: Ended **70,000** seasons ago.
Kan-e-gar: Sonling of *Ose-e-lea* and *Fal-e-gar*(**2**): Mate of *Mat-e-lea*: Grandling of *Del-e-gar*: Born **7260** S.N.
Keaka: Shark of *Edenlea.*
Keaverkack: Similar to sharks but purple in colour: Could grow to more than forty feet in length: Had devastating power of sound at its command: Normally found only in the deepest part of the seas on Delikadove.
Kel-e-lea: Daughterling of *Ser-e-gar* and *Car-e-lea*(**2**): Grandling of *Mel-e-gar*: Water-weaver: Born **7262** S.N.
Kelfa, city of: Situated north-east on the northern continent: Abandoned after the Great Deathsong of **7229** to **7231** S.N.
Kerg: A bird/fish found on *Delikadove*: Nested on many coast lines.
Ket-e-gar: Sonling of *Bel-e-gar* and *Pes-e-lea*: Fatherling of *Syl-e-gar*: *Miy-e-lea*: *Sol-e-lea*: *Aiy-e-gar*: Born **7231** S.N.
Kin-e-gar: Fatherling of *Wel-e-lea*: *Ler-e-lea*: *Jey-e-gar*: Mate of *Cla-e-lea*: Grand-elder of [*See Cla-e-lea*]: Born **7132** S.N. [*No relation to the later Kin-e-gar of the families in Edenlea.*]
Kin-e-gar(2): Grand-elder: Mate of *Pie-e-lea*: Fatherling to *Arl-e-gar*: Grand-elder to *Jux-e-lea*: *For-e-gar*: *Dem-e-lea: Uni-e-lea: Sev-e-gar*: *Mul-e-gar*: Born **7214** S.N.
Kina: Name given to a *Kerg*: Friend and teacher to *Vue-e-lea.*
Klee(s): Kilometre(s)
Knowledge: Secret held in the Crystal of *Pha-e-gar*.
Kor-e-gar: Sonling of *Mel-e-gar* and *Jux-e-lea*(**2**): Born **8** S.E.
Las-e-lea: Daughterling of *Ban-e-lea* and *Jyt-e-gar*(**2**): Mate of *For-e-gar*: Grandling of *Dwe-e-lea*: Born **7261** S.N.
Lay: Female: used by the *Selahw.*
Lea: Female: used by Dolph/ins
Lea-e-lea: Daughterling of *Tag-e-lea* and *Gel-e-gar*(**l**): Grandling of *Fas-e-lea*: Born **7260** S.N.
Leatar: One of the twin moons of *Delikadove*.
Leiner: Plants that reflect sound when any creature passes through them. As with Dolphs they call out the name they are known by.
Ler-e-lea: Daughterling of *Cla-e-lea* and *Kin-e-gar*(**2**): Mate of *Hil-e-gar* : Friend of *Mel-e-gar*: Became Healer after deathsong of mate: Born **7168** S.N. Died **7229** S.N.
Leujan: Type of bird on *Delikadove*: Bird of prey: Hunted the young of the *Muala*: Found only in the forest of *Delikadove*: Golden wings with white tips: A white collar around the neck.
Ley-e-lea: Mate of *Ket-e-gar*: Motherling of [*See Ket-e-gar*]: Born **7233** S.N.
Lon-e-lea: Mate of *Chm-e-gar*: Motherling of *Jan-e-gar*: Grand-elder of *Car-e-lea*: Born **7187** S.N. Died **7262** S.N.
Makeilar: Type of bird on *Delikadove*: Found mostly on the western continent.
Malaroi, city of: On the southeast coast of the Northern Continent.
Mamaling: Mother.
Mat-e-lea: Daughterling of *Set-e-lea* and *Pan-e-gar*(**2**): Mate of *Kan-e-gar*: Grandling of

Uel-e-lea: Born **7260** S.N.

Mate: Wife or Husband: Brought together by the *Joining*.

Mel-e-gar: Fatherling of *Star-e-lay*: *Ser-e-gar: Ien-e-lea: Kor-e-gar*: Grand-elder: Mate of *Cual-e-lay*: *Sye-e-lea*: *Jux-e-lea*: last *Watersinger* of *Delikadove;* Born: **7162** S.N. Died: **9** S.E.

Mel-e-lea: Daughterling of *Ban-e-lea* and *Jyt-e-gar*(**4**): Grandling of *Dwe-e-lea*: Born **5** S.E.

Melegarn, city of: City designed by *Mel-e-gar*: Started **7197** S.N.: Expanded continually until **7268** S.N.: on the Northern continent, west coast.

Miy-e-lea: Daughterling of *Ket-e-gar* and *Ley-e-lea*(**2**): Grandling of *Bel-e-gar*: Born **7263** S.N.

Motherling: Mother.

Muala: Creature that resembled the bear but with hooves.

Mul-e-gar: Sonling of *Arl-e-gar* and *Gis-e-lea*(**6**): Grandling of *Kin-e-gar*: Born **6** S.E.

Nas-e-lea: Daughterling of *Set-e-lea* and *Pan-e-gar*(**5**): Grandling of *Uel-e-lea*: Born **6** S.E.

Neimas: Creature that had the ability to change rock into food: A delicacy of the Dolphs: Would go and share stories and partake of the *Neimas* food: After their destruction by a meteor they named the cycle of seasons after them.

Neimas, age of: Lasted **7268** Seasons: The last cycle of *Delikadove*.

Nek-e-gar: Sonling of *Qeg-e-lea* and *San-e-gar*(**1**): Grandling of *Che-e-gar*: Born **7260** S.N.

Nen-e-lea: Daughterling of *Ose-e-lea* and *Fal-e-gar*(**3**): Mate of *Onn-e-gar*: Grandling of *Del-e-gar*: Born **7261** S.N.

Nes-e-lea: Nursery motherling of *Vue-e-lea*.

Nual-e-gla: A *Selahw* who helped *Mel-e-gar* during the infestation by the *Keaverkack* on *Delikadove*.

Nue-e-lea: Teacher of the *Muala* and *Puga* to *Jer-e-gar.*

Oal-e-gar: The only Dolph to return from the four ill-fated expeditions to the *Frelegar* Mountains from **1345** to **1395** S.N. Date of his return **1398** S.N.: Born **1350** S.N. Died **1398** S.N.

Oilan: Type of tree on *Delikadove*; was tall with upswept canopy, smooth golden-yellow bark, and golden-silver leaves.

Onn-e-gar: Sonling of *Ban-e-lea* and *Jyt-e-gar*(**1**): Mate of *Nen-e-lea*: Grandling of *Dwe-e-lea*: Born **7260** S.N.

Ose-e-lea: Daughterling of *Del-e-gar* and *Tan-e-lea*: Mate of *Fal-e-gar*: Motherling of *Cha-e-gar*: *Kan-e-gar: Nen-e-lea: Wer-e-lea*: *Eis-e-gar* : Born **7225** S.N.

Pan-e-gar: Mate of *Set-e-lea*: Fatherling of [*See Set-e-lea*]: Born **7234** S.N.

Parentling: Parent.

Pel-e-gar: The *Watersinger* before *Mel-e-gar*.

Pel-e-lea: Daughterling of *Ely-e-lea* and *Dag-e-gar*: Mate of *Dal-e-gar*: Motherling of *Ily-e-lea*: *Jer-e-lea*: *Sag-e-lea*: *Teg-e-gar*: *Tes-e-lea*: Born **7235** S.N.

Per-e-gar: Sonling of *Mas-e-gar* and *Sra-e-lea*: Grandling of *Cas-e-lea*: Born **64** S.E.

Pes-e-lea: Mate of *Bel-e-gar*: Motherling of *Ket-e-gar*: Grand-elder of [*See Bel-e-gar*]:

Born **7208** S.N. Died **7261** S.N.

Pha-e-gar: Dolph who went with *Xrl-e-lea* in **1232** S.N. Student of many arts: Born **1200** S.N. in the City of *Gothina* on the western continent. Died **7184** S.N.?

Pie-e-lea: Mate of *Kin-e-gar*: Motherling of *Arl-e-gar*: Grand-elder of [*See Kin-e-gar*]: Born **7211** S.N. Died **7258** S.N.

Plesilea, city of: At the mouth of the river *Jeralea* on the western shore of the Northern continent.

Pon-e-gar: Mate of *Ers-e-lea*: Fatherling of and Grand-elder of [*See Ers-e-lea*]: Born **7176** S.N. Died **7229** S.N.

Puga: Wolf-like creature that hunts the *Muala.*

Punagor: Fifth planet in the system of *Danetar.*

Qeg-e-lea: Daughterling of *Che-e-gar* and *Sil-e-lea*(**2**): Mate of *San-e-gar*: Motherling of *Nek-e-gar*: *Fer-e-gar: Bel-e-lea: Tel-e-gar*: born **7241** S.N.

Qes-e-gar: Sonling of *Set-e-lea* and *Pan-e-gar*(**3**): Grandling *of Uel-e-lea*: Born **7265** S.N.

Que-e-lea: Daughterling of *Ers-e-lea* and *Pon-e-gar*(**2**): Sisterling of *Dag-e-gar*: Auntling to *Jer-e-lea*: Grandling of *Hia-e-lea* and *Tre-e-gar*: Nursery Motherling: Born **7212** S.N.

Qwn-e-lea: Daughterling of *Ban-e-lea* and *Jyt-e-gar*(**3**): Grandling of *Dwe-e-lea*: Born **7264** S.N.

Ran-e-gar: Mate of *Wel-e-lea*: Fatherling of *Chm-e-gar*: Grand-elder of *Jan-e-gar*: Student of Ancient Legends: Born **7163** S.N. Died **7229** S.N.

Rea-e-gar: Sonling of *Tag-e-lea* and *Gel-e-gar*(**3**): Grandling of *Fas-e-lea*: Friend of *Tan-e-lea*: Born **2** S.E.

Reakea: Turtle of *Edenlea.*

Redisea: Tree of *Delikadove.*

Res-e-lea: Mate of *Ion-e-gar*: Motherling to *Vue-e-lea.*

Reul-e-gla: A *Selahw* that *Tan-e-lea* meets.

Rock, the: a creature of *Shakeilar*: Friend of *Mel-e-gar* and later of *Tan-e-lea.*

Roulisad, sea of: Between the West, North and Southern continents on *Delikadove.*

S.E.: seasons of *Edenlea.*

S.N.: seasons of the *Neimas.*

Sag-e-lea: Daughterling of *Pel-e-lea* and *Dal-e-gar*(**3**): Grandling of *Fly-e-lea*: Born **7265** S.N.

San-e-gar: Mate of *Qeg-e-lea*: Fatherling of [*See Qeg-e-lea*]: Born **7246** S.N.

Santiier, city of: [*See Ieulasayer, city of.*]

Sealeta: Found on *Delikadove*: Element which makes the *Watersong* possible.

Season(s): Year(s).

Selahw: A creature of Dolph/in descent discovered by *Mel-e-gar* on *Delikadove.*

Sentinel: A *Shakeilar* who watches either one or a number of colonies of the *Shakeilar* race.

Ser-e-gar: Sonling of *Mel-e-gar* and *Sye-e-lea*(**1**): Mate of *Car-e-lea*: Fatherling of: *Haw-e-gar: Kel-e-lea: Zar-e-gar: Tan-e-lea: Cas-e-lea*: Born **7242** S.N: Died **61** S.E.

Serliker: A creature of *Shakeilar* re-discovered by *Mel-e-gar.*

Set-e-lea: Daughterling of *Uel-e-lea* and *Xeg-e-gar*: Mate of *Pan-e-gar*: Motherling to *Yen-e-lea: Mat-e-lea: Qes-e-gar: Zel-e-lea: Nas-e-lea*: Born **7237** S.N.

Seuma, city of: Situated north-east of the *Bylinkan* mountains on the northern continent: Straddles the river of *Swenerly*.

Sev-e-gar: Sonling of *Arl-e-gar* and *Gis-e-lea*(**5**): Grandling of *Kin-e-gar*: Born **2** S.E.

Seven Cities, the: believed to have been created by *Xrl-e-lea* and her followers in a valley of the *Frelega*r mountains: Discovered in **1397** S.N. Became legend until their re-discovery in **7184** S.N.

Shakeilar: Race of creatures that live in a symbiotic relationship with the Dolphs on *Delikadove*: That all Dolph cities are created from.

Shika: Bird of *Delikadove*: Lived only on the highest peaks of mountain ranges: Always very rare: Now believed to be extinct.

Sil-e-lea: Mate of *Che-e-gar*: Motherling of; Grand-elder of [*See Che-e-gar*]: Born **7210** S.N. Died **7262** S.N.

Sisterling: Sister.

Sky-happy: Mad, crazy.

Sky-flyer: Bird.

Sloona: Snow.

Sleeping-chamber: Bed.

Solarn: Name given *to Edenlea's* Sun: Derived from Sol: Name used by the *Crystal*.

Sol-e-lea: Daughterling of *Ket-e-gar* and *Ley-e-lea*(**3**): Mate of *Zar-e-gar*: Grandling *of Bel-e-gar*: Born **7266** S.N.

Star-e-lay: Daughterling of *Mel-e-gar* and *Cual-e-lay*(**1**): More *Selahw* than Dolph: Born **7184** S.N. Died **7231** S.N.

Starnay, city of: On the isle of *Tethilay* in the *Hederlike* sea: Created by *Mel-e-gar*: A semi-underwater city: In **7252** S.N.

Swenerly, river of: Runs down from the *Bylinkan* mountains through the city of *Seuma*.

Sye-e-lea: Second mate of *Mel-e-gar*: Motherling of *Ser-e-gar*: Grand-elder of [See *Mel-e-gar*]: Born **7204** S.N. Died **7253** S.N.

Syl-e-gar: Sonling of *Ket-e-gar* and *Ley-e-lea*(1): Grandling of *Bel-e-gar*: Born **7260** S.N.

Tag-e-lea: Daughterling of *Fas-e-lea* and *Chi-e-gar*: Mate of *Gel-e-gar*: Motherling of *Lea-e-lea*: *Tey-e-lea*: *Rea-e-gar*: Born **7245** S.N.

Tan-e-lea: Watersinger: Daughterling of *Ser-e-gar* and *Car-e-lea*(**4**): Grandling of *Mel-e-gar*: Mate of *Del-e-gar*: Motherling of *Ose-e-lea*: Born **2** S.E.

Tas-e-lea: Mate of *Jan-e-gar*: Motherling of *Car-e-lea*: Born **7215** S.N. Died **7261** S.N.

Tay(s): Day(s).

Teaka: Food of the Neimas: Normally Yellow and Red but different variations in colour known to have existed: Sweet and light: Can satisfy hunger for two tays or more.

Teg-e-gar: Sonling of *Pel-e-lea* and *Dal-e-gar*(**4**): Grandling of *Ely-e-gar*: Born **2** S.E.

Tel-e-gar: Sonling of *Qeg-e-lea* and *San-e-gar*(**4**): Grandling of *Che-e-gar*: Born **2** S.E.

Tes-e-lea: Daughterling of *Pel-e-lea* and *Dal-e-gar*(**5**): Grandling of *Ely-e-lea*: Born **3** S.E.

Tethilay, isle of: In the southern sea of *Delikadove*.

Tey-e-lea: Daughterling of *Tag-e-lea* and *Gel-e-gar*(**2**): Grandling of *Fas-e-lea*: Helper of

Que-e-lea: Born **7266** S.N.

Tooka: Name for a red and silver fish found in *Edenlea.*

Toomasel, age of: Ended **300,000** seasons ago.

Tor-e-lea: Motherling of *Mel-e-gar*: Mate to *Zes-e-gar*: Born **7143** S.N. Died **7171** S.N.

Tor-e-lea(2): Daughterling of *Ban-e-lea* and *Jyt-e-gar*(**5**): Grandling of *Dwe-e-lea*: Born **5** S.E. [*not to be confused with Tor-e-lea, motherling of Mel-e-gar.*]

Travelling-shelter: Mobile *Shakeilar* Shelter

Tre-e-gar: Mate of *Hia-e-lea*: Fatherling of *Ers-e-lea*: Grand-elder of *Que-e-lea* and *Dag-e-gar*: Born **7147** S.N. Died **7199** S.N.

Tueselaa, city of: On western shore of the western continent: Abandoned during the Great Deathsong of **7229** to **7231** S.N.

Twon: Type of bird on *Delikadove.*

Tynaina, city of: Situated southeast of the northern continent: Abandoned after the Great Deathsong of **7229** to **7231** S.N.

Ual-e-lea: An Ancient ancestor of *Alk-e-lea*: A Watersinger: Born and died during the Cycle of *Kalan.*

Uel-e-lea: Grand-elder: mate of *Xeg-e-gar*: Motherling to *Set-e-lea*: Grand-elder of *Yen-e-lea*: *Mat-e-lea*: *Qes-e-gar: Zel-e-lea: Nas-e-lea*: Born **7221** S.N.

Un-born: To describe youngling(s) inside the womb of a lea or lay.

Un-born, ritual of: The way *Selahw* celebrate the announcement that one of their lays are carrying an Un-born youngling: A dance between the lay and gla who are to be parentlings: The other *Selahw* join in by slapping their flukes on the water to the rhythm of the song.

Un-truth: Lie.

Un-water: Land, ground, etc.

Uni-e-lea: Daughterling of *Arl-e-gar* and *Gis-e-lea*(**4**): Grandling of *Kin-e-gar*: Born **7267** S.N.

Veul(s): Week(s)

Vewala, age of: The name given to the first seasons when Dolphins as Dolphs colonised the land of *Delikadove.*

Vue-e-lea: Daughterling of *Res-e-lea* and *Ion-e-gar*: A student of the *Kerg* on *Delikadove*: Friend and teacher of *Zar-e-gar*: Born **7232** S.N. Died **7268** S.N.?

Water-moving: Only done by a Watersinger: To transport from one place instantly to another.

Watersinger: A Dolphin or Dolph born with the power of the Watersong: Normally occurs every two hundred and fifty seasons: The only exception is *Tan-e-lea* born while another Watersinger still lived [*See Mel-e-gar*].

Watersong: Power used by Watersingers [*See Mel-e-gar, Tan-e-lea*].

Water-time: An expanded state of being from the beginning of mind and thinking: Empathic state to a full Telepathic view through sub sonic sound: When fully developed in Dolphins it also allows the transmission and sharing of full audio-visual experiences including the emotions experienced by the sender to be sent to the receiver:(*Obviously water - [**i.e.; water-time**] being a superb medium for the transmission of telepathic communication, includes apparent silent sound as well as apparent audio emissions;*

salt water in particular being ideal.) Mel-e-gar used it to share the story of their *Exodus* from *Delikadove* to *Edenlea* with the school: Can be used to bond *Water-time* with *Water-time* [*mind to mind*]: A full telepathic sharing can be achieved: Only a few Dolphs such as Watersingers ever achieved a full *Water-time*: Became a natural state for the Dolphins of *Edenlea.*

Waterweaver: To water weave: The ability to shape water into a form of the weaver's choosing. [*See Kel-e-lea*].

Water-weaving: The way a *Waterweaver* binds water together.

Waves of Still Water: Icebergs and Glaciers found in the northern waters of *Edenlea*

Wel-e-lea: Daughterling of *Cla-e-lea* and *Kin-e-gar*(**1**): Mate of *Ran-e-gar*: Motherling of *Chm-e-gar*: Grand-elder of *Jan-e-gar*: Great Grand-elder of *Car-e-lea*: Friend of *Mel-e-gar*: Born **7166** S.N. Died **7229** S.N.

Wer-e-lea: Daughterling of *Ose-e-lea* and *Fal-e-gar*(**4**): Grandling of *Del-e-gar*: Born **2** S.E.

Wunlaka: Type of fish found in the seas of *Delikadove.*

Xeg-e-gar: Mate of *Uel-e-lea*: Fatherling of *Set-e-lea*: Grand-elder of [*See Uel-e-lea*]: Born **7218** S.N. Died **7261** S.N.

Xer-e-gar: Watersinger who established the first Sanctuaries to *Edenlea* during the cycle of *Delikadove*: **100,000,000** seasons ago.

Xrl-e-lea: Dolph who led her two thousand followers to the *Frelegar* mountains in the season of **1232** S.N.: Watersinger: born **1184** S.N. Died **7184** S.N.?

Yen(s): One of the few words of Dolph/in which can have three meanings: Second(s):minute(s):moment(s).

Yen-e-lea: Daughterling of *Set-e-lea* and *Pan-e-gar*(**1**): Mate of Haw-e-gar: Grandling of Uel-e-lea: Born **7258** S.N.

Yengile, city of: On the western shore of the Northern continent of *Delikadove*: Abandoned after the Great Deathsong of **7229** to **7231** S.N.

Yew-e-lea: Distant ancestor of *Del-e-gar*: Watersinger: First guardian of the forest of Duorsilear: Born **2356** S.G.[cycle of Gooma] Died **2430** S.G.

Yewanclas, precipice of: Among the mountains of the western continent: Named after *Yew-e-lea.*

Yol-e-gar: Healer of *Hia-e-lea*: Friend of *Alk-e-lea* and *Bue-e-gar*: Born **7145** S.N. Died **7232** S.N.

Youngling: Child: Used by Grand-elders, Elders and younglings: All Dolphins under 14 seasons: Mark of respect.

Zar-e-gar: Sonling of *Ser-e-gar* and *Car-e-lea*(**3**): Grandling of *Mel-e-gar*: Mate of *Sol-e-lea*: Grand Fisher: Born **7266** S.N.

Zel-e-lea: Daughterling of *Set-e-lea* and *Pan-e-gar*(**4**): Grandling of *Uel-e-lea*: Born **2** S.E.

Zes-e-gar: Fatherling of *Mel-e-gar*: Mate to *Tor-e-lea*: Born **7139** S.N. Died **7171** S.N.

Zyl-e-gar: Mate of *Dwe-e-lea*: Fatherling of *Ban-e-lea*: Grand-elder of [*See Dwe-e-lea*]: Born **7203** S.N. Died **7259** S.N.

Zylasayer, city of: Situated south-west of the city of *Kelfa* at the foot of the *Bylinkan* mountains on the northern continent: Abandoned during the Great Deathsong of **7229** to **7231** S.N. also noted as the place where the Explorer; *Jan-e-gar* died in **7255** S.N.

A Note from the Author.

In 1994, while I was finishing the last revision of this Novel, an event happened which brought the depth of mystery that are the cetaceans to the fore. A mass stranding of eleven Sperm whales (or Selahw) on the Isle of Sanday, Orkney - (which is my home) - defied human reason and died on a dark winter beach.

This was the largest stranding of sperm whales in the history of Europe, and it made headlines around the world. The *Guardian* newspaper featured it on the Home news page on Friday, 9th of December.

Back to that morning of the 8th of December I stood among them, their great forms grey and still, the last life having left in the early hours. Like the giants that they are, the sight of them filled me until I just hoped that they would awaken and return to the deep. But it was not to be. The dark winter sky and the cold wind chilled more than bones and as other tiny humans scurried about them I knew the Selahw were more than overwhelming even in death, they were a message in the sand. Even with the sadness I felt and having talked to others who were there this was an event that should not be forgotten. In the early hours of the morning of the 10th I awoke from a deep dream and started to write. You could say my water-time more than just rippled and the wave took me to that special depth and with a great feeling of the kinship which had been there when Exodus was born - a poem was written.

It has been published twice in the intervening years since then and I felt that as this novel is about to be published that those who have shared the journey of Exodus might appreciate this special water-time. The *sister of time*...In the poem is one Janet Evans who shared their last moments.

Martin A Enticknap, Sanday, 16th May 1999

A WINTER'S WATER-TIME

©10/12/94

We are those that see the final wave,
A mighty ocean roar. From grey to white,
The sea can speak to followers of an ocean's warmth.
For awoken are the great spirits to follow the song,
To share the food for all that come.

It will be the mighty that choose to witness,
The final call. These are the generations,
From old to young to return to the beginning shore.
A curve of sand, a shallow reach of land that speaks,
Of those that tread the lonely walk.
So they may know we are here, in peace once more.

My song of death, the ripeness of an age,
For the rest I shall take upon that wind swept shore.
Those of family to come to stay,
To share my fluid sounds of joy as the stream,
Of my new ocean spills forth.

An echo of the one who knows,
I see as my brothers come to follow my eternal sleep.
She may only be a grey shadow to my winter's eye,
But my sound of wisdom finds the colour and flame,
Of her burning mind.

That song was sung as you danced amongst us,
So small and meek.
Fear not cousin, sister of time.
The joy is upon us as we reach,
To find the communion upon that beach.

For though you, as all on a winter's night,
Only know the world that doesn't sing.
Of one life, one love, one hope.
You dared to allow the fluid touch,
As we all lay waiting, watching as it flows,
From us to you our hope, our love, our eternal lives.

You will hear our final song,
You will wonder why we stay?
You will witness the youngest return to sing,
Of our final winter's day.

As I sing the fallen tone,
So that those that chose freely can follow.
To show the picture of our naked faith,
That now lie waiting within your reach.

From our place among the stars,
We watch the last flicker of life cease,
And wait awhile as the dawn now breaks,
Upon the dark winter beach,
The burden of the mighty are now at peace.

Shed no tear, bear no pain,
For the eleven songs that came,
So those that can be our witness,
That love from us to you,
Is the song you now can sing.

When those that come in winter's days,
To follow, show them how to watch,
How to wait, listen, then to find,
Then your help will open,
Our communion of a winter's water-time.

www.ingramcontent.com/pod-product-compliance
Ingram Content Group UK Ltd.
Pitfield, Milton Keynes, MK11 3LW, UK
UKHW041858190726
13854UKWH00002B/962